Phases of Gravity

PHASES

OF

GRAVITY

Dan Simmons

OLMSTEAD
P R E S S
An [e-reads] Book

Published in 2001 by Olmstead Press: Chicago, Illinois
e-reads: New York, New York

Published in 1989 by Bantam Books: New York, New York

Cover designed by Hope Forstenzer

Text designed and typeset by
Syllables, Hartwick, New York, USA

Printed and bound in Toronto, Ontario, Canada by
Webcom Inc.

ISBN: 1-58754-106-8

Library of Congress Card Number: 2001086674

Editorial Sales Rights and Permission Inquiries should be addressed to:
Olmstead Press, 22 Broad Street, Suite 34, Milford, CT 06460
Email: Editor@lpcgroup.com

Manufactured in Canada
1 3 5 7 9 10 8 6 4 2

Substantial discounts on bulk quantities of Olmstead Press books are available to corporations, professional associations and other organizations. If you are in the USA or Canada, contact LPC Group, Attn: Special Sales Department, 1-800-626-4330, fax 1-800-334-3892, or email: sales@lpcgroup.com.

To Robert and Kathryn Simmons

Part One

Poona

Pan Am Flight 001 left the moonlight behind it and dropped into clouds and darkness as it felt its way toward a landing in New Delhi. Staring out at the port wing, Baedecker felt the weight pulling at him and mixing with the tension of an old pilot being forced to suffer a landing as a passenger. The wheels touched tarmac in an almost perfect touchdown and Baedecker glanced at his watch. It was 3:47 A.M. local time. Tiny motes of pain danced behind his eyes as he looked out past the flashing wingtip light at the dark silhouettes of water towers and service buildings moving past. The massive 747 swung sharply to the right and rolled to the end of its taxi run. The sound of engines swelled one final time and then dropped into silence, leaving Baedecker with the tired pounding of his own pulse in his ears. He had not slept for twenty-four hours.

Even before the shuffling line reached the forward exit, Baedecker felt the wave of heat and humidity strike him. Descending the ramp toward the sticky asphalt, he became aware of the tremendous mass of the planet under him, weighted even further by the hundreds of millions of wretched souls populating the subcontinent, and he hunched his shoulders against the inexorable pull of depression.

I should have done the credit card commercial, thought Baedecker. He stood in the gloom with the other passengers and waited for a blue-and-white jitney to approach them across the dark expanse of pavement. The terminal was a distant blur of lights on the horizon. Clouds reflected the rows of blinking lights beyond the runway.

It would not have been very difficult. All they had asked of him was to sit in front of the cameras and lights, smile, and say, "Do you know me? Sixteen years ago I walked on the moon. That doesn't help me though when I want to reserve an airline seat or pay for dinner in a French café." Two more lines of such drivel and then the standard closing with his name being punched out on the plastic card—RICHARD E. BAEDECKER.

The customs building was a huge, echoing warehouse of a place. Sodium yellow lights hung from metal rafters and made people's skin look greasy and waxlike. Baedecker's shirt was already plastered to his body in a dozen places. The lines moved slowly. Baedecker was used to the officiousness of customs officials, but these black-haired, brown-shirted little men seemed to be reaching for new heights of official unpleasantness. Three places in front of him in the line, an older Indian woman stood with her two daughters, all three in cheap cotton saris. Impatient with their replies, the agent behind the scratched counter dumped their two cheap suitcases on the floor of the shed. Brightly printed cloth, bras, and torn underpants spilled out in a heap. The customs man turned to another agent and said something in rapid Hindi that brought smirks to their faces.

Baedecker was almost dozing when he realized that one of the customs men was talking to him.

"Pardon me?"

"I said—is this all you have to declare? You are bringing in nothing else?" The singsong of Indian English seemed strangely familiar to Baedecker. He had encountered it with Indian hotel-management trainees around the world. Only then the tone was not edged with a strange suspiciousness and anger.

"Yes. That's all." Baedecker nodded toward the pink form they had filled out before landing.

"This is all you have? One bag?" The agent hefted Baedecker's old, black flight bag as if it held contraband or explosives.

"That's all."

The man scowled fiercely at the luggage and then passed it contemptuously to another brown-shirted agent farther along the counter. This man struck an *X* on the bag as if the violence of the motion would drive out whatever evils it held.

"Move along. Move along." The first agent was gesturing.

"Thank you," said Baedecker. He hefted the flight bag and moved out into the darkness beyond the customs shed.

2

The view had been one of blackness. Two black triangles. Not even the stars had been visible during their final descent. Standing in their bulky pressure suits, locked in position by an array of straps and stirrups, they could see only the featureless black sky. During most of its final burn and descent sequence, the landing module had been pitched back so that the lunar surface was invisible beneath them. Only during the final minutes did Baedecker have a chance to look out onto the glare and tumble of the moon's face.

It's just like the simulations, he'd thought. He knew even then that there should be more. He knew even as they were descending that he should be sensing more, feeling more.

But as he automatically responded to Houston's updates and inquiries, obediently punched the appropriate numbers into the computer and read off figures to Dave, the same un-worthy thought returned again and again. *It's just like the simulations.*

∞

"Mr. Baedecker!" It took a minute for the shout to register. Someone was calling his name, had been for some time. Baedecker turned from where he was standing in the alley between the customs shed and the terminal and looked around. Thousands of bugs danced in the glare of the spot-lights. People wrapped in white robes slept on the sidewalk, sat huddled against the dark buildings. Dark men in bright shirts leaned against black-and-yellow cabs. He turned the other way just as the girl caught up to him.

"Mr. Baedecker! Hello." She stopped with a graceful half step, threw her head back, paused to take a deep breath.

"Hello," said Baedecker. He had no idea who the young woman was but was haunted with a strong sense of déjà vu. Who in the world would be greeting him in New Delhi at four-thirty in the morning? Someone from the embassy? No, they didn't know he was coming and wouldn't care if they did. Not anymore. Bombay Electronics? Hardly. Not in New Delhi. And this young blonde was obviously Ameri-can. Always poor at remembering names and faces, Baedecker felt the familiar flush of guilt and embarrassment. He ransacked his memory. Nothing.

"I'm Maggie Brown," said the girl and stuck her hand out. He shook it, surprised at how cool it felt. His own skin felt feverish even to himself. Maggie Brown? She brushed back a loose strand of her shoulder-length hair and again Baedecker was struck with a sense of having seen her be-fore. He would go under the assumption that she worked with NASA, although she appeared too young to have . . .

"I'm Scott's friend," she said and smiled. She had a wide mouth and a slight gap between her front teeth. Somehow the effect was pleasant.

"Scott's friend. Of course. Hello." Baedecker shook her hand again. Looked around again. Several cabbies had come up to them and were proffering rides. He shook his head, but their babble only intensified. Baedecker took the girl's elbow and turned away from the gesticulating mob. "What are you doing here? In India, I mean. And here, too." Baedecker gestured lamely at the narrow street and the long shadow of the terminal. He remembered her now. Joan had shown him a picture of her the last time he had visited Boston. The green eyes had stuck in his memory.

"I've been here for three months," she said. "Scott rarely has time to see me, but I'm there if he does. In Poona, I mean. I found a job as governess . . . not really governess, I guess, but sort of a tutor . . . with this nice doctor's family there? In the old British section? Anyway, I was with Scott last week when he got your cable."

"Oh," said Baedecker. He could think of nothing else to say for several seconds. Overhead, a small jet climbed for altitude. "Is Scott here? I mean, I thought I'd see him in . . . what is it? . . . in Poona."

"Scott's at a retreat at the Master's farm. He won't be back until Tuesday. He asked me to tell you. Me, I'm visiting an old friend at the Education Foundation here in Old Delhi."

"The Master? You mean this guru of Scott's?"

"That's what they all call him. Anyway, Scott asked me to tell you, and I figured you wouldn't be staying long in New Delhi."

"You came out before dawn to give me that message?" Baedecker looked carefully at the young woman next to him. As they moved farther away from the glaring spotlights, her skin seemed to glow of its own accord. He realized that soft light was tinging the eastern sky.

"No problem," she said and took his arm in hers. "My train just got in a few hours ago. I didn't have anything to do until the USEFI offices opened up."

They had come around to the front of the terminal. Baedecker realized that they were out in the country, some distance from the city. He could see high-rise apartments in the distance, but the sounds and smells surrounding them were all of the country. The curving airport drive led to a wide highway, but nearby were dirt roads under multitrunked banyan trees.

"When's your flight, Mr. Baedecker?"

"To Bombay? Not until eight-thirty. Call me Richard."

"Okay, Richard. What do you say we take a walk and then get some breakfast?"

"Fine," said Baedecker. He would have given anything at that moment to have an empty room waiting for him, a bed, time to sleep. What time would it be in St. Louis? His tired mind was not up to the simple arithmetic. He followed the girl as she set off down the rain-moistened drive. Ahead of them the sun was rising.

The sun had been rising for three days when they landed. Details stood out in bold relief. It had been planned that way.

Later, Baedecker remembered very little about actually descending the ladder and stepping off the LM footpad. All those years of preparation, simulation, and expectation had led to that single point, that sharp intersection of time and place, but what Baedecker later remembered was the vague sense of frustration and urgency. They were twenty-three minutes behind schedule when Dave finally led the way down the ladder. Suiting up, going over the fifty-one-point PLS checklist, and depressurizing had taken more time than it had in the simulations.

Then they were moving across the surface, testing their balance, picking up contingency samples, and trying to make up for lost time. Baedecker had spent many hours composing a short phrase to recite upon first setting foot on lunar soil—his "footnote in history" as Joan had called it—but Dave made a joke after jumping off the footpad, Houston had asked for a radio check, and the moment passed.

Baedecker had two strong memories of the rest of that first EVA. He remembered the damned checklist banded to his wrist. They never caught up to the timeline, not even after eliminating the third core sample and the second check of the Rover's guidance memory. He had hated that checklist.

The other memory still returned to him in dreams. The gravity. The one-sixth gee. The sheer exhilaration of bouncing across the glaring, rock-strewn surface with only the lightest touch of their boots to propel them. It awakened an even earlier memory in Baedecker; he was a child, learning to swim in Lake Michigan, and his father was holding him under the arms while he kicked and bounced his way across the sand of the lake bottom. What marvelous lightness, the supporting strength of his father's arms, the gentle rise and fall of the green waves, the perfect synchronization of weight and buoyancy meeting in the ribbon of balance flowing up from the balls of his feet.

He still dreamed about that.

The sun rose like a great, orange balloon, its sides shifting laterally as light refracted through the warming air. Baedecker thought of Ektachrome photos in *National Geographic*. India! Insects, birds, goats, chickens, and cattle added to the growing sound of traffic along the unseen highway. Even this winding dirt road on which they walked was already crowded with people on bicycles, bullock carts, heavy trucks labeled Public Transport, and an occasional black-and-yellow taxi dodging in and out of the confusion like an angry bee.

Baedecker and the girl stopped by a small, green building that was either a farmhouse or a Hindu temple. Perhaps it was both. Bells were ringing inside. The smell of incense and manure drifted from an inner courtyard. Roosters were crowing and somewhere a man was chanting in a frail-voiced falsetto. Another man—this one in a blue polyester business suit—stopped his bicycle, stepped to the side of the road, and urinated into the temple yard.

A bullock cart lumbered past, axle grinding, yoke straining, and Baedecker turned to watch it. A woman in the back of it lifted her sari to her face, but the three children next to her returned Baedecker's stare. The man in front shouted at the laboring bullock and snapped a long stick against a flank already scabrous with sores. Suddenly all other noises were lost as an Air India 747 roared overhead, its metal sides catching the gold of the rising sun.

"What's that smell?" asked Baedecker. Above the general onslaught of odors—wet soil, open sewage, car exhausts, compost heaps, pollution from the unseen city—there rose a sweet, overpowering scent that already seemed to have permeated his skin and clothes.

"They're cooking breakfast," said Maggie Brown. "All over the country, they're cooking breakfast over open fires. Most of them using dried cow dung as fuel. Eight hundred million people cooking breakfast. Gandhi once wrote that that was the eternal scent of India."

Baedecker nodded. The sunrise was being swallowed by lowering monsoon clouds. For a second the trees and grass were a brilliant, false green, made even more pronounced by Baedecker's fatigue. The headache, which had been with him since Frankfurt, had moved from behind his eyes to a point at the base of his neck. Every step sent an echo of pain through his head. Yet the pain seemed a distant and unimportant thing, perceived as it was through a haze of exhaustion and jet lag. It was part of the strangeness—the new smells, the odd cacophony of rural and urban sounds, this attractive young woman at his side with sunlight outlining her cheekbones and setting fire to her green eyes. What was she to his son anyway? How serious was their relationship? Baedecker wished he had asked Joan more questions about the girl, but the visit had been uncomfortable and he had been in a hurry to leave.

Baedecker looked at Maggie Brown and realized that he was being sexist in thinking of her as a girl. The young woman seemed to possess that sense of self-possession, of *awareness*, which Baedecker associated with true adults as opposed to those who had simply grown up. Looking again, Baedecker guessed that Maggie Brown was at least in her mid-twenties, several years older than Scott. Hadn't Joan said something about their son's friend being a graduate student and teaching assistant?

"Did you come to India just to visit Scott?" asked Maggie Brown. They were on the circular drive again, approaching the airport.

"Yes. No," said Baedecker. "That is, I came to see Scott, but I arranged a business trip to coincide with it."

"Don't you work for the government?" asked Maggie. "The space people?"

Baedecker smiled at the image "the space people" evoked. "Not for the past twelve years," he said and told her about the aerospace firm in St. Louis for which he worked.

"So you don't have anything to do with the space shuttle?" said Maggie.

"Not really. We had some subsystems aboard the shuttles and used to rent payload space aboard them every once in a while." Baedecker was aware that he had used the past tense, as if he were speaking about someone who had died.

Maggie stopped to watch the rich sunlight bathe the sides of the New Delhi control tower and terminal buildings in gold. She tucked a wayward strand of hair behind one ear and folded her arms. "It's hard to believe that it's been almost eighteen months since the *Challenger* explosion," she said. "That was a terrible thing."

"Yes," said Baedecker.

∾

It was ironic that he had been at the Cape for that flight. He had been present for only one previous shuttle launch, one of the *Columbia*'s first engineering flights almost five years earlier. He was there in January of 1986 for the *Challenger* disaster only because Cole Prescott, the vice president of Baedecker's firm, had asked him to escort a client who had bankrolled a subcomponent in the Spartan-Halley experiment package sitting in the *Challenger*'s payload bay.

The launch of 51-L had seemed nominal enough and Baedecker and his client were standing in the VIP stands three miles from Pad 39-B, shielding their eyes against the late-morning sun, when things went bad. Baedecker could remember marveling at how cold it was; he had brought only a light cotton jacket, and the morning had been the coldest he could ever recall at the Cape. Through binoculars, he had caught a glint of ice on the gantries surrounding the shuttle.

Baedecker remembered that he had been thinking about getting an early start to beat the leaving crowds when the loudspeaker carried the voice of NASA's public affairs officer. "Altitude four point three nautical miles, down-range distance three nautical miles. Engines throttling up. Three engines now at one hundred four percent."

He had thought fleetingly of his own launch fifteen years before, of his job relaying data while Dave Muldorff "flew" the monstrous *Saturn V*, until he was returned to the present as the loudspeaker carried Commander Dick Scobee's voice saying, "Roger, go at throttle up," and Baedecker had glanced toward the parking lots to see how congested the roads would be and a second later his client had said, "Wow, those SRBs really create a cloud when they separate, don't they?"

Baedecker had looked up then, seen the expanding, mushrooming contrail that had nothing to do with SRB separation, and instantly had recognized the sickening orange-red glow that lit the interior of the cloud as hypergolic fuels ignited on contact as they escaped from the shuttle's destroyed reaction control system and orbital maneuvering engines. A few seconds later the solid rocket boosters became visible as they careened mindlessly from the still-expanding cumulus of the explosion. Feeling sick to his stomach, Baedecker had turned to Tucker Wilson, a fellow *Apollo*-era pilot who was still on active duty with NASA, and had said without any real hope, "RTLS?"

Tucker had shaken his head; this was no return to launch site abort. This was what each of them had silently waited for during their own minutes of launch. By the time Baedecker had looked up again, the first large segments of the destroyed orbiter had begun their long, sad fall to the waiting crypt of the sea.

In the months since *Challenger*, Baedecker had found it hard to believe that the country had *ever* flown so frequently and competently into space. The long hiatus of earthbound doubt in which nothing flew had become the normal state of things to Baedecker, mixing in his own mind with a dreary sense of heaviness, of entropy and gravity triumphant, which had weighed upon him since his own world and family had been blasted apart some months earlier.

"My friend Bruce says that Scott didn't come out of his dorm room for two days after *Challenger* blew up," said

Maggie Brown as they stood in front of the New Delhi air terminal.

"Really?" said Baedecker. "I didn't think that Scott had any interest in the space program anymore." He looked up as the rising sun suddenly was obscured by clouds. Color flowed out of the world like water from a sink.

"He said he didn't care," said Maggie. "He said that Chernobyl and *Challenger* were just the first signs of the end of the technological era. A few weeks later, he made arrangements to come to India. Are you hungry, Richard?"

It was not yet six-thirty in the morning but the terminal was filling with people. Others still lay sleeping on the cracked and filthy linoleum floors. Baedecker wondered if they were potential passengers or merely people seeking a roof for the night. A baby sat alone on a black vinyl chair and cried lustily. Lizards slid across the walls.

Maggie led him to a small coffee shop on the second floor where sleepy waiters stood with soiled towels over their arms. Maggie warned him not to try the bacon and then ordered an omelette, toast and jelly, and tea. Baedecker considered the idea of breakfast and then rejected it. What he really wanted was a Scotch. He ordered black coffee.

The big room was empty of other customers except for one table filled with a loud crew of Russians from an Aeroflot liner Baedecker could see out the window. They were snapping fingers to call over the tired Indian waiters. Baedecker glanced at the captain and then looked again. The big man looked familiar—although Baedecker told himself that a lot of Soviet pilots have such jowls and formidable eyebrows. Nonetheless, Baedecker wondered if he had met him during the three days he had toured Moscow and Star City with the Apollo-Soyuz Test Project crew. He shrugged. It did not matter.

"How is Scott?" he asked.

Maggie Brown looked up and a slightly guarded expression seemed to settle over her like a fine veil. "Fine. He says that he's never felt so good but I think he's lost some weight."

Baedecker had an image of his stocky son, in crew cut and T-shirt, wanting to play shortstop on the Houston Little League team but being too slow, fit only for right field. "How is his asthma? Has this humidity caused it to kick up again?"

"No, the asthma's cured," said Maggie levelly. "The Master cured it, according to Scott."

Baedecker blinked. Even in recent years, in his empty apartment, he had found himself listening for the coughs, the raspy breathing. He remembered the times he had held the boy like an infant through the night, rocking him, both of them frightened by the gurgling in his lungs. "Are you a follower of this . . . of the Master?"

Maggie laughed and the veil seemed to slip from her green eyes. "No. I wouldn't be here if I were. They don't allow them to leave the ashram for more than a few hours."

"Hmmm," said Baedecker and glanced at his watch. Ninety minutes until his flight left for Bombay.

"It'll be late," said Maggie.

"Oh?" Baedecker wasn't sure of what she was talking about.

"Your flight. It'll be late. What are you going to do until Tuesday?"

Baedecker had not thought about that. It was Thursday morning. He had planned to be in Bombay this same afternoon, see the electronics people and their earth station on Friday, take the train to Poona to visit Scott over the weekend, and fly out of Bombay for home on Monday afternoon.

"I'm not sure," he said. "Stay in Bombay a couple of extra days, I suppose. What was so important about this retreat that Scott couldn't take some time off?"

"Nothing," said Maggie Brown. She drank the last of her tea and set the cup down with an abrupt movement that held the hint of anger. "It's the same stuff as always. Lectures from the Master. Solitude sessions. Dances."

"Dances?"

"Well, not really. They play music. The beat picks up. Faster and faster. They move around. Faster and faster. Finally they collapse from exhaustion. It cleanses the soul. That's part of the tantra yoga thing."

Baedecker could hear her silences. He'd read some about this ex-philosophy professor who had become the most recent guru to young rich kids from so many well-to-do nations. According to *Time,* the Indian locals had been shocked at reports of group sex at his ashrams. Baedecker had been shocked when Joan told him that Scott had dropped out of graduate school in Boston to go halfway around the world. In search of what?

"You don't seem to approve," he said to Maggie Brown.

The girl shrugged. Then her eyes lit up. "Hey, I've got an idea! Why don't you spend some time sightseeing with me? I've been trying to get Scott to see something other than the Poona ashram since I got here in March. Come with me! It'll be fun. You can get an Air India in-country pass for next to nothing."

Still thinking about the group-sex rumors, Baedecker was taken aback for a moment. Then he saw the childlike eagerness in Maggie's face and chided himself for being a lecherous old man. The girl was lonely.

"Where would you be going?" he asked. He needed a second to form a polite rejection.

"I'll be leaving Delhi tomorrow," she said brightly. "I'll fly to Varanasi, then to Khajuraho, a stopover in Calcutta, then Agra and back to Poona later in the week."

"What's in Agra?"

"Only the Taj Mahal," said Maggie and leaned toward him with a mischievous look in her eyes. "You *can't* see India and not see the Taj Mahal. It's not *allowed.*"

"Sorry. I'll have to," said Baedecker. "I have an appointment in Bombay tomorrow and you say Scott will be back Tuesday. I need to fly home no later than a week from Friday. I'm stretching this trip out as it is." He could see the disappointment even as she nodded.

"Besides," he said, "I'm not much of a tourist."

The American flag had looked absurd to Baedecker. He had expected to be stirred by it. Once in Djakarta, after being away from the States for only nine months, he had been moved to tears by the sight of the American flag flying from the stern of an old freighter in the harbor. But on the moon—a quarter million miles from home—he could think only of how silly the flag looked with its wire extended stiffly to simulate a breeze in the hard vacuum.

He and Dave had saluted. They stood downsun of the television camera they had erected and saluted. Unconsciously, they had already fallen into the habit of leaning forward in the low-gee "tired ape" position Aldrin had warned them about in briefings. It was comfortable and felt natural, but it photographed poorly.

They had finished the salute and were ready to lope off to other things, when President Nixon talked to them. For Baedecker it had been Nixon's patched-in, impromptu phone call that had pushed an unreal experience into the realm of the surreal. The president obviously had not planned what he would say during his call, and the monologue wandered. Several times it seemed that he had ended his sentence and they would begin to reply only to have Nixon's voice come in again. The transmission lag added to the problem. Dave did most of the talking. Baedecker said, "Thank you, Mr. President," several times. For some reason Nixon thought that they would want to know the football scores from the previous day's games. Baedecker loathed football.

He wondered if this prattle about football was Nixon's idea of how men talked to men.

"Thank you, Mr. President," Baedecker had said. And all the time he stood there in the camera's eye, facing a frozen flag against a black sky and listening to the static-lashed maunderings of his nation's chief executive, Baedecker was thinking about the unauthorized object he had hidden in the contingency sample pocket above his right knee.

∾

The Delhi-Bombay flight was three hours late getting off. A British helicopter salesman sitting next to Baedecker in the terminal said that the Air India pilot and flight engineer had been having a feud for weeks now. One or the other would hold up the flight every day.

Once airborne, Baedecker tried to doze, but the incessant chiming of call-buttons kept him awake. They had no sooner taken off than every other person on the aircraft seemed to be ringing for the saried stewardesses. The three men in the row ahead of Baedecker were loudly demanding pillows, demanding drinks, and snapping their fingers in an imperious manner that went against his Midwestern, egalitarian grain.

Maggie Brown had left him shortly after breakfast. She had scribbled her "Grand Tour Itinerary" on a napkin and stuffed it into the coat pocket of his suit. "You never know," she said. "Something might happen to change your mind." Baedecker had asked a few more questions about Scott before she drove off in a black-and-yellow cab, but his overall impression was of a girl who had mistakenly followed her lover to a strange and alien land and who no longer knew how he felt or thought.

They were flying in a French Air Bus. Baedecker noticed with a professional eye how the wings flexed with greater latitude than a Boeing product and noted with some surprise the steep angle of attack the Indian pilot chose. American airlines would not allow their pilots to horse the machine around like that for fear of alarming their passengers. The Indian passengers did not seem to notice. Their descent toward Bombay was so rapid that it reminded Baedecker of a ride he had hopped into Pleiku in a C-130 where the pilot had been forced to drop in almost vertically during the final approach for fear of small-arms fire.

Bombay seemed composed totally of shacks with tin roofs and factories rotting with age. Then Baedecker caught a glimpse of high-rise buildings and the Arabian Sea, the plane banked at a fifty-degree angle, a plateau rose to greet them out of the shacks, and they were down. Baedecker nodded a silent compliment to the pilot.

The cab ride from the airport to his hotel was almost too much for Baedecker's exhausted senses. Immediately beyond the gates of Bombay's Santa Cruz Airport the slums began. Dozens of square miles of tin-roofed shacks, sagging canvas lean-tos, and narrow, muddy lanes stretched on either side of the highway. At one point a twenty-foot-high water pipeline cut through the tangle of hovels like a garden hose through an anthill. Brown-skinned children ran along the top or reclined on its rusty sides. Everywhere there was the dizzying movement of uncountable bodies.

It was very hot. The humid air pouring in the open windows of the taxi hit Baedecker like a steam-heated exhaust. Occasionally he caught glimpses of the Arabian Sea to his right. A huge billboard in the suburbs proclaimed 0 DAYS TO THE MOONSOON but there was no cooling rain from the low ceiling of clouds, only a reflection of the terrible heat and an ominous sense of weight that settled on his shoulders like a yoke.

The city itself was even more dizzying. Every side street became a tributary of white-shirted humanity pouring into ever-larger streams and rivers of population gone insane. Thousands of tiny storefronts offered their brightly colored

wares to the millions of thronging pedestrians. The cacophony of car horns, motors, and bicycle bells wrapped
Baedecker in a thick blanket of isolation. Gigantic, lurid
billboards touted movies starring actors with pink cheeks
and actresses with raven hair, bee-stung lips, and a purplish
cast to their complexions.

Then they were on Marine Drive, the Queen's Necklace, and the sea was a pounding, gray presence to their
right. To his left, Baedecker caught glimpses of cricket fields,
open-air crematoriums, temples, and high-rise office buildings. He thought that he could see a thin cloud of vultures
circling above the Tower of Silence, waiting for the bodies
of the Parsee faithful, but when he looked away, the specks
continued to circle in the periphery of his vision.

The blast of air-conditioning inside the Oberoi
Sheraton made his sodden skin tremble. Baedecker hardly
remembered registering or following the red-coated porter
to his room on the thirtieth floor. The carpets smelled of
some sort of carbolic, antiseptic cleanser, a group of loud
Arabs in the elevator reeked of musk, and for a second
Baedecker thought that he was going to be sick. Then he
was slipping a five-rupee note to the porter, the drapes were
drawn across the wide window, the door was closed, sounds
were muffled, and Baedecker tossed his seersucker coat on a
chair and collapsed on the bed. He was asleep in ten seconds.

They had taken the Rover almost three miles, a record.
It was a bumpy ride. The powdered moondust flew out from
each wheel in an odd, flat trajectory that fascinated
Baedecker. The world was bright and empty. Their shadow
leaped ahead of them. Beyond the crackle of the radio and
the internal suit sounds, Baedecker sensed a silence cold and
absolute.

The experiment site was well removed from the landing area in a flat spot near a small impact crater designated Kate on their maps. They had been moving uphill gradually with the tiny computer in the Rover memorizing each turn and twist. The landing module was a glitter of gold and silver in the valley behind them.

Baedecker deployed the bulky seismic package while Dave took time to make a full panoramic sweep with his chest-mounted Hasselblad. Baedecker took care in running out the ten-meter gold wires. He watched Dave pivot lightly after each shot, a humanoid balloon tethered to a bright beach. Dave called something to Houston and bounced south to photograph a large rock outcropping. The earth was a small blue-and-white shield in a black sky.

Now, thought Baedecker. He dropped to one knee, found that too difficult in the pressure suit, and went to both knees in the dust to secure the end of the last seismic filament. Dave continued to move away. Baedecker quickly unzipped the sample pocket above his right knee and removed the two objects. His thick gloves fumbled over opening the plastic bag, but he succeeded in shaking the contents into his dusty palm. The small, colored photograph he propped against a small rock about a meter from the end of the sensor filament. It was half in shadow and Dave would not notice it unless he was standing right above it. The other object—the Saint Christopher's medal—he held loosely for a moment, irresolute. Then he bent slightly, touched the metal to the gray soil, dropped it in the bag, and quickly returned it to the sample pocket before Dave returned. Baedecker felt odd kneeling there on the lunar soil, supplicant, his bulking shadow thrown in front of him like a black cloth. The little three-by-five photograph looked back at him. Joan was wearing a red blouse and blue slacks. Her head was turned slightly toward Baedecker, who was smiling directly at the camera. Each had a hand on Scott's shoulders. The seven-year-old was grinning widely. He was wearing a white dress shirt for the photograph, but at the open neck Baedecker could see the blue Kennedy Space Center T-shirt, which the boy had worn almost every day of the previous summer.

Baedecker glanced left at the distant figure of Dave and had started to rise when he sensed a presence behind him. His skin went clammy in his suit. He rose and turned slowly.

The Rover was parked five meters behind him. The television camera, controlled from a console in Houston, was mounted on a strut near the right front wheel. The camera was pointing directly at him. It tilted back slightly to track him as he rose to his full height.

Baedecker stared across the glare and the distance at the small, cabled box. The black circle of the lens stared back at him through silence.

∾

The wide antenna cut a sharp parabola from the monsoon sky.

"Impressive, is it not?" asked Sirsikar. Baedecker nodded and looked down from the hill. Small patches of farmland, none larger than two acres, ran along the narrow road. The homes were untidy piles of thatch atop rough poles. All along the way from Bombay to the receiving station, Sirsikar and Shah had pointed out places of interest.

"Very nice farmhouse," Shah had said, gesturing toward a stone building smaller than the garage in Baedecker's old home in Houston. "It has a methane converter, don't you know."

Baedecker was noticing the men standing on their flat, wooden plows behind their tired-looking oxen. Prongs pushed through the cracked soil. One man had his two sons standing with him so the wooden wedges would dig more deeply into the dry earth.

"We have three now," continued Sirsikar. "Only the *Nataraja* is synchronous. Both the *Sarasvati* and *Lakshmi* are above the horizon for thirty of their ninety-minute transit time and the Bombay station here handles real-time trans-missions from them."

Baedecker glanced at the little scientist. "You name the satellites after gods?" he asked.

Shah shuffled uncomfortably but Sirsikar beamed at Baedecker. "Of course!"

Recruited while *Mercury* flew, trained during *Gemini*, blooded in *Apollo*, Baedecker turned his eyes back to the steel symmetry of the huge antenna.

"So did we," he said.

∾

DAD. WILL BE ON RETREAT UNTIL SAT JUNE 27. BACK POONA SUN. IF YOU'RE THERE, SEE YOU THEN. SCOTT.

Baedecker reread the cable, crumpled it, and shot it at the wastebasket in the corner of his room. He walked to the broad window and stared down at the reflection of lights from the Queen's Necklace on the choppy waters of the bay. After a while he turned and went down to the desk to write out a cable to St. Louis, informing his firm that he would be taking his vacation now after all.

∾

"I knew you'd come," said Maggie Brown. They stepped ashore from the tourist boat and Baedecker recoiled slightly from the onslaught of beggars and peddlers. He wondered again if he had made a mistake by not accepting the credit card commercial. The money would have been welcome.

"Did you guess that Scott would stay at the retreat?" asked Baedecker.

"No. I'm not surprised, but that's not it. I just had a hunch I'd see you again."

They stood on the bank of the Ganges and shared another sunrise. Already crowds were filling the oversized steps that led down into the river. Women rose from the coffee-colored water, wet cotton clinging to their thin forms. Earth-brown pots echoed the color of skin. Swastikas adorned a marble-fronted temple. Baedecker could hear the slap, slap, slap of the washer-caste women beating laundry against the flat rocks upstream. The smoke from incense and funeral pyre floated and mingled in the wet morning air.

"The signs say Benares," said Baedecker as they fell in with the small group. "The ticket was to Varanasi. Which is it?"

"Varanasi was its original name. Everybody calls it Benares. But they wanted to get rid of that because the British called it that. You know, a slave name. Malcolm X. Muhammad Ali." Maggie quit talking and broke into a slight jog as their guide shouted at them to keep up in the narrow lanes. At one point the street became so narrow that Baedecker reached out and touched the opposing walls with his forefingers. People jostled, shouted, shoved, spat, and made way for the ubiquitous cattle that wandered free. A singularly persistent peddler followed them for several blocks, blowing deafeningly on his hand-carved flute. Finally Baedecker winked at Maggie, paid the boy ten rupees, and put the instrument in his hip pocket.

They entered an abandoned building. Inside, bored men held candles to show the way up a battered staircase. They held their hands out as Baedecker passed. On the third floor a small balcony afforded a view over the wall of the temple. A gold-plated temple spire was barely visible.

"This is the holiest spot in the world," said the guide. His skin had the color and texture of a well-oiled catcher's mitt. "Holier than Mecca. Holier than Jerusalem. Holier than Bethlehem or Sarnath. It is the holiest of temples where all Hindus . . . after bathing in the holy Ganges . . . wish to visit before they die."

There was a general nodding and murmuring. Clouds of gnats danced in front of sweaty faces. On the way back down the stairs, the men with the candles blocked their way and were much more insistent with their thrusting palms and sharp voices.

Later, sharing an autorickshaw on their way back to the hotel, Maggie turned to him and her face was serious. "Do you believe in that? Places of power?"

"How do you mean?"

"Not holy places, but a place that's more than just special to you. A place that has its own power."

"Not here," said Baedecker and gestured toward the sad spectacle of poverty and decay they were passing.

"No, not here," agreed Maggie Brown. "But I've found a couple of places."

"Tell me about them," said Baedecker. He had to speak loudly because of the noise of traffic and bicycle bells.

Maggie looked down and brushed her hair back behind her ear in a gesture that was already becoming familiar to Baedecker. "There's a place near where my grandparents live in western South Dakota," she said. "A volcanic cone north of the Black Hills, on the edge of the prairie. It's called Bear Butte. I used to climb it when I was little while Grandad and Memo waited for me down below. Years later I learned that it was a holy place for the Sioux. But even before that— when I stood up there and looked over the prairie—I *knew* it was special."

Baedecker nodded. "High places do that," he said. "There's a place I like to visit—a little Christian Science college—way out in the boonies on the Illinois side of the Mississippi River, not far from St. Louis. The campus is right on the bluffs over the river. There's a tiny chapel right near the edge, and you can walk out on some ledges and see halfway across Missouri."

"Are you a Christian Scientist?"

The question and her expression were so serious that Baedecker had to laugh. "No," he said, "I'm not religious. I'm not . . . anything." He had a sudden image of himself kneeling in the lunar dust, the stark sunlight a benediction.

The autorickshaw had been stuck in traffic behind several trucks. Now it roared around to pass on the right, and Maggie had to almost shout her next comment. "Well, I think it's more than the view. I think some places have a power of their own."

Baedecker smiled. "You could be right."

She turned to him and her green eyes were also smiling. "And I could be wrong," she said. "I could be full of shit. This country will turn anybody into a mystic. But sometimes I think that we spend our whole lives on a pilgrimage to find places like that."

Baedecker looked away and said nothing.

The moon had been a great, bright sandbox and Baedecker was the only person in it. He had driven the Rover over a hundred meters from the landing module and parked it so that it could send back pictures of the lift-off. He undid the safety belt and vaulted off the seat with the one-armed ease that had become second nature in the low gravity. Their tracks were everywhere in the deep dust. Ribbed wheel tracks swirled, intersected themselves, and headed off to the north where the highlands glared white. Around the ship itself the dust had been stamped and packed down like snow around a cabin.

Baedecker bounced around the Rover. The little vehicle was covered with dust and badly used. Two of the light fenders had fallen off, and Dave had jerry-rigged some plastic maps to keep clods of dirt from being kicked up onto them. The camera cable had become twisted a dozen times and even now had to be rescued by Baedecker. He bounced easily to the front of the Rover, freed the cable with a tug, and dusted off the lens. A glance told him that Dave was already out of sight in the LM.

"Okay, Houston, it looks all right. I'll get out of the way here. How is it?"

"Great, Dick. We can see the *Discovery* and . . . ahh . . . we should be able to track you on the lift-off."

Baedecker watched with a critical eye as the camera pivoted to the left and to the right. It aimed at his waist and then tracked up to its full lock position. He could imagine the image it was sending. His dusty space suit would be a glare of white, broken by occasional straps, snaplocks, and the dark expanse of his visor. He would have no face.

"Good," he said. "Okay. Well . . . ah . . . you have anything else you want me to do?"

". . . tiv . . ."

"Say again, Houston?"

"Negative, Dick. We're running a little over. Time to get aboard."

"Roger."

Baedecker turned to take one last look at the lunar terrain. The glare of the sun wiped out most surface features. Even through his darkest visor the surface was a brilliant, white emptiness. It matched his thoughts. Baedecker was irritated to find his mind full of details—the prelaunch checklist, storage procedures, an irritatingly full bladder—all crowding in and not allowing him to think. He slowed his breathing and tried to experience any last feelings that he might be harboring.

I'm here, he thought. *This is real.*

He felt silly, standing there, breathing into his mike, running the schedule even further behind. The sunlight on the gold insulating foil around the lander caught his eye.

Shrugging slightly in his bulging suit, Baedecker bounced effortlessly across the pocked and trampled plain toward the waiting spacecraft.

∞

The half-moon rose above the jungle. It was Maggie's turn to putt. She bent over, knees together, her face a study in concentration. The lightly tapped ball rolled too quickly down the concrete ramp and bounced over the low railing.

"I don't believe this," Baedecker said.

Khajuraho consisted of a landing strip, a famed group of temples, a tiny Indian village, and two small hotels on the edge of the jungle. And one miniature golf course.

The temple compound closed at five P.M. Entertainment other than the temples themselves consisted of a hotel-sponsored elephant ride into the jungle during tourist season. It was not tourist season. Then they had strolled out behind the small hotel and found the miniature golf course.

"I don't believe this," Maggie had said.

"It must have been left behind by a homesick architect from Indianapolis," said Baedecker. The hotel clerk had frowned but provided them with a choice of three putters, two of them bent beyond repair. Baedecker gallantly had offered Maggie the straightest of the lot and they had charged out to the links.

Maggie's missed putt rolled into the grass. A thin green serpent slid away toward higher grass. Maggie stifled a scream and Baedecker held his putter out like a sword. Ahead of them in the humid dusk were peeling plywood windmills and decarpeted putting strips. Cups and concrete water hazards were filled with lukewarm water from the day's monsoon rains. A few yards beyond the last hole

stood a real Hindu temple, seemingly part of the miniature montage.

"Scott would love this," laughed Baedecker.

"Really?" asked Maggie. She rested her weight on her
putter. Her face was a white oval in the dim light.

"Sure. This used to be his favorite sport. We used to
get a season pass to the Cocoa Beach Putt-Putt course."

Maggie lowered her head and sank a ten-foot putt
across pebbly cement. She looked up as something eclipsed
the moon.

"Oh!" she said. A fruit bat with a wingspan of three
feet or more floated out of the trees and coasted black against
the sky.

It was the mosquitoes that drove them inside from the
fourteenth hole.

2

Woodland Heights. Seven miles from the Johnson
Space Flight Center, flat as the Bonneville Salt Flats and as
devoid of trees save for the precariously supported saplings
in every yard, the homes of Woodland Heights stretched in
curves and circles under the relentless Texas sun. Once, flying home from a week at the Cape, early on in the training
for the *Gemini* flight that was never to be, Baedecker banked
his T-38 over the endless geometries of similar houses to
find his own. He finally picked it out by the repainted green
of Joan's old Rambler.

Impulsively, he put the little trainer into a dive and
leveled off at a satisfying and illegal two hundred feet above
the rooftops. The horizon banked, sunlight prismed off
Plexiglas, and he brought the jet back for another run.
Pulling out, he kicked in the afterburner and brought
the T-38 up into a steep climb, arched it into a tight
loop, culminated by the sight of the somehow miracu-

lous emergence of his wife and child from the white ranch house.

It had been one of the few moments in Baedecker's life that he could point to and say that he was truly happy.

∾

He lay awake and watched the strip of moonlight move slowly up the wall of the hotel room in Khajuraho. Baedecker idly wondered if Joan had sold the house or if she was still holding it as rental property.

After a while he rose from the bed and went to look out the window. In so doing he blocked the fragile line of moonlight and let the darkness in.

∾

Basti, chawl, whatever the Calcuttans called it, it was the ultimate slum. Stretching for miles along the railroad tracks, the maze of tin-roofed shacks and gunnysack tents was penetrated only by a few winding paths that served as both streets and sewers. The density of people was almost beyond belief. Children were everywhere, defecating in doorways, chasing each other between huts, and following Baedecker with the light-footed hop of the shy and the barefoot. Women looked away as Baedecker passed, or pulled up the cloth of their saris to cover their faces. Men stared with open curiosity verging on hostility. Some ignored him. Mothers squatted behind their children, intent on pulling lice from matted hair. Little girls crouched next to old women and kneaded cow dung with their hands, shaping it into properly sized patties for fuel. An old man hawked phlegm into his hand as he squatted to shit in an empty lot.

"Baba! Baba!" Children ran alongside Baedecker. Palms were stretched out and hands tugged at him. He had long since emptied his pockets of coins.

"Baba! Baba!"

He had agreed to meet Maggie at two o'clock at Calcutta University but had become lost after getting off the overcrowded bus too soon. It must have been getting close to five o'clock. The paths and dirt streets wound back on themselves, trapping him between the railroad tracks and the Hooghly River. He had captured repeated glimpses of the Howrah Bridge, but he could never seem to get closer to it. The stench from the river was rivaled only by the stink of the slums and mud through which he walked.

"Baba!" The crowd around him was getting larger and not all of the beggars were children. Several large men pushed right behind him, speaking rapidly and thrusting out their hands in jabs that fell just short of landing.

My own goddamn fault, thought Baedecker. *The Ugly American strikes again.*

The huts had no doorways. Chickens ran in and out of the cramped, dark spaces. In a low-lying pond of sewage, a group of boys and men washed the black sides of a sleepy bullock. Somewhere in the tightly packed maze of shacks there was a battery-powered radio playing loudly. The music had been rising to a crescendo of plucked strings that augmented Baedecker's growing anxiety. Thirty or forty people were following him now, and lean, angry men had all but pushed the children away.

One man with a red bandanna around his head screamed loudly in what Baedecker took to be Hindi or Bengali. When Baedecker shook his head that he did not understand, the man blocked his way, waved his thin arms in the air, and shouted more loudly. Some of the phrases were repeated by other men in the crowd.

Much earlier, Baedecker had picked up a small but heavy rock. Now he casually put his hand in the pocket of his safari shirt and palmed the stone. Time seemed to slow and a calm descended on him.

Suddenly there was a screaming from one side, children were running, and the crowd abandoned Baedecker to jog down a side street. Even the man with the red bandanna shouted a parting syllable and moved quickly away. Baedecker waited a minute and then strolled after them, descending a muddy path to the river's edge.

A crowd had gathered around something that had washed up in the mud. At first, Baedecker thought it was a bleached tree stump, but then he saw the awful symmetry of it and recognized it as a human body. It was white—white beyond albino white, beyond fish-belly white—and gases had bloated it to twice normal-size. Black holes seemed to stare out from the puffy mass that had once been a face. Several of the children who had been following Baedecker now squatted close to the thing and ran their hands across it with shrill giggles. The texture reminded Baedecker of white fungus, of huge mushrooms rotting in the sun. Pieces of flesh collapsed inward or broke off as the boys prodded and giggled.

Finally some of the men went closer and prodded the body with sharp sticks. They backed away as gas escaped with an audible hiss. The crowd laughed. Mothers with infants slung on their hips pressed forward.

Baedecker backed away, moved quickly down an alley, made a right turn without thinking about it, and suddenly emerged onto a paved street. A trolley car passed, swaying from its load of hanging passengers. Two rickshaw coolies trotted past, pulling overweight Indian businessmen home for dinner. Baedecker stood in the traffic for a few seconds and then waved down a passing cab.

∾

"How are you doing, Richard?"

"Great, hon. Not much to do for the next couple of days. Tom Gavin's been doing most of the work and taking real good care of us. Dave and I are going to send him out to retrieve the film canisters in a few hours. How are things at home?"

"Just great. We watched the lunar lift-off yesterday from here at Mission Control. You never told us that it went up so quickly."

"Yeah. It was quite a ride."

". . . want to . . . few . . ."

"Sorry. Say again. Didn't copy that."

". . . said that Scott would like to say a few words."

"Okay . . . great! Put him on."

"All right. Good-bye, Richard. We're looking forward to seeing you on Tuesday. Bye!"

"Hi, Dad!"

"Hi, Scott."

"You looked really neat on the TV. Did you really set a speed record like they said?"

"Ahh . . . for land speed . . . for driving on the moon, yeah, I guess we did, Scott. Only Dave was driving. I guess the record's in his name."

"Oh."

"Well, Tiger, we've got to get back to work. It's been real good talking to you."

"Hey, Dad."

"Ah . . . roger, Scott . . ."

"I can see all three of you on the big TV here. Who's driving the command module?"

"Ah . . . That's a good question, isn't it, Tom? I guess . . . Scott . . . I guess that for the next couple of days . . . uh . . . Isaac Newton's doing the driving."

The live transmission of the families talking to the astronauts had been NASA's idea of effective PR in time for the evening news. They did not repeat it on the next flight.

∾

"The illustrious sepulchre of His Exalted Majesty Shah Jahan, the Valiant King, whose dwelling is in the starry Heaven. He traveled from this transient world to the World of Eternity on the twenty-eighth night of the month of Rahab in the year of 1076 of the Hegira."

Maggie Brown closed the guidebook, and they both turned their backs on the white eminence of the Taj Mahal. Neither was in the mood to appreciate beautiful architecture or precious stones inlaid in flawless marble. Outside the gates the beggars waited. Baedecker and the girl crossed the chessboard pavement to lean on the wide railing and look out over the river. A monsoon downpour had driven away all but the most hardy of tourists. The air was as cool as it had been during Baedecker's entire visit—as low as the eighties. The sun was hidden behind bruise-black stratocumulus to the west, but a gray light permeated the scene. The river was broad and shallow, and it moved by with the absorbing serenity of all rivers everywhere.

"Maggie, why did you follow Scott to India?"

She looked at Baedecker, avoided a shrug only by hunching her shoulders, and tucked a stray strand of hair behind her ear. She squinted across the river as if searching for someone on the far bank. "I'm not sure. We only knew each other for about five months before he decided to drop out and come here. I liked Scott . . . I still do . . . but sometimes he seemed so *immature*. Other times he was like an old man who had forgotten how to laugh."

"But you followed him ten thousand miles."

This time she did shrug. "He was hunting for something. We were both serious about that . . ."

"Places of power?"

"Something like that. Only Scott thought that if he didn't find it soon, he never would. He said that he didn't want to piss away his life like . . ."

"Like his old man?"

"Like so many people. So when he wrote me I decided to come and take a look. Only for me it's just time off. *I'm* going to get my master's degree next year."

"Do you think he's found it?" asked Baedecker. His voice was almost trembling.

Maggie Brown brought her head back and took a deep breath. "I don't think he's found anything. I think he's just set on proving that he can be as dumb an asshole as the next guy. Sorry about the language, Mr. Baedecker."

Baedecker smiled. "Maggie, I'll be fifty-three years old next November. I'm twenty-one pounds heavier than I was when I was a wage-earning pilot. My job stinks. My office has the kind of blond furniture in it you used to see in the 1950s. My wife divorced me after twenty-eight years of marriage and is living with a CPA who dyes his hair and raises chinchillas as a hobby. I spent two years trying to write a book before I realized that I had absolutely nothing to say. I've just spent the better part of a week with a beautiful girl who didn't wear a bra the whole time and never once did I make a pass at her. Now . . . just a minute . . . if you want to say that my son, my only begotten son, is as big an asshole as the next guy, why, you go right ahead."

Maggie's laughter echoed off the tall building. An elderly English couple glared at them as if they were giggling in church.

"All right," she said at last. "That's why *I'm* here. Why did you come?"

Baedecker blinked. "I'm his father." Maggie Brown's green eyes did not waver. "You're right," he said. "That's not enough." He reached into his pocket and withdrew the Saint Christopher's medal.

"My father gave this to me when I went off to the Marines," he said. "My father and I didn't have much in common . . ."

"Was he Catholic?"

Baedecker laughed. "No, he wasn't Catholic . . . Dutch Reformed . . . but his *grand*father had been Catholic. This thing's come a long way." Baedecker told her about the medal's trip to the moon.

"Jesus," said Maggie. "And St. Christopher's not even a saint anymore, is he?"

"Nope."

"That doesn't matter, does it?"

"No."

Maggie looked across the river. The light was fading. Lantern lights and open fires gleamed along a line of trees. Sweet smoke filled the air.

"You know what the saddest book I ever read was?" she asked.

"No. What was the saddest book you ever read?"

"*The Boys of Summer*. Ever read it?"

"No. But I remember when it came out. It was a sports book, wasn't it?"

"Yes. This writer—Roger Kahn—he went and looked up a lot of the guys who played for the Brooklyn Dodgers in 1952 and '53."

"I remember those seasons," said Baedecker. "Duke Snider, Campanella, Billy Cox. What's sad about that? They didn't win the Series, but they had great seasons."

"Yeah, but that's just *it*," said Maggie, and Baedecker was amazed at how earnest and tense her voice seemed. "Years later, when Kahn looked up these guys, that was still their best season. I mean, it'd been the best time in their goddamn *lives*, and most of them didn't want to believe it. They were just old farts signing autographs and waiting to die, and they still pretended that the best stuff was ahead of them."

Baedecker did not laugh. He nodded. Embarrassed, Maggie poked through the guidebook. After a silent moment she said, "Hey, here's something interesting."

"What's that?"

"It says here that the Taj Mahal was just for practice. Old Shah Jahan had an even *bigger* tomb planned for himself. Across the river. It was going to be all black and connected to the Taj by a graceful bridge."

"What happened?"

"Hmm . . . evidently when Shah Jahan died, his son . . . Aurangzeb . . . just slid his father's coffin in next to Mumtaz Mahal and spent the money on other things."

They both nodded. As they left they could hear the haunting cries of the Muslim call to prayer. Baedecker looked back before they passed out the main gate, but he was not looking at the Taj or its dim image in the darkened, reflecting pool. He was looking across the river at a tall, ebony tomb and its soaring bridge connecting it to the closer shore.

The moon hung above the banyan trees against the pale of the early-morning sky. Baedecker stood in front of the hotel with his hands in his pockets and watched the street fill with people and vehicles. When he finally saw Scott approaching, he had to look again to make sure it was Scott. The orange robe and sandals seemed appropriate to the long-haired, bearded image, but none of it held a referent for Baedecker. He noticed that the boy's beard, a miserable failure two years earlier, was now full with red streaks in it.

Scott stopped a few feet away. The two stared at each other for a long moment that had just begun to shade into awkwardness when Scott, teeth white against the beard, held out his hand.

"Hi, Dad."

"Scott." The handshake was firm but unsatisfactory to Baedecker. He felt a sudden surge of loss superimposed upon the memory of a seven-year-old boy, blue T-shirt and crew cut, running full tilt from the house and throwing himself into his father's arms.

"How are you, Dad?"

"Good. Very good. How about you? You look like you've lost quite a bit of weight."

"Just fat. I've never felt better. Physically or spiritually."

Baedecker paused.

"How's Mom?" asked Scott.

"I haven't seen her for a few months, but I called her just before I left and she was great. She told me to give you a hug for her. Also to break your arm if you didn't promise to write more often."

The young man shrugged and made a motion with his right hand that Baedecker remembered from Little League games in which Scott had struck out. Impulsively, Baedecker reached out and clasped his son's arm. It felt thin but strong under the flimsy robe.

"Come on, Scott. What do you say we go somewhere to have breakfast and really talk?"

"I don't have a lot of time, Dad. The Master begins his first session at eight and I have to be there. I'm afraid I'm not going to have any free time during the next few days. Our whole group is at a real sensitive stage right now. It doesn't take much to break the life-consciousness. I could slip back a couple of months in my progress."

Baedecker cut off the first response that welled up. He nodded tightly. "Well, we still have time for a cup of coffee, don't we?"

"Sure." There was a slight undertone of doubt in the word.

"Where to? How about the hotel coffee shop? It seems to be about the only place around here."

Scott's smile was condescending. "All right. Sure."

The coffee shop was a shaded, open structure adjoining the gardens and pool. Baedecker ordered rolls and coffee and noticed from the corner of his eye the "Scheduled Class" woman mowing the lawn with a hand sickle. Untouchables remained untouchable in modern India, but they were no longer called that. An Indian family had come to use the pool. Both the father and his little boy were grossly overweight. Again and again they jumped feet-first off the low board and splashed water on the sidewalk. The mother and daughters sat at a table and giggled loudly.

Scott's eyes looked deeper, even more serious than Baedecker had remembered. Even as a baby Scott had been solemn. Now the young man looked tired and his breathing was shallow and asthmatic.

Their food arrived. "Mmmm," said Baedecker, "I haven't cared too much for the Indian food I've had on this trip, but the coffee's been delicious."

"Lots of karma," said Scott. He stared doubtfully at his cup and the two rolls. "You don't even know who prepared this stuff. Who touched it. Could be somebody with really lousy karma."

Baedecker sipped his coffee. "Where are you living here, Scott?"

"Mostly at the ashram or the Master's farm. During solitude weeks I check into a little Indian hostel a few blocks from here. It has open windows and a string bed, but it's cheap. And my physical environment doesn't mean anything to me anymore."

Baedecker stared. "No? If it's so cheap, where has all the money gone? Your mother and I have sent you almost four thousand dollars since you decided to come here in January."

Scott looked out at the pool where the Indian family was making noise. "Oh, you know. Expenses."

"No," said Baedecker softly, "I don't know. What kind of expenses?"

Scott frowned. His hair was very long and parted in the middle. With the beard, his son reminded Baedecker of an eccentric ground crewman he had known while flying experimental aircraft for NASA in the mid-sixties.

"Expenses," repeated Scott. "Getting around wasn't cheap. Most of it I've donated to the Master."

Baedecker felt the conversation slipping out of his control. He felt the anger that he had sworn he would not let come. "What do you mean you give it to the Master? For what? So he could build another auditorium here? Move to Hollywood again? Try to buy another town in Oregon?"

Scott sighed and bit into a roll without thinking about it. He brushed crumbs from his mustache. "Forget it, Dad."

"Forget what? That you dropped out of graduate school to come spend money on this fake guru?"

"I said forget it."

"Like hell. We can at least talk about it."

"Talk about *what?*" Scott's voice was rising. Heads turned. An older man, in orange robe and sandals, his hair tied back in a ponytail, put down his copy of the *Times* and stubbed out his cigarette, obviously interested in the exchange. "What the hell do you know about it? You're so wrapped up in your American materialistic crap that you wouldn't know the truth if it appeared on your fucking desk someday."

"Materialistic crap," repeated Baedecker. Most of the anger was gone now. "And you think that a little bit of tantra yoga and a few months in this ass-backward country is going to lead you to the truth?"

"Don't talk about things you don't know about," snapped Scott.

"I know about engineering," said Baedecker. "I know that I'm not impressed with a country that can't manage a simple phone system or build sewers. I know useless hunger when I see it."

"Bullshit," said Scott, perhaps with more of a sneer than he had intended. "Just because we're not eating Kansas beef you think we're starving . . ."

"I'm not talking about you. Or these others here. You can fly home anytime you want. This is a game for rich kids. I'm talking about . . ."

"Rich kids!" Scott's high laugh was sincere. "This is the first time I've been called a rich kid! I remember when

you wouldn't give me a goddamn fifty-cent allowance because you thought it'd be bad for my self-discipline."

"Come on, Scott."

"Why don't you just go home, Dad. Go home and
watch your color TVs and ride your exerciser in the basement and look at your fucking photos on the wall and leave
me here to go about my . . . my game."

Baedecker closed his eyes for a second. He wished the
day would start over so he could begin again. "Scott. We
want you home."

"Home?" Baedecker watched his son's eyebrows arch.
"Where's home, Pop? Up in Boston with Mom and good-
time Charlie? Your swinging-bachelor pad in St. Louis? No
thanks."

Baedecker reached out and took his son's upper arm
once again. He could feel the tightening there, the resistance. "Let's talk about it, Scott. There's nothing here."

The two men stared at each other. Strangers in a chance
encounter.

"There's sure as hell nothing *there*," said Scott fiercely.
"You've been there, Dad. You know it. Shit, you *are* it."

Baedecker leaned back in his chair. A waiter stood ob-
trusively nearby, uselessly rearranging cups and silverware.
Sparrows hopped across nearby tables, eating from the soiled
plates and sugar cups. The fat boy on the diving board called
loudly and hit the water in a crude belly flop. His father shouted
encouragement, and the women laughed from poolside.

"I have to get going," said Scott.

Baedecker nodded. "I'll walk you there."

The ashram was only two blocks from the hotel. Devotees were walking up the flowered lanes and arriving by
autorickshaw in twos and threes. A wooden gate and tall
fences kept out the curious. Just inside the gate there was a
small souvenir shop where one could buy books, photographs, and autographed T-shirts of the guru.

The two men stood a minute by the entrance.

"Can you get away long enough for dinner tonight?" asked Baedecker.

"Yeah. I guess so. Fine."

"The hotel?"

"No. I know a place downtown that has good vegetarian. Cheap."

"All right. Well, okay, good. Stop by the hotel if you get out early."

"Yeah. I'll be going back to the Master's farm on Monday but maybe Maggie could show you around Poona before you leave. Kasturba Samadhi, the Parvati Temple, all that good tourist shit." The motion with his right hand again. "You know."

Baedecker almost reached out to shake hands again— as with a client—resisted it. The diffuse sunlight was very hot. From the humidity he knew that it would rain hard again before lunch. He would use the time to buy an umbrella somewhere.

"I'll see you later, Scott."

His son nodded. When he turned to join the other robed devotees to enter the ashram, Baedecker noticed how straight the thin shoulders were, how his son's hair caught the light.

∾

On Monday morning Baedecker took the train, the *Deccan Queen*, for the hundred-mile trip down out of the mountains to Bombay. His flight to London was delayed three hours. The heat was very great. Baedecker noticed that the aged airport guards carried ancient bolt-action rifles and wore only sandals over their patched socks.

That morning he had walked through the old British section of Poona until he had found the doctor's house where Maggie worked. Miss Brown was gone—taken the children to the pavilion—did he care to leave a message? He left no message. He left the simply wrapped package holding the flute he'd purchased in Varanasi. The flute and an old Saint Christopher's medal on a tarnished chain.

He boarded about six P.M. and the aircraft was a physical relief. There was an additional maintenance delay, but the stewardesses brought around drinks and the air-conditioning was working well. Baedecker leafed through a *Scientific American* he had bought in Victoria Station.

He dozed off for a while just before they took off. In his dream he was learning to swim and was bouncing lightly over the clear white sand of the lake bottom. He could not see his father, but he could feel the strong, constant pressure of his father's arms buoying him up, keeping him safe from the dangerous currents.

He awoke just as they took off. Ten minutes later they were far out over the Arabian Sea and they broke through the ceiling of cloud cover. It was the first time in a week that Baedecker had seen a pure blue sky. The setting sun was turning the clouds beneath them into a lake of golden fire.

As they reached their cruising altitude and ended their climb, Baedecker felt the slight reduction in g-force as they came over the top of the arc. Looking out the scratched window, searching in vain for a glimpse of the moon, Baedecker felt a brief lifting of spirit. Here in the high, thin air the demanding gravity of the massive planet seemed slightly—ever so slightly—lessened.

Part Two

Glen Oak

Forty-two years after he had moved away, thirty years after he had last visited, sixteen years after his week of fame walking on the moon, Richard Baedecker was invited to come back to his hometown. He was to be guest of honor during the Old Settlers Weekend and Parade. August 8 was to be declared Richard M. Baedecker Day in Glen Oak, Illinois.

Baedecker's middle initial was not *M*. His middle name was Edgar. Nor did he consider the small village in Illinois his hometown. When he did think of his childhood home, which was seldom, he usually remembered the small apartment on Kildare Street in Chicago where his family spent the years before and after the war. Baedecker had lived in Glen Oak for less than three years from late 1942 to May of 1945. His mother's family had owned land there for many years, and when Baedecker's father had gone back into the Marine Corps to serve three years as an instructor at Camp Pendleton, the seven-year-old Richard Baedecker and his two sisters found themselves inexplicably whisked from their comfortable apartment in Chicago to a drafty old rental house in Glen Oak. For Baedecker, memories of those times were as hazy and out of context as the thought of the manic paper and scrap-metal drives that had seemed to occupy his weekends and summers during their entire interlude there. Despite the fact that his parents were buried just outside of Glen Oak, he had not visited or thought of the town in a long, long time.

∾

Baedecker received the invitation in late May, shortly before embarking on a month-long business trip that would take him to three continents. He filed the letter and would have forgotten it if he had not mentioned it to Cole Prescott, vice president of the aerospace corporation for which he worked.

"Hell, Dick, why don't you go? It'll be good PR for the firm."

"You're joking," said Baedecker. They were in a bar on Lindbergh Boulevard, near their offices in suburban St. Louis. "When I lived in that little Podunk town during the war, it had a sign that said POPULATION 850—SPEED ELECTRICALLY TIMED. I doubt if it's grown much since then. Probably gone down in population, if anything. Not many people there would be interested in buying MD-GSS avionics."

"They buy stock, don't they?" asked Prescott and lifted a handful of salted nuts to his mouth.

"Livestock," said Baedecker.

"Where the hell is this Glen Oak, anyway?" asked Prescott.

It had been years since Baedecker had heard anyone say the town's name. It sounded strange to him. "About 180 miles from here as the provincial crow flies," he said. "Stuck somewhere between Peoria and Moline."

"Shit, it's just up the road. You owe it to them, Dick."

"Too busy," Baedecker said and motioned to the bartender for a third Scotch. "Be catching up after the Bombay and Frankfurt conferences."

"Hey," said Prescott. He turned back from watching a waitress bend over to serve a young couple at a nearby table. "Isn't the ninth of August the beginning of that airline confab at the Hyatt in Chicago? Turner got you to go to that, didn't he?"

"No, Wally did. Seretti's going to be there from Rockwell and we're going to talk about the Air Bus modification deal with Borman."

"So!" said Prescott.

"So what?"

"So you'll be going that way anyway, pal. Do your patriotic duty, Dick. I'll have Teresa tell 'em you're coming."

"We'll see," said Baedecker.

∞

Baedecker flew into Peoria on the afternoon of Friday, August 7. The Ozark DC-9 barely had time to climb to eight thousand feet and find the meandering path of the Illinois River before they were descending. The airport was so small and so empty that Baedecker thought fleetingly of the asphalt runway at the edge of the Indian jungle where he had landed a few weeks earlier at Khajuraho. Then he was down the ramp, across the hot tarmac, and was being urgently hailed by a heavy, florid-faced man he had never seen before.

Baedecker groaned inwardly. He had planned to rent a car, spend the night in Peoria, and drive out to Glen Oak in the morning. He had hoped to stop by the cemetery on his way.

"Mr. Baedecker! Mr. Baedecker! Jesus, welcome, welcome. We're really glad to see ya." The man was alone. Baedecker had to drop his old black flight bag as the stranger grabbed his right hand and elbow in a two-handed greeting. "I'm really sorry we couldn't get up a better reception, but we didn't know 'til Marge got a call this morning that you were comin' in today."

"That's all right," said Baedecker. He retrieved his hand and added needlessly, "I'm Richard Baedecker."

"Oh, yeah, Jesus. I'm Bill Ackroyd. Mayor Seaton would've been here, but she's got the Old Settlers' Jaycees Fish Fry to take care of tonight."

"Glen Oak has a woman mayor?" Baedecker resettled his garment bag on his shoulder and brushed away a trickle of sweat on his cheek. Heat waves rose around them and turned distant walls of foliage and the half-glimpsed parking lot into shimmering mirages. The humidity was as bad as St. Louis's. Baedecker looked at the big man next to him. Bill Ackroyd was in his late forties or early fifties. He was sagging to fat and had already perspired through the back of his JC Penney shirt. His hair was combed forward to hide an encroaching baldness. *He looks like me,* thought Baedecker and felt a blossom of anger unfold in his chest. Ackroyd grinned and Baedecker smiled back.

Baedecker followed him through the tiny terminal to the curved drive where Ackroyd had parked his car in a space reserved for the handicapped. The man kept up an amiable stream of small talk that mixed with the heat to produce a not-unpleasant nausea in Baedecker. Ackroyd drove a Bonneville. The engine had been left running, air-conditioning blasting to cool the interior to an unhealthy chill. Baedecker sank into the velvet cushions with a sigh while the other man set his luggage in the trunk.

"I can't tell you what this means to all of us," said Ackroyd as he settled himself. "The whole town's excited. It's the biggest thing that's happened to Glen Oak since Jesse James's gang came through and camped at Hartley's Pond." Ackroyd laughed and shifted the car into gear. His hands were so large that they made the steering wheel and gearshift look like toys. Baedecker imagined that Ackroyd came from the kind of Midwestern stock that had used such huge, blunt hands to string up outlaws.

"I didn't know that the James gang ever went through Glen Oak," said Baedecker.

"Probably didn't," said Ackroyd and laughed his big, unselfconscious laugh. "That makes you the *most* exciting thing ever to happen to us."

∾

Peoria looked like it had been abandoned or bombed. Or both. Storefronts held dust and dead flies. Grass grew up in cracks in the highway and weeds flourished in the untended medians. Old buildings sagged against one another and the few new structures sat like overscaled druid altars amid razed blocks of rubble.

"My God," muttered Baedecker, "I don't remember the city looking like this." Actually Baedecker hardly remembered Peoria at all. Once a year his mother had taken them to town to watch the Thanksgiving Day parade so they could wave at Santa Claus. Baedecker had been too old for Santa Claus, but he would sit with his younger sisters on the stone lions near the courthouse and dutifully wave. One year Santa had arrived in a jeep with the four elves dressed in the uniforms of the different services. Baedecker remembered that the lawn of the city square had risen in a gentle arc to the elaborate stone gingerbread of the courthouse. He would play at being shot and roll down the grassy incline until his mother yelled at him to stop. He noticed now that the square—he thought that it was the same block—had been turned into a fussily landscaped sunken park near a glass box of a city-county building.

"Reagan's recession," said Ackroyd. "Carter's recession before him. Goddamn Russians."

"Russians?" Baedecker half expected to hear a torrent of John Birch propaganda. He thought he remembered reading that George Wallace had carried Peoria County in the 1968 primary. In 1968 Baedecker had been spending sixty hours a week in a simulator as part of the support team for *Apollo 8*. The year had held no meaning for him except in terms of the project deadlines. He had emerged from his cocoon in January of 1969 to find Bobby Kennedy dead, Martin Luther King dead, LBJ a memory, and Richard M. Nixon president. In Baedecker's office in St. Louis, on the wall above the liquor cabinet, between two honorary degrees from colleges he had never visited, there was a photograph of Nixon shaking his hand in a Rose Garden ceremony. Baedecker and the other two astronauts looked tense and ill at ease in the picture. Nixon was grinning, his upper teeth white and exposed, his left hand on Baedecker's elbow in the same salesman's grip Ackroyd had used at the airport.

"Not really their fault," grunted Ackroyd. "Caterpillar's fault for dependin' so much on selling to 'em. When Carter pulled the plug on heavy equipment exports after Afghanistan or whatever the hell it was, it all went downhill. Caterpillar, GE, even Pabst. Everybody was getting laid off for a while. It's better now."

"Oh," said Baedecker. His head hurt. He still felt the motion of the plane as it had banked in over the river. If he couldn't fly an aircraft this day, he wished that he at least could have driven a car to work the cramps out of arms and legs that ached to control something. He closed his eyes.

"You wanta go the quick way or the long way?" asked the big man at the wheel.

"The long way," Baedecker said without opening his eyes. "Always the long way."

Ackroyd obediently took the next exit off I-74 and descended into the Euclidean geometries of cornfields and county roads.

2

Baedecker may have dozed for a few minutes. He opened his eyes as the car stopped at a crossroads. Green signs gave direction and distance to Princeville, Galesburg, Elmwood, and Kewanee. There was no mention of Glen Oak. Ackroyd swung the car left. The road was a corridor between curtains of corn. Dark seams of tar and asphalt patched the road and provided a rhythmic undertone to the air-conditioner. The slight vibration had a hypnotic, equestrian quality to it.

"Into the heart of the heart of the country," said Baedecker.

"Hmmm?"

Baedecker sat up, surprised he had spoken aloud. "A phrase a writer—William Gass, I think—used to describe this part of the country. I remember it sometimes when I think about Glen Oak."

"Oh." Ackroyd shifted uncomfortably. Baedecker realized with a start that he had made the man nervous. Ackroyd had assumed that they were two men, two *solid* men, and the mention of a writer did not fit. Baedecker smiled as he thought about the seminars the various services had given their test pilots prior to the first NASA interviews for the *Mercury* program. *If you put your hands on your hips, make sure your thumbs are toward the back.* Had Deke told him about that or had he read about it in Tom Wolfe's book?

Ackroyd had been talking about his real estate agency before Baedecker had interrupted. Now he cleared his throat and make a cupping gesture with his right hand. "I imagine you've met a lot of important people, huh, Mr. Baedecker?"

"Richard," Baedecker said quickly. "You're Bill, right?"

"Yeah. No relation to that guy on the old *Saturday Night Live* reruns. Lot of people ask me that."

"No," said Baedecker. He had never seen the program.

"So who was the most important, you think?"

"What's that?" asked Baedecker, but there was no way to steer the conversation a different direction.

"Most important person you ever met?"

Baedecker forced some life into his own voice. He was suddenly very, very tired. It occurred to him that he should have driven his own car from St. Louis. The stopover in Glen Oak would not have been much out of his way, and he could have left when he wished. Baedecker could not remember the last time he had driven anywhere except from his town house to the office and back. Travel had become an endless series of airhops. With a slight shock he realized that Joan, his ex-wife, had never been to St. Louis, to Chicago, to the Midwest. Their life together in Fort Lauderdale, San Diego, Houston, Cocoa Beach, the five bad months in Boston, had been near the coast, all in places where the continent clearly ended. He was suddenly curious about what Joan's impressions of this great expanse of fields, farmhouses, and heat haze would be. "The Shah of Iran," he said. "At least he was the most impressive. The court show they put on there, the protocol, and the sheer sense of power he and his retinue conveyed, they put even the White House and Buckingham Palace to shame. Little good it did him."

"Yeah," said Ackroyd. "Say, I met Joe Namath once. I was at an Amway convention in Cincinnati. Don't have time for it since I got involved in the Pine Meadows deal but used to do real well at it. Thirteen hundred one month and that was without really working at it. Joe, he was there for another thing, but he knew a guy who was real good friends with Merle Weaver. So Joe, he told all of us to call him that, he spent the whole two days with us. Went down to the combat zone with us and everything. I mean, he had commitments, but every time he could, he and Merle's friend would go out to dinner with us and pick up a round of drinks and all. A nicer guy you wouldn't want to meet."

Baedecker was surprised to realize that he recognized his surroundings. He knew that around the next curve in the road there would appear a dairy with a floral clock in the center of the driveway. The dairy came into sight. There was no clock, but the parking lot looked newly paved. The purple-shingled house to the left of the road was the one his mother used to refer to as the old stagecoach stop. He saw the sagging second-floor porch and was sure it was the same building. The sudden superimposition of forgotten memories over reality was disturbing to Baedecker, a sense of déjà vu that did not dissipate. He looked straight ahead and knew that it would be only a long sweep of curve and then another mile before Glen Oak would declare itself as a fringe of trees and a single, green water tower visible above the cornfields.

"You ever meet Joe Namath?" asked Ackroyd.

"No, I never have," said Baedecker. On a clear day, from thirty-five thousand feet in a 747, Illinois would be a verdant patchwork of rectangles. Baedecker knew that the right angle ruled the Midwest in the same way that the sinuous, senseless curves of erosion ruled the Southwest where he had done most of his flying. From two hundred nautical miles up, the Midwest had been a smudge of green and brown hues glimpsed between white cloud masses. From the moon it had been nothing at all. Baedecker had never even thought to look for the United States during his forty-six hours on the moon.

"Just a real nice guy. Not stuck-up like some famous people you meet, you know? Damn shame about his knee."

The water tower was different. A tall, white, metal structure had replaced the old green one. It burned in the rich, slanting rays of the late-summer evening sun. Baedecker felt a curious emotion seize him somewhere between the heart and throat. It was not nostalgia or some resurrected form of homesickness. Baedecker realized that the scalding wave of feeling flowing through him was simple awe at an unexpected confrontation with beauty. He had felt the same surprised pain as a child in the Chicago Art Institute one rainy afternoon while standing in front of a Degas oil of a young ballerina carrying an armful of oranges. He had experienced the same sharp slice of emotion upon seeing his son Scott, purple, bruised, slick, and squawking, a few seconds after his birth. Baedecker had no idea why he felt this now, but invisible thumbs pressed at the hollow of his throat, and there was a burning behind his eyes.

"Bet you don't recognize the old place," said Ackroyd. "How long's it been since you been back, Dick?"

Glen Oak appeared as a skirmish line of trees, resolved itself into a huddle of white homes, and widened to fill the windshield. The road curved again past a Sunoco station, past an old brick home, which Baedecker remembered his mother saying had once been a way station on the underground railroad, and past a white sign that read GLEN OAK—POP. 1275—SPEED ELECTRICALLY TIMED.

"Nineteen fifty-six," said Baedecker. "No, 1957. My mother's funeral. She died the year after my father."

"They're buried out in the Calvary Cemetery," said Ackroyd as if he were sharing a new fact.

"Yes."

"Would you like to go out there now? Before it gets dark? I wouldn't mind waiting."

"No." Baedecker glanced quickly to his left, horrified at the idea of visiting his parents' graves while Bill Ackroyd sat waiting in his idling Bonneville. "No, thanks, I'm tired. I'd like to check into the motel. Is the one on the north side of town still called the Day's End Inn?"

Ackroyd chuckled and slapped the steering wheel. "Jesus, that old roadhouse? No, sir, they tore that place down in '62, year after Jackie and I moved here from Lafayette. Nope, the nearest other place is the Motel Six over on I-74 off the Elmwood exit."

"That will be fine," said Baedecker.

"Aw, naw," said Ackroyd and turned a stricken face to Baedecker. "I mean, we'd planned on you staying with us,

Dick. I mean, we've got plenty of room, and I okayed it
with Marge Seaton and the council. The Motel Six's way
the hell gone, twenty minutes by the hardroad."

The hardroad. That was what everyone in Glen Oak
had called the paved highway that doubled as the main street.
It had been four decades since he had heard the phrase.
Baedecker shook his head and looked out the window as
they moved slowly down that main street. Glen Oak's business section was two and a half blocks long. The sidewalks
were raised strips of concrete three tiers high. The storefronts were dark, and the diagonal parking places were empty
except for a few pickup trucks in front of a tavern near the
park. Baedecker tried to fit the images of these tired, flat-
fronted buildings into the template of his memory, but there
was little conjunction, only a vague sense of structures missing like gaps in a once-familiar smile.

"Jackie kept some supper warm, but we could go out
to Old Settlers and get in on the fish fry if you'd like."

"I'm pretty tired," said Baedecker.

"Good enough," said Ackroyd. "We'll take care of all
the formalities tomorrow, then. Marge'd be pretty busy tonight anyway, what with the raffle and all. Terry, my boy
Terry, he's been dying to meet you. He's a real hero to you .
. . I mean, shit, you know what I mean. Terry's real excited
about space and everything. It was Terry that did a school
report on you last year and remembered you'd lived here for
a while. To tell you the truth, that's what gave me the idea
of you being guest of honor at Old Settlers. Terry was so
interested in this being your hometown and all. 'Course
Marge and the others would have loved the idea anyway
but, you know, it would mean an awful lot to Terry if you
could spend the two nights with us."

Even at the crawling pace at which they were moving,
they had already traveled the length of Glen Oak's main
street. Ackroyd turned right and slowed to a stop near the
old Catholic church. It was a part of town Baedecker had

rarely walked in as a boy because Chuck Compton, the school bully, had lived there. It was the only part of town he had come to when he had returned for his parents' funerals.

"It really wouldn't put us out," said Ackroyd. "We'd be real honored to have you, and the Motel Six's probably full with truckers this late on a Friday."

Baedecker looked at the brown church. He remembered it as being much larger. He felt a strange lassitude descend over him. The summer heat, the long weeks of traveling, the disappointment of seeing his son at the Poona ashram, all conspired to reduce him to this state of sad passivity. Baedecker recognized the feeling from his first months in the Marine Corps in the summer of 1951. From there and from the first weeks after Joan had left him.

"I wouldn't want to be any trouble," he said.

Ackroyd grinned his relief and gripped Baedecker's upper arm for a second. "Shoot, no trouble. Jackie's looking forward to meeting you, and Terry'll never forget having a real-life astronaut visit."

The car moved ahead slowly through alternate streaks of cream-rich evening light and stripes of dark tree-shadow.

The bats were out when Baedecker went for a walk an hour later. Their choppy, half-seen flits of movement sliced pieces from the dull dome of evening sky. The sun was gone but the day clung to light the same way that Baedecker, as a boy on such an August evening, had clung to the last sweet weeks of summer vacation. It took Baedecker only a few minutes to walk to the old part of town, to his part of town. He was pleased to be outside and alone.

Ackroyd lived in a development of twenty-or-so ranch houses on the northeast corner of town where Baedecker remembered only fields and a stream where muskrats could be caught. Ackroyd's house was of a pseudo-Spanish design

with a boat and trailer in the garage and an RV in the driveway. Inside, the rooms were filled with heavy, Ethan Allen
furniture. Ackroyd's wife, Jackie, had closely permed curls,
laugh wrinkles around her eyes, and a pleasant overbite,
which made her appear to be constantly smiling. She was
some years younger than her husband. Their only child,
Terry, a pale boy who looked to be thirteen or fourteen, was
as thin and quiet as his father was stout and hearty.

"Say hello to Mr. Baedecker, Terry. Go on, tell him
how much you've been looking forward to this." The boy
was propelled forward by a shove of Ackroyd's huge palm.

Baedecker bent over but still could not find the boy's
gaze, and his open hand felt only the briefest touch of moist
fingers. Terry's brown hair grew longest in front and dropped
over his eyes like a visor. The boy mumbled something.

"Nice to meet you," said Baedecker.

"Terry," said his mother, "go on now. Show Mr.
Baedecker his guest room. Then show him *your* room. I'm
sure Mr. Baedecker will be very interested." She smiled at
Baedecker and he thought of early photos of Eleanor
Roosevelt.

The boy turned and led the way down the stairs, taking them two at a time. The guest room was in the basement. The bed looked comfortable, and there was an attached bathroom. The boy's room was across a carpeted expanse of open area, which might have been planned as a
recreation room.

"I guess Mom wanted you to see this," muttered Terry
and flicked on a dim light in his room. Baedecker looked
in, blinked, and stepped in farther to look again.

There was a single bed, neatly made, a small desk, a
minicomponent stereo, and three dark walls with shelves,
posters, a few books, models, all the usual paraphernalia of
an adolescent boy. But the fourth wall was different.

It was an *Apollo 8* photograph, one of the Earthrise
pictures taken from the external camera's high-speed series

on the first and third lunar orbits. The picture had once captured the imagination of the world but had been so over-used during the intervening years that Baedecker no longer took any notice of it. But here it was different. The photo had been enlarged to make a supergraphic, floor-to-ceiling wallpaper stretching the width of the room. The earth was a bold blue and white, the sky black, the foreground a dull gray. It was as if the boy's basement room opened onto the lunar surface. The dark walls and dim track lighting added to the illusion.

"Mom's idea," mumbled the boy. He tapped nervously at a stack of tape cassettes on his desk. "I think she got it on sale."

"Did you make the models?" asked Baedecker. Shelves were filled with gray plastic dreadnoughts from *Star Wars, Star Trek*, and *Battlestar Galactica*. Two large space shuttles hung from dark thread in a corner.

The boy made a motion with shoulders and hand, an abbreviated half shrug that reminded Baedecker of his son Scott when he had struck out in a Little League game.

"Dad helped."

"Are you interested in space, Terry?"

"Yeah." The boy hesitated and looked up at Baedecker. In his dark eyes there was a brief panic of summoned courage. "I mean, I useta be. You know, when I was younger. I mean, I still like it and all, but that's sort of kid stuff, you know? What I'd really like to be is, well, like a lead guitarist in a group like Twisted Sister." He stopped talking and looked steadily at Baedecker.

Baedecker could not stop a wide grin. He touched the boy's shoulder briefly, firmly. "Good. Good. Let's go up-stairs, shall we?"

∾

The streets were dark except for occasional streetlights and the blue flicker of televisions through windows.

Baedecker breathed in the scent of freshly cut grass and unseen fields. The stars were hesitant to appear. Except for an occasional car passing on the hardroad a block west, the only noise was the muted but excited gabble of the hidden televisions. Baedecker remembered the sound of console radios through some of these same screen doors and windows. He thought that the radio voices had held more authority and depth.

Glen Oak had never had many oak trees, but in the forties it had been resplendent with giant elms, incredibly massive trees arcing their heavy limbs in a latticework of branches which turned even the widest side street into a tunnel of dappled light and shadow. The elms *were* Glen Oak. Even a ten-year-old boy had realized that as he rode his bike toward the town on a summer evening, pedaling furiously toward the oasis of trees and Saturday dinner.

Now most of the elms were gone. Baedecker assumed that various epidemics of disease had claimed them. The wide streets were open to the sky. There was still a proliferation of smaller trees. Given the slightest breeze, leaves danced in front of streetlights and threw shadows across the sidewalk. Large old homes set far back from the sidewalks still had their upper stories guarded by gently rustling foliage. But the giant elms of Baedecker's childhood were gone. He wondered if people returning to former homes in small towns all over the nation had noticed this loss. Like the smell of burning leaves in the autumn, it was something that gnawed at his generation by its absence.

The bats danced and dodged against a violet sky. A few stars had come out. Baedecker crossed into a schoolyard, which occupied an entire block. The tall, old elementary school, its shuttered belfry the home for the ancestors of many of this night's crop of bats, had long since been torn down and replaced by a cluster of brick-and-glass boxes huddled at the base of a larger brick-and-glass box, which filled much of the square block. Baedecker guessed that the larger structure was the gymnasium for the consolidated school. There had been no elementary school gym in his day; when they needed one, they walked the two blocks to the high school. Baedecker remembered the old school as being the centerpiece of acres of grass, half a dozen baseball diamonds, and two playground areas—one for the small children and another boasting the high, three-humped slide for the upper grades. All of this had been guarded by the sentinel-silent line of tall trees along the perimeter of the block. Now the low buildings and monstrous gymnasium claimed most of the space. There were no trees. The playgrounds had been reduced to a strip of asphalt and a wooden, stockadelike structure built in a square of sand. Baedecker walked over and sat on a lower level of the thing. It made him think of a poorly designed gallows.

He could see his old home across the street. Even in the fading twilight he could tell that little had been done to change it. Light spilled from the bay windows on both floors. There was siding now where once there had been old clapboard. A garage and asphalt drive had been added where the gravel driveway had once curved around to the backyard. Baedecker guessed that the barn was no longer behind the house. Near the front walk a tall birch grew where none had been before. For a moment Baedecker searched his memory, trying in vain to remember a sapling there. Then he realized that it could have been planted after he had moved away and the tree still would be forty years old.

Baedecker felt no nostalgia, only a slight vertigo of wonder that such an alien shell of stone and board in such an alien part of the world could once have been home to a boy who felt himself the center of creation. A light went on in a second-story room. Baedecker could almost see his old wallpaper in which clipper ships were locked in endlessly repeating squares of rope, each corner complicated by impossible nautical knots. He remembered lying awake during nights of fever, trying again and again to mentally untie those knots. He also remembered the hanging light bulb and cord, the yellow coffin of a closet in one corner, and the huge Rand McNally world map on the wall by the door where the earnest boy had nightly moved colored pins from one unpronounceable Pacific island to another.

Baedecker shook his head, rose, and walked north, away from the school and house. Full night had come, but the stars were hidden by low clouds. Baedecker did not look up again.

∽

"Hey, Dick, how was it? See the old places?" called Ackroyd as Baedecker crossed the yard to the man's home. The couple were sitting in a small, screened porch between the house and garage.

"Yes. It's cooling off very nicely, isn't it?"

"See anybody you knew?"

"The streets were pretty empty," said Baedecker. "I could see the lights of Old Settlers—at least I presume it was Old Settlers—out southeast of the high school. Sounded like everyone was out there." For Baedecker as a boy, the Old Settlers carnival weekend had been three days that marked the very heart of summer while simultaneously being the last joyous event before the sickening countdown to the resumption of school. Old Settlers had meant the recognition of entropy.

"Oh, heck, yeah," said Ackroyd. "It'll be going strong tonight with the Jaycees barbecue and all. There's still plenty of time to run out there if you want. The American Legion tent serves beer till eleven."

"No, thanks, Bill. Actually I am pretty tired. Thought I might turn in. Say good night to Terry for me, would you?"

Ackroyd led the way inside and turned on the light above the stairs. "Actually, Terry's gone over to his friend

Donnie Peterson's. They've been spending Old Settlers Weekend together since they were in kindergarten."

Mrs. Ackroyd bustled around making sure that Baedecker had extra blankets even though the night was warm. The guest room had a comfortably familiar motel room smell to it. Mrs. Ackroyd smiled at him, softly closed the door, and Baedecker was alone.

The room was almost pitch-black except for the glow of his digital travel alarm-calculator. Baedecker lay back and stared into the darkness. When the softly glowing digits read 2:32, he rose and went out into the empty, carpeted room. There was no sound from the upper stories. Someone had left a light on over the short stairway in case Baedecker wanted to find his way to the kitchen. Instead, Baedecker crossed to the boy's room, hesitated a second outside the half-opened door, and then stepped inside. The light from the stairway dimly illuminated the pockmarked lunar surface and the blue-and-white rising crescent of earth. Baedecker stood there a minute and was turning to go when something caught his eye. He closed the door and sat down on Terry's bed. For a minute there was no light at all and Baedecker was blind. Then he became aware of a hundred softly glowing sparks on the walls and ceiling. The stars were coming out. The boy—Baedecker felt sure it was the boy—had speckled the room with dots of phosphorescent paint. The half globe of the earth began to glow with a milky radiance, which illuminated the lunar highlands and crater rims. Baedecker had never seen a lunar night from the surface—no *Apollo* astronaut had—but he sat on the boy's tightly made bed until the stars burned into his eyes and he thought *yes, yes*.

After a while Baedecker rose, crossed silently to his own room, and slept.

∽

Richard M. Baedecker Day dawned warm and clear. The street outside Ackroyd's home hissed to the sound of Saturday traffic. The sky was so blue that cornstalks in the fields visible beyond the new houses seemed brittle with light.

Baedecker had two breakfasts. The first was with Ackroyd and his wife in their spacious kitchen. The second was with the mayor and city council at a long table in the Parkside Café. Marjorie Seaton struck Baedecker as a small-town version of Chicago's ex-mayor, Jane Byrne. He wasn't sure where the resemblance lay—Seaton's face was as broad and reddened by weather as Byrne's was narrow and pale. Marge Seaton had an open, hearty laugh that bore no similarity to what he remembered of Byrne's tight-lipped chuckles. But there was something about the eyes of both women that made Baedecker think of Apache squaws waiting for the male prisoners to be pegged out for their pleasure.

"The whole town's excited about you being here, Dick," Seaton said and beamed at him. "I should say the entire county. We're going to get folks from as far away as Galesburg today."

"I'm looking forward to meeting them," said Baedecker. He toyed with his hash browns. Next to him, Ackroyd was mopping up runny eggs with a piece of toast. The waitress, a small, bleak-faced woman named Minnie, returned every other moment to refill their coffee cups as if she had distilled the entire definition of hostess down to the dogged completion of that single act.

"Do you have an agenda . . . a schedule?" asked Baedecker. "Some sort of outline for the day?"

"Oh, yeah," said a thin man in a green polyester suit. He had been introduced as Kyle Gibbons or Gibson. "Here you go." He pulled out a folded sheet of mimeograph paper and smoothed it down in front of Baedecker.

"Thanks."

9:00—COUNCIL MTG.—Pksd. (Astronaut?)
10:00—HDBL. TNMT.—(AM. LEG. BALL)

11:30—PARADE FORMS UP (W. 5)
12:00—OLD SETTLERS PARADE
1:00—J.G.C. WEENIE ROAST AND SHOOTOFF (Sh. Meehan)
1:30—SFTBL. TNMT.
2:30—VLT. FIRE DPT. WATERFIGHTS
5:00—OPTIMISTS' BARBECUE
6:00—UP WITH PEOPLE HOUR (Camp. Cr. Singers)
7:00—RAFFLE DRAWING (M. Seaton—H. Sch. Gym)
7:30—STARS OF TOMORROW (H. Sch. Gym)
8:00—ASTRONAUT'S SPEECH (H. Sch. Gym)
10:00—J.G.C. FIREWORKS

Baedecker looked up. "Speech?"

Marge Seaton sipped coffee and smiled at him. "Anything you say'd be just fine, Dick. Don't go to any trouble about it. We'd all like to hear you talk about space or what it was like to walk on the moon or something. Just keep it to twenty minutes or so, okay?"

Baedecker nodded and listened through the open windows as a listless morning breeze moved a few leaves against each other. Some children entered and loudly demanded soft drinks at the counter. Minnie ignored them and hurried over to refill everyone's coffee cups.

The discussion at the table turned to city council matters and Baedecker excused himself. Outside, the midmorning heat was already reflecting up from the sidewalks and beginning to soften the asphalt of the highway. Baedecker blinked and tugged his aviator sunglasses out of his shirt pocket. He was wearing the white linen safari shirt, tan cotton slacks, and desert boots he had worn in Calcutta a few weeks earlier. He found it hard to believe that this world of scalded blue sky, flat white storefronts, and empty highway could coexist with the monsoon mud, endless slums, and crowded insanity of India.

The city park was much smaller than he remembered. In Baedecker's mind the bandstand had been an elaborate

Victorian gazebo, but all that stood there now was a flat-topped slab of concrete raised on cinder blocks. He doubted if the gazebo had ever existed.

On Saturday evenings during Baedecker's two summers there, some rich resident of Glen Oak—he had no idea who it had been—had shown free movies in this park, projecting them onto three sheets nailed high on the side of the Parkside Café. Baedecker remembered watching the Movietone Newsreels, cartoons where no lesser personages than Bugs Bunny and Donald Duck sold war bonds, and such film classics as *Fly by Night, Saps at Sea, Broadway Limited*, and *Once Upon a Honeymoon*. Baedecker could close his eyes and almost recapture the flickering images, the faces of the farm families sitting on benches, blankets, and new-mown grass, the sounds of children running through the bushes near the bandstand and climbing trees, and at least once, memorably, the silent flashes of heat lightning rippling above trees and storefronts, coming closer, the heavy branches of the elms dancing to the breeze fleeing before the coming storm. Baedecker could remember the sweetness of that breeze, coming as it did across so many miles of ripening fields. Baedecker could remember the first real crash of lightning, which, in an uncanny instant of suspended time before everyone ran for shelter, froze people, cars, benches, grass, buildings, and Baedecker himself in a stroboscopic flash of light that briefly made all the world a single frozen frame in an unwatched film.

Baedecker cleared his throat, spit, and walked over to a small boulder on a stone pedestal. Three bronze plaques listed the names of men from Glen Oak who had fought in conflicts ranging from the War with Mexico through Vietnam. Stars designated those who had died during their service. Eight had died during the Civil War, three in World War II, and none in Vietnam. Baedecker glanced at fourteen names listed under Korea, but his name was not among them. He recognized none of the others even though he must have gone to school with some of them. The Vietnam plaque was hardly weathered and only a third filled in. There was room for more wars.

Across the street a farm family had poured out of a pickup truck and were staring into the window of Helmann's Variety Store. Baedecker remembered the place as Jensen's Dry Goods, a long, dark building where fans turned slowly fifteen feet above dusty wood floors. The family was excited, pointing and laughing. More people began filling the sidewalks. Somewhere nearby but out of sight, a band started playing, stopped abruptly, and began again only to halt in mid-cymbal crash.

Baedecker sat down on a park bench. His shoulders ached with the weight of things. He closed his eyes again and tried to summon the often-retrieved sensation of bouncing across a glaring, pockmarked plain, the light throwing a corona around Dave's white suit and PLS pack, gravity a lessened foe, each movement as fluid and effortless as moving tiptoe across the bottom of a sunlit lagoon.

The lightness did not come. Baedecker opened his eyes and squinted at the polarized clarity of things.

The Old Settlers Parade moved out fifteen minutes behind schedule. The consolidated high school's marching band led the way, followed by several rows of unidentified horsemen, then came five homemade floats representing chapters of the FFA, 4-H, Boy Scouts (Creve Coeur Council), the county historical society, and the Jubilee Gun Club. Following the floats came the junior high school band consisting of nine youngsters, then an American Legion contingent on foot, and then Baedecker. He rode in a twenty-year-old white Mustang convertible. Mayor Seaton sat to his right, Mr. Gibbons or Gibson to his left, and Bill Ackroyd rode up front next to the teenaged driver. Ackroyd insisted that the three in back sit up on the trunk with their feet on the red vinyl upholstery. Banners on the sides of the Mustang proclaimed RICHARD M. BAEDECKER—GLEN OAK'S ENVOY TO THE MOON. Beneath the lettering there were Magic-Markered representations of his crew's mission patch. The sun behind the symbolic command-module-with-sails looked like one of the egg yolks Ackroyd had mopped up with such vigor that morning.

The parade flowed out of west Fifth Street by the park and marched proudly down Main Street. Sheriff Meehan's green-and-white Plymouth cleared the way. People lined the high, three-leveled sidewalks that seemed designed for viewing parades. Small American flags were in evidence and Baedecker noticed that a banner had been hung between two light poles above the street: GLEN OAK CELEBRATES RICHARD M. BAEDECKER DAY—OLD SETTLERS PARADE—JUBILEE GUN CLUB SHOOTOFF SAT., AUG. 8.

The high school band turned left on Second Street and took another left by the schoolyard just a block east. Children playing on the wooden gallows-structure waved and shouted. One boy made a pistol of his hand and began firing. Without hesitation, Baedecker pointed his finger and fired back. The boy clutched at his chest, rolled his eyes back in his head, and did a complete somersault off a beam to land on his back in the sandbox six feet below.

They turned right on Fifth Street only a block from where they had started and went east. Baedecker noticed a small white building to his right, which he was sure had once been the library. He remembered the hot attic-smell of the little room on a summer day and the slight frown on the lady-librarian's face when he would check out *John Carter, Mars* for the eighth or tenth or fifteenth time.

Fifth Street was wide enough to carry the parade and still allow two lanes of traffic to move by on their left. There was no traffic. Baedecker again felt the absence of the great elms, especially now that the sun was beating down on the crowned expanse of pavement. Small Chinese elms grew near the grassy drainage ditches, but they seemed out of scale in comparison to the absurdly wide street, long lawns, and large homes. People sat on porches and lawn chairs and waved. Children and dogs ran alongside the horses and dodged back and forth ahead of the band's color guard. Behind Baedecker's Mustang, an informal procession of bicycles, children pulling wagons, and a few gaily bedecked riding lawn mowers added another fifty feet of tail to the parade.

The sheriff's car turned right on Catton Street. They passed the schoolyard again. In front of Baedecker's old home a shirtless man with his belly hanging down over his shorts was mowing the yard. He glanced up as the parade went by and flicked a two-fingered salute at Baedecker's Mustang. Three very old people sat on the shaded porch where Baedecker had once played pirate or held off wave after wave of Japanese banzai attacks.

Two blocks past Baedecker's old home the parade passed the high school and confronted a wall of corn. The band wheeled left onto a county road and led the procession around the high school to acres of open field where the Old Settlers fairground had been erected. Beyond the parking lot were half a dozen large tents, twice that many booths, and a spattering of carnival rides sitting motionless in the midday sun. The high, brown grass of the field had been trampled and littered by the crowds of the night before. Farther north were the baseball diamonds, already occupied by brightly uniformed players and surrounded by cheering crowds. Even farther north, almost back to where the backyard of Baedecker's house had abutted the fields, clusters of fire engines created red-and-green angles on the grass.

The bands stopped playing and the parade dissolved. The fairground area was almost deserted and few people watched as band members and horses milled around in confusion. Baedecker remained seated for a moment.

"Well," said Mayor Seaton, "that was a lot of fun, wasn't it?"

Baedecker nodded and glanced up. The car metal and upholstery were very hot. The sun was almost at its zenith. Near the horizon and just visible in the cloudless sky was the faint disk of a three-quarters moon.

∾

"Dickie!"

Baedecker looked up from the table where he was drinking beer with the others. The woman who stood there was heavy and middle-aged with short blond hair. She wore a print blouse and stretch pants that were approaching the designer's maximum expansion limits. Baedecker did not recognize her. The light in the American Legion tent was dim, softened to a buttered sepia. The warm air smelled of canvas. Baedecker stood up.

"Dickie!" repeated the woman and stepped forward to take his free hand in both of hers. "How are you?"

"Fine," said Baedecker. "How are you?"

"Oh, just great, just great. You look *wonderful*, Dickie, but what happened to all of your hair? I remember when you had this *big* head of *red* hair."

Baedecker smiled and unconsciously ran a hand over his scalp. The men he had been talking with turned back to their beers.

The woman brought her hands up to her mouth and tittered. "Oh, my, you don't remember me, do you?"

"I'm terrible with names," confessed Baedecker.

"I thought you'd remember *Sandy*," said the woman and aimed a playful slap at Baedecker's wrist. "Sandy Serrel. We used to be best friends. Remember, Donna Lou Hewford and I used to hang around you and Mickey Farrell and Kevin Gordon and Jimmy Haines all the time during fourth and fifth grades."

"Of course," said Baedecker and shook her hand again. He had no recollection of her whatsoever. "How are you, Sandy?"

"Dickie, this here is my husband, Arthur. Arthur, this here is my old boyfriend who went to the moon." Baedecker shook hands with a rail-thin man in a Taylor Funeral Home softball uniform. The man was covered with a film of dirt through which red wrinkles were visible at the neck, face, and wrists.

"Bet you never thought I'd get married," said Sandy Serrel. "At least to anyone else, huh?"

Baedecker returned the woman's smile. One of her front teeth was broken.

"C'mon. Next game's starting," said her husband.

The big woman grabbed Baedecker's hand and arm again in a tight grip. "We have to go, Dickie. It was *real* good seein' you again. You gotta come over later tonight and I'll show you off to Shirley and the twins. Just remember, I was praying to Jesus all during that moonwalk thing of yours. If it wasn't for all us folks prayin', Jesus never woulda let you boys all come home safe."

"I'll remember," said Baedecker. She leaned over and kissed him on the cheek. Then she was leaving with her thin husband and Baedecker was left with a scraped sensation on his cheek and a lingering odor of dirty towels.

He sat down and ordered another round of beers.

"Arthur does mostly odd jobs out to the cemetery," said Phil Dixon, one of the council members.

"He's Stinky Serrel's third husband," said Bill Ackroyd. "Doesn't look to be the last one."

"*Stinky* Serrel!" said Baedecker and brought his cup down on the table. "Jesus." His single memory of Stinky Serrel, other than of an unwanted presence following his buddies and him down the street, was of a time in fifth grade when she had walked up to him on the playground one lunchtime when someone had ridden by on a palomino.

"I don't know how you guys do that," she had said and pointed at the stallion.

"Do what?" he'd asked.

"Walk around with a cock banging between your legs," she had said softly into his ear. Baedecker remembered his shock at that, stepping back, blushing, being angry that he had blushed.

"Stinky Serrel," said Baedecker. "Good God." He drank down the rest of his beer and waved at the man in the legion cap for more.

∾

There were no flowers but the two graves were well tended. Baedecker shifted his weight and removed his sunglasses. The gray granite headstones were identical except for the inscriptions: CHARLES S. BAEDECKER 1893–1956, KATHLEEN E. BAEDECKER 1900–1957.

The cemetery was quiet. It was shielded by tall cornfields to the north and by woods on the other three sides. Ravines dropped away to unseen creeks to the east and west. Baedecker remembered hunting in the wooded hills to the south during one of his father's furloughs in the rainy spring of '43 or '44. Baedecker had carried the loaded over-and-under shotgun and .22 for hours but had refused to shoot at a squirrel. It had been during his brief pacifist phase. Baedecker's father had been disgusted but had said nothing, merely handing over the stained canvas sack half-filled with dead squirrels for the boy to carry.

Baedecker dropped to one knee and pulled tendrils of grass away from the sides of his mother's headstone. He put his sunglasses back on. He thought of the body that lay a few feet beneath the rich, black Illinois soil—the arms that had enfolded him when he came, crying, home from kindergarten after the fights, the hands that had held his during nights of terror when he had awakened not knowing where or who he was, crying out, then hearing the soft tread of his mother's slippers in the hallway, the soft touch of her hands in the terrifying dark. Salvation. Sanity.

Baedecker rose, turned abruptly, and left the cemetery. Phil Dixon had been pleased to drop him off there on his way to his farm for supper. Baedecker had told him that he would walk the one and three-quarters miles back to town.

He slipped the black iron bar into the latch of the gate and glanced back at the cemetery. Insects hummed in the grass. Somewhere beyond the trees a cow lowed plaintively. Even from the road, Baedecker could make out the empty rectangles of grass near his parents' graves where space had been set aside for his two sisters and him.

A pickup truck roared up the hill from the east and slid to a stop near Baedecker in a cloud of dust and gravel. A sandy-haired man with a wind-reddened face leaned out from the driver's side. "You're Richard Baedecker, aren't you?" A younger man sat next to him. A gun rack behind their heads held two rifles.

"Yes."

"I thought it was you. Read about you coming in the Princeville *Chronicle-Dispatch*. Me and Galen here are headed into Glen Oak for the Optimists' barbecue. We're going to stop at the Lone Tree for a few cold ones first. I don't see no car. Want a ride?"

"Yes," said Baedecker. He removed his sunglasses, folded them carefully, and set them in the pocket of his shirt. "Yeah, I sure do."

∞

According to Baedecker's driver, the Lone Tree Tavern had once sat a quarter of a mile to the southwest, just across the intersection of gravel roads and county lines. The lone tree, a tall oak, was still there. When Peoria County went dry in the 1930s, Lone Tree had packed itself up and moved into Jubilee County to spend the next forty-five years at the edge of the woods on the top of the second hill west of Calvary Cemetery. The hills were steep, the road was narrow, and Baedecker could remember his mother telling of more than a few patrons of the Lone Tree roaring up to the crest of the cemetery hill only to find another car coming in the other direction. Gas rationing and the shortage of young men had reduced the carnage somewhat during the war. Baedecker's father had gone out to the Lone Tree to drink when he was home on leave. Baedecker remembered drinking a Nesbitt's Orange in the same cool darkness where he now found himself ordering a shot of Irish whiskey and a beer. He glanced down at the broken tiles of the floor as if the small gunnysack of squirrels might still be there.

"You don't remember me, do you?" asked the driver. He had introduced himself in the truck as Carl Foster.

Baedecker drank the whiskey and stared at the red face and transparent blue eyes in front of him. "No," he said.

"Don't blame you," said the farmer with a grin. "You and me went to fourth grade together, but I was held back a year when you and Jimmy and the rest went on to fifth."

"Carl Foster," repeated Baedecker. He reached out and took the other man's hand. "Carl *Foster*. Yes, of course, you sat in front of Kevin and behind what's-her-name, the girl with the bangs and . . . mmm . . ."

"Big tits," said Carl, returning Baedecker's handshake. "At least for fourth grade. Yeah. Donna Lou Baylor. She married Tom Hewford. Say, this here's my son-in-law, Galen."

"Galen," said Baedecker and shook the younger man's hand. "Jesus, we were in Scouts together, weren't we, Carl?"

"Old Man Meehan was scoutmaster," said the farmer. "He was always telling us that a good Scout'd make a good soldier. He gave me a goddamned merit badge for aircraft identification. I used to sit up in the fuckin' hayloft until two A.M. with my silhouette cards, watchin' the skies. Don't know what I would've done if I'd spotted the Luftwaffe coming in to kayo Peoria . . . we didn't get a phone until '48."

"Carl Foster," said Baedecker. He gestured to the bartender for another round.

∾

Later, when the shadows were growing long, they went out back to urinate and shoot rats.

"Galen," said Foster, "get the twenty-two from the truck."

They stood on the edge of the ravine and relieved themselves onto five decades of accumulated junk. Rusted bed springs, old washing machines, thousands of tin cans, and the oxidizing corpse of a '38 Hudson filled the bottom of the dump. More recent relics crawled up the hundred feet of shadowy hillside to mix with actual garbage. Foster zipped up and took the proffered rifle from his son-in-law.

"Don't see any rats," said Baedecker. He set down an empty shot glass and pulled the tab on another beer.

"Gotta stir the little fuckers up," said Foster and fired a shot into an already well-riddled washtub sixty feet down the slope. There was a scurry of dark shapes. The farmer pumped another cartridge into the chamber and fired again. Something leaped into the air and squealed. Foster handed the rifle to Baedecker.

"Thanks," said Baedecker. He took careful aim at a shadow beneath a Philco console radio and fired. Nothing stirred.

Foster had lit a cigarette, and it dangled from his lip as he spoke. "Seems to me like I read somewhere that you were in the Marines." He squeezed off a shot at a cereal box halfway down the hill. There was a shrill cry and black shapes ran across garbage.

"Long time ago," said Baedecker. "Korea. Got to fly with the Navy for a while." The rifle had almost no recoil.

"Never served, myself," said Foster. The cigarette bobbed. "Hernia. Wouldn't take me. You ever have to shoot at a man?"

Baedecker paused with the can of beer half-raised. He set it down as Foster handed the rifle back to him.

"Don't have to answer," said the farmer. "None of my goddamned business."

Baedecker squinted along the sight and fired. There was the flat slap of the .22 and a thud as an old scrub board tumbled over. "You couldn't see much from the cockpit of those old Panthers," said Baedecker. "Drop your ordnance. Go home. It wasn't much more personal in my three confirmed air-to-air kills. I saw the pilots bail out of two of them. On the last one my visor was cracked and spattered with oil so I didn't see much of anything. The gun cameras didn't show anybody getting out. But that's not what you mean. Not quite the same as shooting at a *man*." Baedecker pumped the .22 and handed it to Foster.

"Guess not," he said and fired quickly. A rat leaped straight into the air and fell back writhing.

Baedecker tossed his empty beer can into the ravine. He accepted the rifle from Foster and held it at port arms. Baedecker's voice was a thick monotone. "I did almost shoot someone here in Glen Oak, though."

"No shit? Who?"

"Chuck Compton. Remember him?"

"That fucker. Yeah. How could you forget a fifteen-year-old still stuck in sixth grade? Smoked Pall Malls in the john. Compton was one mean son of a bitch."

"Yes," said Baedecker. "I didn't pay any attention to him until I got into sixth grade. Then he decided he was going to beat the shit out of me every other day. Used to wait for me after school. That sort of thing. I tried to buy him off by giving him quarters, giving him stuff from my lunch—Hershey bars when I had them, even by slipping him answers for geography tests and so forth. He took the stuff, but it didn't help. Compton didn't want things from me. He just got a kick out of hurting people."

"What happened?"

"My mother told me to stand up to him. She said that all bullies were cowards . . . that if you stood up to them, they'd back off. Thanks, Galen." Baedecker accepted the fresh beer and took a long swallow. "So I called him out one Friday and I stood up to him. He broke my nose in two places, knocked out a permanent tooth, and damned near kicked my ribs to splinters. In front of the other kids."

"Yeah, that's Compton."

"So I thought about it for a week or so," said Baedecker. "Then one Saturday morning I saw him on the playground across the street from where I lived. I went upstairs and got my over-and-under out of my mom's closet."

"You had your own gun?" asked Foster.

"My father gave it to me on my eighth birthday," said Baedecker. "Four-ten-gauge shotgun on the bottom. Single-shot twenty-two on top."

"A Savage," said Foster. "My brother used to own one." He threw the stub of his cigarette away. "So what happened?"

"I waited for Compton to get close enough," said Baedecker. "First I took the screen off the window in my mother's bedroom and waited for him to cross the street. He couldn't see me behind the lace curtains. I loaded both barrels but figured I'd use the four-ten. Figured I couldn't miss at ten yards. He was that close."

"A four-ten would give you a nice pattern at that range," said Foster.

"I loaded it with number-six quail shot," said Baedecker.

"Jesus."

"Yes. I wanted Compton's guts spilling out on the ground like with the rabbit my father'd shot with number-six pellets a couple of months earlier. I remember how calm I was as I was sighting down the barrel at Compton's face. I lowered the sights to his belt because I always pulled a little high and to the left. I remember trying to think of any reason why I should let the son of a bitch keep living. I honestly couldn't think of one. I squeezed the trigger the way my father had taught me—holding my breath but not tense, squeezing very slow and easy rather than jerking it. I *pulled* it. The goddamn safety was on. I clicked it down to free the four-ten pin and had to take aim again because Compton had moved a few feet. He stopped to say something to a neighbor girl who was playing hopscotch, and I aimed at his lower back. He was only about seven or eight feet farther away."

"Then what?" asked Foster. He lit a new cigarette.

"Then my mother called me for lunch," said Baedecker. "I unloaded both barrels and put the gun away. I stayed out of Compton's way as best I could for the next few weeks. He got tired of hitting me after a while. We moved the next May."

"Huh," said Foster and took a swig of beer. "Chuck Compton always was an asshole."

"Whatever happened to him?" asked Baedecker and set his beer carefully on the ground. He raised the .22 and took aim down the ravine.

"Married Sharon Cahill over in Princeville," said Foster. "Got born again. Was real religious for a while. He was working for the State Highway in '66 when he fell off his mowin' tractor and his own blades ran over him. Lived a week or so before pneumonia got him."

"Hmmm," said Baedecker and squeezed the trigger. A scurrying shape kicked sideways and squealed in pain. Baedecker returned the rifle to port arms and pumped it three times to make sure the chamber was empty. He handed it over. "I've got to get back," he said. "I have a speech to make at eight."

"Fuckin' A," said Carl Foster and handed the weapon to Galen.

∾

"Are you sure you wouldn't like some coffee?" Bill Ackroyd asked nervously.

"I'm sure," said Baedecker. He stood in front of the hall mirror in Ackroyd's home and tried for the second time to knot his tie.

"How about something to eat?"

"Had a big breakfast," said Baedecker. "Two of them."

"Jackie'll heat up some of the roast."

"No time," said Baedecker. "It's almost eight." They hurried out the door. The twilight bathed the cornfields and Ackroyd's RV in a Maxfield Parish glow. Ackroyd backed the Bonneville out and they roared into town.

∾

Old Settlers was ablaze with lights. The canvas of the big tents seeped light, yellow bulbs were strung between the gaming booths, the softball diamond was bathed in arc-lamp brilliance, and the carnival rides were outlined in colored bulbs. Baedecker suddenly recalled an August night when Jimmy Haines had been sleeping over. It had been the night before Old Settlers. Sometime after midnight the two boys had awakened as if responding to a whispered summons, dressed silently, gone over the wire fence at the back of the property, and pushed through the high grass of the fields behind the high school until they were close enough to hear the soft curses and commands of the carny men assembling the rides. Suddenly the lights of the Ferris wheel and merry-go-round had blinked on, brilliant constellations against the black Midwestern night. Baedecker and his best friend had stood motionless, paralyzed with the wonder of it.

Baedecker remembered standing on the moon, shielding his already-shielded visor with a gloved hand and searching the black sky for a single star. There were none. Only the white glare of the cratered surface and the light from the inconsequential crescent that was the earth had pierced the gold-tinted visor.

Ackroyd parked behind a police car, and the two men joined the crowd filing into the high school gymnasium. Baedecker immediately recognized the wood and varnish smell of the place. He had dribbled basketballs where the folding chairs were set in even rows. The platform that he was ascending had been the stage for his sixth-grade operetta. He had been cast as Billy the Orphan who, in the final act, was revealed to be the Christ child come again to check on a family's charity. Baedecker's father had written from Camp Pendleton to say that it had been the most colossal case of miscasting in the history of the theater.

He sat with Ackroyd on gray metal chairs as Mayor Seaton quieted the crowd. Baedecker estimated that there were three to four hundred people filling the chairs and wooden bleachers. More people milled in the open doorways at the back. The sound of the merry-go-round music came in clearly on the humid air.

". . . of the Apollo Program. Our voyager to the moon. One of America's true heroes and Glen Oak's very own son . . . Richard M. Baedecker!"

∞

Applause filled the gym and momentarily drowned out the midway's music. As Baedecker rose to his feet, Bill Ackroyd gave him a pat on the back that almost sent him to his knees. He recovered, shook the mayor's hand, and faced the crowd.

"Thank you, Mayor Seaton and members of the city council. I'm happy to be back in Glen Oak tonight." There was another round of applause and in the few seconds before he resumed speaking Baedecker realized that he was quite drunk. He had no idea what he would say next.

Baedecker had learned how to lessen his fear of audiences by slightly unfocusing his eyes when he spoke. Crowds became less formidable when they blurred into a colorful sea of faces. But this night he did not do this. Baedecker looked earnestly at the crowd. He saw Stinky Serrel in the second row waving at him with little motions of her hand below her chin. Her husband, still in his softball uniform, was dozing in the chair next to her. Phil Dixon and his family sat three rows farther back. Jackie Ackroyd sat on the aisle of the front row. Next to her, Terry was kneeling on a chair with his back to Baedecker, talking loudly to an older boy. He could not see Carl Foster or Galen, but he sensed that they were there. In the seconds of silence after the applause died away, Baedecker felt a sudden rush of affection for everyone in the crowd.

"The exploration of space has been rewarding to scientists in terms of its payoff in pure knowledge and exciting to engineers because of the technological challenge it has posed," Baedecker heard himself begin, "but many people do not know how tremendously rewarding it has been for the average American in terms of spin-offs, which have improved the quality of all of our lives." Baedecker relaxed as he spoke. He had gotten through the original five-month NASA public relations tour after the mission only by memorizing half a dozen set speeches. What he was starting into now—although updated by him—was the NASA-written piece that he always thought of as his Teflon Speech.

". . . not only those wondrous materials and alloys, but as a result of the NASA-sponsored advances in electronics we can enjoy the benefits of such things as pocket calculators, home computers, and relatively inexpensive video cassette recorders."

Sweet Jesus, thought Baedecker, *we mounted the greatest collective effort of labor and imagination since the pharaohs built the pyramids so we can sit home and watch* Debbie Does Dallas *on our VCRs.*

Baedecker paused, coughed once, and resumed. "Communication satellites . . . some of which were launched by the space shuttle . . . tie our world together in a web of telecommunications. When Dave and I walked on the moon sixteen years ago, we brought along a new, lightweight video camera, which was the prototype for many of today's home video units. When Dave and I drove the Lunar Rover six miles and looked down into a canyon which no human eye had ever been able to see clearly before, our explorations were broadcast live across two hundred forty thousand miles of space."

And were rejected by the networks because they would have interrupted their daytime programming, thought Baedecker. *The Apollo Program died young because it had poor production values and a banal script. After* Apollo 11 *everything looked like reruns. We couldn't compete with* Days of Our Lives.

". . . at that time no one could have foreseen all of the spin-offs created by the project. Our goal was to explore the universe and expand the frontiers of knowledge. Our effect was to create a technological revolution, which, in turn, led to the spin-offs, which have changed the life of the average American consumer."

Joan spinning off from a marriage that had been an illusion for years. Scott spinning off to India, dedicating his life to finding eternal verities in a culture that can't master flush toilets.

"When Dave, Tom, and I flew *Discovery* to the moon, the average business computer cost twelve thousand dollars," said Baedecker. "Today, thanks to the spin-offs of our space program, a home computer costing twelve *hundred* dollars can do the same job. And do it better."

Dave Muldorff spinning off to become a congressman from Oregon. Baedecker remembered a white figure moving lightly across the lunar plain, his suit radiant in a corona of sunlight, leaving footprints in the dust that would be fresh when he and Baedecker would be dust, America not even a memory, the human race forgotten. *Fund-raising rallies. Dave, whose NASA career was cut short by the unpardonable sin of bringing a Frisbee to the surface of the moon and not being repentant.*

". . . and hospitals today can use this kind of device to monitor a patient's vital signs . . ."

Tom Gavin spinning off to his new fundamentalist realities. If God spoke to you while you were up there alone in the command module, Tom, why didn't you tell Dave and me during the flight back? Or mention it during debriefing? Why wait all those years to announce it on the PTL Club?

". . . the thermal tiles and other materials developed for the shuttle will have hundreds of unforeseen uses in commercial and daily life. Other possibilities . . ."

The Challenger *exploding, pieces spinning off toward the waiting sea. The orange hell-glow of burning hypergolics. Fragments falling, falling.*

". . . benefits might include . . ."

Baedecker's wife and son spinning off to other lives, other realities.

". . . might include such things . . ."

Richard E. Baedecker spinning off . . .

". . . such things as . . ."

Spinning off to . . .

". . . such things as . . ."

To what?

Baedecker stopped speaking.

A group of farmers who had been laughing at unheard jokes in the back of the gym stopped talking in the sudden silence and turned toward the stage. The boy, Terry Ackroyd, still kneeling on his chair, stopped talking to his friend and turned his head toward Baedecker.

Baedecker gripped the sides of the podium tightly to keep from falling. The large room pitched and yawed in his vision. A cold sweat broke out on his forehead and lower back. Baedecker's nerves prickled in his neck.

"You all saw the shuttle explode," Baedecker said thickly. "Again and again on videotape. It was like a recurrent dream, wasn't it? A nightmare we couldn't shake." Baedecker was amazed to hear these words. He had no idea what he would say next.

"I was there with NASA when the STS . . . the shuttle system . . . was being designed," he said. "Every step of the way there was a compromise because of money . . . or politics . . . or bureaucracy . . . or sheer corporate stupidity. We killed those seven people as surely as if we had put guns to their heads."

The faces turned toward Baedecker were as translucent as water, as unsteady as candle flames.

"But that's the way evolution works!" cried Baedecker, his mouth too close to the microphone. "The stack . . . the Orbiter and external tank and SRBs and everything, looks so beautiful, so advanced, so technologically *perfect* . . . but it's like us, an evolutionary compromise. Right next to the miracle of the heart or the wonder of the eye, there's some artifact of stupidity like the vermiform appendix just waiting to kill us."

Baedecker swayed slightly and stared at his audience. He was not getting his point across, and it was suddenly very important that he do so.

The silence expanded. The sounds of Old Settlers receded. One person near the back of the gym coughed and the noise echoed like cannonshot. Baedecker could no longer focus on faces. He squeezed his eyes shut tightly and clung to the podium.

"What happened to the fish?"

He opened his eyes. "What happened to the *fish?*" he asked again urgently and raised his voice. "The lungfish. Those first ones to crawl out of the sea. What *happened* to them?"

The silence of the crowd shifted in tone. A tension filled the room. Somewhere outside a girl on one of the rides screamed in mock terror. The cry faded and the audience inside waited.

"They left prints in the mud and then what?" asked Baedecker. His voice sounded very strange even to him. He tried to clear his throat and then he spoke again. "The first ones. I know they probably just gasped on the beach for a while and then went back to the ocean. When they died, their bones joined all the others in the ooze. I know that. I don't mean that." Baedecker half turned toward Ackroyd and the others as if asking for help and then looked back at the crowd. He lowered his head a moment but quickly lifted it to stare at faces. He recognized no one. His eyes would not focus properly. He was afraid that his own face was wet with tears but he could do nothing about that.

"Did they *dream?*" asked Baedecker. He waited but there was no answer.

"You understand, they'd seen the stars," said Baedecker. "Even while they were lying there on the beach, gasping for breath, wanting only to go back to the sea, *they had seen the stars.*

Baedecker cleared his throat again. "What I want to know is . . . before they died . . . before their bones joined the rest . . . did they dream? I mean, of course they dreamed, but were they different? The dreams. What I'm trying to say . . ." He halted.

"I think . . ." began Baedecker and stopped again. His hand banged against the microphone as he turned quickly. "Thank you for the homecoming today," said Baedecker but his head was turned away, the microphone was askew, and no one heard him.

∞

A little before three A.M. Baedecker was quietly and thoroughly sick. He was thankful for the bathroom off the guest bedroom. Afterward he brushed his teeth, rinsed his mouth out, and crossed the basement to Terry's empty room.

The Ackroyds had turned in hours earlier. The house was silent. Baedecker closed the door to block any hint of light and waited for the stars to come out.

They did. One by one they emerged from the darkness. There were at least several hundred of them. The sunlit hemisphere of the earth, three diameters above the lunar peaks, also had been swabbed with phosphorescent paint. The moon's surface glowed in a gentle bath of reflected earthlight. The stars burned. Craters threw impenetrable shadows. The silence was absolute.

Baedecker lay back on the boy's bed, careful not to muss the spread. He thought about the coming day. After he got to Chicago and registered, he would look up Borman and Seretti. With any luck they could get together that night for an informal dinner where they could kick around the Air Bus deal before the convention really got under way.

After dinner, Baedecker would call Cole Prescott at his home in St. Louis. He would tell Prescott that he was resigning and work out the details of the quickest transition possible. Baedecker wanted to be out of St. Louis by early September. By Labor Day if he could.

Then what? Baedecker raised his eyes to the earth shining in a star-deepened sky. The swirls of cloud masses were brilliant. He would trade in his four-year-old Chrysler Le Baron for a sports car. A Corvette. No, something as sleek and powerful as a Corvette but with a real gearbox. Something fast and fun to drive. Baedecker grinned at the profound simplicity of it all.

Then what? More stars were becoming visible as his eyes adapted. *The boy must have worked for hours*, thought Baedecker and stared at the ceiling, seeing distant galaxies resolving themselves in great, glowing strands of stars. He would head west. It had been many years since Baedecker had driven across the continent. He would visit Dave out in Salem, spend some time with Tom Gavin in Colorado.

Then what? Baedecker raised his wrist and let it lie on his forehead. There were voices in his ears, but the background interference made them unintelligible. Baedecker thought of gray headstones in the grass and of dark forms scurrying between the rusted springs of a '38 Hudson. He thought of sunlight striking Glen Oak's water tower and the terrible beauty of his newborn son. He thought of darkness. He thought of the lights of the Ferris wheel turning soundlessly in the night.

Later, when Baedecker closed his eyes and slept, the stars continued to burn.

Part Three

Uncompahgre

"**A**re we all set to climb the mountain?"

Richard Baedecker and the other three hikers stopped in their last-minute adjustments of backpacks and hip belts to look up at Tom Gavin. Gavin was a small man, barely five foot seven, with a long face, short-cropped black hair, and a piercing gaze. When he spoke, even to pose a simple interrogative, his voice seemed propelled up out of his small frame by a wire-taut sense of urgency.

Baedecker nodded and bent over to shift the weight of his pack. He tried again to buckle the padded hip belt, but it would not go. Baedecker's stomach was just ample enough, the belt just short enough, that the metal teeth on the buckle would not secure on the webbing.

"Damn," muttered Baedecker and tucked the belt back out of sight. He would make do with the shoulder straps, although already the weight of the pack was plucking a cord of pain on some nerve in his neck.

"Deedee?" asked Gavin. His tone of voice reminded Baedecker of the thousands of checklists he and Gavin had read through during simulations.

"Yes, dear." Deedee Gavin was forty-five, the same age as her husband, but she had entered that ageless state which some women disappear into between their twenty-fifth and fiftieth birthdays. She was blond and bantam-thin, and although she was constantly animated, her voice and movements held none of the sense of tightly controlled tension that marked her husband's demeanor. Gavin usually appeared to be slightly frowning, as if preoccupied or mentally wrestling with some internal conundrum. Deedee Gavin showed no such signs of intellectual unrest or activity. Of all the various astronauts' wives Baedecker had known, Deedee Gavin had always seemed the least well matched. Baedecker's ex-wife, Joan, had predicted the Gavins' imminent divorce almost twenty years earlier after the first time the two couples had met at Edwards Air Force Base in the spring of 1965.

"Tommy?" asked Gavin.

Tom Gavin Jr. looked away and nodded tersely. He was wearing tattered denim shorts and a blue-and-white Campus Crusade for Christ T-shirt. The boy was already over six feet tall and still growing. At the moment he carried anger like a palpable thing, weighing on him like a second backpack.

"Dick?"

"Yo," said Baedecker. His orange backpack held a tent and rain fly, food and water, extra clothes and rain gear, backpack stove and fuel, mess gear and first-aid kit, rope, flashlight, insect repellent, a Fiberfill sleeping bag and ground cloth, foam pad, and an assortment of other trail necessities. He had weighed it on the Gavins' bathroom scale that morning and it checked out at twenty-eight pounds, but Baedecker was sure that someone had surreptitiously added a few bowling balls and an extensive rock collection to the load since then. The pinched nerve on his neck felt like an overtightened guitar string. Baedecker idly wondered what kind of noise it would make when it snapped. "Ready to go," he said.

"Miss Brown?"

Maggie took a last tug at her pack's shoulder strap and smiled. To Baedecker it seemed that the sun had just come out from behind a cloud even though the Colorado sky had been cloudless all day. "All set," she said. "Call me Maggie, Tom." She had cut her hair since Baedecker had seen her in India three months earlier. She wore cotton shorts and a soft-looking plaid shirt open over a green halter top. Her legs were tan and muscular. Maggie carried the lightest load of any of them, not even a frame pack, just a blue canvas daypack with her goose-down sleeping bag tied beneath it. While everyone else wore massive hiking boots, Maggie wore only her short-topped Nikes. Baedecker half expected her to float away like an untethered balloon while the rest of them continued to trudge along like deep-sea divers.

"Okay, then," said Gavin, "let's get going, shall we?" He turned and led them away from their parked car at a brisk pace.

Above the meadow the road became something less than a jeep trail as it switched back and forth through stands of ponderosa pine, Douglas fir, and occasional aspen groves. Deedee rushed to keep up with her husband. Maggie fell into an easy gait a few paces behind. Baedecker worked hard to keep up, but at the end of the first three hundred yards of hill he was red-faced and staggering, his lungs laboring to find more oxygen than was available in the thin air at nine thousand feet. Only Tom Jr. lagged farther back, occasionally throwing a stone at a tree or carving something into an aspen with the sheath knife from his belt.

"Come on, let's keep up the pace," called Gavin from the next switchback. "We're not even on the trail yet."

Baedecker nodded, too winded to speak. Maggie turned around and bounded back downhill toward him. Baedecker mopped his face, shifted the pack against the sweat-soaked shirt on his back, and wondered at the sheer insanity of anyone going downhill when they would just have to turn around and go back *up* again.

"Hi," she said.

"Hi," managed Baedecker.

"It can't be too long before we camp," she said. "The sun'll be behind the ridge in forty-five minutes or so. Besides, we'll want to stay in the lower part of the canyon tonight, the terrain gets pretty steep in another two miles."

"How do you know that?"

Maggie smiled and pulled a strand of hair back over her ear. It was a gesture Baedecker remembered well from India. He was glad to see that her shorter haircut hadn't eliminated the need for the motion. "I looked at the topo map Tom showed you last night in Boulder," she said.

"Oh," said Baedecker. He had been too disconcerted by Maggie's sudden appearance at the Gavin household to pay much attention to the map. He adjusted his shoulder straps and began moving uphill again. Immediately his heart began pounding, and his straining lungs could find no oxygen.

"What's wrong with him?" asked Maggie.

"Who?" Baedecker concentrated on lifting his feet. He did not remember asking for lead-lined soles when he bought his new hiking boots the week before, but obviously he had.

"Him," said Maggie and nodded her head downhill at the sullen figure of Tom Jr. The boy was staring back the way they had come, his hands thrust deep in his hip pockets.

"Girlfriend problems," said Baedecker.

"Too bad," said Maggie. "Did she walk out on him or what?"

Baedecker stopped again and took a few deep breaths. It did not seem to help. Tiny drummers performed solos in his ears. "No," he said, "Tom and Deedee decided it was getting too serious. They broke it up. Tommy won't be allowed to see her when he gets back."

"Too serious?" asked Maggie.

"The possibility of premarital sex was raising its ugly head," said Baedecker.

Maggie looked back at Tom Jr. "Good grief," she said. "He must be almost seventeen."

"Try eighteen," said Baedecker, moving again, waiting for his second wind to catch up. It was overdue. "Almost your age, Maggie."

She made a face. "Uh-uh, guess again," she said. "I'm twenty-six and you know it, Richard."

Baedecker nodded and tried to pick up his pace so Maggie would not have to take half steps to stay back with him.

"Hey," she said, "where's your hip belt? It helps with those frame packs if you wear it. Gets the load off your shoulders."

"Broken," said Baedecker. He looked up through the trees and saw Tom and Deedee two switchbacks above, moving quickly.

"You still mad?" asked Maggie. Her voice had changed slightly, shifted down a register. The sound of it made Baedecker's straining heart beat even faster.

"Mad about what?" he asked.

"You know, me showing up when I wasn't invited," she said. "Staying to come along on this weekend with your friends."

"Of course not," said Baedecker. "Any friend of Scott's would be welcome."

"Hunh," said Maggie. "We've been over that already. I didn't fly here from Boston just because I used to be your son's friend. I mean, *classes* have started already."

Baedecker nodded. Scott would have received his master's degree this year if he had not dropped out to stay with his Indian guru. Baedecker knew that Maggie was four years older than Scott; she had spent two years in the Peace

Corps after graduating from Wellesley and was now finishing up her graduate degree in sociology.

They emerged into a clearing on a broad switchback and Baedecker stopped and pretended to appreciate the view of the canyon and surrounding peaks.

"I loved the look on your face when I showed up last night," said Maggie. "I thought you were going to drop your teeth."

"My teeth are my own," said Baedecker. He tugged the pack up and tightened a strap. "Most of them."

Maggie threw back her head and laughed. She brushed at his sunburned arm with cool fingers and then she was bounding up the rough road, pausing to turn and beckon him on, then running again. *Running. Uphill.* Baedecker closed his eyes for a second.

"Come on, Richard," she called. "Let's hurry up so we can make camp and have dinner."

Baedecker opened his eyes. The sun was directly behind Maggie, surrounding her with radiance, illuminating even the fine, golden hairs on her arms. "Go ahead," he called. "I'll be there in a week or so."

She laughed and ran up the hill, apparently unruled by the gravity that pulled at Baedecker. He watched her for a minute and then followed, stepping more lightly himself, feeling the load on his back lessen slightly as he moved higher toward the dome of thin, blue Colorado sky.

∾

Baedecker had enjoyed nothing of his life in St. Louis so much as his leaving it.

He resigned his position at the aerospace company where he had worked for the past eight years, his sense of almost complete uselessness there being accidentally confirmed by the way his boss, Cole Prescott, had let him go with deep and obviously sincere regret but without need for an interim period to train someone new. Baedecker sold his town house back to the firm that had built it, sold most of his furniture, stored his books, papers, and the rolltop desk Joan had given him for his fortieth birthday, said good-bye over drinks to his few acquaintances and friends there—most of whom worked for the company—and left, driving west early one afternoon after having a leisurely lunch at the Three Flags Restaurant across the Missouri River in St. Charles.

It had taken Richard Baedecker less than three days to liquidate his life in St. Louis.

He crossed into Kansas at Kansas City during rush hour. The insane flow of traffic did not bother him as he sat back in the leather upholstery and listened to classical music on the car's FM radio. He had originally planned to sell the Chrysler Le Baron and get a smaller, faster car—a Corvette or Mazda RX-7 perhaps—the kind of performance vehicle he would have driven eighteen or twenty years earlier when training for a mission or flying experimental aircraft, but at the last moment he realized how stereotypical it would be for the middle-aged man to go hunting for his lost youth in a new sports car, so he kept the Le Baron. Now he relaxed in its upholstered comfort and air-conditioning while listening to Handel's *Water Music* as he left Kansas City and its grain elevators behind and headed west toward the lowering sun and the endless plains.

He stayed that night in Russell, Kansas, driving into the small town to find a cheaper motel away from the interstate. The sign outside said CABLE TV FREE COFFEE. The old tourist cabins were not air-conditioned, but they were clean and quiet, set back under large trees that created pools of darker shadow in the twilight. Baedecker showered, changed clothes, and went for a walk. He had dinner in the bleachers of the town park, buying two hot dogs and coffee at a concession stand beneath the ball diamond's bleachers. Halfway through the second game the moon rose, orange and waning. Out of old habit, Baedecker looked up and tried to find the Marius Hills in western Oceanus Procellarum, but the site was in darkness. Baedecker sensed a sad, end-of-season flavor to the evening. It was four days past Labor Day and despite the summer's final attempt at a heat wave and the softball tournament, the children had returned to school for the year, the city pool was closed, and the fields of corn beyond the edge of town were growing yellow and brittle as harvest approached.

Baedecker left after the sixth inning of the second game and went back to his motel room. The "CABLE TV" consisted of a small black-and-white television offering two Kansas City channels, WTBS from Atlanta, WGN from Chicago, and three fundamentalist networks.

It was on the second of these religious channels that he saw his old *Apollo* crewmate, Tom Gavin.

∞

A mile and a half above the meadow where they had left their car, the dilapidated jeep road narrowed into a trail and wound its way up through heavy forest. Baedecker was moving more easily now, setting his own pace, enjoying the evening and the movement of shadows across the valley floor. It had become much cooler as the ridge's shadow filled the narrowing canyon up which they were hiking.

Maggie was waiting for him at a curve in the path, and they walked awhile in companionable silence. Beyond the next curve in the trail, Tom and Deedee were busy setting up camp in a clearing ten yards above the stream, which the trail had been paralleling. Baedecker dumped his pack, stretched, and rubbed some of the soreness out of his neck.

"Did you see Tommy back there?" asked Deedee.

Maggie answered. "He was a hundred yards or so down the trail. He should be here in a minute or two."

Baedecker spread the ground cloth and staked down the two-person orange tent he had been carrying. There were several fiberglass poles and wands to connect, and it took Baedecker and Maggie several moments of laughter to get the exoskeleton rigged and the tent properly draped from it. When it was finished, Baedecker's low tent sat a few yards from Tom and Deedee's blue dome.

Gavin came over and kneeled by Maggie, offering her a nylon bundle. "This is Tommy's old one-man tent," he said. "Pretty small. More of a bivouac bag, really, but we thought it would do the trick for one or two nights."

"Sure," said Maggie and went to rig the small tent a few yards downhill from Baedecker's. Tommy had come into camp and was speaking animatedly to his mother as she gathered wood on the far side of the clearing.

"You and Tommy in the two-man, okay?" asked Gavin. He was watching Maggie pound stakes with a rock.

"Fine," said Baedecker. He had removed his hiking boots and was wiggling his toes through his sweat-soaked socks. The relief was a functional definition of heaven.

"Known her long?" asked Gavin.

"Maggie? I met her this summer in India," said Baedecker. "As I said last night, she's a friend of Scott's."

"Hmmm," said Gavin. He seemed about to say more but rose instead and brushed off his jeans. "I'd better get the fire going and the food on the grill. Want to help?"

"Sure," said Baedecker. He stood and walked gingerly across the grass, feeling the pressure of each twig and pebble beneath his feet. "In just a moment. I'll help Maggie get her tent raised and I'll be right there, Tom." Stepping lightly, Baedecker moved down the grassy slope to where Maggie was working.

∞

The cable TV's program had been one of the many clones of the PTL Club that filled the fundamentalist network's schedule. The set was done in K-Mart gothic, the host's gray hair perfectly matched the gray polyester of his suit, and a ten-digit phone number remained permanently affixed on the screen in case a viewer was suddenly moved to pledge money and had forgotten the address which the host's white-wigged wife displayed every few minutes. The wife seemed to be afflicted with some neurological disorder, which set her off on crying jags for no apparent reason. During the ten minutes that Baedecker watched before Tom Gavin appeared, the woman cried while reading letters from viewers who had repented and converted while watching the program, she cried after the paraplegic ex-country-western singer gave a rendition of "Blessed Redeemer," and she cried when their next guest told of a miraculous disappearance of an eight-pound tumor from her neck. Incredibly, the wife's mascara—which looked to have been applied with a trowel—never ran.

Baedecker was in his pajamas and was rising to turn the TV off when he saw his ex-crewmate.

"Our next guest has seen the glory of God's creation in a way which few of us have been privileged to witness," said the host. The man's voice had taken on a sonorous, serious-but-not-quite-solemn tone, which Baedecker had heard all of his life from successful salesmen and middle-level bureaucrats.

"Praise Jesus," said the wife.

"Air Force Major Thomas Milburne Gavin, besides being a war hero in Vietnam . . ."

Tom ferried jets from California to bases in Okinawa, thought Baedecker. *Oh well.*

". . . was decorated with the president's Medal of Freedom after his *Apollo* spacecraft went to the moon in 1971," said the host.

We all got a medal, thought Baedecker. *If we'd had a ship's cat, it would've received one too.*

". . . a test pilot, an engineer, an astronaut, and a respected scientist . . ."

Tom's not a scientist, thought Baedecker. *None of us were until Schmidt flew. Tom got his degree in engineering from CalTech later than most of us. It was either that or drop out of the program at Edwards.*

"... and, perhaps most importantly, the man who may well have been the first *true Christian* to walk on the moon," said the host. "My friends, Major Thomas M. Gavin!"

Tom never walked on the moon, thought Baedecker.

Gavin shook hands with the host, received a kiss from the host's wife, and nodded at the paraplegic singer and the woman who had lost her tumor. He sat down on the end of a long couch while the host and his wife settled themselves into what may have been wing chairs but which—at least on Baedecker's small screen—looked like crushed-velour thrones.

"Tell us, Tom, when was it that you first heard the Lord's voice while you were walking on the moon?"

Gavin nodded and looked at the camera. To Baedecker's eye, his old acquaintance looked no older than he had when the two of them and Dave Muldorff had spent endless hours in simulators in 1970 and '71. Tom was wearing Air Force flight coveralls with an assortment of NASA mission patches sewn on. He looked lean and fit. Baedecker had added twenty pounds since their mission days and could fit into none of his old uniforms.

"I'm looking forward to telling you about that," said Gavin with the thin, tight smile that Baedecker remembered, "but first, Paul, I should mention that I never *walked* on the moon. Our mission called for two members of the crew to descend to the lunar surface in the LM—the lunar excursion module we called it—while the third crew member remained in lunar orbit, tending to the command module's systems and relaying communications from Houston. I was the crew member who remained aboard the command module."

"Yes, yes," said the host, "but, gosh, after going so far, I mean, it was *almost* to the moon, right?"

"Two hundred forty thousand miles minus about sixty thousand feet," said Gavin with another thin smile.

"And the others came back with some dusty moon rocks, while you came back with the eternal truth of God's Word, isn't that right, Tom?" said the host.

"That's right, Paul," said Gavin and proceeded to tell the story of his fifty-two hours alone in the command module, of the time spent out of radio contact behind the moon, and of the sudden revelation over the Crater Tsiolkovsky when God spoke to him.

"By gosh," said the host, "that was a message from the *real* mission control, wasn't it?" The host's wife squealed and clapped her hands together. The audience applauded.

"Tom," said the host, even more serious now, leaning forward and extending one hand to touch the astronaut's knee, "everything you saw on that . . . on that *incredible* trip . . . everything you witnessed during your trip to the stars . . . I've heard you tell young people this . . . it all bore witness to the truth of God's Word as revealed in the Bible . . . it all bore witness to the glory of Jesus Christ, didn't it, Tom?"

"Absolutely, Paul," said Gavin. He looked directly into the camera, and Baedecker saw the same resolve and angry determination there that he remembered from the team handball tournaments held between *Apollo* crews. "And, Paul, as exciting and thrilling and rewarding as it was to fly to the moon . . . that couldn't compare to the reward I found on the day that I finally accepted Jesus Christ as my Lord and personal savior."

The host turned to the camera and nodded his head as if overcome. The audience applauded. The host's wife began to cry.

"And, Tom, you've had many opportunities to bear witness to this and bring others to Christ, haven't you?" asked the host.

"Absolutely, Paul. Just last month I was privileged to be in the People's Republic of China and to visit one of the few remaining seminaries there . . ."

Baedecker lay back on the bed and put his wrist on his forehead. Tom had not mentioned his revelation during the three-day trip back, or in the debriefing during the week-long quarantine they had shared. Actually, Tom had not mentioned it to anyone—or acted upon it—for almost five years after the mission. Then, shortly after his distributor-ship had failed in Sacramento, Gavin had talked about his revelation while on a local radio talk show. Shortly after that he and Deedee had moved out to Colorado to start an evangelical organization. Baedecker wasn't surprised that Tom hadn't talked to Dave or him after the mission; the three of them had made a good crew, but they had not been as close as people might imagine given two years of training time together.

Baedecker sat up and looked at the television. ". . . we had an eminent scientist on our last program," the host was saying, "a Christian and a crusader for equal time for cre-ationism in the schools . . . where children are, I'm sure you're aware, Tom, now being taught only a single, seri-ously flawed, godless theory that man came from monkeys and other lower life forms . . . and this eminent and re-spected scientist made the point that with the number of shooting stars that hit the earth each year . . . and you must have seen a lot of them when you were in space, hey, Tom?"

"Micrometeorites were a concern to the engineers," said Gavin.

"Well, with all those millions of little . . . like little rocks, aren't they? With millions of those striking the earth's atmosphere every year, if the earth was as old as their *theory* says, what? Three billion years?"

Four and a half, thought Baedecker. *Idiot.*

"Somewhere over four billion," said Gavin.

"Yes," smiled the host, "this eminent Christian scien-tist made the point, in fact, he showed us *mathematically*, that if the earth was really *that old*, it'd be buried several miles deep in meteorite dust!"

The audience applauded wildly. The host's wife clasped her hands, praised Jesus over the noise, and rocked back and forth. Gavin smiled and had the good grace to look embarrassed. Baedecker thought of the "orange rock" that he and Dave had brought back from Marius Hills. Argon-39 and argon-40 dating had shown the chunk of troctolite breccia to be 3.95 billion years old.

"The problem with the theory of evolution," Gavin was saying, "is that it goes contrary to the scientific method. There is no way, given the brief human life span, to observe the so-called evolutionary mechanisms they postulate. The geological data is just too doubtful. Gaps and contradictions show up in those theories all the time, whereas *all* of the biblical accounts have been confirmed time and time again."

"Yes, yes," said the host, nodding his head emphatically.

"Praise be to Jesus," said his wife.

"We can't trust science to answer our questions," said Gavin. "The human intellect is just too fallible."

"How true, how true," said the host.

"Praise Jesus," said his wife, "God's truth be made known."

"Amen," said Baedecker and turned off the television.

∾

It was just after dinner, during the last minutes of twilight, when the others entered the clearing. The first two were boys—young men of college age, Baedecker realized—carrying obviously heavy backpacks with aluminum tripods lashed atop them. They ignored Baedecker and the others and hurried to dump their packs and set up the tripods. From the packs they removed foam padding and two sixteen-millimeter movie cameras. "God, I hope there's enough light left," said the overweight one in shorts.

"There should be," said the other one, a tall redhead with a wisp of beard. "This Tri-X is fast enough if he *gets* here pretty quick." They concentrated on attaching their cameras to tripods and focusing on the section of trail from which they had just emerged. High overhead a hawk circled on the last of the day's thermals and let out a lazy screech. A final ray of sunlight caught its wings for a few seconds and then the evening twilight was absolute.

"Wonder what's going on," said Gavin. He scraped out the last of his beef stew and licked the spoon clean. "I chose this old Cimarron Creek approach to the mountain because hardly anyone ever uses it anymore."

"They'd better get their shot pretty soon," said Maggie. "It's getting dark."

"Anyone want S'mores?" asked Deedee.

There was pale movement in the gloom under the fir trees and a man appeared, bent under a long load, moving slowly but surely up the last few yards of trail into the clearing. This man also appeared to be of college age but seemed older than the two bent behind their cameras: he was dressed in a sweat-soaked blue cotton shirt, torn khaki shorts, and solid hiking boots. On his back he carried an oversized blue climbing pack with nylon webbing attached to a long, cylindrical burden wrapped in red-and-yellow sailcloth. The poles must have been fourteen feet long, extending six feet beyond the small man's bent shoulder and dragging in the dust an equal distance behind him. The man's brown hair was long and parted in the middle, hanging down in damp folds to curl in along his sharp cheekbones. As he came closer, Baedecker noticed the deep-set eyes, the sharp nose, and the short beard. The man's posture and obvious exhaustion added to Baedecker's feeling that he was watching an actor reenacting Christ's final journey up the hill to Golgotha.

"Great, Lude, we're gettin' it!" shouted the redheaded boy. "Come on, Maria, before the light's gone! Hurry!" A young woman emerged from the darkening trail. She had short, dark hair, a long, thin face, and was wearing shorts and a halter top that seemed several sizes too large for her. She was carrying a large pack. She moved forward quickly as the bearded hiker dropped to one knee in the meadow, loosened shoulder straps, and lowered the cloth-covered poles to the ground. Baedecker heard the sound of metal striking metal. For a second the man appeared too exhausted to rise or sit; he remained on one knee, head bowed so that his hair covered his face, one arm resting on his other knee. Then the girl named Maria came forward and touched the back of his head gently.

"Great, we got it," shouted the heavyset boy. "Come on, we gotta get all this shit set up." The two boys and the girl went about setting up camp while the bearded man remained kneeling.

"How odd," said Maggie.

"Some sort of documentary," said Gavin.

"I wonder what it's about," said Maggie.

"Marshmallows," said Deedee. "Let's whittle some marshmallow-roasting sticks before it gets too dark to find them." Tom Jr. rolled his eyes and turned his face to the dark woods.

"I'll help," said Baedecker and rose, stretching the cramp out of his muscles. Above the ridgeline to the east, a few faint stars were visible. It was getting cold quickly now. On the far side of the meadow, the two men and the young woman had erected two small tents and were busy gathering firewood in the dark. Farther out, barely visible in the gloom, the one called Lude sat cross-legged and silent in the tall grass.

∾

Baedecker had arrived in Denver at five-thirty in the afternoon on a Wednesday. He knew that Tom Gavin had his office in Denver but lived in Boulder, twenty miles closer to the foothills. Baedecker found a gas station and called Tom's home number. Deedee answered, was excited to heart that he had arrived, would not hear of Baedecker staying at a hotel, and suggested that he catch Tom before he left work. She gave him the phone number and address.

Gavin's evangelical organization was called Apogee and was headquartered on the second floor of a three-story bank building on East Colfax Avenue several miles from downtown Denver. Baedecker parked his car in the lot and followed posters and signs saying ONE WAY with upwardly pointing fingers and JESUS IS THE ANSWER and WHERE WILL YOU BE WHEN THE RAPTURE COMES?

The office was large and staffed with several young people who were dressed and groomed conservatively even to Baedecker's out-of-date eye. "Can I help you, sir?" asked a young man in a white shirt and dark tie. It was very hot in the room—either they had no air-conditioning or it was not working—but the young man's collar was buttoned, the tie firmly knotted.

"I'm here to see Tom Gavin," said Baedecker. "I think he's expecting . . ."

"Dick!" Gavin came into sight from behind a partition. Baedecker had time to confirm how fit and trim his old crewmate looked and to extend his hand before Gavin threw his arms around him in a hug. Baedecker raised one hand in surprise. He remembered Tom Gavin as being anything but a physical person. Baedecker could not even remember seeing Tom hug his wife in public. "Dick, you're looking great," said Gavin, squeezing Baedecker's upper arms. "By gosh, it's good to see you."

"Good to see you, Tom," said Baedecker, feeling pleased and a bit trapped at the same time. Gavin gave him another hug and led the way into his office, a cluttered cubicle formed by four partitions. Office sounds filled the warm air. Somewhere a young woman was laughing. One wall of Gavin's office was covered with framed photographs: a *Saturn V* rocket spotlighted at night on its mobile launch pad, the *Peregrine* command module with the bright limb of the moon beneath it, a group portrait of the crew in their spacesuits, a shot of the LM *Discovery* beginning its descent, and an autographed picture of Richard Nixon shaking Tom's hand in a Rose Garden ceremony. Baedecker knew the photographs well; duplicates or near duplicates had hung on the wall of his own office and den for twelve years. Missing from Gavin's collection was only one of NASA's standard photos from the mission—a color print blown up from a picture taken from the lunar rover's video camera of Baedecker and Dave Muldorff, indistinguishable in their bulky spacesuits, saluting the American flag with the white hills of Marius Crater in the background.

"Talk to me," said Gavin. "Tell me what's going on in your life, Dick."

Baedecker spoke for a minute, telling Gavin about his old job in St. Louis and his departure. He did not explain the reasons for leaving. He was not sure if he knew all the reasons.

"So you're looking for work?" asked Gavin.

"Not right now," said Baedecker. "I'm just traveling. I have enough money saved to be a bum for a few months. Then I'll have to look for something. I have a few offers." He neglected to say that none of the offers interested him at all.

"Sounds great," said Gavin. A framed poster over his desk read SURRENDERING YOUR LIFE TO JESUS IS THE GREATEST VICTORY YOU CAN EVER WIN. "How's Joan? Do you keep in touch at all?"

"I saw her in Boston last March," said Baedecker. "She seems very happy."

"Great," said Gavin. "What about Scott? Still at . . . where was it? Boston University?"

"Not right now," said Baedecker. He paused, debating whether to tell Gavin about his son's conversion to the teach-ings of the Indian "Master." "Scott's spending a semester off, traveling and studying in India," he said.

"India, wow," said Gavin. He was smiling, relaxed, his expression open and affectionate, but in the deep-set, dark eyes Baedecker thought he saw the same cold reservoirs of reserve he could recall from their first meeting more than two decades earlier at Edwards. They had been competitors then. Baedecker did not know what they were now.

"So tell me about this," said Baedecker. "About Apogee."

Gavin grinned and began speaking in a low, firm voice. It was a voice much more used to public speaking and storytelling than the one Baedecker remembered from the mission days. It had been a standing joke that Tom liked to answer in words of one syllable or less. At the time, Dave Muldorff had been nicknamed "Rockford" because of a supposed similarity to a television detective played by James Garner, and for a while the other pilots and ground crew had called Gavin "Coop" because of his laconic "yeps" and "nopes." Tom had not been amused, and the nickname did not stick.

Now Gavin spoke of his years after the lunar mission, of leaving NASA shortly after Baedecker did, of the unsuccessful pharmaceutical distributorship in California. "I was making money hand over fist, we had a big house in Sacramento and a beach house north of San Francisco, Deedee could buy anything she wanted, but I just wasn't happy . . . do you know what I mean, Dick? I just wasn't happy."

Baedecker nodded.

"And things just weren't good between Deedee and me," Gavin went on. "Oh, the marriage was intact, at least it looked that way to our friends, but the deep part . . . the *committed* part, that just wasn't there anymore. We both knew it. Then, it was one day in the fall of 1976, a friend invited Deedee and me to a Bible retreat weekend sponsored by his church. That was the beginning. For the first time—even though I'd been raised a Baptist—for the first time I really heard God's Word and realized that it applied to me. After that, Deedee and I received some Christian marriage counseling and things got better. It was during that time when I did a lot of thinking about the . . . well, the *message* I'd heard, *felt* really, while orbiting the moon. Even so, it wasn't until spring of '77, April fifth, that I woke up one morning and realized that if I was going to go on living that I had to put all of my faith in Jesus. *All* of my faith. And I did it . . . that morning . . . I got down on both knees and accepted Jesus Christ as my personal savior and Lord. And I haven't been sorry since; Dick. Not one day. Not one minute."

Baedecker nodded. "So that led to this?" he asked, nodding at the office all around them.

"Sure did!" Gavin laughed, but his eyes were still intense and unblinking. "Not all at once though. Come on, I'll show you around, introduce you to some of the kids. We've got six people working full-time and another dozen or so volunteers."

"Working full-time at what?" asked Baedecker.

Gavin stood up. "Answering phones mostly," he said. "Apogee's a nonprofit company. The kids arrange my speaking trips, coordinate with local groups—usually ministries and Campus Crusade—put out our monthly publication, do some Christian counseling, run a drug rehabilitation program—we have specially trained people for that—and generally work the Lord's will when He shows it to us."

"Sounds like a busy schedule," said Baedecker. "Sort of like the old days preparing for the mission." Baedecker did not know why he said that; it sounded inane even to him.

"A *lot* like the mission," said Gavin, putting an arm around Baedecker. "Same busy schedule. Same sense of commitment. Same need for discipline. Only this mission is a million times more important than our trip to the moon."

Baedecker nodded and started to follow him out of the office, but Gavin stopped suddenly and turned to face him. "Dick, you're not a Christian, are you?"

Baedecker felt surprise change to anger. He had been asked that before and the question agitated him by its strange combination of aggressiveness and self-serving provincialism. Yet the answer, as always, eluded him. Baedecker's father had been a lapsed member of the Dutch Reformed Church, his mother an agnostic, if anything. Joan had been a Catholic, so for years, while Scott was growing up, Baedecker had attended Mass each Sunday. For the past decade he had been . . . what had he been? "No," said Baedecker, shielding his anger but returning Gavin's stare, "I'm not a Christian."

"I didn't think so," said Gavin and squeezed Baedecker's arm again. Gavin smiled. "I'm going to tell you right up front that I'll be praying that you become a Christian," he said. "I mean that with love, Dick. I really do."

Baedecker nodded and said nothing.

"Come on," said Gavin. "Let's go introduce you to these wonderful kids."

∽

After the cooking pots and utensils were washed in water heated over the campfire, Baedecker, Maggie, Gavin, and Tommy walked over to speak to the other campers. The group sat around their campfire and looked up as the others approached.

"Howdy," said Gavin.

"Hi," said the redheaded boy. The girl and the overweight young man stared up at the visitors. The one called Lude continued to stare into the fire. Firelight illuminated everyone's faces from below.

"Going over the pass and plateau to Henson Creek?" asked Gavin.

"We're going to climb Uncompahgre," said the heavy blond boy in shorts.

Gavin and the others squatted by the fire. Maggie plucked a strand of grass and chewed it. "That's where we're headed tomorrow," she said. "The map says it's about another nine miles to the south ridge of Uncompahgre. That right?"

"Yeah," said the bearded redhead. "That's about right."

Baedecker pointed to the long metal tubing wrapped in sailcloth. "That's quite a load to carry all the way to the mountain," he said.

"Rogallo," said the girl named Maria.

"Ahhh," said Tommy, "I shoulda guessed that. Far out."

"Rogallo," said Gavin. "I see it now."

"What's a Rogallo?" asked Maggie.

"A kite," said the blond boy. "A hang glider."

"What make?" asked Baedecker.

"Phoenix VI," said the redhead. "You know it?"

"No," said Baedecker.

"Going to go off the south ridge?" asked Gavin.

"Off the summit," said Maria. She glanced sideways at the silent, long-haired man next to her. "It's our gig, Lude's and mine."

"Off the top," breathed Tommy. "All *right*."

The redheaded boy stirred the fire. "We're gettin' it on film for our filmmaking course at C.U. We figure about forty-five minutes after editing. We're gonna enter it . . . you know . . . festivals and stuff. Maybe some sports company or something will want it as a promotional thing."

"Should be interesting," said Gavin. "But tell me, why are you taking the long way in?"

"What do you mean?" asked the girl.

"This old jeep trail down the Cimarron is more than twice as long as the way if you'd driven up Henson Creek Road from Lake City and hiked north," said Gavin.

"This is the way," said Lude. His voice made the others pause. It was a deep, raspy voice that did not seem to leave his throat. He still had not looked up from the fire. Looking at him, Baedecker could see flames reflected in the deep orbits of the eyes.

"Well, good luck to you," said Gavin and stood up. "Hope the weather holds." Baedecker and Maggie rose to leave with Gavin, but Tommy remained squatting by the fire.

"I'm going to stay a few minutes," said the boy. "I want to hear more about the hang glider."

Gavin paused. "Okay, see you in a while."

∾

Around their own fire once again, Gavin explained the others' plans to his wife. "Is that safe?" asked Deedee.

"It's idiocy," said Gavin.

"Hang gliders can be pretty elegant machines," said Baedecker.

"They can be murderous," said Gavin. "I knew an Eastern Airlines pilot in California who was killed in one of those things. The guy had twenty-eight years' experience flying, but it didn't help a bit when his kite stalled. He put the nose down to pick up airspeed . . . same thing I'd do, same thing you'd do, Dick. Natural instinct. But that's all wrong in one of those toys. The thing mushed in on him from fifty feet and snapped his neck."

"And off a *mountain*," said Deedee. She shook her head.

"A lot of hang glider pilots fly off mountains these days," said Baedecker. "I used to watch them fly at a sandhill called Chat's Dump south of St. Louis."

"A sandhill or seacoast cliff is one thing," said Gavin. "Uncompahgre Peak is something else. You haven't seen it yet, Dick. Wait till you get a glimpse of it up the canyon tomorrow. Uncompahgre's a big wedding cake of a mountain, shelves and ridges running off it in every which direction."

"Doesn't sound good for thermals," said Baedecker.

"It would be a nightmare . . . plus there's almost always a high wind at fourteen thousand feet. It's a three-thousand-foot drop to the plateau, and even that's over ten thousand feet high . . . and most of the plateau is rocks and boulders. It would be insane to fly there."

"Then why are they doing it?" asked Maggie. Baedecker noticed how green her eyes were in the firelight.

"Did you see that one fellow's—Lude—his arm?" asked Gavin.

Maggie and Baedecker looked at each other and shook their heads.

"Track marks," said Gavin. "He's on something hard."

From the other campfire across the meadow came a sudden burst of laughter and a blast of music from a tape player. "I hope Tommy comes back over soon," said Deedee.

"Let's tell ghost stories around the fire," suggested Maggie.

Gavin shook his head. "No," he said. "Nothing supernatural or demonic. What do you say we sing camp songs?"

"Great," said Maggie, smiling at Baedecker.

Gavin and Deedee led them in a round of "Kum Ba Yah" while from across the darkened meadow came laughter and the taped sounds of Billy Idol singing "Eyes without a Face."

On Thursday evening Baedecker had been in the Gavins' family room, planning the weekend backpacking trip with them, when the front doorbell rang. Gavin had excused himself to answer it, and Baedecker was listening to Deedee tell about the problem with Tommy and his girlfriend when a voice said, "Hello, Richard."

Baedecker looked up and stared. It was impossible that Maggie Brown was standing there in Tom Gavin's family room but there she was, wearing the same white cotton dress she had worn when they had toured the Taj Mahal together. Her hair was shorter, bleached blonder by sunlight, but the tanned and freckled face was the same, the green eyes were the same. Even the slight, somehow pleasing gap between the front teeth attested to the fact that it was, indeed, Maggie Brown. Baedecker stared.

Gavin said, "The lady asked if she'd come to the right house to find the famous astronaut Richard E. Baedecker. I said sho' 'nuff."

Later, while Tom and Deedee watched television, Baedecker and Maggie took a walk down the Pearl Street Mall. Baedecker had come to Boulder once before—a five-day visit in 1969 when their team of eight rookie astronauts had studied geology there and used the university's Fiske Planetarium for astrogation exercises—and the mall had not existed then. Pearl Street, in the heart of old Boulder, had been just another dusty, heavily trafficked western street, populated with drugstores, discount clothing stores, and family restaurants. Now it had been turned into a four-block walking mall, shaded by trees, landscaped with rolling hills and flowers, and bordered by expensive little shops where the cheapest thing one could buy was a single-dip Häagen-Dazs ice cream cone for $1.50. In the two blocks Baedecker and Maggie had already walked, they had passed five street musicians, a chanting Hare Krishna group, a four-person juggling act, a lone tightrope walker stringing his wire between two kiosks, and an ethereal young man wearing only a burlap robe and a gold pyramid on his head.

"Why did you come?" Baedecker asked.

Maggie looked at him, and Baedecker felt a strange sensation, as if a cool hand had suddenly cusped the back of his neck. "You called me," she said.

Baedecker stopped. Nearby a man was playing a violin with more enthusiasm than skill. His violin case lay open on the ground with two dollar bills and three quarters in it. "I called to see how you were," Baedecker said. "How Scott was when you saw him last. I just wanted to make sure you got back from India all right. When the girl at the dorm said that you were still visiting your family, I decided not to leave a message. How did you know it was me? How on earth did you *find* me?"

Maggie smiled, and there was a hint of mischief in her green eyes. "No mystery, Richard. One, I knew it was you. Two, I called your company in St. Louis. They told me you'd recently resigned and moved away, but no one seemed to know where you'd gone until I talked to Teresa in Mr. Prescott's office. She found the emergency forwarding address you'd left. I had the weekend off. Here I am."

Baedecker blinked. "Why?"

Maggie sat on a low redwood bench, and Baedecker sat down next to her. A breeze rustled the leaves above them and set lamplight and shadow dancing across them both. Half a block away there was a burst of applause as the tightrope walker did something interesting. "I wanted to see how your search was going," she said.

Baedecker stared blankly at her. "What search?" he asked.

As if in answer, Maggie unbuttoned the top two buttons of her white dress. She lifted a necklace in the dim light and it took Baedecker a few seconds to recognize the Saint Christopher's medal he had given her in Poona. It was the medal his father had given him in 1952 on the day Baedecker had left for the Marine Corps. It was the medal he had taken to the moon and back. Baedecker shook his head. "No," he said, "you didn't understand."

"Yes, I did," said Maggie.

"No," said Baedecker. "You admitted that you made a mistake following Scott to India. You're making a bigger mistake now."

"I didn't follow Scott to India," said Maggie. "I went to India to see how he was doing because I believed that he was passionately involved in asking questions that I happen to think are important." She paused. "I was wrong. He wasn't interested in asking questions, only in finding answers."

"What's the difference?" asked Baedecker. He felt the conversation slipping out of his control, dropping away from him like an aircraft that had reached stall speed.

"The difference is that Scott took the line of least resistance," said Maggie. "Like most people, he found it too uncomfortable to be out in the open, unsheltered by some shadow of authority. So when the questions got too hard, he settled for easy answers."

Baedecker shook his head again. "This is gobbledygook," he said. "You've got things all mixed up. You have *me* mixed up with somebody else, Maggie. I'm just a middle-aged guy who's tired of his job and just well-off enough to take a few months of unearned vacation."

"Bullshit," said Maggie. "Remember our conversation in Benares? About places of power?"

Baedecker laughed. "Right," he said. He pointed to two young men in ragged shorts who had just passed, weaving their skateboards through the crowd. Behind them came a runner in tight shorts and a self-conscious pride in his body as evident as the sweat that glistened on his tanned skin. Stepping out of his way was a pack of surly-looking teenagers with purple mohawks. "I'm getting closer, aren't I?" he said.

Maggie shrugged. "Maybe this weekend," she said. "Mountains have always been fairly reliable as places of power."

"And if I don't come down off what's-its-name . . . off Uncompahgre Peak with a couple of stone tablets, then you'll go back to Boston on Monday and get on with your education?" asked Baedecker.

"We'll see," said Maggie.

"Look, Maggie, I think we have to . . ." began Baedecker.

"Hey, look, that guy's sitting on a chair up there on his wire," she said. "It looks like he's doing magic tricks. Come on, let's go watch." She tugged Baedecker to his feet. "I'll buy you a chocolate cone after."

"So you like tightrope walkers and tricks?" he asked.

"I like magic," said Maggie and pulled him along with her.

∞

"Six-six-six is the mark of the beast," said Deedee. "It's on my Sears charge card."

"What?" said Baedecker. The campfire had burned down to embers. It was quite cold out. Baedecker had pulled on a wool sweater and his old nylon flight jacket. Maggie huddled next to him in a bulky goosedown coat. The campfire across the meadow had gone out some time earlier, the four young people had gone to their tents, and Tommy had stumbled back and silently crawled into the tent he would be sharing with Baedecker.

"*Revelation* thirteen: sixteen, seventeen," said Deedee. "And he causes all small and great, rich and poor, free and bond, to receive a MARK in their right hand, or in their foreheads: and that no man might buy or sell, save that he has the MARK, or the name of the beast, or the number of a man: and his number is six hundred, threescore and six.'"

"On your Sears card?" asked Maggie.

"Not only there, but on their monthly statements also," said Deedee. Her voice was low, soft, serious.

"The Sears card shouldn't be a problem unless you carry it on your forehead, should it?" asked Baedecker.

Gavin leaned forward and threw two twigs on the fire. Sparks rose and mingled with the stars. "It's really not funny,

Dick," he said. "*Revelation* has been amazingly accurate in predicting events leading up to the beginning of the tribulations era. The code six-six-six is used frequently by computers . . . and on Visa and MasterCard accounts as well. The Bible says that the Antichrist will be the leader of a ten-nation confederation in Europe. Well, it might be coincidence, but the big computer in the Common Market Administration Building in Brussels is called 'the beast' by some of its programmers. It takes up three floors."

"So what?" said Baedecker. "The NASA centers at Huntsville and Houston used more computer space back in '71. It just meant that computers were clumsier then, took up more room, not the coming of an Antichrist."

"Yes," said Gavin, "but that was before the UPC was developed."

"UPC?" asked Maggie. She shivered and shifted a little closer to Baedecker as a cold wind came up.

"Universal Product Code," said Gavin. "Those stripes on all the packages you buy. Like at the supermarket . . . the laser scanner reads the code and the computer records the item price."

"I shop at a little corner market in Boston," said Maggie. "I don't think they even have an electric cash register."

"They will have one," said Gavin. He was smiling, but his lips formed only a thin line. "By 1994 the UPC scanners will be in use everywhere . . . at least in this country."

Baedecker rubbed his eyes and coughed as the smoke drifted his way. "Yes, Tom," he said, "but the scanner reads the price markings on my cans of soup and packages of Tater Tots, not on my forehead."

"Laser tattoos," said Gavin. "Professor R. Keith Farrell of Washington State University developed a laser tattoo gun several years ago for registering fish. It's fast—takes less than a microsecond—is painless, and can be invisible except to UV laser scanners. Social security checks already carry an *F*

or an *H* under their computer coding. It almost certainly
stands for 'forehead or hand.' The next step will be for the
government to begin marking social security recipients themselves for fast identification and coding."

"That would be handy to get back into rock concerts,"
said Maggie.

Deedee leaned forward into the red light of the dying
campfire. Her voice was soft. "'If any man worship the beast
and his image, and receive his mark in his forehead, or in
his hand, the same shall drink of the wine of the wrath of
God; and he shall be tormented with fire and brimstone in
the presence of the holy angels, and in the presence of the
Lamb: and the smoke of their torment ascendeth up for
ever and ever: and they rest no day or night, who worship
the beast and image, and whosoever receiveth the mark of
his name.'" Deedee smiled shyly. "*Revelation* fourteen: nine
to eleven."

"Gosh," said Maggie and there was admiration in her
voice, "how do you memorize all that? I couldn't memorize
the first two stanzas of *Thanatopsis* in high school."

Gavin reached across and took Deedee's hand. "Maybe
an easier verse to memorize is John three: sixteen, seventeen," he said. "'I find no pleasure in the death of the wicked.
Believe in the Lord Jesus Christ and you shall be saved. For
God sent not His Son into the world to condemn the world,
but that the world through Him might be saved.'"

A few heavy raindrops hissed in the fire. Baedecker
looked up to see the stars gone, the sky above as dark as the
black canyon walls. "Damn," he said, "I wanted to sleep
outside tonight."

∾

Baedecker lay in the small tent and thought about his
divorce. It was a topic he rarely tried to bring to mind; the
memories were as blurred and painful as those of the two

months he had spent in the hospital after crashing an F-104 in 1962. He rolled over, but the rough ground poked at him through the sleeping bag and thin foam pad. Tommy Jr. snored next to him. The boy smelled of wine and pot. Outside, a few raindrops pattered on the tent, and the Cimarron River, no wider than a stream, made gurgling sounds thirty feet away.

Baedecker's divorce had been finalized in August of 1986, only two weeks before their twenty-eighth wedding anniversary. Baedecker had flown to Boston for the formalities, coming a day early to stay at Carl Bumbry's house. He had forgotten that Carl's wife had been a closer friend to Joan than Carl had been to him. The next night was spent at the Holiday Inn in Cambridge.

Two hours before going to court, Baedecker dressed in his best three-piece summer suit. Joan liked the suit, had helped him pick it out two years earlier. A few minutes before it was time to leave, Baedecker realized that he knew precisely what dress Joan would wear to the divorce proceedings. She would not have bought a new one, because she would never wear it again. She would not wear her favorite white dress or the more formal green suit. Only the purple cotton dress would be light enough and formal enough for her on this day. And Baedecker had always disliked the color purple.

Baedecker immediately changed into tennis shorts, a blue T-shirt, and tennis shoes. He put his sweat-stained wristband on and threw the racquet and a canister of balls in the backseat of his rented car. Before going into court, he called Carl Bumbry and arranged for a four-thirty game at Carl's club immediately following the divorce action.

Joan wore the purple dress. Baedecker spoke to her before and after the brief ceremony but later could remember nothing of what they said to each other. He did remember the score of the tennis match—Carl had won 6-0, 6-3, 6-4—and Baedecker could recall vividly details of play from each set. After the match Baedecker showered, changed clothes, tossed his clothes into his old military flight bag, and drove north to Maine.

He went alone to Monhegan Island, he realized later, because Joan had always wanted to go there. Long before they had moved to Boston, even back during the hot, Houston days, Joan had been intrigued by the thought of spending time on the little island off the coast of Maine. They had never found the time.

For Baedecker, the image that stuck in his mind was of his arrival after an hour's boat-ride on the *Laura B.* The little boat had entered a thick fog bank a mile or two from the coast and water was beaded along the ship's wires and lines. People had quit conversing; even the youngsters playing near the bow had stopped their shouts and horseplay. The last ten minutes of the ride had been made in silence. Then they passed the two breakwaters of broken concrete slabs and moved into the harbor. Gray-shingled houses and dripping piers shifted in and out of existence as the fog curled, lifted, and settled again. Gulls wheeled and dived above the wake of the boat, their cries ripping the silence into sharp-edged fragments. Baedecker had been standing near the port rail, alone, when he noticed the people standing on the dock. At first he could not be sure they were people; they stood so straight and still. Then the fog lifted and he could make out the colorful sports shirts, the vacation hats, even the make of cameras hanging around some of their necks.

It had given Baedecker a strange feeling. He learned later that the crowd gathered twice a day to meet the boat: tourists heading back to the mainland, islanders greeting guests, and vacationers, bored by the lack of electricity on the island, merely waiting to see the boat. But although Baedecker spent three days on the island, reading, sleeping, exploring the trails and druidish woods, he would later remember only the image of the dock and the fog and the figures standing silently. It was a scene from Hades with shades of the long-dead waiting passively to greet the newly departed. Sometimes, especially when Baedecker was tired and tempted to recall details of the divorce and the painful year that preceded it, he would dream that he was on that dock, in the fog, a gray form in a gray mist, waiting.

∞

The rain stopped. Baedecker closed his eyes and listened to the river moving over rocks in the streambed below. Somewhere in the forest an owl called, but Baedecker heard it as the screech and cry of gulls calling above the sea.

Tommy Jr. was throwing up when Baedecker awoke. The boy had managed to get his head and shoulders out of the tent. Now his legs kicked and his back arched with each series of spasms.

Baedecker pulled on his shirt and jeans and squeezed out the other flap. It was almost seven A.M. but the sunlight had not touched the canyon yet, and there was a deep chill in the air. Tommy had finished vomiting and was resting his face on his arm. Baedecker knelt next to him and asked if there was anything he could do, but already Deedee was bustling over from her own tent, swabbing the boy's face with a damp handkerchief, and murmuring reassurances.

Several minutes later Maggie joined Gavin and Baedecker at the breakfast campfire. Her face was pink from washing at the icy stream and her short hair looked recently brushed. She wore khaki shorts and a bright red shirt. "What's wrong with Tommy?" she asked as she accepted hot water from the pot and stirred instant coffee into her Sierra cup.

"Altitude maybe," suggested Baedecker.

"Not altitude," said Gavin. "Probably something those hippies gave him last night." He gestured to the other side of the meadow where a cold fire ring and trampled grass were the only sign the others had been there.

"When did they leave?" asked Maggie.

"Before dawn," said Gavin. "When *we* should've been moving. We'll never make the summit of Uncompahgre today."

"What's the plan?" asked Baedecker. "Shall we pack back down to the car?"

Gavin looked startled. "No, no, the schedule might work out better this way. Look." He pulled out the topographic map and spread it on a rock. "I'd planned for us to reach *here* last night." He stabbed a finger down on a white area far up the canyon. "But because of the late start from Boulder and our slow pace yesterday, we camped here." He pointed to a green area several miles north. "So we'll take it easy today, pack up to the plateau today, and camp here tonight." He pointed to an area southwest of Uncompahgre Peak. "That way we'll get an early start on Sunday morning. Deedee and I hate to miss church, but we'll be there for the evening services."

"Where was it that you left the other car?" asked Baedecker.

"Right here," said Gavin, pointing to a green area on the map. "It's just a few miles south of the pass and plateau. After we do the mountain, we hike out, pick up the other car on the way north, and we're on our way home."

Maggie studied the map. "That campsite would be high," she said. "Over eleven thousand feet. It looks like it would be pretty exposed if the weather gets bad."

Gavin shook his head. "I checked with the weather service yesterday and there is only a fifteen percent chance of showers in this region through Monday. Besides, there will be plenty of sheltered places as we get close to the south ridge there."

Maggie nodded but did not look satisfied.

"I wonder how the hang glider group is doing," said Baedecker. He looked up the canyon but could see no one on the few stretches of trail visible between the trees. The sunlight was moving down the west wall of rock to their right, exposing strata of pink rock like muscle and tissue opening to a scalpel's blade.

"If they had any sense, they turned around and headed back north toward Cimarron," said Gavin. "Come on, let's get things packed up."

"What about Tommy?" asked Maggie.

"He'll come along with Deedee in a few minutes," said Gavin.

"Do you think he'll feel up to it?" asked Baedecker. "According to the map, the next ten miles are all uphill."

"He'll feel up to it," said Gavin and there was no hint of doubt in his voice.

∾

It was not so bad after the sheer hell of the first hour.

Despite the food consumed, the pack seemed heavier at first than it had the previous day. The canyon continued to narrow and so did the trail, winding along the canyon wall above the stream. Here and there a mudslide or fallen tree had the three of them moving carefully on a steep slope of rock or grass sixty feet above the water. At first Baedecker was convinced that the hang glider group could not have come this way, but then he began noticing bootprints in the soft dirt and furrows in the mud where the poles had been dragged. Baedecker shook his head and continued on.

By nine A.M. the direct sunlight was burning on the rock and filling the air with the scent of heated pine and fir trees. Baedecker poured sweat. He wanted to stop and change from his jeans into a pair of shorts, but he was afraid that if he fell behind the other two he might never catch up. There was no sign of Deedee or Tom Jr. on the trail behind them, but Deedee had been cheery enough when they said good-bye after striking camp. Tom Gavin never really rested, he just stopped moving for a few seconds, fidgeted from foot to foot while squinting ahead up the trail, then only to say "Ready?" and be off and moving before either Maggie or Baedecker could reply.

After the first hour it was not so bad. By the second hour Baedecker had fallen into a rhythm of pain and panting, which seemed tolerable enough. Sometime before noon they came around a bend of rock, and two tall peaks were visible ahead, the summits still holding pockets of snow despite the hot summer just past. Gavin identified the tiered, flat-topped peak as Uncompahgre and the sharper one as the Wetterhorn. A third summit was just visible above the ridgeline. "Uncompahgre looks like a wedding cake, the Wetterhorn looks a little like the real Matterhorn, and the Matterhorn doesn't look at all like the real Matterhorn," said Gavin.

"Gotcha," said Baedecker.

They continued up the deteriorating trail past spires of red rock and occasional waterfalls. The Douglas firs were eighty feet tall in places, rising high above any area flat enough for them. They passed through a thick cluster of ponderosa pine and Maggie had them all sniffing the trees, explaining that the sap of the ponderosa smelled like butterscotch. Baedecker found a recent scar, sniffed the sap, and announced that it was definitely chocolate. Maggie called him a pervert. Gavin suggested that they all move a little faster.

They had lunch where Silver Creek ran into the Cimarron River. The trail had been completely eroded away, and it had taken the three of them half an hour to pick their way down the last few hundred yards of scree to the floor of the canyon. Baedecker looked back down the canyon, but there was still no sign of Deedee or Tommy. To the south the trail resumed on the opposite side of the river, but Baedecker could see no easy way across the twenty-five feet of water. He wondered how Lude and Maria and the others had managed to cross.

Maggie wandered away up Silver Creek and came back a minute later to lead Baedecker to where a dozen violet columbines grew near a fallen log. A ring of Engleman and Blue Spruce enclosed a small clearing carpeted with grass and ferns. A tiny stream bubbled through it, and scores of white-and-purple flowers spotted the grass despite the lateness of the season. Somewhere nearby a woodpecker was tapping out a frenzied code.

"Great place to camp," said Baedecker.

"Yes," said Maggie. "And a great place not to camp, too." She took out a Hershey bar and broke it in half, offering Baedecker the half with more almonds.

Gavin strode into the clearing. He had reshouldered his heavy pack and had binoculars dangling around his neck. "Look," he said, "I'm going to ford the river down there above where the creek comes in. I'll leave a line across it. Then I'm going to reconnoiter the trail up the west side there. It should be about a half mile to that final set of switchbacks. I'll wait for you above tree line, okay?"

"Okay," said Baedecker.

"The map says that the old Silver Jack Mine is up this creek," said Maggie. "Why don't we take a few minutes to hike up to it? Deedee and Tommy should be along pretty soon."

Gavin smiled and shrugged. "Suit yourself. I want to get up on that plateau to find a campsite so we can scout the south ridge before nightfall."

Maggie nodded and Gavin strode away. Baedecker accompanied him down to the river to make sure there were no problems when he forded the quick current. When Gavin reached the other side, he waved and secured his rope to a tree near the bank. Baedecker returned the wave and walked back to the clearing.

Maggie was lying on her red shirt. Her midriff and shoulders were darkly tanned, but her breasts were white, the nipples a delicate shade of pink.

"Oh," said Baedecker and sat down on a log.

Maggie lifted her hand to shield her eyes and looked at him. "Does this make you uncomfortable, Richard?" When Baedecker hesitated, Maggie sat up and pulled on her shirt. "There, decent again," she said with a smile. "Or at least covered up."

Baedecker plucked two long strands of grass, peeled the ends, and offered one to Maggie.

"Thanks." She looked up toward the west wall of the canyon. "Your friends are interesting," she said.

"Tom and Deedee?" said Baedecker. "What do you think?"

Maggie returned his level gaze. "I think they're your friends," she said. "I'm their guest."

Baedecker chewed on his stem of grass and nodded. "I'd like your opinion," he said after a while.

Maggie smiled and looked up at the sun. "Well, after last night's numerology sermon, I was tempted to say that these folks have their porch light on but nobody's home." She chewed off a bit of grass. "But that's not fair. It's unkind. I guess Tom and Deedee just represent a certain type that I have strong reservations about," she said.

"Born-again Christians?" said Baedecker.

Maggie shook her head. "No, people who trade their brains in for sacred truths that can be boiled down to poster slogans."

"It sounds like we're still talking about Scott," said Baedecker.

Maggie did not deny it. "What do *you* think of Tom?" she asked.

Baedecker thought a minute. "Well," he said at last, "there's a story from our early training days that I've been reminded of recently."

"Great," said Maggie. "I'm a sucker for stories."

"It's a long one."

"I'm a sucker for long stories," said Maggie.

"Well, we were out on two weeks of survival training," said Baedecker. "For the grand finale they broke us into teams of three—crews actually—flew us out into the New Mexico desert somewhere northwest of White Sands, and gave us three days to find our way back to civilization. We had our Swiss army knives, some booklets on edible plants, and one compass between us."

"Sounds like fun," said Maggie.

"Yeah," said Baedecker, "NASA thought so too. If we didn't show up in five days, they would've started a search pattern. They weren't too keen on losing any of their second-generation astronauts. So anyway, our team was the same as the crew we had later—me, Dave Muldorff, and Tom. Even then, Tom always worked harder than anyone else. Even after he made the cut . . . getting into the astronaut corps, crew selection, whatever . . . he still would work twice as hard as he had to, as if he was always on the verge of washing out. Well, all of us felt like that some of the time, but it never seemed to let up with Tom.

"Our other teammate was Dave Muldorff—we sometimes called him Rockford back then—and Dave was just the opposite. Dave once told me that the only philosophy he adhered to was Ohm's Law—find the path of least resistance and follow it. Actually, Dave was a lot like Neil Armstrong . . . they'd give a thousand percent and come out on top when they had to, but you'd never see either one of them up at dawn running laps. The main difference between Muldorff and Armstrong was that Dave had a weird sense of humor.

"So anyway, our first day in the boonies went all right. We found a water source and figured out a way to carry some with us. Tom caught a lizard before nightfall and wanted to eat it raw, but Dave and I decided to wait a bit on that. We had our course set to cross a road we knew ran into the mountains, and we were sure we'd find it sooner or later. On the second day, Tom was ready to have the lizard for lunch, but Dave convinced us to get by on plants for a while longer and save the main course for dinner. Then, about two o'clock that afternoon, Dave began acting strange. He kept sniffing the ground and saying that he could *smell* the way to civilization. Tom suggested sunstroke and we both got pretty alarmed. We tried to tie a T-shirt around Dave's head, but he just howled at the sky and took off running.

"We caught up to him within a quarter of a mile; when we came over a rock ridge, there was Muldorff in the middle of this desolate arroyo sitting in a lawn chair under a beach umbrella, drinking a cold beer. He had a transistor radio going, a cooler full of ice and beer under his feet, and a swimming pool—one of those little inflatable ones that kids use—a pool a few feet away with an inflatable raft and a couple of rubber ducks in it. And you have to remember that we were in the middle of nowhere—still about sixty miles from the nearest road.

"After he got through laughing, Dave told us how he did it. He had a WAF clerk at the base commander's office get into the files and find the proposed drop points for the various NASA teams. Then Dave vectored our probable route back and got a friend of his who was flying choppers out of White Sands to ferry the junk out to this arroyo. Dave thought it was funny as hell. Tom didn't. He was so mad at first that he turned his back and walked away from Dave and his beach umbrella and his rock music. At first I sort of agreed with Tom. Dave's stunt was the kind of thing that used to drive NASA absolutely apeshit. The agency had no sense of humor at all as far as we could tell. Our whole team could've been in big trouble.

"But after a beer or two, Dave packed all the stuff in behind a boulder and we got back to survival training. Tom didn't speak to him for twenty-four hours. Worse than that,

I don't think Tom ever completely forgave or forgot for the two years we worked together after that. At first I thought it was just that he was angry about Dave screwing up our training and jeopardizing Tom's perfect record. Then I realized that it was more than that. Dave had broken the rules and Tom could never quite get around that. And there was one other thing . . ."

"What's that?" asked Maggie.

Baedecker leaned forward and whispered. "Well, I think Tom was really looking forward to eating that damned lizard and Dave had taken some of the flavor out of it."

∾

Deedee and Tom Jr. showed up when Baedecker and Maggie were preparing to cross the river, and the four forded together. Tommy looked pale and somewhat subdued but remained as sullen as before. Deedee was chipper enough for both of them. The river was never more than knee-deep, but the current was swift and the water was ice-cold. Baedecker waited until the others were across, untied the rope from the east bank, and brought it across with him.

Forty-five minutes later they passed a waterfall, crossed the stream again—on a fallen log this time—and soon after that they were climbing switchbacks. The summit of the Matterhorn loomed above them and each time they paused to rest, more of Uncompahgre Peak had become visible to the southeast. They were within a few miles of the mountain now, and Baedecker began to realize how large the massif actually was. It reminded him of the huge mesas and buttes he had seen in New Mexico and Arizona, but this one was sharper, steeper, and it rose not from the desert but from a ten-thousand-foot plateau.

By midafternoon they had completed the last series of switchbacks and emerged onto the high tundra. The transformation was startling. The thick pine forests of the canyon had given way to a few aged and stunted fir trees, often weathered to the point there were no branches at all on their western and northern sides, and then to tall clumps of ground juniper, and then even these had disappeared and only grass and the low, red-and-tan gorse covered the rocky tundra. To Baedecker, coming up over the last ridge from the canyon was like stepping from the top rung of a ladder onto the roof of a tall building.

From the high pass they were now traversing, Baedecker could see dozens of greater and lesser mountain peaks and a seemingly endless vista of passes, ridges, high meadows, and softly undulating tundra. Patches of snow mottled the landscape. Overhead, a scattering of fluffy cumulus stretched to the serrated horizon, the white against blue above almost blending into the white against brown below.

Baedecker paused, panting, feeling the sweat pour from him, his lungs still demanding more oxygen than they could supply. "Fantastic," he said.

Maggie was grinning. She removed a red kerchief she had been using as a headband and mopped her face. She touched Baedecker's arm and pointed to the northeast where sheep were grazing along a rolling stretch of alpine meadow several ridges away. The gray bodies mixed with the clouds and snowfields and cloud shadows to give a sense of dappled movement across the entire panorama.

"Fantastic," Baedecker said again. His heart was pounding at his ribs. He felt as if he had left some dark part of him behind in the shadows of the canyon. Maggie offered him her water bottle. He was aware of her arm touching his as he drank.

Tommy slumped down on a rock and poked at a clump of moss campion with his walking stick. Deedee smiled and looked around. "There's Tom," she said and pointed to a small figure far across the pass. "It looks like he's setting up the tent already."

"This is marvelous," Baedecker said softly to himself. For some reason he felt light-headed in the cool, thin air. He gave the water bottle to Maggie and she drank deeply, throwing her head back so that her short, blond curls caught the sunlight.

Maggie offered the water bottle to Deedee, but the older woman took her hand instead. With her other hand she seized Baedecker's fingers. The three stood in a rough circle. Deedee bowed her head. "Thank you, O Lord," she said, "for allowing us to witness the perfection of Your Creation and for sharing this special moment with dear friends who will, with the help of the Holy Spirit, come to know the truth of Thy Word. In Jesus' name we ask. Amen."

Deedee patted Baedecker's hand and looked at him. "It *is* marvelous," she said. There were tears in her eyes. "And admit it, Richard," she said, "don't you wish Joan were here to share this with us?"

∞

Their campsite had three tents arranged around a tall, flat-topped boulder that stood alone at the locus of a great circle of tundra. There was no firewood at that altitude except for the branches of the low shrubbery that grew between the rocks, so they set their two backpack stoves on a flat rock next to the boulder and watched the blue propane flames as the stars came out.

Before dinner they had reconnoitered their route as the shadows of the Wetterhorn and the Matterhorn covered the plateau and moved up the terraced sides of Uncompahgre. "There," said Gavin and handed the binoculars to Baedecker. "Right at the base of the south ridge."

Baedecker looked and could make out a low, red tent set back in the shadows of the rocks. Two figures moved around it, storing equipment and working over a small stove. Baedecker handed back the binoculars. "I see two of them," he said. "I wonder where the girl and the guy carrying the hang glider are."

"Up there," said Maggie and pointed toward the high ridge just at the point where sunlight still struck the massif.

Gavin focused his binoculars. "I see them. That idiot is still dragging the kite along."

"He can't be planning to fly it tonight, can he?" asked Maggie.

Gavin shook his head. "No, he's still hours from the summit. They're just getting as high as they can before nightfall." He handed the binoculars to Maggie.

"The early-morning conditions would be best for what he wants to do," said Baedecker. "Strong thermals. Not too much wind." Maggie gave him the binoculars and Baedecker swept the ridge twice before finding the small figures high on the jagged spine of the mountain. Sunlight illuminated the red-and-yellow carrying bag as the little man bent under the burden of the aluminum and Dacron bundle. The woman followed several paces behind, bent under her own load of a large frame pack with two sleeping bags. As Baedecker watched, the sunlight left the mountain and the two struggling silhouettes became indistinguishable from the tumble of spires and boulders along the ridge.

"Uh-oh," said Maggie. She was looking toward the west. The sun had not set, but along the horizon lay a band of blue-black clouds that had swallowed the last light of day.

"Probably miss us," said Gavin. "The wind is to the southeast."

"I hope so," said Maggie.

Baedecker turned the binoculars back on the south ridge, but the two human figures there were too insignificant to stand out as storm and nightfall approached.

Stars continued to burn overhead, but in the west all was darkness. The four adults huddled near the stoves and drank hot tea while Tommy sat four feet above them on the boulder and stared off to the north. It was very cold, and there was no hint of wind.

"You've never met Dick's wife, Joan, have you, Maggie?" asked Deedee.

"No," said Maggie, "I haven't met her."

"Joan's a wonderful person," said Deedee. "She has the patience of a saint. Her personality is perfectly suited to a camping trip like this because nothing phases her. She takes things in her stride."

"Where are you going after Colorado?" Gavin asked Baedecker.

"Oregon. I thought I'd stop and see Rockford."

"Rockford?" said Gavin. "Oh, Muldorff. It's too bad about his illness."

"What illness?" asked Baedecker.

"Joan was the most patient of all the wives," Deedee said to Maggie. "When the men would be gone for days . . . *weeks* . . . all of us would get a little cranky . . . even me, I'm afraid . . . but Joan never complained. I don't think I once heard Joan complain in all of the years I knew her."

"He was hospitalized last June," said Gavin.

"I know," said Baedecker. "I thought that was for appendicitis. He's all right now, isn't he?"

"Joan was a Christian then, but she hadn't really given herself to Jesus," said Deedee. "Now she and Phillip . . . he's an accountant . . .? I understand that they're very active in an evangelical church in Boston."

"It wasn't appendicitis," said Gavin. "I talked to Jim Bosworth who lobbies on the Hill in Washington. He says that Muldorff's friends in the House know that he has Hodgkin's disease. He had his spleen removed last June."

"Do you attend a church there, dear? In Boston, I mean."

"No," said Maggie.

"Oh, well," said Deedee. "I just thought you might have run into Joan if you did. The world is such a small place that way, isn't it?"

"Is it?" asked Maggie.

"The prognosis isn't good, I don't think," said Gavin. "But then, there's always the possibility of a miracle."

"Yes, it really is," said Deedee. "One time when we were all getting ready for the men's mission, Joan called me and asked if I'd come over to stay with their little boy while she went out shopping for Dick's birthday present. I had a friend visiting from Dallas but I said, 'Sure, we'll both come over.' Well, Scott was about seven then and Tommy was three or four . . ."

Baedecker stood up, crossed to his tent, crawled inside, and heard no more.

∾

When Baedecker was seven or eight, sometime early in the war, he had accompanied his father on a fishing trip to a reservoir somewhere in Illinois. It had been the first overnight fishing trip he had been allowed to go on. He remembered sleeping in the same bed with his father in a tourist cabin near the lake and going out in the morning into a hot, brilliant late-summer day. The broad expanse of water seemed to both muffle and amplify all sounds. The foliage along the gravel road going down to the dock seemed too dense to penetrate, and the leaves were already covered with dust by six-thirty in the morning.

The small ritual of preparing the boat and outboard motor was exciting, a leave-taking within the larger trip. The life jacket was reassuring in its bulky, fish-smelling clumsiness. Their little boat moved slowly across the reservoir, cutting through the calm water, stirring sluggish rainbows where oil had been spilled, the throb of the ten-horsepower motor blending with the smell of gasoline and fish scales to create a perfect sense of place and perspective in Baedecker's young consciousness.

The old highway bridge had been stranded far out from shore when the dam had bottled up the river some years before. Now only two broken fragments of the span remained, glaring white as exposed thighbones against the blue sky and dark water.

The young Baedecker was fascinated with the idea of boarding the bridges, of standing on them far out on the hot expanse of lake, of fishing from them. Baedecker knew that his father wanted to troll. He knew the infinite patience with which his father would fish, watching the line for hours almost without blinking, letting the boat creep across the lake or even drift with the motor off. Baedecker did not have his father's patience. Already the boat seemed too small, their progress far too slow. The compromise was to let the boy off—still wrapped in his bulky life jacket— while his father explored the nearby inlets for a promising hole. He made Baedecker promise that he would stay in the center of the larger of the two spans.

The sense of isolation was wonderful. He watched as his father's boat disappeared from sight around a point and continued watching until the last echoes of the outboard faded away. The sunlight was very hot, and the effect of watching his fish line and bobber soon became hypnotic. The small waves lapping at the moss-covered undersides of the bridge six feet below created an illusion of movement, as if the two segments of bridge were moving slowly across the reservoir. Within half an hour the heat and sense of motion created a slight nausea in the boy, a throbbing pulse of vertigo. He pulled in his line, propped the pole against the cracked concrete railing, and sat on the roadbed. It was too hot. He took off his life jacket and felt better as sweat dried on his back.

He was not aware of the instant when the idea of jumping from one section of the bridge to the other occurred to him. The two pieces of the shattered span were separated by no more than eight feet of water. The smaller span's roadbed was six feet above the water, but the larger section upon which Baedecker stood had not settled as much as the other and was almost a foot higher, making the jump seem even easier.

The thought of jumping quickly became an obsession, a pressure swelling in Baedecker's chest. Several times he paced his steps to the edge of his span, planning his run, rehearsing his leap. For some reason he was sure that his father would be pleased and amused when he returned to find his son on the different section of bridge. Several times he worked up his nerve, began the run, and stopped. Each time he felt the fear rise in his throat and he would stop, his sneakers making rough sounds on the concrete. He stood there panting, his fair skin burning in the hot sunshine, his face flushed with embarrassment. Then he turned back, took five long steps, and leaped.

He tried to leap. At the last possible second he tried to stop his forward momentum, his right foot slid out over the edge of the span, and he fell. He managed to twist in midair, there was a tremendous blow to his midsection, and then he was dangling—his feet and lower legs hanging above the water, his elbows and forearms flat on the roadbed.

He had hurt himself. His arms and hands were badly scraped, there was the taste of blood in his mouth, and his stomach and ribs ached more than he had ever imagined possible. He did not have the strength left to pull himself up onto the bridge surface. His knees were under the slab of the roadbed and try as he might he could not lift his legs high enough to find purchase on the cracked concrete. The lake water seemed to create a suction that threatened to pull him in. Baedecker quit struggling and hung there with only the friction against his torn hands and arms keeping him from sliding backwards into the lake. With his child's imagination he could see the great depths of darkness that lay beneath the bridge, could sense the submerged trees far below the surface, and could feel his descent to the muddy lake bottom. He could imagine the drowned streets and houses and graveyards of the valley turned reservoir, all waiting beneath the dark waters. Waiting for him.

Two feet in front of Baedecker's eyes, a weed grew out of a narrow fissure in the bridge surface. He could not reach it. It would not hold him if he did. He felt the saving pressure on his torn hands and arms lessening. His shoulders ached and he knew that it was only minutes, perhaps seconds, until his trembling upper arms gave way and he would slide backward with a terrible rasping of palms and forearms across the burning concrete.

Then, dreaming but rising from his dream like a diver rising from depths, Baedecker became aware of the wind rising and the tent flapping and of the smell of rain approaching, but he could also clearly hear—as he had heard forty-five years before—the steady throb of the approaching outboard motor, falling into silence now, and then the touch of strong hands on his side and the calm sound of his father's voice. "Let go, Richard. Jump. It's all right. I've got you. Let go, Richard."

∾

Thunder was rumbling. A cold wind blew in when the tent flap was parted. Maggie Brown slid in, settled her foam pad and sleeping bag next to his.

"What?" said Baedecker. His palms and arms were sore.

"Tommy wanted to trade places," whispered Maggie. "I think he wants to do some solitary drinking. I said okay. Shhh." Maggie touched her finger to his lips. The darkness in the tent was broken by sudden, brilliant flashes of lightning, followed scant seconds later by thunder so loud that it seemed to Baedecker that freight trains were rumbling across the high tundra toward them. The next explosion of light showed Maggie slipping out of her shorts, tugging them over her hips and down. Her underpants were small and white.

"Storm's here," said Baedecker, blinking away afterimages of the lightning flash that had illuminated Maggie removing her shirt. Her breasts had looked pale and heavy in the brief, stroboscopic flash.

"Shhh," said Maggie and slid against him in the darkness. He had fallen asleep wearing only his jockey shorts and a soft flannel shirt. Her fingers unbuttoned the shirt in the darkness, pulled it off. He was rolling next to her on the soft jumble of sleeping bags, his arms enfolding her, when her hand slid under the elastic waistband of his shorts. "Shhh," she whispered and pulled off his underpants, using her right hand to free him. "Shhh."

The lightning illuminated their lovemaking in images of frozen light. The thunder drowned all sound except heartbeats and whispered entreaties. At one point Baedecker looked up at Maggie as she straddled him, their arms extended like dancers', fingers intertwined, the nylon of the tent bright behind her as lightning flash followed lightning flash and the waves of thunder rolled through them and across them. A second later, rocked tight in her arms, resisting the explosion of his own orgasm, he was sure he heard her whisper above the cascade of external sound, "Yes, Richard, let go. I've got you. Let go."

Together, still moving slightly, they rolled over in the tangle of sleeping bags and foam pads, and listened as the wind rose to terrible heights, the tent strained and flapped wildly against its restraints, and the lightning flash and thunder crash were no longer separated by so much as a second. Together they huddled against the storm.

"COME ON, GODDAMN YOU GODS, LET'S SEE YOU DO YOUR WORST! COME ON, YOU COWARDS!" The scream came from just outside the tent and was followed by a blast of thunder.

"Good God," whispered Maggie. "What is that?"

"COME ON, LET'S HAVE A GODDAMN GOD OLYMPICS. SHOW YOUR STUFF. YOU CAN DO BETTER THAN THAT! SHOW US, YOU SHITS!" This time the scream was so raw and shrill that it barely sounded human. The last words were followed by a lightning flash and a sound so great that it seemed the sky's fabric was being torn by giant hands. Baedecker tugged on his shorts and stuck his head out of the tent flap. A second later Maggie joined him, pulling on Baedecker's flannel shirt. It was not raining yet, but both of them had to squint against dust and gravel thrown up by the gale-force winds.

Tommy Gavin Jr. was standing on the boulder between the tents. He was naked, legs apart for balance against the wind, arms raised, head thrown back. In one hand he was clutching an almost-empty bottle of Johnny Walker whiskey. In the other he held a three-foot section of aluminum tent pole. The metal glowed blue. Behind the boy Baedecker could see lightning coursing through the belly of thunderclouds looming darker and closer than the mountain peaks illuminated by each flash.

"Tommy!" Gavin yelled. He and Deedee had thrust their heads and shoulders from their writhing tent. "Get down here!" The words were whipped away by the wind.

"COME ON, GODS, SHOW ME SOMETHING!" screamed Tommy. "YOUR TURN, ZEUS. DO IT!" He held the tent pole high.

A blue-white bolt of lightning seemed to leap upward from a nearby summit. Baedecker and Maggie flinched as the shell fire of thunder rolled over them. A few feet away, the Gavins' tent collapsed in the rising wind.

"THAT'S A SIX POINT EIGHT," screamed Tommy as he held up an imaginary scorecard. He had dropped the bottle, but the tent pole still waved. Gavin was struggling to free himself from the collapsed tent, but the fabric was wrapped around him like an orange shroud.

"OKAY, SATAN, SHOW YOUR STUFF," shouted Tommy, laughing hysterically. "LET'S SEE IF YOU'RE AS GOOD AS THE OLD MAN SAYS." He pirouetted, almost fell, and caught his balance five feet above them on the lip of the boulder. Baedecker saw that the boy had an erection. Maggie yelled something in Baedecker's ear, but the words were lost in thunder.

The two forks of lightning seemed to strike simultaneously, one on either side of the camp. Baedecker was blinded for several seconds during which he found himself incongruously reminded of electric trains he had owned as a boy. *The ozone*, he thought. When he could see again, it was to watch Tommy leaping and laughing atop the boulder, his hair whipping in the still-rising gale. "NINE POINT FIVE!" screamed the boy. "FUCKING AYE!"

"Get your ass down here," yelled Gavin. He was out of the tent and reaching, his hands inches short of Tommy's bare ankle. The boy danced backward on the boulder.

"GOTTA GIVE JESUS HIS TURN," cried Tommy. "GOTTA GIVE THE MAN A TRY. SEE WHAT SHIT HE CAN THROW. SEE IF HE'S STILL AROUND."

Gavin ran around to the low end of the rock and grabbed for handholds. Lightning rippled through a dark billow of cloud low above, exploded outward, and struck the summit of Uncompahgre Peak a mile to the east.

"FIVE POINT FIVE!" screamed Tommy. "BIG FUCKING DEAL."

Gavin slipped on the rock, slid back, began climbing again. Tommy danced back to the highest corner of the boulder. "ONE MORE!" he yelled over the wind. Baedecker could hear and smell the rain approaching now, dragging over the tundra like a heavy curtain. "YAHWEH!" screamed Tommy. "COME ON! LAST CHANCE TO GET IN THE GAME IF YOU'RE STILL AROUND, YAHWEH, YOU OLD FART, LAST CHANCE TO SCORE IN THE . . ."

It all happened simultaneously. The tent pole in the boy's upraised hand glowed as bright as a neon sign, Tommy's hair rose from his head and writhed like a nest of snakes, and then the dark form of Gavin merged with boy and the two tumbled off the boulder just as the world exploded in light and noise and a great implosion pressed Baedecker into the ground and submerged his senses in pulses of pure energy.

Whether the lightning struck the boulder or not, Baedecker was never to know. There was no mark on the rock in the morning. When he could hear and see again, Baedecker realized that he had shielded Maggie with his body at the same instant she had attempted to do the same to him. They sat up together and looked around. It was pouring rain now. Only Baedecker's tent had withstood the storm. Tom Gavin was on his hands and knees, head down, panting, face pale in the retreating flashes of light. Tommy was shivering and curled tightly into a fetal position on the wet ground. His hands were clasped together tightly over his eyes and he was sobbing. It was Deedee who crouched above him, half-holding him, half-shielding him from the darkened skies. Her T-shirt was plastered against her back so that each vertebra showed. Her face was upraised and in the final flashes of lightning before the storm disappeared to the east, Baedecker saw the exultation there. And the defiance.

Maggie leaned toward Baedecker until the wet tangle of her hair touched his cheek. "Ten point oh," she said softly and kissed him.

The rain fell the rest of the night.

∞

They reached the south ridge shortly before sunrise.

"This is odd," said Maggie. Baedecker nodded and they continued to climb, staying ten yards behind Gavin. Gavin

had been packed and moving before five A.M. long before
the first, gray light of morning had penetrated the drizzle.
He had said only, "I came to climb the mountain. I'm going
to do it." Neither Maggie nor Baedecker had understood,
but they had come along. Baedecker could see their two
tents far below, still in the shadow of Uncompahgre. They
had been able to repitch Gavin's tent in the night, but
Tommy's had been a total loss with shreds of nylon strewn
far over the tundra. When Gavin and Baedecker had gone
out in the dark to bring back the boy's sleeping bag and
clothing, they had discovered two more whiskey bottles in
the debris of the tent. It was Deedee who mentioned that
they had come from the bar that the Gavins kept stocked
for company.

Now Gavin paused on the ridge as they caught up to
him. They were well above twelve thousand feet. They had
climbed directly east to the ridgeline, ignoring the easier
approach from the south. Baedecker's heart was pounding
and he was exhausted, but it was an exhaustion that he could
deal with and still function adequately. Next to him, Maggie
was flushed and breathing hard from the exertion. Baedecker
touched her hand and she smiled.

"Somebody," said Gavin and pointed far up the ridge
to where someone was struggling on a steep section of trail.

"It's Lude," said Baedecker. He could see the man slip,
fall, and struggle to his feet again. "He still has the hang
glider."

Gavin shook his head. "Why would anyone kill themselves to do something as useless as that?"

"How I yearn to throw myself into endless space," said
Maggie, "and float above the awful abyss."

Both Baedecker and Gavin turned to stare at her.

"Goethe," she said as if in self-defense.

Gavin nodded, adjusted his climbing pack, and moved
on up the trail. Baedecker grinned at her. "Can't memorize
the first stanza of *Thanatopsis*, eh?" he said.

Maggie shrugged and grinned back. Together they moved up the trail toward the beckoning band of sunlight.

∾

They found the tattered remains of the small backpack tent near the thirteen-thousand-foot level. A hundred yards farther on they found the girl named Maria. She was huddled against a rock, her hands clasped between her clenched knees, and, despite the direct sunlight now bathing them all in gold, she was shivering violently. She did not stop shaking even after Maggie wrapped her in a goosedown coat and sat hugging her for several minutes.

"St . . . st . . . storm t . . . tore the t . . . tent all to shit," she managed, the words coming through clenched and chattering teeth. "Got all . . . w . . . w . . . wet."

"It's okay," said Maggie.

"G . . . got . . . t . . . to get up the h . . . hill."

"Not today, young lady," said Gavin. He was rubbing the girl's hands. Baedecker noticed that the girl's lips were gray, her fingers white at the tips. "Hypothermia," said Gavin. "You've got to get down the hill as soon as possible."

"Tell L . . . L . . . Lude I'm s . . . sorry," she said and began crying. Her sobs were punctuated with fits of shivering.

"I'll go down with you," said Maggie. "We have hot coffee and soup down below." The two women stood, the smaller one still trembling uncontrollably.

"I'll go down with you," said Baedecker.

"No!" Maggie's voice was firm. Baedecker looked at her in surprise. "I think you should go on," she said. "I think you both should go up." Her eyes were sending Baedecker a message, but he was not sure what it was.

"You're positive?" he asked.

"Positive," she said. "You have to go, Richard."

Baedecker nodded and had turned to follow Gavin when Maria called out. "Wait!" Still shaking, she fumbled in her pack and came out with a rectangular plastic case. She handed it to Baedecker. "Lude for . . . forgot I was carrying it. He's g . . . got to have it."

Baedecker opened the case just as Gavin walked back to join him. Inside the carrying case, set into niches in foam, were two disposable syringes and two bottles of clear liquid.

"No," said Gavin. "We're not carrying that to him."

Maria looked uncomprehendingly at them. "You've g . . . g . . . got to," she said. "He'll n . . . need it. He forgot yesterday."

"No," said Gavin.

"We'll get it to him," said Baedecker and put the case in the pocket of his flight jacket. He did not flinch when Gavin wheeled to confront him. "It's insulin," said Baedecker. He touched Maggie's hand again and moved ahead of Gavin up the narrowing ridge.

∾

Lude had made it to within fifteen hundred feet of the summit before collapsing. They found him curled under the heavy pack with the long, sailcloth-covered poles across his shoulder. His eyes were open, but his face was parchment white and he was breathing in short, shallow gasps.

Baedecker and Gavin helped him out from under the unassembled hang glider, and the three sat on a large rock next to a two-thousand-foot drop to the high meadow below. The shadow of Uncompahgre reached well more than a mile now, touching the steep flanks of the Matterhorn. High peaks and snow-dappled plateaus were visible as far as Baedecker could see. He looked back down the ridge and picked out Maggie's red shirt. The two women were moving slowly but separately as they picked their way down the south ridge.

"Thanks, man," said Lude, handing the canteen back to Gavin. "I needed some of that. Ran out of water last night before the storm hit."

Baedecker gave him the syringe case.

The little man shook his head and ran a shaking hand through his beard. "Hey, yeah, thanks," he said softly. "Stupid. Forgot Maria had that stuff. And all that crap I ate yesterday."

Baedecker looked away as the injection was administered. Gavin glanced at his watch and said, "Eight forty-three. Why don't I go on up? You can help our friend down, Dick, and I'll catch up to you."

Baedecker hesitated, but Lude laughed loudly. He was packing away the syringe case. "No way, man. I didn't come fifteen fucking miles to pack this stuff back down. Uh-uh." He struggled to his feet and tried to lift the long bundle. He was able to take five steps up the steep and sandy slope before falling to his knees.

"Here," said Baedecker, unlashing the sailcloth-covered poles from the pack and helping him to his feet. "You get the pack. I'll carry this." Baedecker started uphill, surprised at how light the long poles were. Tom Gavin made a noise and moved ahead of them.

The incline became steeper, the trail narrower, the exposure more dramatic just below the summit. But it was the altitude that almost did Baedecker in during the last hundred meters. His lungs could not pull in enough air. His ears would not stop ringing. Baedecker felt his vision blur to the heavy throbbing of his pulse. In the end he forgot everything except the task of setting one foot farther uphill than the other and then lifting his weight against the terrible gravity that threatened to press him down into the rocky mountainside. He had crossed a wide expanse of flat area and almost stumbled over the precipitous northwestern face before he realized that they were on the summit.

He sat down heavily and lowered the poles just as Lude collapsed to a sitting position next to him.

Gavin sat on a wide rock nearby. He had one leg up and was smoking a pipe. The smell of tobacco was sharp and sweet in the clear air. "Shouldn't spend too much time up here, Dick," he said. "We have to pack down to Henson Creek."

Baedecker said nothing; he was watching Lude. The little man was still pale, and there was a tremor in his large hands, but now he crawled over to the long carrying bag and removed sections of aluminum tubing. He spread out a square of red nylon, took a cloth tool case from his pack, and began laying out parts.

"Cable," said Lude. "Stainless steel. Nico swedged."

Baedecker moved over next to him and watched as more bags and baggies were brought out.

"Prone harness," said Lude. "Knee hangers fasten with Velcro. Attached with this carabiner."

Baedecker touched the metal ring and felt the sun's warmth on the steel surface, sensed the colder steel beneath.

"Nuts and bolts," said Lude, laying bags and pieces on the red nylon according to some prearranged pattern. His voice had taken on the cadence of a litany. "Cable tensioners. Saddles, brushings, tangs, nut covers." He removed larger pieces. "Wingposts, noseplates, brackets, crossbar, control bars." He patted the mass of folded Dacron. "Sail."

"We should be heading down," said Gavin.

"In just a minute," said Baedecker.

Lude had connected the long aluminum tubes at their apex and swung them out to an angle of a hundred degrees. Orange-and-white Dacron unfolded like a butterfly's wings opening to the sun. It took him only a few minutes to secure a vertical post and cross-spar. He began working on wires connecting the various components. "Give me a hand, man?" He was speaking to Baedecker.

Baedecker accepted the tools and followed the young man's lead, securing eyebolts, attaching flying wires to the control bar, and tightening nuts. Lude inflated pockets under the leading edge of the wing and Baedecker noticed for the first time that the camber there was adjustable. Thirty years of flying advanced aircraft made him appreciate the elegant simplicity of the Rogallo wing: it was as if the essence of controlled flight had been distilled into these few yards of steel, aluminum, and Dacron. When they were finished, Lude checked all of Baedecker's connections and adjustments and the hang glider sat there like some bright, oversized insect ready to leap into space. Baedecker realized with a shock how large it was, spanning fourteen feet from noseplate to keel, twenty-nine feet across the delta wing.

Gavin tapped his pipe out against the rock. "Where's your helmet?"

"Maria's got the helmet," said Lude. He looked at Gavin and then at Baedecker. Suddenly he laughed. "Hey, man, you don't get it. I don't fly. I just build them, modify them, and show the way. Maria's going to fly it."

It was Gavin's turn to laugh. "Not today she isn't," he said. "She went down to our camp. She's in no shape to walk, much less fly."

"Bullshit, man," said Lude. "She's right behind me."

Baedecker shook his head. "Hypothermia," he said. "Maggie took her down."

Lude jumped up and ran to the southwest corner of the summit. When he saw the two figures just leaving the ridge three thousand feet below he grabbed his head with both hands. "Damn, I don't believe it." He sat down heavily, his long hair falling over his face. Sounds emerged which Baedecker first interpreted as sobs; then he realized that the man was laughing. "Fifteen fucking miles with that thing on my back," he said and laughed. "All this way up and it's off."

"Messes up your movie-making," said Gavin.

"Screw the movie," said Lude. "It fucks up the celebration."

"Celebration?" said Gavin. "What celebration?"

"Come here," said Lude, standing and turning to the west. He led Gavin and Baedecker to the edge of the precipice. "Celebration of *that*," said Lude and swung his right arm in an arc that took in peaks, plateau, and sky.

Gavin nodded. "God's creation is beautiful," he agreed. "But it doesn't take a foolhardy act to celebrate either the Creator or His handiwork."

Lude looked at Gavin and slowly shook his head. "No, man, you missed it," he said. "It ain't somebody's *thing*. It just *is*. And we're part of it. That deserves a celebration, you know?"

It was Gavin's turn to shake his head, pityingly, as if at a child. "Rocks and air and snow," he said. "It means nothing by itself."

Lude looked at the ex-astronaut for a long moment while Gavin shouldered his pack. Finally he smiled. His long hair was blowing in the gentle breeze. "Your mind's really fucked, you know that, man?"

"Come on, Dick," said Gavin, turning his back on the other. "Let's get started down."

Baedecker walked back to the Rogallo wing, crawled under the leading edge, and lifted the harness. "Help me," he said.

Lude ran over. "You sure, man?"

"Help me," said Baedecker. Lude's large hands were already buckling, cinching nylon webbing, and securing waist and shoulder straps. The crotch straps and D-rings reminded Baedecker of all the parachutes he had worn over the years.

"You can't be serious," said Gavin.

Baedecker shrugged. Lude fastened the Velcro leg straps and showed him how to shift forward to get into a prone flying position. Baedecker stood and took the weight of the glider on his shoulder at the apex of the metal triangle while Lude held the keel parallel to the ground.

"You're insane," said Gavin. "Don't kid around, Dick. You don't even have a helmet. We'll have to get a mountain rescue team to get your body off the cliff face."

Baedecker nodded. The wind was gusting gently out of the west at less than ten miles per hour. He took two steps toward the drop-off. The kite bounced slightly and settled on his shoulders. He could feel the play of wind and gravity in the taut wire and billowing Dacron.

"This is preposterous, Dick. You're acting like an adolescent."

"Keep your nose up, man," said Lude. "Shift your body to bank."

Baedecker walked to within eight feet of the edge. There was no slope; the rock dropped vertically for a hundred feet or more to terraces of jagged rock and then fell away to more vertical faces. Baedecker could see Maggie's red shirt a mile below, a small speck of color against the brown and white of the boulder-strewn tundra.

"Dick!" said Gavin. It was a barked command.

"Don't start any three-sixties unless you got a thousand feet of air under you," said Lude. "Away from the hill, man."

"You're a goddamned fool," Gavin said flatly. It was a final assessment. A verdict.

Baedecker shook his head. "A celebrant," he said and took five steps and leaped.

Part Four

Lonerock

The funeral is on New Year's Eve, the clouds are low, and the short procession of vehicles has driven the four-and-a-half-hour ride from Salem, Oregon, through intermittent attempts at snow. Although it is still morning, the light seems tired and desultory, absorbed by trees and stones and farmhouse wood until only gray outlines of reality remain. It is very cold. The white exhaust from the idling hearse flows over the six men as they wrestle the casket from the vehicle and carry it across a brittle expanse of frozen grass.

Baedecker feels the cold of the bronze handle through his glove and wonders at how light the body of his friend seems. Carrying the massive casket is no effort at all with the other five men helping. Baedecker is reminded of a child's game where a group would levitate a supine volunteer, each person placing only a single finger under the tense and waiting body. Inevitably, the reclining child would rise several feet from the floor to a chorus of giggles. To Baedecker as a boy, the sensation of lifting someone that way had carried with it a slight flush of fear at the sense of gravity defied, of unbreakable laws being broken. But always, at the end, the squealing, wiggling child would be lowered, carefully or abruptly, the weight returned; gravity obeyed at last.

Baedecker counts twenty-eight people at graveside. He knows that there could have been many more. There had been talk of the vice president attending, but the offer carried the odor of an election year, and Diane had put a quick end to that. Baedecker looks to his left and sees the spire of the Lonerock Methodist Church in the valley two miles below. The wan light ebbs and flows with each passing layer of cloud, and Baedecker is fascinated with the sense of shifting substance in the distant spire. The church had been closed for years before this morning's funeral there, and when Baedecker had been packing kindling into the metal stove prior to the arrival of the other mourners, he had noticed the date on an old newspaper: October 21, 1971. Baedecker had paused a moment then and had tried to remember where he and Dave might have been on October 21 of that year. Less than three months before the flight. Houston or the Cape, most probably. Baedecker cannot remember.

The graveside services are brief and simple. Colonel Terrence Paul, an Air Force chaplain and old friend, makes a few remarks. Baedecker speaks for a moment, remembering his friend moving across the surface of the moon, buoyant, haloed in light. A telegram from Tom Gavin is read aloud. Others speak. Finally Diane talks softly about her husband's love of flying and of family. Her voice breaks once or twice, but she recovers and finishes.

In the silence that follows, Baedecker can almost hear the snowflakes settling on coats and grass and coffin. Suddenly there is a roar, which shakes the entire hillside, and the group looks up to see four T-38s in tight formation coming in low from the northwest, no more than five hundred feet high in order to stay under the overcast. As the formation shrieks overhead with a scream that echoes in bone and teeth and skull, the jet in the wingman's position suddenly veers out of formation and climbs almost vertically to be swallowed by the gray ceiling of clouds. The other three T-38s disappear to the southeast, the scream of their after-burners fading to a low moan and then to silence.

The sight of the missing man formation has, as it always does, moved Baedecker to tears. He blinks in the cold air. General Layton, another family friend, nods to the Air Force honor guard, and the American flag is removed from the coffin and ceremoniously folded. General Layton hands the folded flag to Diane. She accepts without tears.

Small groups and individuals murmur to the widow, and then people pause a moment and move slowly toward the idling automobiles beyond the fence.

Baedecker remains behind for a few minutes. The air is cold in his lungs. Across the valley he sees the brown hills mottled with patterns of gray snow. The county road cuts across the face of the bluff like a scar. Farther west, a hog-back ridge rises from the pine-forested hills, and Baedecker is reminded of a stegosaurus's scales. He glances toward the small shack at the far end of the cemetery and sees the yellow backhoe parked there in semiconcealment. Two men in heavy gray overalls and blue stocking caps are smoking and watching. *Waiting for me to leave*, thinks Baedecker. He looks down at the surface of the gray coffin poised above the hole dug out of the frozen earth and then he turns and walks to the cars.

Diane is waiting at the open door of her white Jeep Cherokee, and she beckons Baedecker over after the last of the other mourners have turned to their own cars. "Richard, would you ride down the hill with me?"

"Of course," says Baedecker. "Shall I drive?"

"No, I'll drive." They are the last car to leave. Baedecker glances at Diane as they turn down the narrow gravel road; she does not look back at the cemetery. Her bare hands are white and firm on the wheel. It begins to snow more heavily as they switch back down the rough lane and she clicks the windshield wipers on. The metronomic tick of the wiper blades and the purr of the heater are the only sounds for several minutes.

"Richard, do you think it went all right?" Diane unbuttons her coat and turns down the heater. Her dress is a very dark blue; she had not been able to find a black maternity dress in the three days prior to the funeral.

"Yes," says Baedecker.

Diane nods. "I think it did too."

They rumble over a cattleguard. Brake lights flare as the car ahead of them slows to avoid a large rock protruding from the rutted path. They pass through a rancher's field and turn right onto a gravel road that heads into the valley.

"Will you stay with us tonight in Salem?" asks Diane. "We're going to have some hot food here at the house and then head back."

"Of course," says Baedecker. "I told Bob Munsen that I'd meet him up at the site this afternoon, but I could be back by seven."

"Tucker will be there tonight," she says quickly, as if still in need of convincing him. "And Katie. It would be good to have the four of us together one last time."

"It doesn't have to be the last time, Di," says Baedecker.

She nods but does not speak. Baedecker looks at her face, sees the freckles visible against pale skin, and is reminded of a porcelain doll from Germany, which his mother had kept on her bureau. He had broken it one rainy day while roughhousing with Boots, their oversized springer spaniel. Although his father had carefully glued it back together, from that time on Baedecker had always been aware of the infinitesimal tracery of fracture lines on the white cheeks and forehead of the delicate figurine. Now Baedecker searches Diane's features as if seeking new fracture lines there.

Outside, the snow falls more heavily.

∞

Baedecker arrived in Salem in early October. He hobbled off the train, set his luggage down, and looked around. The small station was fifty yards away. No bigger than a large picnic pavilion, it looked as if it had been built in the early twenties and abandoned shortly thereafter. There were clumps of moss growing on the roof shingles.

"Richard!"

Baedecker looked past a family exchanging hugs and could make out the tall form of Dave Muldorff near the station. Baedecker waved, picked up his old military flight bag, and moved slowly in his direction.

"Damn, it's good to see you," said Dave. His hand was large, the handshake firm.

"Good to see you," said Baedecker. He realized with a sudden surge of emotion that he *was* happy to see his old crewmate. "How long has it been, Dave? Two years?"

"Almost three," said Dave. "That Air and Space Museum thing that Mike Collins hosted. What the hell did you do to your leg?"

Baedecker smiled ruefully and tapped at his right foot with the walking stick he was using as a cane. "Just a sprained ankle," he said. "Twisted it when I was up in the mountains with Tom Gavin."

Dave picked up Baedecker's flight bag and the two began the slow walk to the parking lot. "How is Tom?"

"Just fine," said Baedecker. "He and Deedee are doing very well."

"He's in the salvation business these days, isn't he?"

Baedecker glanced at his ex-crewmate. There had never been any love lost between Gavin and Muldorff. He was curious about Dave's feelings now, almost seventeen years after the mission.

"He runs an evangelical group called Apogee," said Baedecker. "It's pretty successful."

"Good," said Dave and his voice sounded sincere. They had reached a new, white Jeep Cherokee and Dave tossed Baedecker's flight bag and garment bag in the back. "Glad to hear that Tom's doing okay."

The Jeep smelled of new upholstery heated by the sun. Baedecker rolled the window down. The early October day was warm and cloudless. Brittle leaves rustled on a large oak tree just beyond the parking lot. The sky was a heart-stoppingly perfect shade of blue. "I thought it was always raining out here in Oregon," said Baedecker.

"Usually is." Dave pulled the Jeep out into traffic. "Three or four days a year the sun comes out and gives us a chance to scrape the fungus out from between our toes. The cops, TV stations, and local Air Force base hate days like this."

"Why's that?" asked Baedecker.

"Every time the sun comes out, they get three or four hundred calls reporting a big, orange UFO in the sky," said Dave.

"Uh-huh."

"I'm not shitting you. All over the state vampires are scurrying for their coffins. This is the one state in the Union where they can go about their business in daytime without encountering any sunlight. These few sunny days are a big shock to our Nosferatu population."

Baedecker lay his head back against the seat and closed his eyes. It was going to be a long visit.

"Hey, Richard, can you tell that I've recently had oral sex with a chicken?"

Baedecker opened one eye. His old crewmate still resembled a leaner, craggier version of James Garner. There were more lines on the face now, and the cheekbones were sharper against the skin, but the wavy black hair showed no hint of gray. "No," said Baedecker.

"Good," said Dave in a relieved tone. Suddenly he coughed twice into his fist. Torn-up bits of yellow Kleenex fluttered into the air like feathers.

Baedecker closed his eye.

"Real good to have you here, Richard," said Dave Muldorff.

Baedecker smiled without opening his eyes. "Real good to be here, Dave."

∾

Baedecker had sold his car in Denver and taken the train west with Maggie Brown. He did not know whether the decision was wise—he suspected that it was not—but for once he attempted simply to carry out an action without analysis.

The Amtrak California Zephyr left Denver at nine A.M. and he and Maggie breakfasted in the dining car while the long train burrowed under the continental divide through the first of fifty-five tunnels awaiting them in Colorado. Baedecker looked at the paper plates, paper napkins, and paper tablecloth. "The last time I traveled by train in America, there was real linen on the table and the food wasn't microwaved," he said to Maggie.

Maggie smiled. "When was that, Richard, during World War II?" She meant it as a joke—a not-so-subtle jibe at his constant mentioning of their age difference—but Baedecker blinked in shock as he realized that it *had* been during the war. His mother had taken his sister Anne and him from Peoria to Chicago to visit relatives over the holidays. Baedecker remembered the train seats that faced backward, the hushed tone of the porters and waiters in the dining car, and the strange thrill that passed through him as he peered out the window at streetlights and the orange-lit windows of homes in the night. Chicago had been constellations of lights and rows of apartment windows flashing by as the train moved along elevated tracks through the southside. Despite the fact that he had been born in Chicago, the view had given the ten-year-old Baedecker a sense of displacement, a not unpleasant feeling of having lost the center of things. Twenty-eight years after the trip to Chicago, he was to feel the same sense of uncenteredness as his *Apollo* spacecraft passed out of radio contact with the earth as the rough limb of the moon filled his view. Baedecker remembered leaning against the small window of the command module and wiping away condensation with his palm, much as he had four and a half decades earlier as the train carrying his mother, his sister, and him pulled into Union Station.

"You folks done?" The Amtrak waiter's voice bordered on belligerence.

"All done," said Maggie and swallowed the last of her coffee.

"Good," said the waiter. He flipped the red paper tablecloth up from opposite corners, enclosed the paper plates, plastic utensils, and Styrofoam cups in it, and tossed the entire mass into a nearby receptacle.

"Progress," said Baedecker as they moved back through the shifting aisle.

"What's that?" asked Maggie.

"Nothing," said Baedecker.

∾

Late that night, while Maggie slept against his shoulder, Baedecker watched out the window as they changed engines in a remote corner of the switching yard in Salt Lake City. Under an abandoned overpass, bounded about by tall weeds made brittle by the autumn cold, hobos sat by a fire. *Are they still called hobos?* wondered Baedecker.

In the morning both he and Maggie awoke just before dawn as the first false light touched the pink rocks of the desert canyon through which the train was hurtling.

Baedecker knew instantly upon awakening that the trip would not go well, that whatever he and Maggie had shared in India and rediscovered in the Colorado mountains would not survive the reality of the next few days.

Neither of them spoke while the sun rose. The train rushed on westward, the rocks and mesas flying by, the morning wrapped in a temporary and fragile hush.

∞

Dave and Diane Muldorff lived in a well-to-do suburb on the south side of Salem. Their patio looked down on a wooded stream and Baedecker listened to water running over unseen rocks as he ate his steak and baked potato.

"Tomorrow we'll take you over to Lonerock," said Dave.

"Sounds good," said Baedecker. "I look forward to seeing it after hearing about it all these years."

"*Dave* will take you over," said Diane. "I have a reception at the Children's Home tomorrow night and a fundraiser on Sunday. I'll see you on Monday."

Baedecker nodded and looked at Diane Muldorff. She was thirty-four, fourteen years younger than her husband. With her tousled mane of dark hair, startling blue eyes, snub nose, and freckles, she reminded Baedecker of all the girls-next-door he had never known. Yet there was a solid streak of adult in Diane, a quiet but firm maturity, which was now emphasized as she entered her sixth month of pregnancy. This evening she wore soft jeans and a faded blue Oxford shirt with the tails out. "You look good, Di," Baedecker said on impulse. "Pregnancy agrees with you."

"Thank you, Richard. You look good, too. You've lost some weight since that party in Washington."

Baedecker laughed. He had been at his heaviest then, thirty-six pounds over his flying weight. He was still twenty-one pounds over that weight.

"Are you still jogging?" asked Dave. Muldorff had been the only one of the second generation of astronauts who did not run regularly. It had been the point of some contention. Now, ten years after leaving the program, he looked thinner than he had then. Baedecker wondered if Dave's illness was the cause.

"I run a little," said Baedecker. "Just started up a few months ago after I got back from India."

Diane carried several icy bottles of beer to the table and sat down. The last of the evening light touched her cheeks. "How *was* India?" she asked.

"Interesting," said Baedecker. "Too much to take in in so short a time."

"And you saw Scott there?" asked Dave.

"Yes," said Baedecker. "Briefly."

"I miss seeing Scott," said Dave. "Remember our fishing trips off Galveston in the early seventies?"

Baedecker nodded. He remembered the endless afternoons in rich light and the slow, warm evenings. He and his son would both return home with sunburns. "The redheads return!" Joan would cry out in mock dismay. "Get out the ointment!"

"Did you know that what's-his-name, Scott's holy man, is coming to stay full-time in that ashram of his not far from Lonerock?" asked Diane.

Baedecker blinked at her. "Full-time? No, I didn't."

"What was the ashram like in Poona where Scott was staying?" asked Dave.

"I don't really know," said Baedecker. He thought of the shop outside the main building where one could buy T-shirts with images of the Master's bearded face on them. "I was just in Poona two days and didn't see much of the ashram."

"Will Scott be coming back to the States when the group moves over here?" asked Diane.

Baedecker tasted his beer. "I don't know," he said. "Maybe he's here now. I'm afraid I'm out of touch."

"Hey," said Dave. "Want to come inside to the billy yard room for a fast game?"

"Billy yard room?" said Baedecker.

"What's the matter, Richard," said Dave, "didn't you ever watch *The Beverly Hillbillies* back during the golden age of the tube?"

"No," said Baedecker.

Dave rolled his eyes at Diane. "That's the problem with this lad, Di. He's culturally deprived."

Diane nodded. "I'm sure you'll fix that, David."

Muldorff poured more beer and carried both mugs with him to the door of the patio. "Luckily for him, I've got twenty episodes of *The Beverly Hillbillies* on tape. We'll start watching as soon as I thrash him in a fast but expensive game of pool. Come wiz me, mon sewer Baedecker."

"Oui," said Baedecker. He picked up some of the dishes and carried them toward the kitchen. "Einen Augenblik, por favor, mon ami."

∾

Baedecker parks his rented car and walks the two hundred yards to the crash site. He has seen many such sites before; he expects this one to hold no surprises. He is wrong.

As he reaches the top of the ridge, the icy wind strikes him and at the same instant he sees Mt. St. Helens clearly. The volcano looms over the valley and ridgeline like a great, shattered stump of ice. A narrow plume of smoke or cloud hangs above it. For the first time, Baedecker realizes that he is walking on ash. Under the thin layer of snow the soil is more gray than brown. The confusion of footprints on the hillside reminds him of the trampled area around the lunar module when he and Dave returned from their last EVA at the end of the second day.

The crash site, the volcano, and the ash make Baedecker think of the inevitable triumph of catastrophe and entropy over order. Long strands of yellow-and-orange plastic tape hang from rocks and bushes to mark locations that investigators had found interesting. To Baedecker's surprise, the wreckage of the aircraft has not yet been moved. He notices the two long, scorched areas, about thirty meters apart, where the T-38 had initially struck the hill and then bounced even while disintegrating. Most of the wreckage is concentrated where a low band of rocks rises from the hillside like new molars. Snow and ash had been flung far out in rays that remind Baedecker of the secondary impact craters near their lunar landing site in the Marius Hills.

Only vague and twisted remnants of the aircraft remain. The tail section is almost intact; five feet of clean metal from which Baedecker reads the Air National Guard serial number. He recognizes a long, blackened mass as one of the twin General Electric turbojet engines. Pieces of melted plastic and shards of twisted metal are everywhere. Tangles of white, insulated wire are strewn randomly around the shattered fuselage like the discarded entrails of some slaughtered beast. Baedecker sees a section of fire-blackened Plexiglas canopy still attached to a fragment of fuselage. Except for the colored tape and footsteps concentrated there, there is no sign that a man's body had been fused into these broken pieces of baked alloy.

Baedecker takes two steps toward the canopy, steps on something, looks down, and recoils in horror. "Jesus." He raises a fist in reflex even as he realizes that the bit of bone and roasted flesh and singed hair under the concealing bush must be part of a carcass of a small animal unlucky enough to have been caught in the impact or ensuing fire. He crouches to look more closely. The animal had been the size of a large rabbit, but the unsinged remnants of fur were strangely dark. He reaches for a stick to prod the tiny corpse.

"Hey, no one's allowed in this area!" A Washington state trooper is wheezing his way up the hill.

"It's all right," Baedecker says and shows his pass from McChord Air Force Base. "I'm here to meet the investigators."

The trooper nods and stops a few feet from Baedecker. He hooks his thumbs in his belt as he struggles to catch his breath. "Hell of a mess, isn't it?"

Baedecker raises his face to the clouds just as it begins to snow again. Mt. St. Helens is gone, hidden by clouds. The air smells of burnt rubber even though Baedecker knows that except for the tires, there had been very little rubber aboard the aircraft.

"You with the investigation team?" asks the trooper.

"No," says Baedecker. "I knew the pilot."

"Oh." The state trooper shuffles his feet and looks back down the hill toward the road.

"I'm surprised they haven't transferred the wreckage," Baedecker says. "Usually they try to get it into a hangar as soon as possible."

"Problem with transport," says the trooper. "That's where Colonel Fields and the government guys are this afternoon, trying to get the truck situation straightened out down at Camp Withycombe in Portland. And there's the jurisdiction problem, too. Even the Forest Service is involved."

Baedecker nods. He crouches to look at the dead animal again but is distracted by a bit of orange fabric fluttering from a nearby branch. *Part of a backpack*, he thinks. *Or a flight suit.*

"I was one of the first ones here after the crash," says the state trooper. "Jamie and me got the call just as we were heading out of Yale going west. Only guy here before us was that geologist who's got his cabin over toward Goat Mountain."

Baedecker straightens up. "Was there much fire?"

"Not by the time we got here. The rain must've put it out. There wasn't a hell of a lot to burn up here. Except the plane, of course."

"It was raining hard before the crash?"

"Shit, yes. We couldn't see fifty feet coming up the road. Real strong winds, too. Like I always pictured a hurricane was like. You ever seen a hurricane?"

"No," says Baedecker and then remembers the hurricane in the Pacific that he and Dave and Tom Gavin had looked down on from two hundred miles up just before the translunar injection burn. "So it was already dark and raining hard?" he asks.

"Yeah." The trooper's tone suggests that he is losing interest. "Tell me something. The Air Force guy—Colonel Fields—he seems to think that your friend flew over the park here because he knew the plane was going down."

Baedecker looks at the state trooper.

The man clears his throat and spits. The snow has stopped and the soil still visible looks even grayer to Baedecker in the waning afternoon light. "So if he knew the thing was having problems," says the trooper, "how come he just didn't punch out of it once he got the plane over the boonies here? Why'd he ride it down into the mountain?"

Baedecker turns his head. On the highway below, several military vehicles, two flatbed trucks, and a small crane have pulled to a stop near Baedecker's rented Toyota. An enclosed jeep with someone in Air Force blue at the wheel begins its climb up the hill. Baedecker walks away from the trooper and moves downhill to meet them.

"I don't know," he says to himself, the words spoken so softly that they are lost in the rising wind and sound of the approaching vehicle.

∾

"How long to Lonerock?" asked Baedecker. They were headed north on Twelfth Street in Salem. It was already three P.M.

"About a five-hour drive," said Dave. "You have to take I-5 north to Portland and then follow the Gorge up past the Dalles. Then it's another hour and a half past Wasco and Condon."

"Then we'll get there after dark," said Baedecker.

"Nope."

Baedecker refolded the road map he had been wrestling with and raised an eyebrow.

"I know a shortcut," said Dave.

"Through the Cascades?"

"You might say that."

They pulled off Turner Road onto a lane leading into a small airport. Several executive jets were parked near two large hangars. Across a wide strip of taxi apron sat a Chinook, a Cessna A-37 Dragonfly with Air National Guard markings, and an aging C-130. Dave parked the Cherokee near the military hangar, pulled their luggage out of the back, and tossed Baedecker a quilted goosedown jacket. "Suit up, Richard. It'll be cold where we're going."

A sergeant and two men in mechanic overalls emerged from the hangar as Dave approached. "Howdy, Colonel Muldorff. All set and prechecked," said the sergeant.

"Thanks, Chico. Meet Colonel Dick Baedecker."

Baedecker shook hands, and then they were moving across the tarmac to where the mechanics were sliding back the side door of a helicopter parked behind the larger Chinook. "I'll be damned," said Baedecker. "A Huey."

"A Bell HU-1 Iroquois to you, tenderfoot," said Dave. "Thanks, Chico, we'll take it from here. Nate's got my flight plan filed."

"Have a good trip, Colonel," said the sergeant. "Nice meetin' ya, Colonel Baedecker."

As Baedecker followed Dave around the ship, he felt a slight sinking sensation in the region of his solar plexus. He had ridden in Hueys scores of times—even clocked thirty-five hours or more flying them during the early days of his

NASA training—and he had hated every minute of it. Baedecker knew that Dave loved the treacherous machines; much of Muldorff's experimental flying had been in helicopters. In 1965, Dave had been on loan to Hughes Aircraft to sort out problems in their prototype TH-55A trainer. The new helicopter had a tendency to drop nose first into the earth without warning. The research led to comparison field studies on the flight characteristics of the older Bell HU-1, already in service in Vietnam. Dave was sent to Vietnam for six weeks of observation flying with the army pilots who were reported to be doing unusual things with their machines there. Four and a half months later he was recalled after it was discovered that he had been flying combat missions with a medevac squadron on a daily basis.

Dave had used his experience to solve Hughes's problem with the TH-55As, but he had been passed over for promotion as a result of his unauthorized flying with the 1st Cav. He also received notes from both the Air Force and Army informing him that under no circumstances could he put in for retroactive combat flight pay. Dave had laughed. He had been notified two weeks before leaving Vietnam that he had been accepted into NASA's training program for post-*Gemini* astronauts.

"Not bad," said Baedecker as they finished the external checks and moved into the cockpit. "Got your own slick for weekend jaunts. One of the perks of being a congressman, Dave?"

Muldorff laughed and tossed Baedecker a clipboard with the cockpit checklist. "Sure," he said. "Goldwater used to get his free rides in F-18s. I've got my Huey. Of course, it helps that I'm still on active reserve out here." He handed Baedecker a baseball cap with the insignia AIR FORCE 1½ sewn on it. Baedecker tugged it on and set the radio headset in place. "Also, Richard," continued Dave, "it might reassure you to know—as a concerned taxpayer—that this particular pile of rusted bolts did its duty in 'Nam, ferried around weekend warriors out here for ten years, and is now officially on the spare-parts list. Chico and the boys keep it around in case anybody has to run up to Portland to buy cigarettes or something."

"Yeah," said Baedecker. "Great." He strapped himself into the left seat as Dave waggled the cyclic control stick and reached down with his left hand to squeeze the starter trigger on the collective pitch control lever. It had been the constant interplay of controls—cyclic, collective, rudder pedals, and throttle thrust grip—that had given Baedecker fits when he had been forced to fly the perverse machines twenty years earlier. Compared to a military helicopter, the *Apollo* lunar module had been a simple machine to master.

The gas-turbine engine roared, the high-speed starter motor whined, and the two forty-eight-foot rotor blades began to turn. "Yowzuh!" called Dave over the intercom. Various dials registered their appropriate readings while the *whop-whop-whop* of the main rotors reached a point of almost physical pressure. Dave pulled up on the collective control and three tons of well-aged machinery lifted off its skids to hover five feet above the tarmac.

"Ready to see my shortcut?" Dave's voice was flat and metallic over the intercom.

"Show me," said Baedecker.

Dave grinned, spoke quickly into his mike, and confidently pitched the ship forward as they began their climb into the east.

∞

San Francisco was rainy and cold for the two days Baedecker and Maggie Brown were there. At Maggie's suggestion, they stayed in a renovated old hotel near Union Square. The halls were dimly lit and smelled of paint, the showers were jerry-rigged onto massive bathtubs with claw feet, and everywhere hung the exposed pipes of the building's sprinkler system. Baedecker and Maggie took turns show-ering to remove the grime of their forty-eight-hour train trip, lay down to take a nap, made love instead, showered again, and went out into the evening.

"I've never been here before," said Maggie with a wide grin. "It's marvelous!" The streets were busy with rushing theater-goers and couples—mostly male—walking hand in hand under neon signs promising topless and bottomless delights. The wind smelled of the sea and exhaust fumes. The cable-car system was down for repairs, and all of the cabs in sight were either filled or beyond hailing distance. Baedecker and Maggie took a bus to Fisherman's Wharf where they walked without speaking until a cold drizzle and Baedecker's injured ankle forced them into a restaurant.

"The prices are high," said Maggie when the main course had been served, "but the scallops are delicious."

"Yes," said Baedecker.

"All right, Richard," said Maggie and touched his hand. "What's wrong?"

Baedecker shook his head. "Nothing."

Maggie waited.

"I was just wondering how you were going to make up this week's worth of classes," he said and poured more wine for both of them.

"Not true," said Maggie. In the candlelight her green eyes seemed almost turquoise. Her cheeks were sunburned even under their tan. "Tell me."

Baedecker looked at her a long moment. "I've been thinking about when Tom Gavin's son pulled that stupid stunt in the mountains," he said.

Maggie smiled. "You mean dancing naked on a rock during a lightning storm? With a tent pole in one hand? *That* stupid stunt?"

Baedecker nodded. "He could have been killed."

"This is true," agreed Maggie. "Especially since he seemed intent upon taking the names of all the gods in vain until he pissed off the wrong one." She seemed to notice Baedecker's intensity and her voice changed. "Hey, it turned out all right. Why are you letting it bother you now?"

"It's not what he did that bothers me," said Baedecker. "It's what I did while he was up on that boulder."

"You didn't do anything," said Maggie.

"Exactly," said Baedecker and finished his glass of wine. He poured more. "I did nothing."

"Tommy's father got him down before either one of us could react," said Maggie.

Baedecker nodded. At a nearby table several women laughed loudly at an unheard joke.

"Oh, I see," said Maggie. "We're talking about Scott again."

Baedecker wiped his hands on a red linen napkin. "I'm not sure," he said. "But at least Tom Gavin saw his son doing something stupid and saved him from possible disaster."

"Yes," said Maggie, "and little Tommy was . . . what? . . . seventeen, and Scott will be twenty-three in March."

"Yes, but . . ."

"And little Tommy was ten feet away," said Maggie. "Scott is in Poona. India."

"I know that . . ."

"Besides, who are you to say what Scott's doing there is disaster? You've had your chance, Richard. Scott's a big boy now, and if he wants to spend a few years chanting mantras and giving away his lunch money to some bearded horse's ass with a Jehovah Complex, well, you've had *your* chance to help him, so what do you say you just get on with your screwed-up life, Richard E. Baedecker." Maggie took a long drink of wine. "Oh, shit, sometimes, Richard, you give me such a . . ." She stopped and began to hiccup violently.

Baedecker gave her his ice water and waited. She sat silently for a second, opened her mouth to speak, and hiccuped again. Both of them laughed. The group of ladies at a nearby table looked over at them disapprovingly.

The next day in Golden Gate Park as they peered out from under their newly purchased umbrella at orange metal columns appearing and disappearing in the low clouds, Maggie said, "You're going to have to work out this thing about Scott before we get on with our own feelings, aren't you, Richard?"

"I'm not sure," said Baedecker. "Let's just let it rest for a few days, all right? We'll talk about it later in the week."

Maggie brushed a raindrop from her nose. "Richard," she said, "I love you." It was the first time she had said that.

In the morning, when Baedecker awoke to bright sunlight sifting through the hotel curtains and to the sound of traffic and pedestrian bustle from the street below, Maggie was gone.

∾

They flew east and then north and then east again, gaining altitude even as the forested land rose under them. When the altimeter read 8,500 feet, Baedecker said, "Don't Air National Guard regs call for oxygen somewhere around here?"

"Yup," said Dave. "In case of sudden loss of cabin pressure, oxygen masks will fall from the overhead compartments and hit you on the head. Please place them over your snout and breathe normally. If you are traveling with a child or infant on your lap, quickly decide which of you has the right to breathe."

"Thanks," said Baedecker. "Mt. Hood?" They had been approaching the volcanic peak for some time. Now it loomed tall to the left of their flight path, the snow-crested summit still two thousand feet higher than their own altitude. The shadow of the Huey rippled across the carpet of trees below and ahead of them.

"Uh-huh," said Dave, "and that's Timberline Lodge where they did the exterior shots for *The Shining*."

"Mmmm," said Baedecker.

"Did you see the movie?" asked Dave over the intercom.

"No."

"Read the book?"

"No."

"Ever read any Stephen King?"

"No."

"Jesus," said Dave, "for a literate man, Richard, you're incredibly poorly versed in the classics. You *do* remember Stanley Kubrick, don't you?"

"How could I forget him?" said Baedecker. "You dragged me to see *2001: A Space Odyssey* five times the year it was at the Cinerama theater in Houston." It was not an exaggeration. Muldorff had been obsessed with the movie and had insisted on his crewmates repeatedly seeing it with him. Before their flight, Dave had talked enthusiastically about smuggling an inflatable black monolith along only to "discover it" buried under the lunar surface during one of their EVAs. A shortage of inflatable black monoliths had frustrated that plan so Dave had contented himself with having Mission Control awaken them at the end of each sleep period by playing the opening chords of *Also Sprach Zarathustra*. Baedecker had thought it mildly amusing the first few times.

"Kubrick's masterpiece," said Dave and banked the Huey to the right. They flew low over a pass where tents and camper-trailers huddled around a small mountain lake, late afternoon sunlight dappling the water, and then the land was falling away from them, the pine forest looked less green to Baedecker, and low brown hills became visible to the south and east. They flew on at a steady five thousand feet as the land changed to irrigated farmland and then to high desert. Dave spoke softly into his microphone to traffic control, joked once with someone at a private airport south of Maupin, and then switched back to the intercom. "See that river?"

"Yeah."

"That's the John Day. Scott's guru bought up a little town to the southwest of there. The same one Rajneesh put in the papers a few years ago."

Baedecker flipped open a navigation map and nodded. He unzipped his goosedown coat, poured coffee from a thermos, and handed Dave his cup.

"Thanks. Want to take the stick for a while?"

"Not especially," said Baedecker.

Dave laughed. "You don't like helicopters, do you, Richard?"

"Not especially."

"I don't know why not," said Dave. "You've flown about everything with wings including VTOLs and STOLs and that damn Navy pogo plane that killed more men than it was worth. What do you have against helicopters?"

"Do you mean other than the fact that they're treacherous, untrustworthy pieces of shit just waiting to slam you into the ground?" said Baedecker. "You mean other than that?"

"Yeah," said Dave and laughed again. "Other than that." They dropped to three thousand feet and then to two. Ahead of them, their sides golden and chocolate in the horizontal light, a small herd of cattle moved sluggishly across a wide expanse of dry grassland.

"Hey," said Dave, "remember that press conference we went to before *Apollo 11* to watch Neil, Buzz, and Mike show their stuff?"

"Which one?"

"The one right before the launch."

"Vaguely," said Baedecker.

"Well, Armstrong said something during it that really pissed me off."

"What was that?" asked Baedecker.

"That reporter—what's-his-name, he's dead now—Frank McGee asked Armstrong a question about dreams and Neil said he'd had a recurring dream since he was a boy."

"So?"

"It was the dream where Neil could hover off the ground if he held his breath long enough. Remember that?"

"No."

"Well, I do. Neil said that he'd first had the dream when he was a little kid. He'd hold his breath and then he'd begin to hover, not fly, just hover."

Baedecker finished his coffee and set the Styrofoam cup into a trash bag behind his seat. "Why did that piss you off?" he asked.

Dave looked over at him. His eyes were unreadable behind his sunglasses. "Because it was *my* dream," he said.

The Huey nosed over and dropped until they were flying only three hundred feet above the rough terrain, well below FAA minimum altitude requirements. Sagebrush and piñon pines flicked by, reasserting a sense of speed to their passage. Baedecker looked down past his feet, through the chin bubble, and watched a lone house flash by. It had been brown and weathered, its tin roof rusted, its barn collapsed, its only access suggested by two drifted ruts stretching off to the horizon. There had been a new, white satellite dish next to the shack.

Baedecker clicked on the intercom. There was no intercom floor switch for the left seat, so he had to reach out and touch the switch on the cyclic each time he wanted to talk. "Tom Gavin told me that you were pretty sick last spring," he said.

Dave glanced to his left and then looked back at the ground rushing past them at one hundred knots. He nodded. "Yeah, I was having some problems. I thought I had the flu—just running a fever with swollen glands in my neck. Instead, my doctor in Washington said I had Hodgkin's disease. I didn't even know what it was until then."

"Serious?"

"They grade the thing on a four-point scale," said Dave. "Level One is take some aspirin and mail in the forty dollars. Level Four is G.Y.S.A.K.Y.A.G."

Baedecker did not have to ask about the abbreviation. During the hundreds of hours they had shared in cramped simulators, there had been too many times when he had heard Dave's suggested response to some newly inserted emergency as G.Y.S.A.K.Y.A.G.—grab your socks and kiss your ass good-bye.

"I was a Level Three," said Dave. "Caught fairly early. They got me feeling better with medication and a couple of chemotherapy sessions. Took out my spleen for good measure. Everything looks real good now. If they get it on the first pass, they generally get it for good. I passed my flight physical three weeks ago." He grinned and pointed to a town just visible to the north. "That's Condon. Next stop, Lonerock. Home of America's future Western White House."

They crossed a gravel county road and Dave banked sharply to follow it, dropping to fifty feet. There was no traffic. Short, sagging telephone poles ran along the left side of the road, looking as if they had stood there forever. There were no trees; the barbed wire fences had some sort of metal boilers or discarded water heaters as fence posts.

The Huey passed over the lip of a canyon. One second they were fifty feet above a gravel road, and the next instant they were eight hundred feet above a hidden valley where a stream ran through cottonwood groves, and fields lay pregnant with winter wheat and grass. There was a ghost town in the center of the valley. Here and there a tin roof poked above bare branches or fall foliage and at one place a church steeple was visible. Baedecker noticed a large old school looking west from high ground above the town. It was only five

P.M., but it was obvious that the valley had been in shadow for some time.

Dave kicked the Huey over in a diving turn that had the rotor blades almost perpendicular to the ground for several seconds. They flew low over a main street that appeared to consist of five abandoned buildings and a rusted gas pump. They banked left and passed over a white church, its spire dwarfed by a jagged tooth of a boulder behind and beyond the churchyard.

Baedecker's intercom clicked. "Welcome to Lonerock," said Dave.

∞

Most of the friends and mourners are gone by the time Baedecker returns to Dave and Diane's house in Salem. The snow he had seen near Mt. St. Helens now falls as a light drizzle.

Tucker Wilson greets Baedecker at the door. Before that morning, he had not seen Tucker since the day of the *Challenger* disaster two years earlier. An Air Force pilot and a backup member of the *Apollo* team, Tucker had finally commanded a Skylab mission a year before Baedecker had left NASA. Tucker is a short man with a wrestler's build, rubicund face, and only a trace of sandy hair left above the ears. Unlike so many test pilots who tended to speak with southern or neutral accents, Tucker's speech was accented with the flat vowels of New England. "Di's upstairs with Katie and her sister," Tucker says. "Come on in Dave's den for a drink."

Baedecker follows him. The book-lined room with its leather chairs and old rolltop desk is a study rather than a den. Baedecker sinks into a chair and looks around while Tucker pours the Scotch. The shelves hold an eclectic mix of expensive collectors' editions, popular hardbacks, paperbacks, and stacks of journals and papers. On a stretch of clear wall near the window are a dozen or so photographs: Baedecker recognizes himself in one, smiling next to Tom Gavin as Richard Nixon stiffly extends his hand to a grinning Dave.

"Water or ice?" asks Tucker.

"No," says Baedecker. "Neat, please."

Tucker hands Baedecker his glass and sits in the antique swivel chair at the desk. He seems uncomfortable there, picks up a typewritten sheet on the desk, puts it down, and takes a long drink.

"Any problems with the flight this morning?" asks Baedecker. Tucker had flown in the missing man formation.

"Uh-uh," says Tucker. "But there might've been if that overcast had got any lower. We were frying chickens in the barnyard as it was."

Baedecker nods and tastes his Scotch. "Aren't you in line for a ride after the shuttle program resumes?" he asks Tucker.

"Yep. Next November if things get back on track the way they're supposed to. We're carrying a DOD payload so we'll get to skip all that conquering heroes preflight press conference crap."

Baedecker nods. The Scotch is The Glenlivet, unblended, Dave's favorite. "What do you think, Tucker," he says, "is the thing safe to fly?"

The shorter pilot shrugs. "Two and a half years," he says. "More time to fix things than the hiatus after Gus and Chaffee and White died in *Apollo 1*. Of course, they gave the SRB fix to Morton Thiokol and they're the ones who certified the O-rings safe in the first place."

Baedecker does not smile. He had seen the strange, incestuous dance between contractors and government agencies and, like most pilots, was not amused. "I hear they'll have the new escape system in place for the first flight."

Now Tucker does laugh. "Yeah, have you seen it, Dick? They've got a long pole stowed in the lower bay, and while the command pilot holds the ship straight and level and subsonic, the crew hitches up and slides out like trout on a line."

"Wouldn't have helped *Challenger*," says Baedecker.

"It reminds me of the AIDS joke about the heroin junkie who isn't afraid of catching anything when he uses dirty needles because he's wearing a condom," says Tucker. He drinks the last of his Scotch and pours more. "Well, hell," he says, "there are more than seven hundred Criticality One items in the shuttle stack, and my guess is that the goddamn O-rings are the only ones we *don't* have to worry about."

Baedecker knew that a Criticality One item was a system or component, which had no reliable backup; if that item failed, so did the mission. "You won't be landing at the Cape anymore?" says Baedecker.

Tucker shakes his head. On his first shuttle mission, Wilson had landed *Columbia* on the long strip at Cape Canaveral only to have a tire blow and two brakes wear to the rim. "They know now that it's too damn risky," he says. "We'll be ferrying from Edwards or White Sands for the foreseeable future." He takes a long drink. "But what the hell," he says and grins, "no guts, no glory."

"What's the thing like to fly?" asks Baedecker. For the first time in days, he is able to think about something other than Dave.

Tucker leans forward, animated now, his hands making open-fingered gestures in the air. "It's damned incredible, Dick," he says. "Coming down is like trying to deadstick in a DC-9 at Mach 5. You have to argue with the damn computers to make them let you fly it, but, by God, when you're flying it you're really *flying*. Have you been in the updated simulator?"

"Had a tour," says Baedecker. "Didn't take time to sit in the left seat."

"You've got to try it," Tucker says. "Come down to the Cape next fall and I'll clear some time for you."

"Sounds good," says Baedecker. He finishes his drink and turns the glass in his hands, allowing it to catch the lamplight. "Did you see Dave much down at the Cape?"

Tucker shakes his head. "He hated the idea of all those congressmen and senators getting free rides while us ex-fighter pukes waited years for another go. He was on all the right committees and worked hard for the program, but he disagreed with the Teacher in Space and Journalist in Space crap. He said the shuttle was no place for people who put their pants on one leg at a time."

Baedecker chuckles. The allusion was to one of the first incidents to get Dave in trouble with NASA. During Muldorff's first flight in an *Apollo* module, an earth-orbital engineering flight, Dave had held a live TV broadcast for the folks at home. Tucker Wilson had been there with him when Dave said something to the effect, "Well, folks, for years we astronaut-types've been telling you that we're just regular folks. Not heroes, but just like everybody else. Guys who put their pants on one leg at a time like everyone else. Well, today I'm here to show you otherwise." And with that Muldorff had pirouetted in zero-g, wearing only his in-flight "long johns" and Snoopy cap, and with a single, graceful move, had tugged on his flight coveralls . . . two legs at a time.

Baedecker crosses to a bookshelf and pulls out a volume of Yeats. Half a dozen slips of paper serve as markers.

"You learn anything this afternoon?" asks Tucker.

Baedecker shakes his head and slides the book back. "I talked to Munsen and Fields. They're just getting around to transferring the last of the wreckage up to McChord. Bob's going to arrange it so I can hear the tape tomorrow. The Crash Board has some preliminary ideas already but they're taking tomorrow off."

"I heard the tape yesterday," says Tucker. "Not much to go on there. Dave reported the hydraulics problem about fifteen minutes out of Portland. They were using the civil airport because Munsen had come down for that conference . . ."

"Yeah," says Baedecker. "Then he decided to stay another day."

"Right," says Tucker. "Dave went east alone, reported the hydraulics glitch about fifteen minutes out, and made his turn about a minute later. Then the goddamned starboard engine overheated and shut down. That was about eight minutes out, I think, on the way back. Portland International was closer so they went with that. There was some ice buildup, but that wouldn't have been serious if he could have climbed out of it. Dave didn't do too much talking, and the controller sounds like a young asshole. Dave reported seeing lights just before he went down."

Baedecker swallows the last of his Scotch and sets the glass on the liquor cart. "Did he know he was going in?"

Tucker frowns again. "Hard to say. He wasn't saying much, asking for altitude confirmation mostly. The Portland Center controller reminded him that the ridges ran up to five thousand feet around there. Dave acknowledged and said that he was coming out of cloud at sixty-two hundred and could see some lights. Then nothing until they lost him on radar a few seconds later."

"What was his voice like?"

"Gagarin all the way," says Tucker.

Baedecker nods. Yuri Gagarin, the first man to orbit the earth, had died in a crash of a MiG during a routine training flight in March of 1968. Word had spread through the test-flying community of the extraordinary calmness of Gagarin's voice on tape as he flew the flamed-out MiG into an empty lot between homes in a crowded suburb. It was only after Baedecker had gone to the Soviet Union as part of an administrative team a year before the *Apollo-Soyuz* Test

Project that he heard from a Soviet pilot that Gagarin had
gone down in a remote forest area and the cause of the crash
had been listed as "pilot error." There were rumors of alco-
hol. There had been no voice tape. Still, among test pilots
of Baedecker's and Tucker's generation, "Gagarin all the way"
remained the ultimate compliment of coolness in an emergency.

"I just don't get it," says Tucker and there is anger in
his voice. "The T-38's the safest goddamn plane in the
goddamn Air Force."

Baedecker says nothing.

"It averages two goddamn accidents per one hundred
thousand hours in the air," says Tucker. "Name me one other
supersonic aircraft with that sort of record, Dick."

Baedecker crosses to the window and looks out. It is
still raining.

"And it doesn't matter a goddamn bit, does it?" says
Tucker. He pours himself a third drink. "It never does, does
it?"

"No," says Baedecker. "It doesn't."

There is a knock and Katie Wilson enters. Tucker's wife,
frizzy-blond and sharp-featured, at first might be mistaken
for an aging cocktail waitress with little on her mind, but
then one would notice the sharp intelligence and alert sen-
sitivity behind the heavy makeup and southern drawl. "Richard," she says, "I'm glad you're back."

"Sorry I'm so late," he says.

"Diane wants to talk to you," says Katie. "I made her
get ready for bed because I knew she'd be up all night playing the perfect hostess otherwise. She's been awake for forty-
eight hours straight, and her due date is in another week,
for heaven's sake."

"I won't keep her up long, Katie," says Baedecker and
goes up the stairs.

Diane Muldorff is in her robe, sitting in a blue chaise
longue, reading a magazine. She looks very pregnant to

Baedecker. She beckons him in.

"I'm glad you're here, Richard."

"Sorry I'm so late, Di," he says. "I rode up to McChord with Bill Munsen and Stephen Fields."

Diane nods and sets the magazine down. "Close the door, will you, Richard?"

He does so and then comes closer to sit on the low chair near her dresser. He looks at her. Diane's dark hair is freshly brushed, her cheeks pink from a recent scrubbing, but her eyes cannot hide the fatigue and sorrow of the past few days.

"Will you do me a favor, Richard?"

"Anything," Baedecker says truthfully.

"Colonel Fields, Bob . . . the others . . . they've promised to keep me informed about the crash investigation . . ." She breaks off.

Baedecker watches her and waits.

"Richard, will you look into it yourself? I mean, not just follow the official inquiry, but look into it yourself and tell me everything you find out?"

Baedecker hesitates a second, puzzled, and then he reaches across and takes her hand. "Of course I will, Di. If you want me to. But I doubt that I'll find anything that the Crash Board won't."

Diane nods, but her grip is cool and insistent. "But you'll *try?*"

"Yes," says Baedecker.

Diane touches her cheek and looks down as if suddenly dizzy. "There are so many little things," she says.

"What do you mean?" asks Baedecker.

"Things I don't understand," she says. "David took the helicopter out to Lonerock, did you know that?"

"No."

"The weather got worse so he came back in the car we'd stored there," she says. "But why did he go there at all?"

"I thought he worked on his book out there," says Baedecker.

"He was supposed to stop by Salem one night after the fund-raising meeting in Portland," Diane says. "Instead, he flew out to Lonerock when the house was all closed up. We weren't planning to stay there until weeks after the baby was born."

Baedecker touches her arm, holds it gently.

"Richard," she says, "did you know that David's cancer had returned? I didn't think he had told anyone, but I thought perhaps he might have called . . ."

"I didn't even have a phone where I was, remember, Di?" he says. "You had to send that telegram."

"Yes, I remember," she says, her voice ragged with exhaustion. "I just thought . . . He didn't tell me, Richard. His doctor in Washington is a friend. . . . He called the day after the accident. The disease had spread to David's liver and bone marrow. They had wanted to do a complete chemotherapy treatment in the spring, using a combination of drugs called MOPP. David had refused. That kind of chemotherapy causes sterility in most cases. Dave had had some radiation and the laparotomy, I knew that. I didn't know about the other . . ."

"Dave told me in October that they were pretty sure they'd caught it all," says Baedecker.

"Yes," says Diane, "they found it again just before Christmas. David didn't tell me. He was supposed to have a flight physical next week. He never would have passed it."

"Richard!" comes Katie's voice up the stairs. "Telephone!"

"In a minute," calls Baedecker. He takes Diane's hand again. "What are you thinking, Di?"

She looks directly at him. In spite of her tiredness and pregnancy, she does not look vulnerable to Baedecker, only beautiful and determined.

"I want to know why he went out to Lonerock when he didn't have to," she says firmly. "I want to know why he flew that T-38 by himself when he could have waited a few hours for a commercial flight. I want to know why he stayed in that plane when he must have known it was going down." Diane takes a breath and smoothes her robe. She squeezes his hand hard enough for it to be painful. "Richard, I want to know why David is dead rather than here with me waiting for our child to be born."

Baedecker stands up. "I promise I'll do my best," he says. He kisses her on the forehead and helps her up. "Come on now, get in bed and go to sleep. You're going to have guests for breakfast. I may be out early, but I'll call you before I come back."

Diane looks at him as he pauses by the door. "Good night, Richard."

"Good night, Di."

Downstairs, Katie is waiting for him. "It's long distance, Richard. I told them to call back, but they're waiting."

He walks into the kitchen to take it there. "Thanks, Kate," he says. "Know who it is?"

"Someone named Maggie," calls Katie. "Maggie Brown. She says that it's important."

∾

Dave landed the Huey on a ranch half a mile beyond Lonerock. There was a short grassy field, a tattered windsock hanging limp from the cupola of an old barn, and an ancient Stearman two-seater tied down between the barn and the ranch house. "Welcome to Lonerock International Airport," said Dave as he switched off the last of the circuit breakers. "Please remain seated until the aircraft comes to a complete stop at the terminal." The rotors turned more slowly and then stopped.

"Does every ghost town have an airport?" asked Baedecker. He took off his earphones and cap, ran his fingers through his thinning hair, and shook his head. He could still hear the roar of the turbine in his ears.

"Only where the ghosts are fliers," said Dave.

A man walked slowly from the barn to meet them. He was younger than either Muldorff or Baedecker, but his face had been darkened and textured by years of working in the sun. He wore western boots, faded jeans, a black cap, and an Indian-turquoise belt buckle. The left sleeve of his plaid shirt was pinned at the shoulder. "Hullo, Dave," he called. "Wondered if you was comin' over this weekend."

"Evening, Kink," said Dave. "Kink, meet Richard Baedecker, friend from the old days."

"Kink," said Baedecker as they shook hands. He liked the restrained strength in the man's handshake and the creased laugh lines around his blue eyes.

"Kink Weltner here served three tours as a helicopter crew chief in 'Nam," said Dave. "He lets me park the bird here now and then. Somehow he came into the possession of a big, underground tank of aviation-grade kerosene."

The rancher walked over and ran his hand lovingly along the cowling of the Huey. "I can't believe this rusted pile of shit's still flying. Did Chico replace that omni gauge?"

"Yeah," said Dave, "but you might want to take a look inside."

"I'll pull the hell-hole cover when I refuel it," said Kink.

"See you later," said Dave and led the way toward the barn. It was cool here in the valley. Baedecker carried his goosedown coat in one hand and his black flight bag in the other. He looked up to watch the hills to the east catch the last bands of evening sunlight. Brittle cottonwood leaves stood out against the fragile blue sky. There was a jeep parked near the barn, keys in the ignition, and Dave threw his stuff in the back and hopped in. Baedecker joined him, grabbing the roll bar as Dave pulled out onto the gravel road at high speed.

"Nice to have your own crew chief way out here," said Baedecker. "Did you know him in Vietnam?"

"Nope. Met him after Di and I bought the house here in '76."

"Did he lose his arm in the war?"

Dave shook his head. "Never got touched over there. Three months after he was discharged, he got drunk and rolled a pickup outside of the Dalles."

∾

They drove into Lonerock past the jagged tooth of a boulder and the closed-up church. Far across the valley, the road they had followed from Condon was a white line on the shadowed wall of the cliff. Baedecker noticed several abandoned houses set back in weeds along the street, caught a glimpse of the old school to the right through the trees, and then Dave pulled to a stop in front of a white house with a tin roof and a low picket fence out front. The lawn was well tended, there was a flagstone patio to one side, and a hummingbird feeder hung from a young lilac tree out front. "Casa Muldorff," announced Dave and lifted Baedecker's bag out of the jeep.

The guest room was on the second floor, tucked under the eaves. Baedecker could imagine the sound of rain on the tin roof above. He respected the amount of work that had gone into the old structure. Dave and Diane had ripped out walls, reinforced the floors, added a fireplace in the living room and a stove in the kitchen, repaired the foundation, added electrical wiring and indoor plumbing, remodeled the kitchen, and turned a low attic into a small but comfortable second floor. "Other than that," Dave had said, "the house is pretty much the way we found it." Back in the days when the Oregon Trail was a recent memory, the house had served as a post office, then sheriff's office, and even a morgue for a while before sagging into disrepair with the rest of the little town. Now the guest bedroom had clean white walls, crisp white curtains, a high brass bed, and an antique dresser with a white bowl and pitcher on it. Baedecker looked out the window through baring branches at the small front yard and dirt street beyond. He could imagine buggies passing by but little other traffic. The remnants of a low, board sidewalk lay rotting in the grass outside the picket fence.

"Come on," called Dave from downstairs. "I'll show you the town before it gets too dark."

It did not take long to see the entire town, even on foot. A hundred feet beyond Dave's house, the dirt road doglegged to the north and became Main Street for one block. The county road hooked left from it, crossing a low bridge and continuing off through wheat and alfalfa fields to the cliff two miles west. The stream Baedecker had seen from the air curved around through Dave's property past the weathered shed he called a garage.

The silence was deep enough that Baedecker heard their footsteps on the gravel of Main Street as intrusive. A few houses in town looked occupied, and there was an old mobile home parked behind one boarded-up structure, but most of the buildings were weedchoked and weathered, rafters open to the elements. Three stores sat closed and idle on the west side of Main Street, two with rusted light fixtures sans bulbs over their doorways. A gas pump outside the abandoned store offered high-test at thirty-one cents a gallon. The fly-specked sign hanging diagonally in the window read *Coke* CLOSED *The Pause That Refreshes*

"Is it officially a ghost town?" asked Baedecker.

"Sure is," said Dave. "The official census is four hundred eighty-nine ghosts and eighteen people at the height of the summer season."

"What about the people who stay here year 'round? What do they do?"

Dave shrugged. "There are a couple of retired farmers and ranchers. Solly in the trailer back there won the Washington lottery a few years ago and settled out here with his two million."

"You're kidding," said Baedecker.

"Never kid," said Dave. "Come on, I want you to meet someone."

They walked a block and a half east to the edge of town and then up a sharp grade to where the brick school sat. It was an imposing structure, two stories tall and then some with an oversized, glass-enclosed belfry atop it. As they came closer, Baedecker could see that much care had gone into the old building's rehabilitation. A well-tended garden filled part of what had been the schoolyard, the bricks had been sandblasted clean some years ago, the front door was nicely carved, and white curtains were tied back in the tall windows.

Baedecker was puffing slightly when they reached the front door. Dave grinned. "Need to jog more, Dickie." He tapped loudly with a brass knocker. Baedecker jumped slightly as a voice came from a metal tube set into the doorframe near his ear.

"It's Dave Muldorff, Miz Callahan," shouted Dave into the tube. "Brought a friend with me."

Baedecker recognized the antiquated mouthpiece as part of an old speaking-tube system such as he had seen only in movies and once in a tour of Mark Twain's home in Hartford.

There was a muffled reply that Baedecker translated as "come up" and then a buzz as the door opened. Baedecker was reminded of the entrance foyer to his family's apartment building on Kildare Street in Chicago before the war. As he entered, he half expected to smell the mixture of moldy carpet, varnished wood, and boiled cabbage that had meant homecoming to him for the years of his early childhood. He did not. The interior of the school smelled of furniture polish and the evening breeze coming through open windows.

Baedecker was fascinated by the glimpses of rooms as they ascended the two flights of stairs. A large classroom on the first floor had been transformed into an oversized living room. Part of the long blackboard remained but was now bracketed by built-in bookcases holding hundreds of volumes. A few pieces of quality antique furniture sat here and there on a polished wood floor, and a small area had been set off by a Persian carpet and comfortably overstuffed sofa and chairs.

On the second story, as far above the ground as a normal third story, Baedecker caught a glimpse of a book-filled study behind sliding doors and a bedroom with a single, canopied bed alone in the center of six hundred square feet of polished wood. Two cats moved quickly into the shadows at the sound of footsteps. Baedecker followed Dave up a wrought-iron spiral staircase that obviously had been added after the building ceased functioning as a school. They passed through a trapdoor cut into the ceiling and suddenly they were in light again, emerging onto what might have been the pilothouse of a tall stern-wheeler.

Baedecker was so surprised and struck by the view that for several seconds he could not focus his attention on the elderly woman who sat smiling at him from a wicker chair. He looked around, not bothering to hide his expression of delight.

The old school belfry had been enlarged into a glass cupola at least fifteen feet by fifteen feet, and even the top of the belfry had been glassed in with skylights. Baedecker could tell from the quality of light that all of the glass was polarized. Now it merely enhanced the already-rich evening colors of sky and foliage, but he knew that in the daytime the glass would be opaque from the outside while hues would be clarified and exaggerated to an observer within. Outside, running east and west along the crest of two gables leading from the belfry, a narrow widow's walk was set off by an intricate wrought-iron railing. Inside, there were several pieces of wicker furniture, a table with a tea service and star charts laid out, and an antique brass telescope on a tall tripod.

But it was the view that struck Baedecker the most. From this vantage forty feet above the town, he could see over rooftops and treetops to the canyon walls and foothills and beyond them to the high ridges where slabs of ancient sediment thrust through the soil like thorns through tired cloth. The polarized sky was such a dark shade that it reminded Baedecker of those rare flights above 75,000 feet where the stars become visible in the daytime and the cobalt blue curve of the heavens blends to black. Baedecker realized that the stars *were* becoming visible now, entering the sky in pairs and small clusters like early theatergoers searching for the best seats.

A breeze came through screens set low in the glass wall, the wind ruffled the pages of a book on the arm of a chair, and Baedecker focused his attention on the woman who sat smiling at him.

"Miz Callahan," said Dave, "this is Richard Baedecker. Richard, Miz Elizabeth Sterling Callahan."

"How do you do, Mr. Baedecker," said the woman and extended her hand palm downward.

Baedecker took it and looked carefully at the old woman. His initial impression had been of a woman in her late sixties, but now he revised that age upward by at least a decade and perhaps more. Still, despite the assault of years, Elizabeth Sterling Callahan retained a beauty too entrenched to be overthrown by time alone. Her hair was white and cropped short, but it stood out in electric waves from her strong-featured face. Her cheekbones pressed sharply against skin freckled by sun and age, but the small, brown eyes were lively and intelligent, and her smile still had the power to intrigue.

"Very pleased to meet you, Miz Callahan," said Baedecker.

"Any friend of David's is a friend of mine," she said and Baedecker smiled at the rich huskiness of her voice. "Sit down, please. Sable, say hello to our friends."

Baedecker noticed for the first time that a black Labrador was curled in the shadows behind her chair. The dog looked up eagerly as Dave crouched to pet it.

"How long?" said Dave, patting the dog's side.

"Patience, patience," laughed Miz Callahan. "Good things take time." She looked at Baedecker. "Is this your first visit to our town, Mr. Baedecker?"

"Yes, ma'am," said Baedecker, feeling like a boy in her presence and not necessarily disliking the feeling.

"Well, it's a quiet little place," said Miz Callahan, "but we hope you will find it to your liking."

"I do already," said Baedecker. "I also very much like your house. You've done wonderful things with it."

"Why thank you, Mr. Baedecker," she said and Baedecker could see her smile in the dimming light. "My late husband and I did most of the work when we first retired here in the late 1950s. The school had been abandoned for almost thirty years at that point and was in terrible shape. The roof had collapsed in places, pigeons were roosting in all of the second-floor rooms . . . oh, my, it was in terrible shape. David, there is a pitcher of lemonade there on that table. Would you mind pouring us each some? Thank you, dear."

Baedecker sipped the lemonade from a crystal wineglass as full night fell outside. There were a few house-lights visible in town and two pole lights, one not far from Dave's house, but their glow was shielded by branches and did not detract from the beauty of the sky as more stars took their places.

"There's Mars rising," said Dave.

"No, dear, that's Betelgeuse," said Miz Callahan. "You see, it's opposite Rigel and above Orion's Belt."

"You're interested in astronomy?" asked Baedecker, smiling at Dave's embarrassment. He had had to coach his crewmate during the astrogation exercises for months prior to the mission.

"Mr. Callahan was an astronomer," said the old woman. "We met when he was a professor at DePauw University in Greencastle, Indiana. I had gone there to teach history. Have you ever seen DePauw, Mr. Baedecker?"

"No, ma'am."

"A very pretty little school," said Miz Callahan. "Second-rate academically and buried in the seventh circle of desolation out there in the cornfields of Indiana, but a very pretty little campus. More lemonade, Mr. Baedecker?"

"No, thank you."

"Mr. Callahan was a Chicago Cubs fan," she said. "We used to travel to Chicago on the Monon Railroad every August to watch games at Wrigley Field. That was our vacation. I remember in 1945, when they did so well, Mr. Callahan made plans to stay over in the Blackstone Hotel for an extra week. Traveling to the Cubs' games was the one thing Mr. Callahan missed when he took early retirement and we moved out here in the fall of 1959."

"What made you decide on Lonerock?" asked Baedecker. "Did you have family in Oregon?"

"Oh, heavens, no," said Miz Callahan. "Neither of us had ever been out west before we moved here. No, Mr. Callahan simply had calculated on his maps that this was the best place for magnetic lines of force, and we loaded up the DeSoto and came out."

"Magnetic lines of force?" said Baedecker.

"Are you interested in watching the sky, Mr. Baedecker?" she asked.

Before Baedecker could respond, Dave said, "Richard walked on the moon with me sixteen years ago."

"Oh, David, don't start up with that again," said Miz Callahan and gave his wrist a playful slap.

Dave turned to Baedecker. "Miz Callahan doesn't believe that Americans walked on the moon."

"Really?" said Baedecker. "I thought everyone accepted that."

"Oh, now, don't you start teasing me as well," said the old woman. Her husky voice held mild amusement. "David's bad enough."

"It was on television," said Baedecker and immediately realized how lame the statement sounded.

"Yes," said Miz Callahan, "and so was Mr. Nixon's so-called Checkers Speech. Do you believe everything you see and hear, Mr. Baedecker? I've not owned a television since our picture tube failed. It was on a Sunday. Right in the middle of *Omnibus*. We had a Sylvania Halolite. The halo continued to work after the screen went black. It was rather restful, actually."

"The lunar landings were in all the papers," said Baedecker. "Remember the summer of 1969? Neil Armstrong? 'One small step for man, one giant leap for mankind?'"

"Yes, yes," chuckled the woman. "Tell me, Mr. Baedecker, does that sound like something a person would make up on the spur of the moment? Or say at such a time? Of course not. It sounds like just what it is, a poorly written drama."

Baedecker started to speak, looked at Dave, and closed his mouth.

"David, how is dear Diane?" asked Miz Callahan.

"Just fine," said Dave. "I was with her when they did the sonogram."

"Amniocentesis as well?" asked the old woman.

"No, just the sonogram."

"That was wise," said Miz Callahan. "Diane's young enough, there's no reason to run the one percent risk of miscarriage if the procedure is not necessary. When is the due date again?"

"The doctor says January seven," said Dave. "Di thinks it'll be later. I'm voting for a little earlier."

"First baby probably later if anything," said Miz Callahan.

Baedecker cleared his throat. "Ah, what were you saying about magnetic lines of force?"

Miz Callahan patted her dog and rose to walk slowly and carefully to the table. She glanced at the sky, looked down at her charts, nodded as if satisfied, and returned to her seat. "Yes, electromagnetic lines, actually," she said. "I never understood it all, but after Mr. Callahan first made contact, he wrote it all down. You may look at it someday if you wish. At any rate, Mr. Callahan confirmed that they were correct and that this would be the best spot in the United States . . . in North America, really . . . so we moved. Mr. Callahan passed on in 1964, but since they don't speak to *me* directly the way they did to him, I have to rely on his early calculations. Wouldn't you agree?"

"I guess so," said Baedecker.

"Mr. Callahan was undoubtedly correct about the *place*," continued the woman, "but was never quite sure about the *time*. They simply would not commit themselves to a date. I've seen them fly over hundreds of times, but they have yet to come all the way down. Well, I have to tell you, they had best get on with it. I am not getting any younger, and some days it is all I can do to drag these old bones up the stairs. Tonight will not be a good night for watching because the full moon will be rising soon and . . . oh, my, look!"

Baedecker followed the shadowy line of her arm to a point near the zenith where a satellite or an extremely high-flying aircraft glowed briefly for several seconds as it tracked from west to east. The three of them watched its progress until it disappeared against the background of stars, and then they sat in the comfortable darkness and silence for several minutes.

"More lemonade, anyone?" Dave said at last.

∾

After Baedecker's mother died of a stroke in the fall of 1956, his father moved from their Chicago house to their "log cabin" in Arkansas. Baedecker's parents had won the land in a *Herald Tribune* contest and had been working on the house for almost five years, spending summers there when possible, sometimes traveling down for Christmas. Baedecker's father had retired from the Marine Corps in 1952, the same year his son had begun flying F-86 Sabres in Korea, and had held a part-time sales job with Wilson's Sporting Goods ever since. They had planned on retiring to Arkansas in June of 1957. Instead, Baedecker's father had gone there alone in November of 1956.

Baedecker had strong memories of two trips there: the first in October of 1957, two months before his father's death from lung cancer, and the second, with Scott, during the hot Watergate summer of 1974.

Scott was ten that year, but he had already entered the growth spurt that would not end until he was six feet one, two inches taller than his father. Scott had let his red hair grow that year so that it was touching his shoulders. Baedecker disliked it—he thought it made the thin boy look effeminate—and he disliked even more the nervous tic his son had developed in constantly flipping the hair out of his face, but Baedecker did not think it important enough to make an issue of.

The drive from Houston had been hot and uneventful. It had been the first summer of Joan's dissatisfaction, or so Baedecker later thought of it, and he was glad to be away for a few weeks. Joan had decided to stay in Houston because of commitments she had made to various women's clubs. Baedecker had left NASA a month earlier and would begin his new job with a St. Louis–based aerospace firm in September. It was his first vacation in more than ten years.

Scott was not pleased. During the first few days of work around the cabin—clearing the underbrush, repairing damaged windows, replacing shingles, and generally shoring up the exterior of a cabin that had been empty for years—Scott had been quiet and obviously sulking. Baedecker had brought a transistor radio along, and the news was filled with urgent speculation on Nixon's impeachment or imminent resignation. Joan had been absorbed in the Watergate story since the televised hearings had begun over a year earlier. At first she resented them because network coverage interfered with her favorite soap operas, but soon she was looking forward to them, watching the evening's replay on PBS, and talking to Baedecker of little else. To Baedecker, on the verge of ending a flying career he had been in since he was eighteen, Nixon's final agonies were graceless and embarrassing, evidence of an unraveling society that Baedecker already viewed with some sadness.

The log cabin was actually a two-story log home quite out of fashion with the stone-and-brick ranch houses and A-frames appearing in developments around the new reservoir. The cabin sat on a hill amidst three acres of forest and meadow. Down a long stretch of hill there was a narrow lake frontage and a short dock Baedecker's father had built the summer Eisenhower was reelected. Baedecker's parents had been working on finishing the second-floor rooms and adding a rear deck, but when he moved there after his wife's death, Baedecker's father left the work unfinished.

Baedecker and Scott tore down the rotting remnants of the deck on the August day that Richard Nixon announced his resignation. Baedecker remembered sitting in front of the cabin that Thursday evening, eating hamburgers he and Scott had grilled, and listening to the last, lame expressions of self-pity and defiance from the departing president. Nixon ended with the phrase, "To have served in this office is to have felt a personal kinship with each and every American. In leaving it, I do so with this prayer: May God's grace be with you in all the days ahead." Immediately, Scott said, "Just get it over with, you lying shit. We won't miss you."

"Scott!" barked Baedecker. "Until noon tomorrow, that man is President of the United States. You will *not* speak that way."

The boy had opened his mouth to respond, but two decades of Marine Corps–instilled authority had gone into Baedecker's command, and Scott was able only to throw down his plate and run away, his face reddening. Baedecker had sat alone in the last vestiges of the Arkansas twilight, watching his son's white shirt receding down the hill toward the dock. Baedecker knew that Scott's sulking would deepen for their few remaining days together. He also knew that Scott's statement, while phrased somewhat differently, adequately expressed Baedecker's own feelings about Nixon's departure. Baedecker had looked at the cabin and remembered the first time he had seen it—the first time he had been in Arkansas—driving straight through from Yuma, Arizona, in his new Thunderbird, being reminded of New England as he passed through small towns with names like Choctaw and Leslie, Yellville and Salesville, and half expecting to see the ocean rather than the long lake where his parents had won their property.

His father's appearance had shaken him; although sixty-four years old, Baedecker's father had always appeared at least a decade younger. Now his hair had remained jet-black, but gray stubble mottled his cheeks, and his neck had gone loose and lined since Baedecker had seen him in Illinois eight months earlier. Baedecker realized that in twenty-four years he had never seen his father unshaven before.

Baedecker had arrived for the visit on the night of October 5, 1957, the day after *Sputnik* was launched. Late that night his father had gone down to the dock to fish and "to look for the satellite," even though Baedecker had assured him it was too small to see with the naked eye. It was a cool, moonless night, and the forest three miles away across the expanse of lake was a black line against the starfield. Baedecker watched the glow of his father's cigarette and listened to the crisp sound of the reel and line. Occasionally a fish would jump in the darkness.

"Who's to say that thing isn't carrying atomic bombs," his father suddenly had said.

"Pretty small bombs," said Baedecker. "The satellite's about the size of a basketball."

"But if they can send up something that size, they can put a bigger one up with bombs aboard, can't they?" said his father, and Baedecker thought that the deep voice sounded almost querulous.

"True," said Baedecker, "but if they can launch that much weight into orbit, they don't need to put bombs aboard. They can use the boosters as ballistic missiles."

His father said nothing, and Baedecker wished he had also kept quiet. Finally his father coughed and spoke again, reeling in the line and swinging it out again. "I read in the *Tribune* about that new rocket plane, the X-15, they've got on the drawing boards. Supposed to go up into space, go around the earth, and land like a regular plane. You going to be flying it when it's ready?"

"Don't I wish," said Baedecker. "Unfortunately, there are a bunch of guys ahead of me with names like Joe Walker and Ivan Kincheloe. Besides, that's out at Edwards. I spend most of my time at Yuma or back at Pax River. I'd hoped to be on the first string by this time, but I haven't even made varsity yet."

Baedecker saw the glow of his father's cigarette go up and down. "Your mother and I had hoped to be getting ready for our first winter down here by now," he said. "Sometimes it doesn't matter what you hope or plan for. It just doesn't matter."

Baedecker ran his hand across the smooth wood of the dock.

"The mistake is waiting and waiting for the payoff like it's a reward you've got coming," said his father and the querulous note was gone now, replaced by something infinitely sadder. "You work and you wait and you work some more, all the while telling each other and yourself that the good times are coming, and then everything falls to pieces and you're just waiting to die."

A cold wind blew across the lake and Baedecker shivered.

"There it is," said his father.

Baedecker looked up, following the pointing finger, and there in the dark gaps between the cold stars, impossibly bright, orange as the tip of his father's cigarette, moving west to east far too high and too fast to be an aircraft, moved the *Sputnik* too small to be seen.

∽

Dave made chili, and they had a late dinner after they got back from Miz Callahan's, sitting in the long kitchen and listening to Bach on a portable cassette player. Kink Weltner dropped by and drank a beer while they ate. Dave and Kink talked about football while Baedecker tuned out, football being one of the few sports that bored him senseless. When they went outside to see Kink off, the full moon was rising, outlining rock outcroppings and pine trees on the ridgeline to the east.

"I want to show you something," said Dave.

In a small back room on the first floor, there were mounds of books, a crude desk made of a door set on sawhorses, a typewriter, and several hundred sheets of manuscript stacked under a paperweight made from part of the abort switch from a *Gemini* spacecraft.

"How long have you been working on this?" asked Baedecker, thumbing through the first fifty pages or so.

"A couple of years," said Dave. "It's funny, but I only work out here in Lonerock. I have to drag my research stuff back and forth."

"Going to work on it this weekend?"

"No, I'd like you to look at it if you would," said Dave. "I want your opinion. You're a writer."

"Nuts," said Baedecker. "Some writer. I spent two years fiddling with that stupid book and never got past chapter four. It finally occurred to me that to write something you have to have something to say."

"You're a writer," repeated Dave. "I'd appreciate your opinion of this." He handed the rest of the stack to Baedecker.

Later, Baedecker lay on his bed and read for two hours. The book was unfinished—entire chapters existing only in outline form, a few scribbled notes—but what was there, fascinated Baedecker. The manuscript's working title was *Forgotten Frontiers*, and the opening segments dealt with the early exploration of both the Antarctic and the moon. Parallels were drawn. Some were as obvious as the races to plant the flag, the hunger to be *first,* taking precedence over any serious or systematic scientific programs. Other similarities were more subtle, such as the stark beauty of the south polar desert drawn in comparison to firsthand accounts of the moon. The information was drawn from diaries, notes, and recorded statements. With both Antarctica and the moon, the inadequate accounts—the descriptions of the Antarctic explorers being, by far, the better expressed—told of the mysterious clarity of desolation, the overwhelming beauty of a new place totally foreign to mankind's previous experience, and of the seductive attraction inherent in a place so inclement and so hostile as to be completely indifferent to human aspirations and frailties.

In addition to exploring the aesthetics of exploration, Dave had woven in minibiographies and psychological portraits of ten men—five Antarctic explorers and five space voyagers. The Antarctic profiles included Amundsen, Byrd, Ross, Shackleton, and Cherry-Ganard. For their modern-day counterparts, Dave had chosen four of the lesser-known *Apollo* astronauts, three of whom had walked on the moon and one who had—like Tom Gavin—remained in lunar orbit aboard the Command Module. He had also included one Russian, Pavel Belyayev. Baedecker had met Belyayev at the Paris Air Show in 1968, and he had been standing with Dave Muldorff and Michael Collins when Belyayev had said, "Soon, perhaps, I will see first-hand what the backside of the moon looks like." Now Baedecker was interested to read that, according to Dave's research, Belyayev had indeed been chosen to be the first cosmonaut to go on a circumlunar flight in a modified Zond spacecraft. The launch date was only a few months after Baedecker and the others had spoken to him in the spring of 1968. Instead, *Apollo 8* became the first spacecraft to circle the moon that Christmas, the Soviet lunar program was quietly scrapped under the pretense they had never planned to go to the moon, Belyayev died a year later as a result of an operation for a bleeding ulcer, and—instead of becoming famous as the first man to see the backside of the moon in person—the luckless cosmonaut received the minor distinction of being the first dead Russian "space hero" *not* to be buried in the Kremlin Wall. Baedecker thought of his father . . . "then everything falls to pieces and you're just waiting to die."

The sections on the four American astronauts were—at best—only sketched in, although the direction these chapters would take was obvious enough. As with the portraits of the Antarctic explorers, the *Apollo* segments would deal with the astronauts' thoughts in the years following their missions, new perspectives they may have gained, old perspectives lost, and a discussion of any frustration they might feel at the impossibility of their ever returning to this particular frontier. Baedecker agreed with the choice of astronauts, he found himself very curious what they might say and share, but he felt that this would be the heart of the book when it was done . . . and by far the most difficult part to research and write.

He was thinking about this, standing at the window looking at the moonlight on the leaves of the lilac tree, when Dave knocked and entered.

"Still dressed, I see," said Dave. "Can't sleep?"

"Not yet," said Baedecker.

"Me either," said Dave and tossed him his cap. "Want to go for a ride?"

∾

Driving north on I-5 toward Tacoma, Baedecker thinks about Maggie's call the previous evening.

"Maggie?" he had said, surprised that she had gotten hold of him at the Muldorff's. He realized that it was almost one A.M. on the east coast. "What's the matter, Maggie? Where are you?"

"Boston," said Maggie. "I got the number from Joan. I'm sorry about your friend, Richard."

"Joan?" he said. The thought of Maggie Brown having talked to his ex-wife seemed unreal to Baedecker.

"I called about Scott," said Maggie. "Have you been in touch with him?"

"No," said Baedecker. "The last couple of months I've been trying. I cabled the old address in Poona and sent letters, but there was no response. I called out here to Oregon in November, but somebody at their ranch said they didn't have Scott's name on their residents' list. Do you know where he is?"

"I'm pretty sure he's there," said Maggie. "In Oregon. At the ashram-ranch there. A friend of ours who was in India came back to B.U. a few days ago. He said that Scott came back to the States with him on the first of December. Bruce said that Scott had been pretty sick in India and that he'd spent several weeks in the hospital there—or at least in the infirmary that passes for a hospital there on the Master's farm outside of Poona."

"Asthma?" said Baedecker.

"Yes," said Maggie, "and a bad case of dysentery."

"Did Joan say Scott'd been in touch with her?"

"She said she hadn't heard from him since early November . . . from Poona," said Maggie. "She gave me the Muldorffs' number. I wouldn't have called, Richard, but I didn't know where else to get in touch with you, and Bruce—my friend who came back from India—said that Scott's been pretty sick. He wasn't able to walk off the plane when they landed in Los Angeles. He's pretty sure that Scott's at the ranch in Oregon."

"Thanks, Maggie," said Baedecker. "I'll call out there right away."

"How are you, Richard?" Something in the tone of Maggie's voice changed, deepened.

"I'm all right," he said.

"I'm so sorry about your friend Dave. I loved the stories you told me about him in Colorado. I'd hoped to meet him someday."

"I wish you had," said Baedecker and realized how much truth there was in the statement. Maggie would have loved Dave's sense of humor. Dave would have enjoyed her enjoyment. "I'm sorry I haven't been in touch," he said.

"I got your postcard from Idaho," said Maggie. "What have you been doing since you were there at your sister's in October?"

"I spent some time in Arkansas," said Baedecker, "working on a cabin my father built. It's been empty for a long time. How are *you?*"

There was a pause, and Baedecker could hear vague, electronic background noises. "I'm fine," she said at last. "Scott's friend Bruce came back to ask me to marry him."

Baedecker felt the wind go out of him much as it had four days earlier when Di's telegram had reached him. "Are you going to?" he said after a minute.

"I don't think I'll do anything precipitous until I get my master's in May," she said. "Hey, I'd better go. Please take care of yourself, Richard."

"Yes," Baedecker had said, "I will."

∾

The fragments of Dave's T-38 take up a significant amount of space on the floor of the hangar. Smaller and more important pieces lie tagged on a long row of tables.

"So what will the Crash Board findings be?" Baedecker asks Bob Munsen.

The Air Force major frowns and sticks his hands in the pockets of the green flight jacket. "The way it looks now, Dick, is that there was a slight structural failure on takeoff that caused the hydraulic leak. Dave got a red light on it about fourteen minutes out from Portland International and turned back immediately."

"I still don't see why he was flying out of Portland," says Baedecker.

"Because that's where I'd parked the goddamned thing right before Christmas," says Munsen. "I was scheduled to ferry it to Ogden on the twenty-seventh and Dave wanted to ride. He was going to catch a commercial flight out of Salt Lake."

"But you got hung up for forty-eight hours," says Baedecker. "At McChord?"

"Yeah," says Munsen, and there is disgust and regret in the syllable, as if he should have been in the aircraft when it crashed.

"So why didn't Dave use his priority status to bump someone on a commercial flight if he had to get back so quickly?" Baedecker says, knowing no one there has the answer.

Munsen shrugs. "Ryan wanted the T-38 at Hill Air Force Base in Ogden by the twenty-eighth. Dave had my clearance and wanted to fly it. When he called, I told him go ahead, I'd deadhead back to Hill."

Baedecker walks over and looks at the charred metal on the table. "Okay," he says, "structural failure, hydraulic leak. How serious?"

"We figure he'd lost about sixty percent of assist by the time he went down," says Munsen. "Have you heard the tape?"

"Not yet," says Baedecker. "What about the starboard engine?"

"He got a light about a minute after the hydraulic problem showed up," replies Munsen. "He shut it down about eight minutes before impact."

"Jesus Fucking Christ!" shouts Baedecker and slams his fist into the table hard enough to send tagged pieces flying. "Who the fuck crewed this thing?"

"Sergeant Kitt Toliver at McChord," says Munsen in a thin voice. "Best crew chief heading the best crew we've got. Kitt flew down with me for this seminar in Portland over Christmas. The weather closed in, and I drove back up to McChord on the twenty-sixth, but Kitt was in town. He did two inspections of it the day Dave flew. *You* know how these things are, Dick."

"Yeah," says Baedecker, and there is no lessening of the anger in his voice, "I know how these things are. Did Dave do a complete preflight?"

"He was in a hurry," says the major, "but Toliver says he did."

"Bob, I'd like to talk to Fields and the others," says Baedecker. "Could you get them together for me?"

"Not today," says Munsen. "They're spread all over the place. I could do it by tomorrow morning, but they wouldn't be very happy about it."

"Do it, please," says Baedecker.

"Kitt Toliver's here now," says Munsen. "Up at the NCO mess. Do you want to talk to him now?"

"No," says Baedecker, "later. First I have to listen to
the flight tape. Thanks, Bill, I'll see you tomorrow morning." Baedecker shakes hands and goes to listen to his friend's
voice for the last time.

∾

"Let's get drunk and stick beans up our noses!" shouted
Dave. His voice echoed down the dark streets of Lonerock.
"Sweet Christ on a stick, what a beautiful night!"

Baedecker zipped up his goosedown jacket and leaped
into the jeep as Dave gunned the engine.

"Full moon!" shouted Dave and howled like a wolf.
From somewhere in the hills beyond the town came the
high yelping of a coyote. Dave laughed and drove east past
the boarded-up Methodist church. Suddenly he slammed
the jeep to a stop and grabbed Baedecker by the arm. He
pointed to the white disk of the moon. "We *walked* up there,"
he said, and although his voice was low, there was no denying the urgency and pleasure there. "We walked up there,
Richard. We left our little anthropoid, hindpawprints in
the moon's *dirt,* man. And they can't take that away from
us." Dave revved the engine and drove on, singing *They Can't
Take That Away from Me* at the top of his voice.

The jeep ride lasted for less than a mile and ended in
Kink Weltner's field. Dave pulled clipboards and flashlights
out of the back of the Huey and ran a careful inspection,
even crawling under the dark mass of the ship to make sure
there was no condensation in the fuel line. They were on
the flat roof deck of the ship, checking rotor hub, mast,
control rods, and the Jesus nut when Baedecker said, "We
don't really want to do this, do we?"

"Why not?" said Dave.

"It'll wake up Kink." It was the only thing Baedecker
could think of on short notice.

Dave laughed. "Nothin' wakes Kink up. Come on."

Baedecker climbed downward and in. He settled himself in the left seat, clicked the shoulder straps to the broad lap belt, tugged on the regulation National Guard helmet that he had left off on the flight out, wiggled the earphones in place, and blinked at the circles of red light glowing at him from the center console. Dave leaned forward to do the cockpit check while Baedecker read off the positions of circuit breakers. When he finished, Dave slid a piece of equipment into metal brackets on his side of the console and ran radio jacks to it.

"What the hell is that?"

"Tape deck," said Dave. "No self-respecting Huey flies without it."

The starter whined, rotors turned, and the turbine coughed and caught. Dave clicked in the intercom. His voice was muffled. "Next stop, Stonehenge."

"How's that?"

"Just watch and wait, amigo. Oh, are my goggles on straight?"

Baedecker glanced over to his right. Dave was wearing bulky night-vision goggles, but the face under the goggles and helmet was not Dave's. It was not even human. In the red cockpit glow, Baedecker could make out two huge eyes protruding at forty-five-degree angles on short, fleshy stalks, a wide, lipless frog's mouth, no chin, and a neck as lined and wattled as an aged turkey's.

"Yeah, they're on straight," said Baedecker.

"Thanks."

Three minutes later they were hovering twenty-five hundred feet above Lonerock. A few lights shone below. "You didn't care for my Admiral Ackbar?" asked Dave.

"Au contraire," said Baedecker, "it was the best Admiral Ackbar mask I've seen in weeks. Why are you doing that?"

Dave had triggered the landing-light extension switch on the collective pitch control lever. Now he was flicking the on-off switch. Baedecker could see the flashes through his chin bubble.

"Just sendin' extraterrestrial greetings and felicitations to Miz Callahan," said Dave, "so she can call it a night and go to bed." He retracted the light and pitched the Huey over in a banking turn.

They passed over Condon at five thousand feet. Baedecker saw lights glowing around an empty bandstand in a small park, an abandoned main street frozen in the glow of mercury-vapor lamps, and darkened side streets dappled with glimpses of streetlights through tall old trees. It suddenly occurred to Baedecker that small towns in America were saner than cities because they were allowed to sleep.

"Put this in, would you, Richard?" Dave handed him an audiocassette. Baedecker held it up to the glow of the omni gauge. It said only *Jean-Michel Jarre*. He popped it into the cassette player. He was reminded of the small tape player they had brought along in the Command Module. Each of them had supplied three cassettes; Tom Gavin had brought country-western tunes and Barry Manilow hits, Baedecker had brought Bach, Brubeck, and the Preservation Hall Jazz Band, and Dave had brought—well, he had brought the damnedest stuff—tapes of whale songs, Paul Winter's group Consort playing *Icarus*, the Beach Boys, a duet of Japanese flute and Indian sitar, and a recording of some sort of Masai tribal ceremony.

"What now?" said Baedecker.

Dave punched the tape player on and looked at him, the ends of the tubular goggles glowing redly. "G.Y.S.A.K.Y.A.G.," he said gleefully.

The first pulse of music filled Baedecker's earphones in the same instant that Dave pitched the Huey nose-over in a dive. Baedecker slid forward until he was held in position only by the shoulder harness and seat belt. The dive provided precisely the same sensation he had enjoyed as a kid at Riverview Park in Chicago when the roller coaster ended its long, clattering climb and plunged over the top for its high-speed plummet, only this roller coaster had a five-thousand-foot drop beneath it and there were no rails curving up and away in a reassuring swerve from destruction, only the moonlit hills a mile below, darkened here and there by patches of black vegetation, forest, river, and rock.

Baedecker kept his hands off the left-hand cyclic control stick and collective pitch lever, his feet back from the pedals, and this made the dive seem that much more out of control. The hills rose quickly to meet them, and the descent rate did not lessen until the Huey was at zero altitude, then below zero altitude, banking at the last moment past hills and cliff sides, moonlight bright out Baedecker's open window, black shadows beyond Dave's, and then they were in a valley, a canyon, the cyclic moved back and forth between Baedecker's legs and then centered itself, dark trees flashed by thirty feet on either side, their tops higher than the Huey, and they were hurtling along at 125 knots, fifteen feet above a rapid-rippled, moonlit stream, banking steeply when the canyon curved, now level again, then banking so the rotor blades threw an iridescent wake of spray into the air behind them.

The music meshed with the kaleidoscope of scenery rushing at them and past them. The music was electronic, unearthly, yet driven by a solid and insistent beat that seemed to have throbbed up out of the pulse of turbine and rotors. There were other sounds to the music, laser echoes, the rush of an electronic wind, surf sliding on a rocky shore, but all of it was orchestrated to the demanding drive of the central beat.

Baedecker sat back as the Huey banked steeply to the right, rotors almost touching the river, following a wide curve of canyon. He knew there was no room or time at this altitude for a safe autorotation should the engine fail. Worse, if there were a single cable, high-tension wire, bridge, or pipeline spanning the canyon, there would be no time to avoid it. But Baedecker glanced right at Dave sitting comfortably at the controls, his right hand almost casually moving the cyclic, his attention perfectly focused ahead of him, and he knew that there would be no cables, wires, bridges, or pipelines; that every foot of this canyon had been flown in daylight and dark. Baedecker relaxed, listened to the beat of the music, and enjoyed the ride.

And remembered another ride.

They had come down feet forward, faces up toward the half disk of the earth, the LM engines flaming before them in a 260-mile-long braking burn. They were standing in their bulky pressure suits, minus helmets and gloves, restrained by straps and stirrups while their strange device kicked and clattered and pushed up against their booted feet like the deck of a small boat on an uncertain sea. Dave was to his left, right hand on the ACS stick, left hand poised over the thrust translator, while Baedecker watched the six hundred instrument dials and readouts, spoke to controllers 219,000 miles away across static-filled emptiness, and tried to anticipate every whim and alarm of the overworked PGNS guidance computer. Then they were pitching over, upright at last, eight thousand feet above the lunar highlands and still descending, their trajectory as certain and unrelenting as a falling arrow's, and just then, in spite of the demands of the moment, he and Dave had both lifted their eyes from the instruments and stared for five eternal seconds out the triangular windows at the glaring peaks, death black canyons, and earthlit foothills of the moon's mountains. "Okay," Dave had whispered then, with the peaks drifting toward them like teeth, the hills coming up at them like frozen, white waves of rock, "I could use some help here, amigo."

The music ended and the Huey emerged from the canyon and then they were crossing a wide river, which Baedecker realized must be the Columbia. Wind buffeted the ship, and Dave rode the pedals, compensating easily. They climbed to a hundred feet as a dam flashed underneath. Baedecker looked down through the chin bubble and watched a string of lights go by, saw moonlight on white-caps. They climbed to five hundred feet and banked right, still climbing. Baedecker saw the north shore pass under them, noticed a steep cliff to their right, and then they climbed again, spun on the Huey's axis, and hovered.

They hovered. There was no sound. The wind pushed once at the stationary aircraft and then relented. Dave pointed, and Baedecker slid his window back and leaned out for a better view.

A hundred feet below them, the only structure on a hill high above the wind-tossed Columbia, the stone circle of Stonehenge sat milk-white and shadow-bound in the light of the full moon.

"Okay," said Dave, "I could use some help here, amigo."

Dust billowed up as they descended through thirty feet. The landing light extended and flashed on, illuminating the interior of a swirling cloud. Baedecker caught a glimpse of a graveled parking lot set on an uneven patch of hilltop below, and then dust surrounded them again and pebbles beat like hailstones on the belly of their craft.

"Talk to me," Dave said calmly.

"Twenty-five feet and drifting forward," said Baedecker. "Fifteen feet. Looks all right. Ten feet. Wait, back up ten, there's a boulder there. Right. Okay. Down. Five feet. You're okay. Two feet. Okay. Ten inches. Contact."

The Huey rocked slightly and settled firmly on its skids. Dust surrounded them and then dissipated in the strong breeze. Dave shut down the ship, the red cockpit glow disappeared, and Baedecker realized that they were in gravity's realm once again. He took off his helmet, undid his straps, and opened the door. Baedecker stepped off the skid and walked around the front of the helicopter to where Dave stood, his dark hair damp with sweat, his eyes alive. The wind was stronger now, ruffling Baedecker's thin hair and cooling him quickly. Together he and Dave walked to the circle of stones.

"Who built this?" Baedecker asked after several minutes of silence. The full moon hung just above the tallest arch. Shadows fell across the large stone lying in the center of the circle. This was Stonehenge as it must have looked shortly after the druids finished their labors, before time and tourists took their toll on the pillars and stones.

"A guy named Sam Hill," said Dave. "He was a road builder. Came out here early in the century to found a town and vineyards. A sort of Utopian colony. He had a theory that this section of the Columbia Gorge was perfect for wine grapes—rain from the west, sunlight from the east slopes. Perfect harmony."

"Was he right?"

"Nope. Missed it by about twenty miles," said Dave. "The town's lying in ruins over the hill there. Sam's buried down there." He pointed to a narrow trail leading down a steep section of hillside.

"Why Stonehenge?" asked Baedecker.

Dave shrugged. "We all want to leave monuments. Sam borrowed his. He was in England during World War I when the experts thought that Stonehenge had been a sacrificial altar. Sam made this into a sort of antiwar memorial."

Baedecker went closer and could see names set into the stones. What first had appeared to be rock was actually cement.

They walked to the south of the circle and looked out over the river. The lights of a town and bridge glowed several miles to the west. The wind gusted strongly, bending brittle spears of grass on the hillside, carrying the cold scent of autumn with it.

"The Oregon Trail ends a few miles down there," said Dave, pointing toward the lights. A little later he said, "Did you ever wonder why they would come so far, pass up two thousand miles of perfectly good land, just to follow a dream?"

"No," said Baedecker. "I don't think I have."

"I do," said Dave. "I've wondered that since I was a kid. Christ, Richard, I drive across this country and can't imagine crossing it on foot or in those pissant wagons, at an ox's pace. The more I see of it, the more I realize that any man who wants to be president of the United States is committing the ultimate hubris. Wait here a minute, I'll be right back."

Dave walked back through the circle of stones, and Baedecker stood at the edge of the cliff, letting the breeze cool him, listening to the sounds of some night bird far below. When Dave returned, he was carrying a Frisbee that glowed slightly from its own fluorescence.

"Jesus," said Baedecker, "that's not *the* Frisbee, is it?"

"Sure enough," said Dave. During their last EVA, while performing for the TV camera on the rover, Dave had produced a Frisbee from his contingency collection bag, and he and Baedecker had tossed it back and forth, laughing at its tumbling in a vacuum and its odd trajectory in one-sixth g. Great fun at the time. When they came home four days later, they returned to the Great Frisbee Controversy. NASA was upset because Dave had used the term Frisbee—a brand name—thus providing priceless advertising to a company not affiliated with NASA. Media newscasters and commentators generally approved of the frivolity, one calling it "a rare human touch in an otherwise heartless undertaking," but questioned the need for a *manned* lunar exploration program and pointed to the Soviet robot probes as a cheaper and more sensible approach. A Connecticut senator had discussed "the six-billion-dollar Frisbee tournament," and black leaders were incensed, calling the event both callous and insensitive to the needs of millions. "Two white college boys playing games in space at the taxpayers' expense," said one black leader on the *Today* show, "while black babies die of rat bites in the ghettos."

Capcom had radioed up some of this during their daily news update at the end of their sleep period four hours before reentry. Then the communicator asked if any of them had any opinion on the whole affair or any suggestions for mollifying the agency's critics.

"This channel secure?" Dave had asked.

Houston assured him that it was.

"Well, fuck 'em all," Dave had said laconically, thus going down—at least for the astronaut corps—into the program record books for the first live-mike use of that particular pilot's term. It had also almost certainly cost Dave a future ride in the Skylab program. Nonetheless, he had waited five more years for a flight, watching Skylab end and the single, obsolete gesture of *Apollo-Soyuz* go by before finally resigning.

Now Dave tossed the Frisbee to Baedecker. The phosphorescent plastic glowed green-white in the bright moonlight. Baedecker backed up ten steps and snapped it back.

"Works better in air," said Dave.

They threw the glowing disk back and forth silently for several minutes. Baedecker felt a tide of affection tug at him.

"Do you know what I think?" Dave said after a while.

"What do you think?"

"I think old Sam and all those others had the right idea. You pass all those other places by and keep on going because the place you're headed *is* perfect." He caught the Frisbee and held it two-handed. "But what they didn't understand is that you *make* it that way just by dreaming about it."

Dave walked to the edge of the cliff and briefly held the Frisbee toward the stars, an offering. "Everything ends," he said and pulled back, pivoted, and threw the disk hard out over the drop-off. Baedecker stepped up next to him and the two watched as the Frisbee soared an impossible distance, banked gracefully in the moonlight, and silently fell into the darkness above the river.

∾

Baedecker walked from the cabin to the dock where his son sat on the railing looking out over the lake. The radio had been filled with commentary about the grace of Nixon's resignation and speculation about Gerald Ford. Several reporters had commented glowingly about a statement by Ford that after all of his years in Congress, he had not made a single enemy. Baedecker understood the reporters' relief—after years of abiding with Nixon's obvious belief that he was surrounded by enemies, the change was welcome—but Baedecker remembered his father telling him that you can judge a man by his choice of enemies as well as or better than by his choice of friends, and he wondered if Ford's disclaimer was truly a recommendation of integrity.

Scott was sitting on the railing at the far end of the dock. His white T-shirt glowed slightly in the light from the waning moon. The dock itself sagged in several places and had a stretch of missing railing. Baedecker remembered the new-wood smell of it when he had stood there talking to his own father seventeen years before.

"Hello," said Baedecker.

"Hi." Scott's voice was no longer sullen, only distant.

"Let's forget that blowup, okay?"

"Okay."

Baedecker leaned against the railing and the two looked out at the lake for several minutes. Somewhere an outboard motor growled, the sound coming flat and pure across the still water, but no running lights showed. Baedecker could see lightning bugs flickering on the far shore like the flash of small arms fire.

"I visited your granddad here once not long before he died," said Baedecker. "The lake was smaller then."

"Yeah?" There was little interest in Scott's voice. He had been born eight years after Baedecker's father had died and rarely showed any curiosity about him or his grandmother. Scott's other grandparents were both alive and well in a Florida retirement community and had happily spoiled the boy since birth.

"Tomorrow I thought we'd clear out the last of the old furniture in the morning and take the afternoon off. Want to go fishing?"

"Not especially," said Scott.

Baedecker nodded, trying not to give in to his sudden flush of anger. "All right," he said. "We'll work on the driveway in the afternoon."

Scott shrugged and said, "Are you and Mom going to get divorced?"

Baedecker looked at his ten-year-old son. "No," he said. "What on earth gave you that idea?"

"You don't like each other," said Scott, still assertive but with a slight quaver in his voice.

"That's not true," said Baedecker. "Your mother and I love each other very much. Why are you saying these things, Scott?"

The boy shrugged again, the same one-shouldered little motion Baedecker had seen too many times when Scott had been hurt by a friend or had failed at some simple task. "I don't know," he said.

"You know why you said it," Baedecker said. "Tell me what you're talking about."

Scott looked away and flipped the hair out of his eyes with a snap of his head. His voice was high but not yet a whine. "You're never home."

"My job made me travel, you know that," said Baedecker. "That's going to change now."

"Yeah, sure," said Scott. "But that's not it anyway. Mom's never happy, and you don't even notice. She hates Houston, she hates the Agency, she hates your friends, and she hates my friends. She doesn't like anything but her goddamn clubs."

"Watch what you're saying, Scott."

"It's *true*."

"Watch how you say it anyway."

Scott snapped his head away and silently stared out at the lake. Baedecker took a deep breath and tried to focus on the August evening. The smell of water and fish and oil on the water reminded him of his own summers of childhood. He closed his eyes and remembered the time after the war when he was about thirteen and he and his father had gone up to Big Pine Lake in Minnesota for three weeks of hunting and fishing. Baedecker had been shooting at cans with the .22 on his Savage over-and-under, but when it came time to clean the weapon, he realized that he had left his cleaning rod at home. His father had only shaken his head in that unexpressed disappointment that was more painful than a slap to the young Baedecker, but then his father put down the fishing tackle he was working with, tied a small lead sinker to a string, dropped it through the barrel of his son's .22, and tied a cloth to the string. Baedecker was ready to clean the rifle by himself, but his father kept the other end of the string and the two had pulled the rag through, back and forth, speaking softly about nothing important. They had continued long after the barrel was clean. Baedecker remembered it all: his father's red-and-tan plaid shirt, sleeves rolled to the elbows, the mole on his father's sun-browned left arm, the soap and tobacco smell of him, the pitch of his voice—and he remembered more than that— he remembered the sad, insistent *awareness* of everything he was feeling at the moment, his inability, even then, simply to experience it. Even while cleaning the rifle in near-perfect contentment, he had been aware of that contentment, aware that someday his father would be dead and he would remember everything about the moment, even his own awareness.

"You know what I hate?" said Scott and his voice was calm.

"What do you hate?" asked Baedecker.

The boy pointed. "I hate the fucking moon."

"The moon?" said Baedecker. "Why?"

Scott turned so that he was straddling the railing. He flipped the hair out of his eyes. "When I was in first grade? I told the class during sharing time that you'd been put on the primary crew for the mission? Miss Taryton, she said that was great, but there was this kid named Michael Bizmuth? He was a shit, nobody'd play with him or anything. He came up to me during recess and said, 'Hey, your Dad's gonna die up there and they're gonna bury him and you're gonna have to look at it your whole *life*.' So I hit him in the mouth and got in trouble and Mom wouldn't let me watch TV for two weeks. But every night for a year before you went, I'd get down on my knees and pray an hour. An hour each night. My knees'd hurt but I'd stay the whole hour."

"You never told me this, Scott," said Baedecker. He wanted to say something else but could think of nothing.

Scott did not seem to be listening. He pushed the hair out of his eyes and frowned in concentration. "Sometimes I prayed that you wouldn't go, and sometimes I prayed that you wouldn't die up there . . ." Scott paused and looked right at his father. "But most of the time, you know what I prayed? I prayed that when you did die there, they'd bring you back and bury you in Houston or Washington, D.C., or somewhere so I wouldn't have to look up at night and see your grave hanging up there for the rest of my life."

"Do you ever think about suicide, Richard?" asked Dave.

It was Sunday morning. They had risen early, eaten a large breakfast, and were taking a pickup truck borrowed from Kink into the hills above Lonerock to cut firewood.

"No," said Baedecker. "At least not much."

"I do," said Dave. "Not my own, of course, but about the concept."

"What's there to think about?" said Baedecker.

Dave slowed the pickup to ford a small stream. The road up Sunshine Canyon had gone from gravel to dirt to ruts to a vague, two-pronged path between the trees. "A lot of things to think about," said Dave. "Why, when, where, and—maybe most important—how."

"I don't see why it would matter too much about the how," said Baedecker.

"But it does!" cried Dave. "One of my few heroes is J. Seltzer Sherman. You've heard of him . . ."

"No."

"Sure you have. Sherman was a proctologist in Buffalo, New York, who got deeply depressed about his life in 1965. Said he couldn't see the light at the end of the tunnel any more. Flew out to Arizona, bought a telephone pole, sharpened it on one end, took it by mule down into the Grand Canyon. Surely you remember that."

"No."

"It was in all the papers. It took him ten hours going down. He buried that pole sharp end up, spent fourteen hours coming back up the trail, took aim, and jumped off the south rim."

"And?" said Baedecker.

"Missed it by that much," said Dave, showing half an inch of space between finger and thumb.

"I suppose it's still there as a challenge," said Baedecker.

"Exactly," said Dave. "Although old J. Seltzer himself says that he might try it again someday."

"Uh-huh," said Baedecker.

"When Di was a social worker in Dallas, she used to see lots of teenage suicide attempts," said Dave. "She said that boys were a lot more efficient than girls. Their methods were more final—guns, hanging, that sort of thing. Girls tended to take overdoses of Midol after calling their boyfriends to say good-bye. Di says that a lot of kids classified as gifted kill themselves. They're almost always successful when they try, she says."

"Makes sense," said Baedecker. "Can we slow down a little? This ride's killing my kidneys."

"The two men I admired most killed themselves with guns," said Dave. "One was Ernest Hemingway. I guess the why was because he couldn't write anymore. The when was July '61. The where was the foyer of his house in Ketchum, Idaho. The how was a double-barreled Boss shotgun he'd used to shoot pigeons. He used both barrels against his forehead."

"Jesus, Dave," said Baedecker. "It's too pretty a morning for this stuff." They bounced along for a minute. The road ran along a wooded ridgeline where Baedecker could look out and see valleys ahead. "Who was the other man you admired?" he asked.

"My father," said Dave.

"I didn't know your father killed himself," said Baedecker. "I thought you told me once that he died of cancer."

"No," said Dave. "I said that cancer led to his death. So did booze. So did terminal loneliness. You want to see his ranch?"

"It's near here?" asked Baedecker.

"About six miles north," said Dave. "He and Mom got divorced back when it wasn't so fashionable. When I was a little kid, I used to take the train out from Tulsa to spend summers on his ranch. He's buried in a cemetery a couple of miles above Lonerock."

"That's why you bought a house out here," said Baedecker.

"That's why I knew the area. Di and I had been interested in ghost towns and such down in Texas and California. When we came out to Salem, I showed her this part of the state and we found the house for sale in Lonerock."

"And that's why you think about suicide?" said Baedecker. "Hemingway and your father?"

"Naw, it's just a topic of interest to me," said Dave. "Like building models or poking around in ghost towns."

"But you don't see it in relation to yourself?"

"Not at all," said Dave. "Well, wait a minute, that's not quite true. Remember on the mission, when we had that eight-minute live-broadcast spot to fill during the last EVA? I did give some thought to it then. Dave Scott'd done that Galileo experiment shtick with the rock hammer and the falcon's feather, remember? That was a hard act to follow, so I figured, what if I just say something like, 'Well, folks, one of the things we don't know much about up here on the moon is the effect of explosive decompression in hard vacuum on your basic government employee. Here goes nothing.' And then I'd pop open the urine transfer collector valve on my EMU and go squirting out of it like toothpaste out of a stomped-on tube of Colgate right there on prime-time, three-network, live American television."

"I'm glad you didn't do that," said Baedecker.

"Yeah," said Dave and drove on in thoughtful silence for a minute. "Yeah, I decided that if we couldn't think of anything else to do to fill the eight minutes, I'd go through pretty much the same song and dance and then I'd open *your* UTC valve."

"Scott?"

"Dad, is that you?"

"Yes," says Baedecker. "My God, it's hard to get hold of you. I've called five times and been put on hold each time, then I was cut off. How *are* you, Scott?"

"I'm okay, Dad," says Scott. "Where are you?"

"Right now I'm up at McChord Air Force Base in Tacoma," says Baedecker, "but I'm staying down in Salem for a few days. Scott, Dave Muldorff was killed last week."

"Dave?" says Scott. "Oh, shit, Dad. I'm really sorry. What happened?"

"Aircraft accident," says Baedecker. "Look, that's not why I called. I heard that you were sick, even in the hospital for a while. How are you feeling now?"

"I'm okay, Dad," Scott says, but Baedecker can hear the hesitation. "A little tired still. Look, Dad, how'd you know I was here?"

"Maggie Brown told me," says Baedecker.

"Maggie? Oh, yeah, Bruce probably talked to her. Dad, I'm sort of sorry about your visit to Poona last summer."

The pay phone clunks, and for a second Baedecker can hear nothing. "Scott?"

"Yeah, Dad."

"What is it? Your asthma worse again?"

Several seconds of silence pass. "Yeah. I thought the Master'd cured it last summer, but I've been having some trouble at night. That and some other stuff I picked up in India."

"Do you have your medication and inhalator?" asks Baedecker.

"No, I left that stuff back at school last year."

"Have you seen a doctor?"

"Sort of," says Scott. "Hey, Dad, are you just out here because of Dave, or what?"

"For now," says Baedecker. "I quit my . . ."

"Please deposit seventy-five cents for the past two minutes overtime," says a synthesized voice.

Baedecker fumbles for change and feeds in the quarters. "Scott?"

"What'd you say, Dad?"

"I said I quit my job last summer. I've been traveling since then."

"Jesus," says Scott, "you not working? Where have you been?"

"Here and there," says Baedecker. "I spent Thanksgiving in Arkansas working on Dad's cabin. Look, Scott, I'm going to be over in your neck of the woods tomorrow and I want to stop by and talk to you."

There is a hiss of interference and a muted buzz of voices.

"What, Scott?"

"I said . . . I said, I don't know, Dad."

"Why not?"

"Well, there's been some trouble around the ashram here . . ."

"What sort of trouble?"

"Not here exactly," Scott says quickly. "But in the area. Some of the ranchers and locals are all upset. There've been some shots fired. The Master's thinking of closing the grounds to outsiders." There is the sound of another voice speaking to Scott. "Uh, Dad, I've got to get going now . . ."

"Just a second, Scott," says Baedecker. He feels an inexplicable panic rise in him. "Look, I'm going to stop by tomorrow. Scott, I could use some help finishing the job on the cabin. That place could be very nice if I could get it fixed up this spring. Would you think about taking a few weeks off and working on it with me?"

"Dad, I don't . . ."

"Just think about it, please," says Baedecker. "We'll talk tomorrow."

"Dad, I'm afraid that . . ."

The line goes dead. Baedecker tries to call back several times and gives up.

He goes into the other room where Kitt Toliver is sitting. Toliver is in his mid-thirties, tall and solidly built. He reminds Baedecker a bit of Deke Slayton because of his crew cut and intensity of gaze. "Thanks for waiting, Sergeant," says Baedecker.

"No problem, Colonel."

"You understand that I'm not part of the official inquiry," he says. "I have no official status whatsoever. I'm just trying to find some answers because Dave was a friend of mine."

"Yessir," says Toliver. "I'll be glad to tell you everything I told Colonel Fields and the others."

"Good," says Baedecker. "You did the preflight on the Talon?"

"Yessir, twice," says Toliver. "Once in the morning and again after I got the call from Major Munsen telling me that Congressman Muldorff would be flying it."

"Did Dave do a preflight?"

"Sure did," says Toliver. "He said he had to connect with a commercial flight in Salt Lake, but he still took time to look at my PIF and did his own look-see. Did it right, too."

"And you're convinced that the aircraft was airworthy?"

"*Yessir,*" says Toliver and there is steel in his voice. "You can read my PIF 720, *sir*. They say there was a structural failure after takeoff and I can't argue with what happened, but as far as we could tell from the external inspection and cockpit check, that machine was in perfect order. The engines were new, sir. Less than twenty flying hours on them."

Baedecker nods. "Kitt, did Dave do anything or say anything during the preflight that you thought was unusual?"

Toliver frowns slightly. "During the preflight? No, sir. Oh, he told me a joke about . . . uh . . . well, about having oral relations with a chicken. But other than that, no sir."

Baedecker grins. "Did he have luggage with him?"

"Yes, sir. An Air Force flight bag. And the big package."

"Big package?" says Baedecker.

"Yessir, I told Colonel Fields and the team all about that."

"Tell me," says Baedecker.

Toliver lights a cigarette. "Not much to tell, sir. I went back to the wardroom to get a jacket, and when I came back Congressman Muldorff had loaded a box out of his car.

"How big a box?"

Toliver holds out his hands to signify a shape about two feet by two feet.

"Did it go into the storage locker?" asks Baedecker.

"No, sir," says Toliver. "When I got back to the plane, the congressman was settling in and the box was strapped in the backseat."

"Well strapped in?" asks Baedecker. "Any chance it could have come loose in flight?"

"No, sir," replies Toliver. "It was well secured. Seat belt and harness."

"Was the backseat armed?" asks Baedecker.

Toliver shakes his head. "No, no reason for it to be."

"But Dave's seat was?"

"Yes, sir," says Toliver and the silent *of course, idiot,* is all but audible.

Baedecker takes some notes on a small pad. "Did he tell you what was in the box?"

"Yessir," says Toliver and grins. "He said it was a birthday present for his son. I said, 'How old's your boy?' The congressman sort of smiled and said, 'He'll be one minute old in about two weeks.' Said his wife was due about January seven."

"Did he say what the present was?" asks Baedecker.

"No, sir. I just said, 'Congratulations, sir,' and we got him ready for takeoff."

Baedecker closes the notebook and holds out his hand. "Thanks, Kitt. I appreciate your time. If you think of anything else, you can get in touch with me through Major Munsen."

"Will do," says Toliver. He turns to go and then pauses. "Colonel, there was the one unusual thing I told the team about. I thought you'd probably heard about what the congressman'd said, but maybe you haven't yet."

"What's that?" asks Baedecker.

"Well, when I was ready to pull the ladder off, I said 'Have a good flight, sir.' I always say that. And Congressman Muldorff, he sort of grins and says, 'Thanks, Sergeant, I'm planning on it. This is going to be my last one.' I didn't think about it much at the time, but it's been bothering me since the crash. What do you think he meant, sir?"

"I'm not sure," says Baedecker.

Toliver nods but does not leave. "Yessir. Did you know him well, sir?"

Baedecker starts to reply but pauses. "I'm not sure," he says at last. "We'll see."

"Hey," said Dave, "I'm feeling a bit *beaucoup* drunk."

"Affirmative," said Baedecker.

They had cut firewood all Sunday morning in the hills above Lonerock. Baedecker had enjoyed the hard work, the sweat evaporating quickly in the high, cool air. Then they had loaded the pickup, eaten a lunch of thick corned-beef sandwiches with plenty of mustard, had a couple of beers from the cooler, driven back to Lonerock, had a beer or two on the way, unloaded the truck, stacked the wood in the shed behind Dave's house, had a beer, brought the truck back, and had a couple of beers with Kink. Then they had returned to the house to sit on the porch and drink beer.

It was about four o'clock in the afternoon when Dave made his announcement. "Jesus, drunk from beer," he said. "That's high school stuff, Richard."

"Affirmative," said Baedecker.

"Hey, you know what we forgot to do? We forgot to tell you to have me remind you to remind me to take you up to see my dad's ranch."

"Yes," said Baedecker. "Remind me to remind you to do that tomorrow."

"Nuts with that," said Dave. "Let's do it now."

Baedecker followed him down to the jeep and watched as Dave tossed things into the backseat. Baedecker eased himself into the passenger seat, taking care not to spill his beer. "What're we, moving up there or what?"

"Have dinner there," said Dave, setting the last of the cargo in place and clambering into the left seat. "Ignition sequence countdown."

"Check," said Baedecker, swiveling to look at the heaped backseat.

"Cooler?"

"Check."

"Beer?"

"Check."

"Barbecue grill?"

"Check."

"Hamburgers?"

"Check."

"Buns?"

"Check . . . no, wait a minute. Red light on the . . . no, there they are, under the charcoal. Check."

"Charcoal?"

"Check."

"Lighter fluid?"

"Check."

"Flashlight?"

"Check."

"Winchester?"

"Check. What the hell do we need that for?"

"Rattlesnakes," said Dave. "Lots of rattlers up there. Lots of rattlers down here, come to think of it. Been real warm this fall. Still out."

"Oh."

"S-IVB LH$_2$ precool and fast fill, S-IC LOX tank replenish, glycol fuel jacket topping."

"Check," said Baedecker. He pulled a tab on a beer and handed it to Dave.

"We have ignition," said Dave and started the jeep, backed out of the drive, turned in a cloud of dust, and accelerated north down Main Street at high speed. They sped past the rusted gas pump. "Houston, we have cleared the tower," drawled Dave.

"Roger," said Baedecker.

Dave swung onto a narrow road leading northeast into a canyon. The jeep bounced along the ruts for a quarter of a mile and then emerged onto smoother ground. "Roll and pitch program completed," said Dave. "Stand by for Mode One Charlie."

"Affirmative," said Baedecker. They rattled over a cattleguard, and some charcoal bounced out of the bag and disappeared into the dust cloud behind them. "Inboard cut-off," said Baedecker. "Stand by for staging."

The jeep's right wheel jolted over a large rock, Dave's AIR FORCE 1½ cap flew off his head and ended up in the backseat under the small charcoal grill. "Tower jettison," said Dave.

"Roger."

They rounded a hairpin curve and began climbing a steep grade. Dave shifted down into second gear and then into first. "Be advised, Houston," he said, "we are GO for staging."

They leveled off on a ridge far above the valley. The jeep trail led along a narrow strip with boulders to the left and a sheer dropoff to the right. "Affirmative," said Baedecker. "G.Y.S.A."

"K.Y.A.G.," said Dave.

It was more than six miles. The road ran along treeless ridgetops, dropped into a shadowed canyon, and climbed out across a flat expanse of high desert so that it was half an hour before Dave turned onto a graveled county road and the ranch finally came into view. They drove across a broken cattleguard and down a lane overgrown with sagebrush before pulling to a stop in front of an abandoned wood-frame building. Baedecker could see a barn and a huddle of smaller outbuildings beyond.

They walked through the brittle grass to the house with Baedecker watching for snakes every inch of the way. The ranch house showed signs of long abandonment—windows gone, plaster fallen in most of the rooms, banister missing on the stairway, a rear porch collapsed on one side—but it was also easy to see that it had been built with care and precision. The porch continued around three sides of the building and there the hand-carved gingerbread remained, the interior woodwork had been meticulously crafted, and the large stones in the central fireplace obviously had been set by hand.

"How long has it been empty?" asked Baedecker as they stepped through the litter of plaster in the kitchen.

"Pop died in '56," said Dave. "A couple of families owned it for a while right after that, but they never had a chance of making a go of it. It's damn hard to make a living around here on a small spread. Pop could never decide if he wanted to be a farmer or a rancher. He didn't have enough water to make a go of the farm, and never had enough pasture to do justice to ranching."

"How old were you when your father died?"

Dave took a long drink of beer and stood looking out the kitchen window. "Seventeen," he said. "That was the first summer I didn't take the train out and stay here. I had a girlfriend and a summer job in Tulsa. Important things to do." He tossed the beer can in the sink. "Come on out back. I want to show you something."

They walked past the barn and smaller buildings. As with the main house, the barn had been built to last. Baedecker read the place of manufacture on the large hinges—Lebanon, Pennsylvania, Patented 1906. They crossed a section of field and Baedecker was just beginning to think about snakes again when Dave stopped, pointed to a large, circular depression in the pasture, and said, "Coot Lake."

It took Baedecker a minute to see it. The mound they were standing on would have been part of the east bank, the rotted wood underfoot a trough to the south part of the irrigation ditch that fed water to the pond, and the washed-out gully to the north the dam itself. Fifty yards across the sunken area was the other dike with half a dozen dusty cottonwoods hanging over the weed-strewn slope that had been the west bank.

"Richard," said Dave, "do you ever wonder how much of your life you've spent trying to please the dead?"

Baedecker sipped his beer and thought about this as Dave sat on a rock and stripped a long strand of grass for chewing.

"I think we underestimate how much of our own lives we devote to trying to meet the expectations of the dead," continued Dave. "We don't even think about it, we just do." He pointed to a cluster of weeds and bushes twenty yards across the low meadow. "That's where we had our old raft tied. Sort of a float. The water was only about seven or eight feet deep there, but I wasn't allowed to swim on the south side of it because it was filled with reeds and water plants so your feet'd get all tangled up. Pop'd rip 'em out every year and they'd be back every summer. He lost one of his old hunting dogs out there before I was born. Then one summer—it must've been during my third summer out here, I was about nine, I think—my dog Blackie got all tangled up in the stuff when he was swimming out to join me on the raft."

Dave paused and chewed on his stalk of grass. The sun was almost setting, and the shadows from the cottonwoods stretched far out over the dead pond. "Blackie was mostly a Lab," he said. "Pop gave him to me when I was born, and for some reason that was very important to me. Maybe that's why he stayed *my* dog even though I only saw him summers after I was six and Ma and I moved away. We didn't have room for him in Tulsa. Still, it's like he waited all year for those ten weeks each summer. I don't know why it was so important that he and I were the same age, that he'd been born almost the same time I was, but it was.

"So this one day I'd finished my morning chores and was lying on the raft on my stomach, almost asleep, when I hear Blackie swimming out to the raft, then suddenly the noise is gone and I look up and there's no sign of him, just ripples. I knew right away what must've happened, the reeds, and I dove off after him without even thinking. I heard Pop shout at me from near the barn when I came up, but I dove down again, three, maybe four times, pushing through the weeds, getting stuck down there, kicking loose and trying again. You couldn't see anything, and the mud alone would grab you up to ankle and try to keep you down there. The last time I came up I had the stinking water up my nose and I was covered with mud and I could see Pop yelling at me from the shore over there, but I went down again and just when I was out of air and the weeds were all wrapped around me and I was sure there wasn't any use of trying more, I *felt* Blackie, right on the bottom, not even struggling any more, and I didn't even go back up for air, I just kept pulling at weeds and kicking at the mud, still holding on to him because I knew I wouldn't find him again if I let go for a second. I ran out of air. I remember swallowing some of that stinking water, but goddamn it, I wasn't going back up without my dog. And then somehow I got both of us free and was pulling him into the shallow end there and Pop was dragging us both on shore and fussing over me and yelling at me at the same time, and I was coughing water and crying and trying to get Blackie to breathe. I was sure he was drowned, he was so limp and heavy he *felt* full of water. He felt dead. But I kept pushing at his ribs while I was throwing up water myself and I'll be damned if that dog didn't all of a sudden cough up about a gallon or so of pond water and start whimpering and breathing again."

Dave took the stalk of his grass out of his mouth and tossed it away. "I guess that's about as happy as I've ever been," said Dave. "Pop said he was mad at me for jumping in—he threatened to wallop me if I ever went swimming there again—but I knew that he was proud. Once when we went into Condon I was sitting in the truck and I heard him telling a couple of his friends about it, and I knew he was proud of me. But I don't think that was why I felt so happy about it. You know, Richard, I used to think about it when I was flying medevac in 'Nam and knew it was something more than just pleasing Pop. I hated being there in Vietnam. I was scared shitless almost all of the time and I knew it was going to kick the hell out of my career when they found out what I was doing. I hated the weather, the war, the bugs, *everything*. And I was happy. I thought about it then and I realized that it just made me damn *happy* to be saving things, saving people. It's like everything in the universe was conspiring to drag those poor sons of bitches down, drag them under, and I'd come along in that fucking chopper and grab on and we'd just *refuse* to let them go under."

They walked back past the house, set up the grill next to the jeep, and cooked their dinner. The evening chill struck the instant the direct sunlight was gone. Baedecker could see two volcanic peaks catching the last light far to the north and east. They waited until the charcoal glowed white, singed the outside of their hamburger patties, added thick slices of onion, and ate ravenously, each opening a fresh beer with dinner.

"Did you ever consider buying the ranch and rebuilding it?" asked Baedecker.

Dave shook his head. "Too many ghosts."

"Still, you came back to live nearby."

"Yeah."

"I have a friend," said Baedecker, "who said that there might be places of power. She thinks we could do worse than to spend our lives searching for them. What do you think?"

"Places of power," said Dave. "Like Miz Callahan's magnetic lines of force, huh?"

Baedecker nodded. The idea did sound absurd.

"I think your friend is right," said Dave. He pulled another beer from the cooler and shook the ice off it. "But I bet it's more complicated than that. There're places of power—yeah—no doubt about that. But it's like we were talking about last night. You have to help *make* them. You have to be in the right place at the right time and *know* it."

"How do you know it?" asked Baedecker.

"By dreaming about it but not thinking about it," Dave said.

Baedecker pulled the tab on another beer and put his feet up on the dash. The house was only a silhouette against a fading sky now. He zipped up his coat. "By dreaming about it but not thinking about it," he said.

"Right. Have you ever practiced any Zen meditation?"

"No," said Baedecker.

"I did for a few years," said Dave. "The idea is to get rid of all the thinking so there's nothing between you and *the thing*. By not looking you're supposed to *see* clearly."

"Did it work?"

"Nope," said Dave, "not for me. I'd sit there chanting my mantra or whatever and think about every damned thing in the universe. Half the time I'd have a hard-on from erotic daydreams. But I did find something that worked."

"What's that?"

"Our training for the mission," said Dave. "The endless simulations worked pretty much the way meditation was supposed to and didn't."

Baedecker shook his head. "I don't agree. That was just the opposite. The whole goddamn thing, when it finally happened, was just like the *simulations*. I didn't experience *any* of it because of all the preprogramming the simulations had stuck in me."

"Yeah," Dave said and took the last bite of his hamburger, "that's the way I used to feel. Then I realized that that wasn't the case at all. What we did was turn those two days on the moon into a sacrament."

"A sacrament?" Baedecker tugged his cap down low and frowned. "A sacrament?"

"Joan was Catholic, wasn't she?" asked Dave. "I remember you used to go to Mass with her occasionally in Houston."

"Yes."

"Well, you know what I mean then, although it's not as well done these days as when I was a kid and used to go with Ma. The Latin helped."

"Helped what?"

"Helped the ritual," said Dave. "Just like the mission, the simulations helped. The more ritualized it is, the less thought gets in the way. You remember the first thing Buzz Aldrin did when they had a few minutes of personal time after *Apollo 11* landed?"

"Celebrated communion," said Baedecker. "He brought the wine and stuff in his personal preference kit. He was . . . what? . . . Presbyterian?"

"It doesn't matter," said Dave. "But what Buzz didn't realize is that the mission itself was already the ritual, the sacrament was already in place, just waiting for someone to celebrate it."

"How so?" said Baedecker but already the truth of what Dave was saying had struck him on some internal level.

"I saw the photograph you left there," Dave said. "The picture of you and Joan and Scott. By the seismic experiment package."

Baedecker said nothing. He remembered kneeling there in the lunar dusk before the snapshot, the layers of pressurized moonsuit stiff and clumsy around him, the stark sunlight a benediction.

"I left an old belt buckle of my father's," said Dave. "I set it right next to the laser reflecting mirrors."

"You did?" said Baedecker, truly surprised. "When?"

"When you were getting the Rover ready for the trip to Rill 2 on the first EVA," said Dave. "Hell, I'd be amazed if every one of the twelve of us who walked up there didn't do something like that."

"I never thought of that," said Baedecker.

"The rest of it was all preparation, just clearing away inconsequentials. Even places of power are useless unless you're prepared to *bring* something to them. And I don't mean just the things we brought—they're to the real sacrament what the lump of bread is to the Eucharist. Then, if you come away the same person you were, you know it wasn't really a place of power."

"That's it then, that's the problem," said Baedecker. "Nothing changed."

Dave laughed and grasped Baedecker's upper arm through the thick jacket. "Are you serious, Richard?" he said softly. "Do you remember who you *were* and have any idea who you are now?"

Baedecker shook his head.

Dave said nothing. He jumped out to dump the last of the embers, bury them carefully in the sand, and stow the gear in the back of the jeep. He came around to

Baedecker's side. "Move over," he said. "You're driving. I'm too drunk."

Baedecker, who had matched Dave beer for beer through the afternoon and evening, nodded and shifted to the driver's side.

The jeep's headlights picked out sagebrush and scrub pines as they drove slowly back. Clouds obscured the stars and the full moon would not rise for hours yet.

"Tom Gavin will never understand," said Dave. "The poor son of a bitch is so desperate for the sacramental element that he'll never find it. I've seen him on TV talking about being born again in lunar orbit. Shee-it. He talks about it and talks about it and doesn't have the least fucking idea of what being born again means. *You* were the one, Richard. I saw it."

Baedecker shook his head slowly. "No," he said. "I didn't feel it. I don't know what any of it meant."

"You think a newborn knows what it all means?" asked Dave. "It just happens and then you go about the mean business of being alive. Awareness comes later, if it comes at all."

They emerged from the canyon and headed across the last ridge before the switchbacks. Baedecker shifted into first gear and crept along the narrow jeep trail as slowly as the vehicle would allow. He felt sober, but he kept seeing rattlesnakes wiggling at the edge of the headlight beams.

"Being born again doesn't mean that you've arrived somewhere," said Dave. "It means you're ready to start the trip. The pilgrimage to more places of power, the doomed quest to keep the people and things you love from being caught by the weeds and dragged under. Stop here, please."

Baedecker stopped and watched while Dave leaned over, was quietly sick over the side of the jeep, and sat up to clean his mouth with water from an old canteen under the seat. Dave slumped back down, burped once, and pulled his cap low over his eyes. "Thus endeth the gospel according to Saint David. Drive on."

Baedecker slowed the jeep on the ridge before the switchbacks leading to the last canyon. Lonerock was visible two miles below, a few lights glowing between dark trees.

"Flick your headlights a few times," Dave said.

Baedecker did.

"Okay, drive on."

"Does Miz Callahan think the aliens drive UFOs with headlights?" said Baedecker.

Dave shrugged without lifting his cap. "Maybe they take EVAs."

Baedecker shifted down, missed his shift, ground gears, shifted again.

"Mmm, smooth," said Dave. "What did you think of my book idea?"

"*Frontiers?*" said Baedecker. "I liked it."

"You think it's a worthwhile project?"

"Definitely."

"Good," said Dave. "I want you to help me write it."

"Why, for chrissakes? You're doing fine."

"No, I'm not," said Dave. "I can't write the parts about the people for shit. Even if my work on the Hill gave me time to travel and do the research—which it won't—I couldn't write that part."

"The part about the Russian, Belyayev, was great," said Baedecker.

"I picked up all that crap when I was over there for the ASTP," said Dave. "The most recent parts are ten years old. The important part of the book will be what the four American guys are up to. And I don't want any of that *Reader's Digest* pap either—'Lieutenant Colonel Brick Masterson has since left the Agency to pursue a successful career combining his Austin beer distributorship and his part ownership in a string of lesbian mud-wrestlers.' Uh-uh, Richard, I want to know what these suckers are *feeling*. I want to know what they don't tell their wives in the middle of the night when they can't sleep. I want to know what moves them right down to the seat of their meat. I don't care how inarticulate we poor ex–jet jockeys are, I expect you to get in there with your little epistemological proctoscope . . . damn, that's good . . . I can't be too drunk if I can say that, huh? I want you to get in there and find out what we need to know about our-selves, okay, Richard?"

"I don't think so . . ." began Baedecker.

"Shut up, please," said Dave. "Think about it. Let me know by, say, right after the baby's born. We're coming back out to Salem and Lonerock a few weeks after that. Think about it until then. That's an order, Baedecker."

"Yassuh."

"Jesus," said Dave. "You ran over that poor snake back there and it wasn't even a rattler."

Lying on the sleeper sofa in Dave's study, Baedecker watches rectangles of light from passing cars move across the bookshelves and he thinks about things. He remembers Dave's comment, "I guess that's about as happy as I've ever been," and he tries to remember a comparable point in time for himself. Dozens of memories come to mind—from child-hood, with Joan in the early years, the night Scott was born—but, as important and satisfying as each one is, it is ulti-mately rejected. Then he recalls a single, simple event that he has carried with him over the years like a well-worn snap-shot, bringing it out in times of loneliness and displace-ment.

It was a minor thing. A few minutes. He was flying back to Houston from the Cape some time during the last months of training. He was alone in his T-38—just as Dave had been a week ago—when, on an impulse, he overflew the sprawling subdivision in which he lived. Baedecker re-members the perfect timing of the emergence of his wife and seven-year-old child, the clarity with which he saw them from an altitude of eight hundred feet at five hundred miles per hour. He remembers the sunlight dancing on the Plexiglas canopy as he pulled the T-38 into a victory roll, and then another, celebrating the sky, the day, the coming mission, and his love for the two small figures seen so far below.

Someone in the household coughs loudly and Baedecker starts from the edge of sleep, conditioned by years of listening for his son's labored breathing in the night. He watches a rectangle of white light moving across the dark line of books and tries to relax.

Eventually he sleeps. And the dream comes.

It is one of only two or three dreams that Baedecker has that he knows is not a dream. It is a memory. He has had it for years. When he comes awake, gasping and clutching at the headboard, he knows immediately that it has been *the dream*. And, sitting up in the darkness of Dave's study, feeling the sweat already drying on his face and body, he knows that this time—for the first time—the dream has been different.

Until now the dream had always been the same. It is August of 1962 and he is taking off from Whiting Field near Pensacola, Florida. It is a sickeningly hot day, muggy beyond belief, and it is a relief when he is sealed into the cockpit of the F-104 Starfighter and begins breathing cool oxygen. He is not involved in flight-testing. There is nothing untested about this F-104; the chrome-alloyed aircraft is all stock-block equipment, scheduled to join an Air Force squadron at Homestead Air Force Base south of Miami. Baedecker has spent two weeks ferrying it cross-country on an "interservice courtesy call," his first political job for NASA, giving rides to Navy and Army VIPs curious about the new first-line fighter. A retired admiral here at Pensacola—a hulk of a man too fat for his flight suit and almost too fat for the rear seat—had patted Baedecker on the back after his joyride and proclaimed, "Absolutely first-rate flying machine." Like most pilots who had flown the F-104, Baedecker did not totally agree. The aircraft was impressive for its power and brute force—indeed, it was used out at Edwards as a proficiency trainer for the X-15 that Baedecker had flown for the first time earlier that summer—but it was not a first-rate flying machine; it was an engine with an ejection seat attached, two seats in this case, and two stubby wings offering about as much lift surface as fins on an arrow.

Sitting in the cockpit on this particularly hot August day, Baedecker is glad that the tour is over; he has a ten-minute solo flight to Homestead and then he will be heading back to California by C-130 transport. He does not envy the Air Force pilots who will be flying the F-104 on a daily basis.

Heat waves rise in rippling billows and distort the runway and line of mangrove trees beyond. Baedecker taxis into position, radios the tower for clearance, and sets the brakes on while he brings the engine up to full power. He can feel that everything is copacetic even before the dials register their proper readings. The machine strains at its mechanical tether like a half-mad thoroughbred pushing at the starting gate.

Baedecker radios the tower again and releases the brakes. The machine leaps forward, slamming him back into his seat while the runway centerline blurs together under the nose of the aircraft. Still, the monster uses an ungainly amount of runway before it reaches rotation speed. Baedecker lifts the nose sharply onto an invisible line twenty degrees above the advancing wall of trees, feels the aircraft solidly off the ground, pulls the gear up, and kicks in the afterburner.

Things happen simultaneously then. Power drops to ten percent of what is needed, Baedecker's board goes red, he knows without thinking that the flanges around the afterburner have popped open and that thrust is spilling uselessly in a blazing fountain behind him, and the stall buzzer screams in panic. Baedecker instinctively throws the nose down, sees he has neither time nor altitude for this, and pulls back sharply on the stick at precisely the same instant the first branches snap off under the belly of the dying F-104. Baedecker hunches in a near fetal position, pulls the D-ring, sees the canopy fly off in a strangely silent act of levitation and waits a full eternity of 1.75 seconds before the charge in his ejection seat fires and he is following the canopy up but too late, the plane is striking heavy branches now, is shearing off entire trunks of pine trees, and the cartwheeling tail section slams into the base of the rising ejection seat, not a solid hit but a foul tip that sends the seat spinning ass-over-tail, Baedecker flying out of it upside down, his spring-loaded chute deploying toward the foliage forty feet below, both of his ankles already broken by the impact, his head ringing. Then the main chute is opening, Baedecker's feet tug toward the sky like a child swinging too high, the impact is too strong, breaking his left shoulder upon opening and his right shoulder after swinging him almost completely around, the main chute side-slipping below him now, an inverted, orange umbrella trying to close in on itself, no reason for it not to close and drop him to the flame and flying carnage below, but it does not and he swings forward in another full arc, his broken feet almost striking the upper branches and flowers of flaming aviation fuel this time, his lungs already breathing in the unbreathable vapors and heat. And then, for two endless seconds, he is hanging under the silk canopy the way God and man had meant, drifting forward like a tourist under a para-glide chute being towed by a KrisKraft, but it is not water under him but half an acre of jagged stumps and branches, ten thousand *punji* stakes created in three seconds of violent aircraft impact, and flame as far as he can see, flame rising around him and above him, already licking razor-tongues at his suit and shroudlines and pain-dead feet hanging at impossible angles beneath him, and in two more seconds he will *land* in that conflagration of sharpened stakes and flesh-melting fuel fire, he will *land* on those broken ankles, bones splintering, body and parachute sputtering into flame in the heat, skin broiling like a mantis boiling and popping through its own shell in the flames.

And Baedecker awakes.

He awakes—as he always does—reaching above him for shroudguides and finding headboard and wall. He awakens—as he always does—silent and sweating and remembering each detail of what he had not been able to remember in the pain-wracked hours of consciousness after the crash or in the pain-measured ten weeks of slow recovery in the hospitals after that . . . or even in the three years following that August day until that first night when he had had *the dream* for the first time and came awake, just like this, reaching and sweating and remembering perfectly what could not be remembered.

But this time the dream had been different. Baedecker swings his feet to the floor, rests his head in shaky hands, and tries to find the difference.

And does.

The board is red, the stall buzzer is screaming, Baedecker feels the aircraft wallow belly-first toward the trees. There is no reprieve from this heavy pull, the earth is calling him down and under. But Baedecker pulls the stick back into his stomach, hunches and pulls the D-ring, knowing there is not enough time, seeing shattered branches fly up with the lifting canopy, but then—in slow motion—the familiar salvation as the ejection seat rises from the coffin of disintegrating fuselage, rises as slowly as a Victorian elevator in no particular rush to leave, and as his helmeted head passes the line of sight of the deflection mirror set above the cockpit instruments he sees himself for a second there, visor reflecting mirror reflecting visor, and rising farther he sees what he has forgotten, sees what he did not think about in the exigency of the survival instant—which, of course, he had always known, had never really forgotten only abandoned in the reflexive instinct of survival—he sees Scott in the backseat; Scott along for the ride today and still trusting, Scott, about seven years old in crew cut and his Cape Canaveral T-shirt, and his eyes in the mirror, still trusting, waiting for his father to *do something* but no fear there yet, only trust, and then Baedecker is up and out and safe—but such painful safety!—and screaming Scott's name even as he drifts slowly down to the churning waves of fire.

Baedecker stands and takes two steps to the window. He sets his cheek and forehead against the coolness of the rain-streaked glass and is surprised to feel tears streaking his cheek.

In the deep hours of the morning, Baedecker sets his face against the cold glass and knows exactly now why Dave had died.

Baedecker leaves before dawn so as to be in Tacoma by 7:30 A.M. Some of the members of the Crash Board are not happy to be there but by 8:15 A.M. Baedecker is sitting and listening to the six of them, speaking briefly when they are finished, and by 9:00 A.M. he is on his way south and east, crossing into Oregon above the Dalles. It is a gray, windy day with the smell of snow in the air, and although he scans the northern bluffs for some glimpse of the Stonehenge monument, he sees nothing.

It is a little after 1:00 P.M. when Baedecker looks down at Lonerock from the hilltop to the west of it. There are patches of snow on the steep incline, and he keeps the rented Toyota in second gear. The town seems even emptier than usual as he drives down the short main street. Solly's mobile home is closed up for the winter; Miz Callahan's school has heavy curtains pulled across the windows; and pockets of snow on the side streets have not been disturbed. Baedecker parks in front of the picket fence and lets himself into the house with the keys Di had loaned him two days earlier. The rooms are tidy, still smelling faintly of the ham they had heated up there after the funeral. Baedecker goes into the small writing room at the back of the house, gathers up the stack of manuscript and notes, packs them in a box that had held nine-by-twelve envelopes, and carries it out to the car.

Baedecker walks the hundred yards to the schoolhouse. There is no response either to his knock or to calls into the speaking tube. He backs away to look up at the belfry, but the windows are gray slabs reflecting the low clouds. The garden still holds brittle, broken cornstalks and a decomposing scarecrow dressed in a tuxedo.

He drives the short distance to Kink Weltner's ranch. He has parked the Toyota and is about to go up to the house when he catches sight of the Huey tied down in the field beyond the barn. The presence of the helicopter shakes him in some obscure way; he had forgotten that Dave had flown it there. Baedecker walks to it, runs his hand along the tie-down wires, and peers into the cockpit. The windshield is frosted, but he can see the Air National Guard helmet propped on the back of the seat.

"Hullo, Dick."

Baedecker turns to see Kink Weltner walking toward him. Despite the cold, Kink is wearing only a dark suit, the left sleeve neatly pinned back.

"Hello, Kink. Where are you headed all dressed up?"

"Headed down to Las Vegas for a few days to get rid of this cabin fever," says Kink. "Fucking weather gets tiresome."

"I'm sorry we didn't get to talk after the funeral," Baedecker says. "I had a few things to ask you."

Kink blows his nose with a red kerchief and slips it back into the breast pocket of his suit. "Yeah, well, I had a lot of chores to finish up. Goddamn, I wish that hadna happened to Dave."

"Me too," says Baedecker. He taps the side of the fuse-lage. "I'm surprised this is still here."

Kink nods. "Yeah. I've called 'em twice about it. Talked to Chico both times because nobody wants to take respon-sibility for a machine that's not supposeta exist. They're waiting for a patch of good weather, I guess. I'm not sure if nobody wants to drive this far or if they're afraid to fly it over the mountains. It's all fueled and ready to go when they want it. I'd fly it back myself, but it's sort of hard to handle a Huey with one arm."

"I never mastered it with two arms," says Baedecker. "Kink, you talked to Dave when he got here, didn't you?"

"Just said hello. I was surprised to see him right after Christmas an' all. I knew he and Diane was comin' up some-time after the baby was born, but I didn't expect him before that."

"Did you see him again before he left?"

"Nah, the weather'd already closed in when he landed, an' he said he had the Cherokee stored over to the house. He said he'd be back in a couple of weeks to get the Huey if nobody else picked it up before then."

"Did he say why he'd come out to Lonerock?"

Kink shakes his head and then stops as if he had re-membered something. "I did ask him how his Christmas was and he said fine but that he left one of the presents out here. That didn't make a whole lot of sense since they hadn't been out here—far as I know—since you was here with 'em back before Halloween."

"Thanks, Kink," says Baedecker as they walk back to-ward the house. "Can I use your phone?"

"Sure, just slam the door shut on your way out. Don't bother to lock it," says Kink as he climbs into his pickup. "See ya around, Dick."

"So long, Kink." Baedecker goes into the house and tries calling Diane. There is no answer. The afternoon light makes it seem like late evening, as if there is no energy left in the universe.

Baedecker drives back through Lonerock, passes the closed-up house, and turns right toward the school. He sees the curtains still closed, makes a U-turn in the snow out front, and is heading back toward Main Street when he sees the thin figure with its shock of white hair come around the building from the field behind. He stops and is out of the car jogging uphill toward her, thinking that in her long, dark coat, Miz Callahan resembles the scarecrow in her frozen garden.

"Mister Baedecker," she says and takes his hand in both of hers. "I was just getting my automobile ready for the trip. I have decided to drive to the coast and spend a few weeks with Mr. Callahan's sister's daughter."

"I'm glad I caught you," says Baedecker.

"Isn't it terrible about David?" she says and her hands clench with emotion.

"Yes, it is," says Baedecker and watches the large Labrador—Sable—come bounding around the side of the building.

And then there they are—four of them—barely big enough to walk, and Baedecker is on one knee, petting them, rubbing behind their ears, and he does not even need the old woman's next words to confirm what he knows.

"So terribly sad," she says, "and David had come so far to pick out just the right one for his little boy."

∾

Baedecker calls from Condon. Diane answers on the third ring.

"I'm sorry I wasn't there for breakfast this morning," he says. "I decided to go talk to Bill and the rest of them and get a preliminary report."

"Tell me," she says.

Baedecker hesitates a second. "We can talk tonight when there's more time, Di. I hate to go into it all over the phone."

"Please, Richard. I want to know the important parts now." Her voice is gentle but firm.

"All right," says Baedecker. "First, the starboard engine had shut down completely just like they thought, but they're pretty sure now that Dave got it restarted just a few seconds before the crash. The hydraulics problem was a result of a stress, structural failure . . . no one could have caught it . . . but even that seems to have stabilized at about thirty-five percent assist. I don't know if the gear would've gone down, but Dave was planning to deal with that when the time came.

"Second, he couldn't see a damn thing, Di. He said on the tape that he could see lights when he came out of the clouds at sixty-two hundred, but that was for about two seconds. The mountain ridge he hit was in the center of a squall, heavy rain and zero visibility down to the deck for at least eight miles to the north.

"Third—and this is the important part, Di—the Portland Center controller handling the emergency told Dave that there were ridges up to five thousand feet there. The ridge he hit was at fifty-six hundred; it ran all the way east to Mt. St. Helens. I'd bet anything that Dave had fifty-five hundred as his punch-out altitude. Maybe higher, but the thing is, he'd just got the beast back in the corral—he was on top of the hydraulics problem, he was out of the ice, he'd just got the engine relit, and he was less than four minutes out from Portland. He was doing the best he could, Di, and he would've had it if it hadn't been for that ridge."

Baedecker pauses, seeing . . . no, *feeling* those last few seconds. Fighting a stick gone as heavy as a crowbar in a box of rocks, pedals trying to kick his knees back into his belly, no time to look out the rain-streaked canopy, watching the tumbling ball, checking the airspeed indicator and altimeter while handling the throttle and waiting for *just* the right second to try again on the engine restart. And all the time, above the grind and storm, aware of the small noises from the backseat.

Baedecker, knowing in his gut and soul that Dave was no fool, could see him being the first to snort derision at the sentimental suggestion of a pilot spending two seconds too long in a dying airplane because of a dog, but Baedecker could remember the tone of Dave's voice three months earlier, saying, "I can't remember ever being any happier," and in that tone he hears the possibility of a pause of one second or two where no pause is permissible, sees that final straw added to the already significant weight of a test-pilot's determination to save a salvageable aircraft.

". . . appreciate your doing it and telling me; Richard," Diane is saying. "I never doubted, really. There were just so many little questions I couldn't answer."

"Di," says Baedecker, "I know why Dave came out to Lonerock. He had a special present he wanted to give you and the baby." Baedecker pauses. "It wasn't . . . ah . . . wasn't ready when he was here," he lies. "But I'm going to bring it in tonight if that's all right." Baedecker glances at the Toyota where the puppy is making scrabbling sounds in the box in the backseat next to the box holding Dave's manuscript.

"Yes," says Diane and takes a breath. "Richard, you know the sonogram said we're going to have a boy."

"Dave told me," says Baedecker.

"Did he tell you the names we've been considering?" she asks.

"No," says Baedecker. "I don't think so."

"We both agreed that Richard is nice," Diane says. "Especially if you think so too."

"Yes," says Baedecker. "I think so too."

∾

Baedecker drives south on County Road 218, past Mayville and Fossil, crossing the John Day River just past Clarno. The road to the ashram-ranch is wide and graveled, running north from the paved county road. Baedecker drives three miles along it, thinking about Scott. He remembers the drive back to Houston that Watergate summer so long ago, Baedecker wanting to talk more to his son, unable to, feeling—in spite of everything—that Scott also wanted to talk, to change things.

There is a roadblock where the road narrows between two ditches several feet deep. A blue, airport-type limousine is parked diagonally, blocking the road. To the left is a small building with a sloping roof, brown sides, and a single window. It is meant to be a guardhouse, but it makes Baedecker think of the covered school-bus stops that sit by the side of the road in Oregon. He stops and gets out of the Toyota. The puppy is sleeping in the backseat.

"Yessir, may we help you?" says one of the three men who emerge from the shack.

"I'd like to get by," says Baedecker.

"Sorry, sir, no one beyond this point," says the man. Two of the three are large and bearded, but the speaker is the larger of the two, at least six-two. He is in his early thirties, and wears a red shirt under his goosedown vest. There is a medallion on the outside of the vest, and Baedecker can see a photograph of the guru there.

"This is the road to the ashram, isn't it?" asks Baedecker.

"Yeah, but it's closed," says the second man. He wears a dark plaid shirt and Baedecker notices a cheap security-service badge pinned to it.

"The ashram's closed?"

"The road's closed," says the big man, and Baedecker hears the change in his tone. There will be no more "sirs." "Now turn your vehicle around," he says.

"I'm here to see my son," says Baedecker. "I talked to him yesterday on the phone. He's been sick, and I want to see him and talk awhile. I'll leave my car here if you want to drive me in."

The big man shakes his head and takes three steps forward and in that brief motion comprised of swagger and expectation, Baedecker knows that he will not be allowed to pass. He has never met the man, but he knows him well; he has seen his type in bars from San Diego to Djakarta. He has known several like him—far too many—in the Marines. For a while, as a young man, Baedecker had considered becoming him.

Baedecker glances at the third man—little more than a boy really—thin and pockmarked. He is wearing only a red cotton shirt and is shivering in the cold breeze coming out of the north.

"Nope," says the big man and comes closer, too close for psychological comfort and knowing it. "Turn it around, Pop."

"I'd like to see my son," says Baedecker. "If you have a phone in there, let's call someone."

Baedecker makes a move to step around him, but the big man stops him with a thrust of three fingers, hard, in Baedecker's chest. "I said turn it around," he says. "Back it up to that wide spot down there, and turn it around."

Baedecker feels something sharp and cold and familiar well up inside of him, but he stops and backs up two steps. The big man is all shoulders, chest, and arms, broad neck under a wild beard, but his belly is big and soft even under the vest. Baedecker glances down at his own stomach and shakes his head. "Let's try it again," Baedecker says. "This road is still a county road, I asked in Condon. Now if you have a phone or radio, let's talk to somebody who can think and make grown-up decisions. If not, drive me into the ashram and we'll find someone."

"Uh-uh," says the big man and shows his teeth. The other one with a beard takes a step closer to his friend while the youngest one moves back into the doorway of the guardhouse. "Move *now*, Pops," says the big man. The same three fingers hit Baedecker's chest again. Baedecker takes another step back.

The man shows more teeth, pleased by Baedecker's retreat, steps forward again, and brings his whole palm forward in what will be a straight-armed shove. Baedecker goes with it, takes the offered arm, brings it around and back and up, not quite hard enough to break bone but quickly enough to let softer things rip inside. The big man yells and pulls, Baedecker steps with it, watching the second man, and lifts higher, only his right hand busy now, leaning on the big man a bit as the other goes cheek down onto the hood of the Toyota.

The man with the badge yells something as he moves in, both arms held out wide like a wrestler beginning a match. Baedecker hits him three times with his left hand, the first two blows fast and useless with no extension and little weight behind them, the third solid and satisfying, landing deep in the other's throat. The man backs away with both hands up to his neck, catches the heels of his cowboy boots in the gravel at the edge of the road, and sits down heavily in the deep ditch.

The big man is still puffing and sliding along the hood, kicking now and trying to get his arm back. Baedecker is sliding with him, ready to get both hands into play, when he sees the youngest man come out of the shack with a twelve-gauge pump shotgun.

Ten feet separate Baedecker and the boy. The kid is holding the weapon somewhere between port arms and the way Scott used to hold a tennis racket when he was little before Baedecker taught him better. Baedecker did not see the boy pump the first shell into the chamber, and he feels strongly that it was not done before the boy emerged from the shack. Baedecker hesitates a second, but already the cold, sharp-edged anger he had felt a second earlier is fading to be replaced by the hot flush of anger at himself. He spins the big man around and propels him back toward the boy hard enough that the man stumbles forward, forgets that his right arm will no longer work to break his fall, and goes face first into the gravel and mud at the feet of the boy with the gun.

The kid is shouting something, waving the shotgun like a magic wand, but Baedecker ignores him, gets back into the Toyota, backs it down the gravel road, turns it around where the road is wide enough, and drives back the way he came.

∾

Baedecker had listened to the tape alone, in a small room at McChord Air Force Base. There was not much on it. The young controller's voice was professionally brisk, but there was the sharp edge of fear just under the surface. Dave's voice was in the mode that Baedecker had always thought of as his in-flight voice; speech lazy and unhurried, the Oklahoma accent out of his boyhood quite pronounced.

Six minutes before the crash. The controller: Ah, Roger that, Delta Eagle two-seven-niner, ah, engine shutdown. Do you wish to declare an emergency at this time? Over.

Dave: Negative that, Portland Center. I'll bring it back your way and we'll do some thinking about it before we mess up all the airline schedules. Over.

Two minutes before the crash. The controller: Ah, affirmative on clearance for runway three-seven, Delta Eagle two-seven-niner. Ah, are you . . . do you have confirmation that landing gear is operational at this time? Over.

Dave: Negative, Portland Center. No green light at this time, but no red light either. Over.

Controller: Roger, Delta Eagle two-seven-niner. Do you have procedure if you receive no down and locked indication? Over.

Dave: Affirmative on that, Portland Center.

Controller: Very good, Delta Eagle two-seven-niner. What is procedure? Over.

Dave: Procedure as follows, Portland. G.Y.S.A.K.Y.A.G. Over.

Controller: Say again, please, Delta Eagle two-seven-niner. We did not copy that. Over.

Dave: Negative, Portland. Busy right now. Over.

Controller: Roger, Delta Eagle. Please be advised . . . ah . . . be advised that your current altitude reads seven-five-two-zero and that there are ridges in your flight path up to five thousand feet. Repeat, ridges to five triple zero. Over.

Dave: Roger. Dropping through seven thousand feet now. Copy bumps ahead to five triple zero feet. Thank you, PC.

Sixteen seconds before the crash. Dave: Coming out of clouds at sixty-two hundred now, Portland Center. See some lights to the right. Okay, now . . .

Then nothing.

Baedecker listened to the tape three times and on the third he heard the final "Okay, now . . ." differently. There was triumph under the drawl. Something had begun to go right for Dave in those last few seconds.

The voice recording reminded Baedecker of another time, another flight. He thought of the date on the old newspaper the morning of Dave's funeral—October 21, 1971. It could have been. It would have been in late October, not long before the mission.

They were flying home to Houston from the Cape in a T-38, Baedecker in the front seat. They were over the Gulf, but the only sea visible was the sea of clouds three thousand feet below them, glowing milk white from horizon to horizon in the light from the not-quite-full moon. They had been flying in silence for some time when Dave came on the intercom. "We're going up *there* in a couple of months, amigo."

"Not unless you get the Pings high-gate sequence right in the simulator next time," said Baedecker.

"We're *going*," said Dave. "And things ain't never gonna be the same."

"Why not?" asked Baedecker, glancing up. The light prismed on the canopy, distorting the moon's shape.

"Because, Richard," came the slow reply, "*we're* not going to be the same. People who tred on sacred ground come away changed, my friend."

"Sacred ground?" said Baedecker. "What the hell are we talking about?"

"Trust me," said Dave.

Baedecker had been silent a minute, letting the steady pulse of the engines and oxygen flow surround him. Then he had said, "I do trust you."

"Good," said Dave. Then, "Give me the stick, please."

"You've got it."

Dave pitched the T-38 into a steep climb, adding throttle as they climbed, until Baedecker was on his back staring straight at the moon as they clawed skyward. The Marius Hills region would be perfectly illuminated in the lunar sunrise. Dave held the climb until the straining aircraft was twelve miles high—six thousand feet above its official ceiling capability—and then, instead of leveling off, he pulled back on the stick until they hung there vertically, unable to gain more altitude, unwilling to fall, the T-38 hanging by its nose between space and the sea of clouds 55,000 feet below, gravity not defied but nullified, all forces in the universe equalized and harmonized. It could not last. An instant before the aircraft stalled into a spin, Dave kicked off with hard left rudder and the little trainer shuddered once like an animal pulled back on its leash, and then they tumbled over into a forty-five mile fall that would end in Houston and home.

∾

Baedecker reaches Lonerock a half an hour before sunset, but the gray day is already drained of light. He drives to Kink's ranch, parks the Toyota, and carries the barking puppy into the house. He feeds it milk, sets the box by the still-warm stove in the kitchen, and is satisfied that the house will stay warm enough for the dog until he returns.

Outside, Baedecker pulls off the tie-down wires, gets the clipboard from the cockpit, and does an external pre-flight inspection on the Huey as the cold wind blows in from the north. It takes him three times longer than when he and Dave had done it, and when he is down on his knees trying to find the fuel-drain valve, his left hand begins to throb with cold and pain. Three fingers there are swollen to twice their normal size. Baedecker sits on the frozen ground and wonders if any of the fingers are broken. He remembers once when he was about twelve, coming home to the apartment on Kildare Street after a schoolyard fight. His father had looked at his bruised hand, shaken his head, and said only, "If you absolutely have to fight and if you insist on hitting someone in the face, don't hit them with an empty hand."

Finished with the exterior checks, Baedecker begins to enter by the left door, stops, and goes around to the right side. He steps up on the skid, reaches across to grab the far edge of the seat, and pulls himself in. It is cold in the helicopter. The machine has a heater and defrosters, but he cannot waste battery power on them before the turbine starts. If it starts.

Baedecker straps himself in, releases the inertial reel lock so that he can lean forward, and does the check of console switches and circuit breakers. When he is finished, he leans back and his head taps the flight helmet set atop the shoulder harness bracket. He pulls the helmet on, setting the earphones in place. He has no intention of using the radio, but the headset warms his ears.

Baedecker sits back in the heavy chair, wiggles the cyclic stick between his legs, and grips the collective pitch lever with his left hand. The hand will not quite close on it, but he decides that the grip is adequate. He practices using his finger and thumb to manage the throttle.

He lets out a deep breath. The truth is, he realizes, that he has not flown a powered aircraft in more than three years and he is glad that telemetry is not sending his heart rate back to a bank of doctors; they would diagnose tachycardia after one look at the monitors. Baedecker opens the throttle with his throbbing left hand and squeezes the trigger switch with his good finger. There is a loud whine, the turbine fires up with a loud hiss like the pilot light on a huge hot-water heater catching, and the exhaust-gas temperature gauge shoots into the red while the rotors begin to turn. In five seconds the turbine is humming smoothly, and the rotors are only a blur and a half-sensed pressure overhead.

"Okay, good," Baedecker mutters into his dead microphone. "Now what?" He turns on the heating fan and defroster, waits thirty seconds for the windshield to clear, and pulls up lightly on the collective control stick. Even that slight pull—it reminds Baedecker of the finicky parking brake on Joan's old Volvo—increases the pitch angle sufficiently to raise the Huey six feet off its skids.

A hover would be nice, Baedecker thinks. He gives it more throttle to compensate for the increased pitch angle, his left hand protesting with pain at being asked to do two things at once. He slacks off at ten feet, planning to hold the Huey there for a minute, his windshield on level with the open hayloft door of Kink's barn fifty feet away. Immediately the torque tries to spin the machine counterclockwise on its axis. Baedecker gives it some right pedal, overcompensates, and causes the tail rotor to push the Huey around the opposite direction. He brings the rotation to a stop 180 degrees from where he started, but in the meantime the reduced pitch angle has dropped the ship five feet, now eight, and Baedecker is tugging the cyclic stick back too far, leveling off three inches above the ground only to hop fifteen feet into the air as the controls respond.

Baedecker lets it sink back to ten feet, feverishly work-ing throttle, cyclic, pitch control, and pedals in an effort to achieve a simple hover. Just as he thinks he has achieved it, he glances left and sees that he is sideslipping smoothly, as if on frictionless glass rails ten feet above the cold ground, headed directly and implacably for Kink's barn.

He kicks the pedal hard enough to bring the heavy machine around in a yawing, wallowing turn, tucks the stick forward and then quickly back, and flares the Huey into an inelegant, molar-grinding excuse for a landing that sends it skipping twice in four-foot hops before it settles shakily on its skids in the center of the barnyard.

Baedecker mops the back of his hand across his brow and feels sweat running down his neck and ears. He releases the stick and collective and sits back, the harness moving with him, holding him snugly. The rotors continue their senseless spin.

"Okay," Baedecker says softly, "I could use some help here, amigo."

Try holding your breath, dummy. It is Dave's voice over the inactive intercom, through Baedecker's silent earphones. It is Dave's voice in his mind.

Baedecker relaxes, lets the air go out of him in a long exhalation, does not inhale, and lets his mind wander while his *body* remembers those many hours of instruction seven-teen years earlier. Still easily holding his breath, he lifts the pitch lever, pulls back gently on the cyclic stick, adjusts the throttle and pedals as he rises, and hovers effortlessly ten feet above the ground. He carefully takes a breath. The hover is solid, easily held, as simple as sitting in a small boat on a smooth sea. Baedecker swings the Huey around, pitches the nose down to pick up speed, and begins a long, climbing turn that will bring him back across Lonerock at about two thousand feet.

It is not dark yet, the sun is still up, actually becoming visible below the clouds for the first time all day, but

Baedecker fumbles on the collective lever for the switch and then trips the landing light on and off several times. Below him, the dark cube of the cupola atop the school remains dark. Baedecker levels off at twenty-five hundred feet and aims the nose of the Huey west-southwest.

At one hundred knots, the trip will take Baedecker less than fifteen minutes. The setting sun glares directly into his eyes. He clicks down the helmet-visor, but the view is too darkened that way, so he slides it back up and squints. Mount Hood gathers a gold corona in the west, and even the underbelly of the clouds glow now in rose and yellow hues as if releasing the colors they had spent the week absorbing.

Baedecker drops to three hundred feet as the John Day River falls behind. He smiles. He can almost hear Dave's voice, "You're doing the oldest kind of IFR flying, kid. 'I Follow Roads.'" He almost misses the ashram access road because he is watching a string of cattle to the south, but then he swings to the right in a comfortable bank, feeling the machine working with him now and he with it, glancing sideways almost straight down out his right window at sagebrush and snowbanks and low pines casting long shadows across a dry creek bed.

He passes over the roadblock at a steady 150 feet, seeing two men emerge and resisting the impulse to swing around and make a pass at 120 knots with skids eight feet above the ground. He has not come for that.

Two miles farther he crosses a rise, sees the ashram-ranch, and realizes his error.

It is a goddamn city. The road becomes asphalt through the long valley, and hundreds of permanent tents sit in rank and file along one side while buildings and parking lots line the other. There is a gigantic structure at the junction of two streets, a veritable town hall, rows of buses sit parked behind it, and scores of people are in the streets. Baedecker makes two passes over the main thoroughfare at a hundred feet, but the noise of his rotors only brings more people out of buildings and tents. The muddy streets fill with red-shirted ants. Baedecker half expects the flash of small-arms fire to begin at any moment. He holds the Huey in an indecisive hover above what might be the main hall—a long building with permanent roof and foundations and canvas sides—and thinks, *What now?*

Relax.

Baedecker does. He rotates the helicopter to watch the sun disappear behind the hills. The sudden twilight is somehow more gentle than the gray day had been. Looking quickly at the mile-long complex below, he picks a flat-topped hill near an unfinished wooden building on the southeast corner of town. The hill and the lone structure are off the main lanes, separated by several hundred yards from the rest of the maze.

He circles once and begins descending carefully. He is still thirty feet above the rough hilltop when he catches a glimpse of red out of the corner of his eye. Five people have emerged from the unfinished building, but Baedecker has eyes only for the one in front. The figure is still sixty yards away, half-hidden in the shadow of the building, but Baedecker knows instantly that it is Scott—Scott thinner than he has ever seen him, Scott without the beard he had worn in India and with hair shorter than Baedecker has seen it in a decade, but Scott nonetheless.

The landing is smooth, the Huey settling onto its skids without a jar. Baedecker has to concentrate on the console for a minute, leaving the rotors turning in a hot whisper but making sure the machine will stay earthbound for a few minutes. When he looks out and down, he sees four of the figures still motionless in shadow, but Scott is moving quickly uphill now, breaking into a slow jog up the rough and rocky hillside.

Baedecker kicks open the door, leaves his helmet in the seat, and moves out from under the rotors in an instinctive crouch. At the edge of the hill he stands upright for a minute, hands on his hips, watching. Then, moving quickly but surely on treacherous footing, Baedecker starts down so as to meet his son halfway.

Part Five

Bear Butte

Baedecker ran. He ran hard, the sweat stinging his eyes, his sides aching, his heart pounding, and his panting an audible thing. But he continued to run. The last mile of the four should have been the easiest, but it was by far the hardest. Their running path took them through the dunes and back onto the beach for the last three-quarters of a mile, and it was here that Scott chose to pick up the pace. Baedecker fell five yards behind his son but refused to allow the distance to widen farther.

As their Cocoa Beach motel came into sight, Baedecker felt the effort draining the last reservoirs of his energy, felt his straining heart and lungs demanding a lessening of the pace, and it was then that he accelerated, kicking hard to close the gap between the thin redhead and himself. Scott glanced to his right as his father moved alongside, grinned at Baedecker, and broke into a faster sprint that brought him off the hard, wet shore onto the soft sand of the beach. Baedecker kept up with his son for another fifty paces and then fell back, making the last hundred yards to the low cement wall of the motel in a staggering lope.

Scott was bending and doing stretching exercises as Baedecker collapsed to the sand and set his back against the cement blocks. He dropped his head to his arms and panted.

"Best run yet," said Scott after a minute.

"Hnrh," agreed Baedecker.

"Feels good, doesn't it, Dad?"

"Hnnh."

"I'm going to go in for a swim. Want to come with me?"

Baedecker shook his head. "Go ahead," he panted. "I'll stay here and throw up."

"Okay," said Scott. "See you in a while."

Baedecker watched his son jog across the beach to the water. The Florida sun was very bright, the sand as dazzlingly white as lunar dust at midday. Baedecker was pleased that Scott felt so well. Eight months earlier they had seriously considered another hospital stay for him, but the asthma medicine had quickly begun to help, the dysentery had resolved itself after several weeks of rest, and while Baedecker had been losing weight during the months of diet and work in Arkansas, Scott had steadily put on pounds so that he no longer looked like a redheaded concentration camp survivor. Baedecker squinted at the ocean where his son was swimming with strong strokes. After a minute, Baedecker rose with a slight groan and jogged slowly down the beach to join him.

It was evening when Baedecker and Scott drove north along U.S. 1 to the Space Center. Baedecker glanced at the new developments and shopping centers along the highway and recalled the raw look of the place in the mid-sixties.

The huge Vehicle Assembly Building was visible even before they turned onto the NASA Causeway.

"Does it all look the same?" asked Baedecker. Scott had been a fanatic about visiting the Cape. He had worn the same blue KSC T-shirt through all of his sixth and seventh summers. Joan used to have to wash it at night to get it away from the boy.

"I guess so," said Scott.

Baedecker pointed to the gigantic structure to the northeast. "Remember when I brought you out here to watch the VAB being constructed?"

Scott frowned. "Not really. When was that?"

"Mmm. 1965," said Baedecker. "I was already working for NASA, but it was the summer before I was chosen for flight status with the Fifth Group of astronauts. Remember?"

Scott looked at his father and grinned. "Dad, I was one year old."

Baedecker smiled at himself. "Come to think of it, I do remember you on my shoulders for most of that tour."

They were stopped at two checkpoints before they reached the KSC industrial area. The spaceport, usually wide open to tour groups and the curious, had been closed up tight for the imminent Department of Defense launch. Baedecker showed the IDs and passes Tucker Wilson had provided, and they were quickly waved through.

They drove slowly past the sprawling Headquarters Building and turned off the parkway into the lot of the Manned Spacecraft Operations Building. The huge, three-story complex looked as ugly and functional as it had during Baedecker's stay there during the training and prelaunch phases of his *Apollo* mission. Ribbons of glass on the west side caught the last gleam of the sunset as they parked the car.

"This is sort of a big deal, isn't it?" said Scott as they walked toward the main entrance. "Thanksgiving dinner with the astronauts and all."

"It's not really Thanksgiving dinner," said Baedecker. "The members of the crew had dinner with their families earlier. This is just coffee and pie . . . sort of a traditional gathering the night before a flight."

"Isn't it unusual for NASA to fly on a holiday like this?" asked Scott.

"Not really," said Baedecker as they stopped to show their identification to a guard just inside the door. An Air Force aide led the way up a narrow staircase. "*Apollo 8* flew around the moon over Christmas," Baedecker continued. "Besides, the DoD set the date for this launch because of the satellite deployment windows."

"And besides that," said Scott, "Thanksgiving is today and the launch is tomorrow."

"Right," said Baedecker. There were two more checkpoints before they were shown into a small waiting room outside of the crew dining quarters. Baedecker looked around at the green sofa, uncomfortable chairs, and low coffee table covered with magazines, and was pleased for some reason that the private quarters area had maintained the same late-sixties feel to it that he had known two decades earlier.

The door opened and a group of businessmen emerged from the dining room. They were guided by a young Air Force major. One of the men wearing a dark suit and carrying an attaché case stopped when he saw Baedecker. "Dick," he said, "goddammit, it's true then that Rockwell got you."

Baedecker stood up and shook hands. "Not true, Cole," he said. "Just stopping by for a social call. Cole, I don't know if you've met my son. Scott, this is Cole Prescott, my boss back in St. Louis."

"We met years ago," said Prescott as he shook hands with Scott. "At the company picnic right after Dick started working for the company. You were about eleven, I think."

"I remember the three-legged race," said Scott. "Nice to see you again, Mr. Prescott."

Prescott turned to Baedecker. "So what have you been up to, Dick? We haven't heard from you in . . . what? Six months?"

"Seven," said Baedecker. "Scott and I spent last spring and summer fixing up an old cabin in Arkansas."

"Arkansas?" said Prescott and winked at Scott. "What the hell is in Arkansas?"

"Not much," said Baedecker.

"Hey," said Prescott. "I heard tell that you were out talking to people at North American. *¿Es verdad?*"

"Just talking."

"Yeah, that's what they all say," said Prescott. "But look, Dick, if you haven't signed with anybody . . ." He paused and looked around. The others had left. Through the slightly opened door to the dining room came laughter and the clink of dishes. "Cavenaugh's retiring this January, Dick."

"Yes?"

"Yes." Prescott leaned over as if about to whisper. "I'll be filling his chair when he goes. That leaves room on the second level, Dick. If you had any thoughts about coming back in, now'd be the time."

"Thanks, Cole," said Baedecker, "but I have a job right now. Well, not exactly a job, but a project that will be keeping me pretty busy for the next few months."

"What's that?"

"I'm finishing work on a book that David Muldorff began a couple of years ago," said Baedecker. "The part remaining involves quite a bit of traveling and interviewing. In fact, I have to fly to Austin on Monday to start work on it."

"A book," said Prescott. "Got an advance on it yet?"

"A modest one," said Baedecker. "Most of the royalties will go to Dave's wife Diane and their little boy, but we're using the advance to cover some of the expenses."

Prescott nodded and glanced at his watch. "Okay," he said, "but keep in mind what I said. It was nice seeing you again. Dick, Scott."

"You too," said Baedecker.

Prescott paused by the door. "It was a damn shame about Muldorff."

"Yes," said Baedecker. "It was."

Prescott departed just as a NASA PR man in shirtsleeves and a black tie came to the open door of the dining room. "Colonel Baedecker?"

"Yes."

"The crew's just about ready for dessert. Would you and your son like to come in now?"

∾

There were five astronauts and seven other men at the long table. Tucker Wilson made the introductions. Besides Tucker, Baedecker knew Fred Hagen, the copilot on this mission, and Donald Gilroth, one of the NASA administrators present. Gilroth had put on considerable weight and corporate status since Baedecker had last seen him.

The three other astronauts, two mission specialists and a payload specialist, were also Air Force. Tucker was the only full-time NASA pilot involved in this mission, and despite recent efforts to include women and minorities in the space effort, this all-military flight was a step back to the WASP-male tradition. Conners and Miller, the mission specialists, were quiet and serious but the youngest crewmember, a blond youngster named Holmquist, had a high, infectious laugh that made Baedecker like him immediately.

There were a few minutes of obligatory discussion of the old *Apollo* days as the pie and coffee arrived, and then Baedecker turned the conversation to the upcoming mission. "Fred, you've been waiting quite a while for this, haven't you?"

Hagen nodded. He was a few years younger than Baedecker, but his crew cut had gone completely gray so that he looked a bit like Archibald Cox. Baedecker realized with a start that most of the shuttle pilots were approaching his age. Space, once a frontier so frightening that the experts had worried that the youngest, boldest, and strongest of the nation's test pilots might not withstand its rigors, had now become the property of men with bifocals and prostate worries.

"I've been waiting since the MOL folded," Hagen said. "With a little luck, I'll help to fly up its successor as part of the space station."

"What was the MOL?" asked Scott.

"Manned Orbiting Laboratory," said Holmquist. The blond mission specialist was only two or three years older than Scott. "It was one of the Air Force's pet projects, like the X-20 Dyna Soar, that never got off the ground. Before our time, Scott."

"Yeah," said Tucker and lobbed a wadded-up napkin at the younger astronaut, "back in pretransistor days."

"I suppose you could look at the shuttle orbiter as a bigger, better Dyna Soar," said Baedecker and even as he said it, he saw the word in his mind as "dinosaur." He had flown powerless lifting bodies at Edwards in the mid-sixties as part of NASA's contribution to the defunct Air Force program.

"Sure," said Hagen, "and Spacelab's sort of an updated, international version of the MOL . . . a couple of decades late. And Spacelab itself has become a sort of a test project for the space station components we'll start ferrying up in a couple of years."

"You're not carrying Spacelab on this mission though, are you?" asked Scott.

There was a silence in which several men shook their heads. The DoD payload was out-of-bounds for this conversation, and Scott knew it.

"Is weather still a worry?" asked Baedecker. Thunderstorms across the Gulf had been building up by midmorning for days.

"Little bit," said Tucker. "Last word from meteorology was go, but they didn't sound too sincere. What the hell. The windows are brief, but we've got them for three days in a row. You two going to be in the VIP stands tomorrow, Dick?"

"Wouldn't miss it," said Baedecker.

"What do you think of all this, Scott?" asked Hagen. The Air Force colonel was looking at the redhead with friendly interest.

Scott started to shrug and stopped himself. He glanced at his father and then looked right at Hagen. "To be honest, sir, I find it very interesting and a little sad."

"Sad?" It was Miller, one of the mission specialists, a dark, intense man who reminded Baedecker a bit of Gus Grissom. "Why sad?"

Scott opened the fingers of his left hand and took a breath. "You're not broadcasting the launch tomorrow, right? Not allowing reporters on the Cape? Not announcing any part of the mission progress except the absolute minimum. Not even telling the public when exactly the launch is going to take place, right?"

"That's correct," said Captain Conners. There was the clipped quality of the Air Force Academy in his voice. "That seems the least we can do for national security in what has to be a classified mission." Conners glanced at the others as a waiter picked up the pie plates and refilled coffee cups. Holmquist and Tucker were smiling as they looked at Scott. The others were just looking.

Scott did shrug, but he grinned before he spoke and Baedecker felt that some of the fierce, unrelenting *intensity* that he had felt emanating from his son for years had lessened somewhat in recent weeks. "I understand that," said Scott, "but I remember the days when Dad flew . . . when the press knew about it every time a crew member farted . . . excuse me, but that's what it was like. For the families, too. At least during the missions. What I'm trying to say is I just remember how *open* it was and how we kept comparing that to the secrecy of the Russians' program. We were *proud* to let it all hang out for everybody to see. Now, I guess, it makes me a little sad that we're getting to be more like the Soviets."

Miller opened his mouth to speak, but Holmquist's laugh cut him off. "*Too* true," said Holmquist. "But I tell you, my man, we've got a long way to go before we're like the Russians. Did you see the reporters down at Melbourne Airport taking notes as all the defense contractors' baggage came in? That's all they needed to let them know what kind of payload's flying. Have you seen the *Washington Post* or *New York Times* today?"

Scott shook his head.

The young payload specialist went on to describe the articles appearing in press and TV, never confirming or denying their veracity but elaborating in humorous detail the frustrated efforts of Air Force press officers to stick their fingers in a dike that had become a sieve. One of the NASA administrators told a story about the press boats that were being chased from the area when all the while Soviet intelligence-gathering ships were deployed just beyond the restricted zone.

Fred Hagen offered a tale about his X-15 days when an enterprising reporter disguised himself as a visiting Brazilian Air Force officer to get an exclusive. Baedecker told about his trip to the Soviet Union prior to the *Apollo-Soyuz Test Project* and how, late one wintry night, Dave Muldorff had walked up to a lampshade in their living quarters in Star City and suggested loudly that a nightcap sure would hit the spot, but they were all out of the complimentary booze their hosts had provided. Ten minutes later a Russian orderly had shown up with bottles of vodka, Scotch, and champagne.

There was more laughter as the dinner group broke up into small conversations and several of the administrators took their leave. Holmquist and Tucker were talking to Scott when Don Gilroth walked around the table and put his hand on Baedecker's shoulder. "Dick, could we take a minute? Outside here?"

Baedecker followed the other man into the empty waiting room. Gilroth closed the door and hitched his belt up over his ample stomach. "Dick, I didn't know if we'd get a chance to talk tomorrow, so I thought I'd get to you tonight."

"Talk about what?" said Baedecker.

"About coming back to work for NASA," said the administrator.

Baedecker blinked in surprise. The idea had never occurred to him.

"I talked to Cole Prescott and Weitzel and some of the others, and I hear you're considering some other things, but I wanted you to know that NASA's interested too," said Gilroth. "I know we'll never be competitive with private industry, but these are exciting times around here. We're trying to rebuild the whole program."

"Don," said Baedecker, "I'll be fifty-four years old before long."

"Yeah, and I'll be fifty-nine in August," said Gilroth. "Don't know if you've noticed, Dick, but the shop isn't being run by teenagers these days."

Baedecker shook his head. "I've been out of touch for too many years . . ."

Gilroth shrugged. "We're not talking about going back onto active flight status, you know," he said. "Though God knows with all the work comin' up in the next couple of years, anything's possible. But Harry could sure use someone with the experience over in the Astronaut Office. Between the leftovers and the trainees, we've got close to seventy astros running around here. Not like the old days when Deke and Al had to keep an eye on just a dozen or so of you hell-raisers."

"Don," said Baedecker, "I've just begun work on a book that Dave Muldorff didn't have time to finish and . . ."

"Yep, know all about that," said Gilroth and tapped Baedecker on the upper arm. "There's no rush on this, Dick. Think it over. Get back to me anytime this year. Oh . . . and Dick . . . Dave Muldorff must've thought it was a good idea, you're coming back. I got a letter from him last November where he mentioned it. Sort of confirmed my own thinking about trying to get some of the old pros back."

Baedecker was digesting this when Tucker and Scott came through the door.

"There you are," said Tucker. "We were planning to take a little ride up to the pad. Want to come along?"

"Yes," said Baedecker. He turned to the departing Gilroth. "Don, thanks for the idea. I'll get back to you."

"Good enough," said the administrator and gave the three of them a two-fingered salute.

∽

Tucker drove them in a green NASA-owned Plymouth for the eight miles up the four-laned Kennedy Parkway to Pad 39-A. The VAB, illuminated from above and below by floodlights, loomed impossibly large as they approached. Baedecker looked up at an American flag painted on one corner of the south face and realized that the flag alone was big enough to play a football game on. Beyond the assembly building, the space vehicle became visible, enclosed in a protective web of gantries. Searchlights cut beams through the humid air, lights glowed throughout the latticework of pipes and girders, and Baedecker thought that the whole thing looked like a gigantic oil derrick filling some interplanetary supertanker.

They passed through security checkpoints, and Tucker drove up the long ramp to the base of the Service and Access Tower. Another guard approached them, saw Tucker, saluted, and stepped back into the shadows. Baedecker and

Scott got out of the car and stood looking up at the machine poised above them.

To Baedecker's eye the shuttle—or the SSTS, Space Shuttle Transportation System as the engineers liked to call the entire package of orbiter, external tank, and solid rocket boosters—looked jerry-rigged and awkward, an unlikely coupling of species neither aircraft nor rocket, creating a sort of interim evolutionary form. Baedecker realized, not for the first time, that he was looking at a space-faring platypus. Now it struck him with full force how much the space shuttle—that much-vaunted symbol of America's technology—already had become an assemblage of aging, almost obsolete equipment. Like the older command pilots who flew them, the surviving shuttles carried the dreams of the 1960s and the technology of the 1970s into the unknowns of the 1990s, substituting wisdom from painfully learned lessons for the unlimited energy of youth.

Baedecker liked the look of the rust-colored external fuel tank. It made sense not to burn precious fuel lifting tons of paint into the fringes of space only to have the expendable, thin-skinned tank burn up seconds later, but the effect of such common sense was to make the shuttle look more workaday, almost battered, a good, used pickup truck rather than the classy showroom models flown in earlier space programs. Despite—or perhaps because of—this new-paint-over-the-old-rust feel to the entire ungainly machine, Baedecker realized that if he were still a flying member of the team, he would love the shuttle with the kind of pure and unreasonable passion men usually reserved for wives or lovers.

As if reading Baedecker's mind, Tucker said, "She's beautiful, isn't she?"

"She is that," agreed Baedecker. Without thinking about it, he let his gaze wander to the aft field joint of the right-hand solid rocket booster. But if there were O-ring demons lurking there, waiting to destroy ship and crew by raking sudden tongues of flame across the hydrogen-primed bomb of the external tank, there was no sign of them today. But then, Baedecker realized, there had been no sign of them to the *Challenger* crew either.

Around them, men in white went about their business with the insect-intensity of technicians everywhere. Tucker pulled three yellow hard hats from the back seat of the Plymouth and tossed one to Baedecker and another to Scott. They moved closer and craned their necks to look up again.

"She's something, isn't she," said Tucker.

"Quite a sight," murmured Baedecker.

"Frozen energy," Scott said to himself.

"What's that?" asked Tucker.

"When I was in India," Scott said, speaking so softly that his voice was barely audible above background work noises and the soft chug of a nearby compressor, "I guess, for some reason, I started to think of things . . . to really *see* things sometimes . . . in terms of energy. People, plants, everything. Used to be, I'd look at a tree and see branches and leaves. Now I tend to see sunlight molded into matter." Scott hesitated, self-conscious. "Anyway, that's what this is . . . just a huge fountain of frozen kinetic energy, waiting to thaw into motion."

"Yeah," said Tucker. "There's energy waiting there, all right. Or at least there will be when the tanks are topped off in the morning. About seven million pounds of thrust when those two strap-on roman candles get lit." He looked at the two of them. "Want to go up? I promised you a look-see, Dick."

"I'll wait here," said Scott. "See you later, Dad."

Baedecker and Tucker rode up in the pad elevator and stepped out into the white room. Half a dozen Rockwell International technicians in white coveralls, white overboots, and white caps were working in the brilliantly illuminated space.

"This access is a little easier than mounting the *Saturn V*," said Baedecker.

"Had that little boom arm, didn't it?" said Tucker.

"Three hundred and twenty feet up," said Baedecker, "I used to lurch across that damn number nine swing arm in full pressure suit, carrying that little portable ventilator that weighed about half a ton, and hold my breath until I got into the white room. I was sure I was the only *Apollo* hero who was fast developing a fear of heights."

"We're a little closer to the ground here," said Tucker. "Evening, Wendell." Tucker greeted a technician with earphones connected to a cable jacked into the hull of the shuttle.

"Evening, Colonel. Going inside?"

"For a few minutes," said Tucker. "I want to show this old *Apollo* fossil what a real spacecraft looks like."

"All right, but wait just a second, please," said the technician. "Bolton's on the flight deck running the communications check. He'll be coming down in just a second."

Baedecker ran his hand across the skin of the shuttle. The white tiles were cool to the touch. Close up, the spacecraft showed signs of wear—subtle discolorations between the tiles, flakes of black paint missing, a well-used polish to the fittings on the open entry hatch. The used pickup had been washed and waxed, but it was still a used pickup.

A technician emerged from the round hatch and Wendell said, "Okay, it's all yours."

Baedecker followed Tucker in, wondering as he did so what had become of Gunter Wendt. The old-hand *Mercury* and *Gemini* crews had held Wendt, the first white-room "pad führer," in such esteem that they had coerced North American Rockwell into hiring him away from McDonnell when the *Apollo* program came in.

"Watch your head, Dick," said Tucker.

They crossed the middeck and climbed to the forward seats on the flight deck. To someone trained in *Apollo*, the shuttle interior seemed huge. There were two additional couches set behind the pilot's and copilot's seats, and a ladder had led to a single seat on the lower deck.

"Who gets the lonesome spot down there?" asked Baedecker.

"That's Holmquist and he's sick about it," said Tucker as he slid into the horizontal command pilot's couch. "He's done everything but bribe one of the other two for a window seat."

Baedecker edged carefully into the right seat. In his center seat in the *Apollo* Command Module, clumsiness would just have gotten him stuck. A slip now would drop him five or six feet to the windows and instrument bay below him at the rear of the flight deck. He pulled the shoulder harnesses on out of habit, secured the lap belt, but ignored the wide crotch strap.

Several trouble lights hung from hooks, throwing a bright light on the instruments and shadows into the corners. Tucker clicked one of these lamps off and activated several cockpit switches, bathing them both in a red-and-green glow. A cathode ray display directly in front of Baedecker lit up and began running through a litany of meaningless data. The quickly changing lines of data reminded Baedecker of the PanAm passenger shuttle with its flashing cockpit graphics in *2001: A Space Odyssey*. Dave had insisted they see that movie a dozen times during the winter of 1968. They had been putting in fourteen-hour shifts supporting *Apollo 8*, and then in the evenings they would drive pell-mell across Houston to watch Keir Dullea, Gary Lockwood, HAL, and the austro-lopithecines perform to the sounds of Bach and Strauss and Ligeti. Dave Muldorff had been quite irritated one night when Baedecker had fallen asleep at the beginning of the fourth reel.

"Like it?" asked Tucker.

Baedecker ran his gaze over the console. He set his hand lightly on the rotational hand controller. "Very elegant," he said and meant it.

Tucker tapped at the computer keys on the low console that separated them. New information filled all three of the cathode displays. "He's right, you know," Tucker said.

"Who's right?"

"Your boy." Tucker ran a hand over his face as if he were very tired. "It *is* sad."

Baedecker looked at him. Tucker Wilson had flown forty missions over Vietnam and shot down three enemy MiGs in a war almost devoid of aces. Wilson was a career Air Force man, only transferred to duty with NASA.

"I don't mean it's sad that the services are finally flying missions," Tucker said. "Shit, the Russians have had a pure military presence up there in the second *Salyut* station for . . . what? Ten years at least. But it's still sad what's happening here."

"How so?"

"It's just different, Dick," said Tucker. "Back when you were flying and I was on backup, things were simpler. We knew where we were going."

"To the moon," said Baedecker.

"Yeah. Maybe the race wasn't all that friendly, but somehow it was more . . . shit, I don't know . . . more *pure*. Now even the size of the damn bay doors back there was dictated by the DoD."

"You're just carrying an intelligence-gathering satellite back there," said Baedecker. "Not a bomb." He remembered his father standing on a darkened dock in Arkansas thirty-one years earlier, searching the skies for *Sputnik* and saying, "If they can send up something that size, they can put up a bigger one with bombs aboard, can't they?"

"No, it's not a bomb," agreed Tucker, "and now that Reagan is history, chances are we won't be spending the next twenty years ferrying up SDI parts either."

Baedecker nodded and glanced toward the windows, hoping to catch a glimpse of the stars, but the special glass was shielded for the launch. "You didn't think it would work?" he asked, referring to the Strategic Defense Initiative—what the press still called, with some derision, Star Wars.

"No, I think it would," said Tucker. "But even if the country could afford it—which we can't—a lot of us feel it's too risky. I know that if the Russians started orbiting X-ray lasers and a bunch of other hardware that *our* technology couldn't match in twenty years . . . or defend against . . . most of the brass I know would be calling for a preemptive attack on whatever they put up."

"F-16-launched antisatellite stuff?" asked Baedecker.

"Yeah," said Tucker. "But say we didn't get everything. Or they replaced it faster than we could shoot it down. What would *you* advise the president to do, Dick?"

Baedecker glanced at his friend. He knew that Tucker was a personal friend of the man who had just won the election to replace Ronald Reagan. "Threaten surgical strikes of their launch sites," said Baedecker. The entire shuttle stack seemed to sway slightly in the evening breeze, making Baedecker feel a hint of nausea.

"Threaten?" said Tucker with a grim smile.

Baedecker, knowing from his childhood in Chicago as well as from his years in the Marines just how useless threats can be, said, "All right, *launch* surgical strikes against Baikonur and their other launch facilities."

"Yeah," said Tucker and there was a long silence broken only by the creaks and groans of the 150-foot external tank lashed to the orbiter's belly. Tucker flicked off the cathode displays. "I love the Cape, Dick," he said softly. "I don't want it blown to shit in a game of tit for tat."

In the sudden darkness, Baedecker breathed in the smell of ozone, lubricant, and plastic polymers; the cockpit smell that had replaced ozone, leather, and sweat. "Well," he said, "the arms deals the last couple of years are a beginning. The satellite you're carrying back there will allow a degree of verification that would've been impossible even ten years ago. And killing ICBMs with good treaties—*before* the weapons are built—seems more efficient than putting a trillion dollars worth of X-ray lasers in space and hoping for the best."

Tucker laid his hands on the console as if he were sensing with his palms the data and energy that lay dormant there. "You know," he said, "I think the president-elect missed a bet during the campaign."

"How so?"

"He should've made a deal with the American people and the Soviets," said Tucker. "For every ten dollars and ten rubles saved by negotiating away missiles or cutting back SDI, the Russians and us should put ten rubles or ten bucks toward joint space projects. We'd be talking tens of billions of dollars, Dick."

"Mars?" said Baedecker. When he and Tucker had been training for *Apollo*, Vice President Agnew had announced that NASA's goal was to land men on Mars by the 1990s. Nixon had not been interested, NASA soon came down from its drunken euphoria, and the dream had receded to the point of invisibility.

"Eventually," said Tucker, "but first get the space station going and then put a permanent base on the moon."

Baedecker was amazed to find that his breathing seemed to catch at the thought of men returning to the moon in his lifetime. Men *and* women, he amended silently. Aloud, he said, "And you'd be willing to share it with the Russians?"

Tucker snorted. "As long as we don't have to *sleep* with the bastards," he said. "Or fly in their ships. Remember *Apollo-Soyuz?*"

Baedecker remembered. He and Dave had been part of the first team to sightsee the Soviet space program prior to the *Apollo-Soyuz* mission. He still remembered Dave's subtle commentary on the flight back. "State of the art. Jesus, Richard, they call this *state of the art!* To think we've spent all that energy scaring ourselves and Congress into believing all that stuff about the Soviet space juggernaut, the supertechnologies they're always on the verge of building, and then what do we see? Exposed rivets, electronic packages the size of my grandmother's old Philco radio, and a spacecraft that couldn't perform a docking maneuver if it had a hard-on."

Their written report had been a bit less pointed, but during the *Apollo-Soyuz* mission the American spacecraft had done all of the chasing and docking and—contrary to original plans—the crews had *not* switched ships for the landing.

"I don't want to fly in their tubs," repeated Tucker, "but if cooperating with them would get NASA back in the space-exploring business, I could put up with the smell." He unstrapped himself and began climbing down, taking care to use the proper handholds.

"A camel pissing out, eh?" said Baedecker, following carefully.

"What's that?" said Tucker as he crouched in front of the low, round hatch.

"Old Arab proverb," said Baedecker. "It's better to have the camel inside your tent pissing out than outside pissing in."

Tucker laughed, removed a stogie from his shirt pocket, and clamped it between his teeth. "Camel pissing out," he said and laughed again. "I like that."

Baedecker waited until Tucker exited and then he crouched, grabbed a metal bar above the hatch, and swung himself out into the delivery-room brightness of the white room.

∾

Early on the morning of the launch, Baedecker sat alone in the coffee shop of his Cocoa Beach motel, watching the surf break and rereading the letter he had received from Maggie Brown three days earlier.

November 17, 1988
Richard,

I loved your last letter. You write so rarely but every letter means so much. I know you well enough not to know how much you think about and how much you care about . . . and how little you say. Will you ever allow anyone to share the full depths of your insights and feelings? I hope so.

You make Arkansas sound beautiful. The descriptions of early mornings on the lake with the mists rising and crows calling in the bare branches along the shore made me want to be there.

Boston is all slush and traffic and tired brick right now. I love teaching and Dr. Thurston thinks that I'll be ready to begin work on my thesis next April. We'll see.

Your book is fantastic—at least the bits and pieces you've let me read. I think your friend Dave would be very proud. The character studies make the pilots come alive in a way I've never seen equaled in print, and the historical perspectives allow a lay person (me, for instance) to understand our current era in a new light—as a culture choosing between a frightening future of exploration and discovery, or a retreat into the safe and familiar harbors of internecine wars, stagnation, and decline.

As a sociologist I have more than a few questions (not answered by your book . . . or the fragments I've seen) concerning you astronaut-critters. Such as—why do so many of you hail from the Midwest? And why are almost all of you only children or the oldest siblings? (Is this true of the new mission specialists—especially the women—or just the ex-test pilots among you?) And what are the long-term psychological effects of belonging to a profession (test pilot) where the on-the-job mortality rate is one in six? (Could this lead to a certain reticence in showing feelings?)

Your references to Scott in the last letter sound more optimistic than anything I've heard previously. I'm so pleased he's feeling better. Please give my warm greetings to him. From the tone of your letter, Richard, it sounds like you're rediscovering how complex and thoughtful your son can be. I could have told you that! Scott was indulging his stubbornness when he wasted a year in that stupid ashram, but as I've suggested before, part of that stubbornness comes from his reluctance to let any experience pass unexamined or to remain less than totally understood.

Where could he have gotten that trait do you think?

Speaking of stubbornness, I will not comment upon the mathematical section of your letter. It's not worthy of a reply. (Other than to point out that when you're 180, I'll just be a spry 154. It may be a problem then.) (But I doubt it.)

You asked me in your letter about my own philosophical/religious views on some things. Are we still talking about the places-of-power idea we confronted in India eighteen months ago?

You know about my love of magic, Richard, and about my own obsession with what I think of as the secrets and the silences of the soul. For me, our quest for places of power is both real and important. But you know that.

All right, my belief system. I composed a twelve-page epistle on this since your letter posed the question, but then I tossed it away because I guess my whole system of beliefs can be boiled down to this:

> *I believe in the richness and mystery*
> *of the universe; and I don't believe*
> *in the supernatural.*

That's it. Oh, and I also believe that you and I have some decisions to make, Richard. I won't insult both of us with clichés or the travails of keeping Bruce at bay seven months after the deadline I promised him, but the fact is that you and I have to decide if we have a future together.

Until recently, I felt that we did. The few hours and days we have spent together over the past year and a half convinced me that the universe was richer—and, strangely, more mysterious—when we encountered it together.

But, one way or the other, life is beckoning to each of us right now. Whatever we decide, you need to know that our time together has widened and deepened everything for me, backward and forward in time.

I think I'll go for a walk now to watch the sculls on the Charles.

Maggie

Scott joined him at the table. "You're up early today, Dad. What time are we going over for the launch?"

"About eight-thirty," said Baedecker and folded away Maggie's letter.

The waitress came over and Scott ordered coffee, orange juice, scrambled eggs, wheat toast, and a side order of grits. When she left, he glanced at Baedecker's solitary cup of coffee and said, "Is that all you're having for breakfast?"

"I'm not very hungry this morning," said Baedecker.

"You didn't eat anything yesterday either, come to think of it," said Scott. "I remember you didn't have dinner on Wednesday either. And you didn't touch the pie last night. What's wrong, Dad? Are you feeling all right?"

"I feel fine," said Baedecker. "Honestly. Just not much appetite recently. I'll have a big lunch."

Scott frowned. "Just be careful, Dad. When I used to go on long fasts in India I'd get to the point after a few days where I didn't *want* to eat anything."

"I feel fine," Baedecker said again. "I feel better than I have for years."

"You *look* better," Scott said emphatically. "You must have lost twenty pounds since we started running at the end of January. Tucker Wilson asked me last night what kind of vitamins you've been taking. Jesus, you look *great*, Dad."

"Thanks," said Baedecker. He took a sip of coffee. "I was rereading Maggie Brown's letter and remembered that she said to say hello to you."

Scott nodded and looked out at the ocean. The sky was a flawless blue to the east, but there was already a haze in front of the rising sun. "We haven't talked about Maggie," said Scott.

"No, we haven't."

"Let's talk," said Scott.

"All right."

At that second Scott's breakfast arrived and the waitress filled their coffee cups. Scott took a bite of toast. "First of all," he said, "I think you've got the wrong idea about Maggie and me. We were friends for a few months before I went over to India, but we weren't all that close. I was surprised when she showed up to visit that summer. What I'm trying to say is, even though the idea occurred to me a few times, Maggie and I never got it on."

"Look, Scott . . ." began Baedecker.

"No, now listen a minute," said Scott, but as soon as he said it, he took time to eat some scrambled eggs with that total focus of attention that Baedecker remembered from as far back as his son's first feedings in his high chair. "I've got to explain this," Scott said at last. "I know it'll sound weird, Dad, but from the first time I met Maggie on campus she reminded me of you."

"Of me?" said Baedecker, at a loss. "How?"

"Maybe reminded isn't the right word," said Scott. "But something about her made me think of you all the time. Maybe it was the way she used to listen so hard to people. Or the habit she had of picking up on little things people do or say and remembering them later. Maybe it was the way she never seemed satisfied with explanations that satisfied the rest of us. So anyway, when I had the chance in India, I tried to arrange it so you and she could have a few days to get to know each other."

Baedecker stared at his son. "Are you saying that's why you had her meet my plane in New Delhi? *That's* why you kept me waiting a week before I could see you in Poona?"

Scott finished his egg, dabbed at his mouth with a linen napkin, and shrugged ever so slightly.

"Well I'll be damned," said Baedecker and scowled at his son.

Scott grinned and continued grinning until Baedecker found himself grinning back.

∾

The launch was scrubbed with three minutes remaining before ignition.

Baedecker and Scott sat in the VIP stands near the Vehicle Assembly Building and watched across the turning basin canal as high cirrus from the west quickly were replaced by cumulonimbus. The launch was scheduled for 9:54 A.M. By 9:30 the clouds were overhead and the wind gusts had risen to twenty-five knots, close to the maximum allowed. At 9:49 there were lightning strikes visible to the north and rain began to fall intermittently. Baedecker remembered sitting in these same stands when lightning had struck *Apollo 12* as it lifted off, knocking out every instrument in the Command Module and causing Pete Conrad to say some candid things into a live mike. At 9:51 A.M. the voice of NASA's Public Affairs Officer came over the loudspeakers to announce that the mission had been postponed. Because of a very tight launch window—less than an hour— they would recycle the countdown for a launch the next day between two and three P.M. At 10:03 the speakers announced that the astronauts had been removed from the shuttle, but the voice was talking to an empty grandstand as the would- be spectators ran through the growing rain squall to reach automobiles or shelter.

Baedecker let Scott drive the rented Beretta as the flood of vehicles inched its way west across the causeway. "Scott," he said, "what are your plans if the launch goes off tomorrow?"

"Just what I'd planned before," said Scott. "Go up to Daytona for a few days to visit Terry and Samantha. Then fly to Boston next week to see Mom when they get back from Europe. Why?"

"Just wondering," said Baedecker. He listened to the windshield wipers tick away in their useless effort against the downpour. Brake lights flashed in the long line ahead of them. "Actually," said Baedecker, "I was considering flying to Boston today. If I wait until after the launch tomorrow afternoon, there won't be enough time before my appointment in Austin on Monday."

"Boston?" said Scott. Then, "Oh, yeah . . . that might not be a bad idea."

"Would you go up to Daytona tonight, then?"

Scott thought for a second, tapping his fingers on the steering wheel. "No, I don't think so," he said. "I already told Terry I'd be there tomorrow night or Sunday. I think I'll stay here and watch the launch."

"You don't mind?" asked Baedecker, looking at his son. The months they had spent together the previous spring and summer had helped him become much better at gauging Scott's true reaction to things.

"Naw, I don't mind a bit," said Scott and his grin was sincere. "Let's go by the motel and get your stuff."

∞

The rain had let up considerably by the time they turned south on Highway 1.

"I hope Thanksgiving wasn't too much of a letdown," said Baedecker. They had eaten alone at the hotel before going to the crew's dessert gathering.

"Are you kidding?" said Scott. "It was great."

"Scott," said Baedecker, "do you mind if I ask what your plans are? Long-term plans, I mean."

His son ran his fingers through his short, wet hair. "See Mom for a while, I guess. Get through this semester."

"You're definitely going to finish?"

"With five weeks left before graduation? Damned right I am."

"What about after?" said Baedecker.

"After graduation? Well, I've been thinking about it, Dad. I got a letter from Norm last week and he said I can get back on his construction crew and work right on up until mid-August. It would help pay for the doctoral program in Chicago."

"Are you planning on that?"

"If the philosophy program is as good as Kent says it is, I'm very tempted," said Scott. "And even though the scholarship offer is partial, it's the best deal I've seen. But I've also been thinking about going into the service for a couple of years."

Baedecker stared at his son. He could not have been more surprised if Scott had calmly announced that he was flying to Sweden for a sex-change operation.

"It's just a thought," said Scott, but there was something in his voice that suggested otherwise.

"Don't commit yourself to anything like that unless I get a few hours . . . or weeks . . . to try and talk you out of it, okay?" said Baedecker.

"I promise," said Scott. "Hey, we're still going to spend Christmas vacation at the cabin, aren't we?"

"I'm planning on it," said Baedecker.

They drove east over the 520 Causeway and turned south again past endless rows of Cocoa Beach motels. Baedecker wondered how many times he had driven this way from Patrick Air Force Base in a mad rush to get back to the Cape. He said, "What branch?"

"Hmmm?" asked Scott, searching for their motel entrance through a renewed downpour.

"Which branch of the service?"

Scott pulled into the drive and parked in front of their unit. The rain pounded on the roof. "Gee, Dad," he said. "You need to ask that of me? What with me growing up in a family proud of three generations of Baedeckers in the U.S. Marine Corps?" He opened the door and jumped out, hunkering down in the rain just long enough to say, "I was thinking Coast Guard," and then ran toward the protective overhang of the motel balcony.

∾

It was snowing in Boston and already growing dark by the time Baedecker took a cab from Logan International to the address near Boston University. Still sunburned from the three days in Florida, he looked out through the gloom at the brown, icy water of the Charles River and shivered. Lights were coming on along the dark banks. The snow turned to dirty slush to be thrown up by the cab's tires.

Baedecker had always pictured Maggie living near the campus, but her apartment was some distance to the east, not too far from Fenway Park. The quiet side street was lined with stoops and bare trees, a neighborhood that looked to have been on the edge of decay in the sixties, saved by young professionals in the seventies, and now would be on the verge of invasion by the middle-aged affluent with an urge to homestead.

Baedecker paid the driver and ran from the cab to the door of the old brownstone. He had tried calling from Florida and again from Logan, but to no avail. He had pictured Maggie out shopping for groceries, returning home just as he arrived, but now he glanced up at the dark windows and wondered why he thought he would find her home on the Friday evening after Thanksgiving.

The second-floor hallway was warm but dimly lit. Baedecker checked the apartment number on the envelope, took a deep breath, and knocked. There was no answer. He knocked again and waited. A minute later he walked to the end of the hallway and looked out a tall window. Through an alley opening he could see snow falling heavily in front of a neon sign above a darkened shop.

"Hey, mister, were you the one knocking?" A young woman in her early twenties and a young man with horn-rimmed glasses were leaning out into the hall from an apartment two doors down from Maggie's.

"Yes," said Baedecker. "I was looking for Maggie Brown."

"She's gone," said the woman. She turned into the apartment and shouted, "Hey, Tara, didn't Maggie go to Bermuda with what's-his-name . . . Bruce?" There was a muffled reply. "She's gone," said the young woman as Baedecker took a step closer.

"Would you know when she'll be back?"

The woman shrugged. "Thanksgiving break just started yesterday. Probably a week from Sunday."

"Thank you," said Baedecker and went down the hall and stairway. An attractive young woman with short brown hair passed him in the foyer.

Baedecker stepped out onto the sidewalk and paused, looking up at the snow. He wondered how far he would have to go to find a phone or a taxi. The cold cut through his raincoat and he shivered. He turned right and began walking back toward Massachusetts Avenue.

He had gone a block and a half and his shoes were soaked through when he heard a voice calling behind him. "Hey, you, mister, wait up a second, please."

Baedecker stopped at the curb while the young woman he had passed in the foyer ran across the street to him. "Are you Richard, by any chance?" she asked.

"Richard Baedecker," he said.

"Wow, I'm glad I stopped to chat with Becky," she said and stopped to catch her breath. "I'm Sheila Goldman. You talked to me once on the phone."

"I did?"

Sheila Goldman nodded and brushed a snowflake from her eyelash. "Yes," she said. "Way back last September right at the beginning of the school year. Maggie was with her family that night."

"Oh, yes," said Baedecker. It had been the briefest of conversations; he had not even left his name.

"Becky told you that Maggie was gone for break?"

"Yes," said Baedecker. "I didn't know the university's schedule."

"Becky said that she thought Maggie had gone with Bruce Claren, right?" She paused and brushed more snow from her lashes. "Well, Becky doesn't know much. Bruce had been hanging around for weeks, but there was no chance that Maggie was going anywhere with him."

"Are you a friend of Maggie's?" asked Baedecker.

Sheila nodded. "We've been roommates for a while," she said. "We're pretty close." She rubbed her nose with her mitten. "But we're not so close that Maggie wouldn't kill me if she found out that you'd come to visit and . . . well, anyway, she's not down in Bermuda with Brucie."

A car took the turn at high speed, splashing slush at both of them. Baedecker took Sheila Goldman's elbow and they backed away from the curb together. "Where did Maggie go for Thanksgiving?" he said. He knew that her parents lived only an hour's drive away in New Hampshire.

"She left yesterday for South Dakota," said Sheila. "She flew out late in the afternoon."

South Dakota? thought Baedecker. Then he remembered a conversation they had had in Benares many months before. "Oh, yes," he said. "Her grandparents."

"Just Memo, her grandmother, now," said Sheila. "Her grandfather died in January."

"I didn't know that," said Baedecker.

"Here's their address and everything," said Sheila and handed him a slip of yellow paper. The handwriting on it was Maggie's. "Hey, you want to come back to our apartment to call a cab or anything?"

"No, thanks," said Baedecker. "I'll call from down the street if I can't flag one down on Mass Avenue." Impulsively he took her hand and squeezed it through the mitten. "Thank you, Sheila."

She reached up on her tiptoes and kissed him on the cheek. "You're welcome, Richard."

∞

Baedecker flew into Chicago shortly before midnight and spent a sleepless six hours in the airport Sheraton. He lay in the dark room listening to vague motel sounds and breathing motel smells and he thought about his last conversation with Scott.

Waiting with him in the Melbourne Airport near the Cape for Baedecker's connecting flight to Miami, Scott had suddenly said, "Do you ever think about what your epitaph might be?"

Baedecker had lowered his newspaper. "That's a reassuring question right before flight time."

Scott grinned and rubbed his cheeks. He was letting his beard grow back, and the red stubble caught the light. "Yeah, well, I've been thinking about mine," he said. "I'm afraid it will read—'He came, he saw, he screwed up.'"

Baedecker shook his head. "No pessimistic epitaphs allowed until you're at least twenty-five," he said. He began reading again and then set the paper down. "Actually," he said, "that's not too far from a quote I've carried around in my head for years, half suspecting that it might end up serving as *my* epitaph."

"What's that?" asked Scott. Outside, the rain was letting up, and they could see bright sky silhouetting palm trees.

"Have you ever read John Updike's 'Music School'?"

"No."

Baedecker paused. "I guess it's my favorite short story," he said. "Anyway, there's a place in it where the narrator says, 'I am neither musical nor religious. Each moment I live I must press my fingers down without confidence of hearing a chord.'"

Scott said nothing for half a minute. The airport PA system was busy paging people and disavowing any collusion with religious solicitors. "So how does it end?" asked Scott.

"The story?" said Baedecker. "Well, the narrator remembers when he was a boy going to Holy Communion and had been taught not to touch the Host with his teeth . . ."

"Uh-uh," said Scott. "That's not what they taught me at Saint Malachy's."

"No," agreed Baedecker, "now they bake the wafer so thick that it has to be chewed. That's what the narrator decides about his life at the end of the story. I think the closing lines are—'The *World* is the Host. And it must be chewed.'"

Scott stared at his father for some time. Then he said, "Have you read any of the Vedic holy books, Dad?"

"No," said Baedecker.

"I did," said Scott. "I read quite a bit from them last year in India. They didn't have much of anything to do with the stuff the Master was teaching, but somehow I think I'll remember the books longer. One of my favorite things was from the *Tattireeya Upanishads*. It goes—'I am this world, and I eat this world. Who knows this, knows.'"

At that moment the boarding call was announced for Baedecker's flight. He stood, hefted his flight bag with his left hand, and held out his right hand to his son. "Take care, Scott. I'll see you at Christmas break if not before."

"You take care, too, Dad," said Scott and, ignoring the offered handshake, threw his arms around Baedecker and hugged him.

Baedecker put his hand on his son's strong back and closed his eyes.

∞

Baedecker caught a 7:45 A.M. United flight out of O'Hare. It was bound for Seattle but had a scheduled stop in Rapid City, South Dakota, which was as close as Baedecker could get to Maggie's grandparents' ranch near Sturgis without bailing out. Tired as he was, Baedecker noticed that the aircraft was one of the new Boeing 767s. He had not flown in one before.

They served breakfast somewhere over southern Minnesota. Baedecker stared at the tray of reheated scrambled eggs and sausage and decided that appetite or no appetite, it was time to eat after almost three days. He could not do it. He was sipping coffee and looking down at glimpses of brown landscape between the clouds when the stewardess came up to him and said, "Mr. Baedecker."

"Yes?" said Baedecker and felt a stab of alarm. How did she know his name? Had something happened to Scott?

"Captain Hollister wonders if you would like to come up to the flight deck."

"Sure," said Baedecker and followed her forward through the first-class section with relief slowing his heart rate. He searched his memory, trying to recall if he had met an airline pilot named Hollister. He could remember no one with that name, but he did not trust his memory.

"Here you are, sir," said the stewardess and opened the door for him.

"Thank you," said Baedecker and stepped through.

The pilot looked up and grinned. He was a florid-faced man in his early forties with thick hair, a boyish grin, and a pleasant, Wally Schirra-like expression. "Welcome, Mr. Baedecker, I'm Charlie Hollister. This is Dale Knutsen."

Baedecker nodded a greeting at both men.

"Hope we didn't disturb your breakfast," said Hollister. "I noticed your name on the passenger list and just wondered if you'd like to see how our new baby here compares to your *Apollo* hardware."

"My God," said Baedecker. "I'm amazed you made the connection with my name."

Hollister smiled again. Neither pilot nor copilot appeared to be involved with flying the aircraft.

"Here," said Knutsen and released his straps. "Have my seat, sir. I'm going back to the galley for a minute."

Baedecker thanked him and settled into the fleece-lined right seat. Except for the yoke in place of a hand-controller, the cockpit could have been a close relative of the space shuttle's. Video display terminals flashed instrument readings, lines of data, and colored maps onto three screens in front of him. A computer keyboard filled the console between Hollister and him. Baedecker looked out at the blue sky, distant horizon, and layer of clouds far below. He looked back at the pilot. "I am surprised that you made the connection," he said. "We haven't met, have we?"

"No, sir," said Hollister. "But I know all of the names from the various missions and remember seeing you on television. The only thing I ever really wanted in life was to be an astronaut myself, but, well . . ."

Baedecker extended his hand. "Let's drop the sirs," he said. "They make me feel a little old. My name's Richard."

"Howdy, Richard," said Hollister as they shook hands across the computer.

Baedecker glanced at the flashing data screens and moving yoke. "The aircraft seems to be flying itself pretty well," he said. "Does it let you do anything?"

"Not much," said Hollister with a rueful laugh. "She's a doozy, ain't she? State of the art. I can program her on the ground at O'Hare and wouldn't have to do a thing until we're setting down in Seattle. Only thing she can't do herself is lower the gear."

"You don't actually go on full automatic like that, do you?" asked Baedecker.

Hollister shook his head. "We argue that we need to keep our hand in, and the union supports us. The airline argues back that they bought the seven-six-seven so that the Flight Management Computer System will save money on fuel and that every time we take over manual, we piss that away. Fact is, they're right."

"Is it fun to fly?" asked Baedecker.

"She's a good ship," said Hollister. He punched a button and the displays changed. "Safe as sitting on Grandma's back porch. But fun . . . naw." He proceeded to show Baedecker details of the Automatic Flight Control System, the Engine Indicating and Crew Alert System, and the computerized color radar displays that incorporated maps of their position relative to VHF Omni-Range stations, waypoints, and Instrument Landing System beams. The same map showed the location of weather fronts, kept a running count of wind velocity, and let them know which direction they were flying at all times. "It'll tell me who my wife's sleeping with if I ask it real politely," said Hollister. "So how does this stack up with the gear you took to the moon?"

"Impressive," said Baedecker, not telling Hollister that he had worked for a company producing military avionics light-years ahead of even this system. "To answer your question, we had a lot of crude gauge and dial instrumentation and the LM computer we depended on to guide our butts to the surface had a total capacity of only thirty-nine thousand words . . ."

"Sweet Christ," said Hollister and shook his head.

"Exactly," said Baedecker. "Your FMCS here can work rings around our old PGNS. And most of ours was locked in. If a new problem came up, we could only call on a couple of thousand words."

"It makes you wonder how we got there at all," said Hollister. He took the controls, threw a switch high on the instrument board, and set his right hand on the throttles. "Want to take it a second?"

"Won't United shit a brick?" asked Baedecker.

"No doubt about it," said Hollister. "But the only way they're going to find out is if they hear our voices on the black-box flight recorder, and it won't make any difference to us then. Want it?"

"Sure," said Baedecker.

"You've got it."

Baedecker handled the yoke gingerly, thinking of the hundred-some passengers juggling their coffee cups behind him. Far ahead, the clouds were dissipating enough that the brown line of the horizon was visible.

"Was it true that Dave Muldorff wanted to name the lunar module *The Beagle*?" asked Hollister.

"Sure was," said Baedecker. "He almost had them convinced, too. He said it was in the tradition of Darwin, voyage of the *Beagle* and all that. You see, when the crews first started naming the machines, they had names like *Gumdrop* and *Spider* and *Snoopy*. Then after Neil and the-*Eagle*-has-landed and all that, the names kept getting more serious and pretentious . . . *Endeavor* and *Orion* and *Intrepid* and *Odyssey*. At the last minute they didn't trust Dave's intentions and strongly suggested that he go with *Discovery*."

"What was wrong with *Beagle*?" asked Hollister.

"Nothing," said Baedecker, "but they knew Dave and they were right. He'd worked out a whole shtick starting with, 'Houston, the *Beagle* has landed,' and getting worse. He was trying to get Tom Gavin to go with *Lassie* for the CM. He would've called our wheeled lunar vehicle *Rover* and told everybody it was a reliable little son of a bitch. We would probably have gone down in NASA history as the Beagle Boys. No, they were right to head him off at the pass, Charlie."

Hollister laughed. "I remember watching that Frisbee thing you two did up there. Jesus, that must have been a fun time to be flying."

The copilot returned with Styrofoam cups of coffee for each of them. Baedecker returned the controls to Hollister, gave up his seat to Knutsen, and stood a minute, leaning on the back of the copilot's seat and looking out at the vast expanse of cloud and sky. "Yes," he said and raised his cup in a silent toast and drank some of the rich, black coffee. "It was fun."

∾

The Rapid City Airport appeared to be a landing strip in search of a town. The approach took them over weathered pastureland, dry streambeds, and ranches. The single runway sat atop a grassy mesa, which held only a tiny terminal, low tower, and an almost-empty parking lot.

As Baedecker settled into his rented Honda Civic, he decided that he had had enough of scheduled flights and rental cars. He would use the bulk of his savings to buy a 1960 Corvette and have done with it. Better yet, when the money came in, a nice little Cessna 180 . . .

It was a forty-minute drive from Rapid City along Interstate 90 to the Sturgis exit. The highway ran along the foothills separating the dark mass of the Black Hills in the south from the prairie and pastureland stretching north to the horizon. The housing developments and mobile home parks perched on hillsides along the way looked as raw as open wounds on the landscape.

It was twelve-thirty when Baedecker asked directions at a Conoco station near the I-90 exit and almost one P.M. by the time he drove under a wooden arch and down a long lane to the Wheeler Ranch.

The woman who approached him as he got out of the car and stretched reminded him somewhat of Miz Elizabeth Sterling Callahan of Lonerock, Oregon. In her seventies, at least, but still fluid in her movements, this woman had her long, gray hair tied back in a scarf and wore a red mackinaw jacket over dark blue pants. Her face was lined but placid. A collie trotted at her heels. "Hello there," she called. "Can I help you?"

"Yes, ma'am. Are you Mrs. Wheeler?"

"Ruth Wheeler," said the woman as she came close. There were deep laugh lines around eyes as startlingly green as Maggie's.

"My name's Richard Baedecker," he said and offered his hand for the collie to smell. "I'm hunting for Maggie."

"Richard . . . oh, Richard!" said the woman. "Oh, my, yes. Margaret has mentioned your name. Well, welcome, Richard."

"Thank you, Mrs. Wheeler."

"Ruth, please," she said. "Oh, my, Margaret will be surprised. She's gone right now, Richard. She went into town to run some errands. Won't you come in the house for some coffee while we wait for her. She should be back soon."

On the verge of accepting, Baedecker felt a tremendous impatience seize him, as if he could not rest, could not stop until a long voyage was finished. "Thank you, Ruth," he said. "If you have an idea where she might be, I think I'll run into town and try to find her."

"Try the Safeway in the shopping center or the hardware store on Main," she said. "Margaret's driving our old blue Ford pickup with a big, red generator in the bed. It has my Dukakis sticker on the rear bumper."

Baedecker grinned. "Thank you, ma'am. If I don't find her and she gets back first, tell her I'll be back soon."

Mrs. Wheeler walked up and put her hand on the open window after he turned the Civic around. "One other place she might be," she said. "Margaret likes to stop by Bear Butte. It's a big old hill just outside of town. Just go to the north end and follow the signs."

∞

The blue pickup was not in the Safeway lot or parked along Main Street. Baedecker drove slowly back and forth through the small town, half expecting to see Maggie step out of a doorway at any moment. The one-thirty news on the radio talked about the secret launch of the space shuttle that should be lifting off sometime in the next two hours. The reporter incorrectly referred to the KSC as "Cape Kennedy" and reported that the area had high clouds but that the weather should hold for the launch.

Baedecker turned around in the parking lot of a beef jerky plant and drove back through Sturgis, following the green signs to Bear Butte State Park.

The small lot was empty of cars. Baedecker parked the Civic near a closed-up information building and looked up at Bear Butte. It was an impressive hill. If his geology training still served, Baedecker estimated that the mountain was a well-weathered volcanic cone rising in a long ridge to a summit he guessed to be at least eight hundred feet above the surrounding prairie, perhaps more. The mountain was separated from the foothills to the south and it leaped out of the grasslands quite dramatically. Baedecker had to use his imagination to see a bear in the long hill, and when he did it was a bear hunkered forward with its haunches in the air.

On a whim, Baedecker grabbed his old flight jacket out of the back seat and began walking up the trail from the visitors' center.

Although patches of snow lay here and there in shaded areas, the day was warm and Baedecker could smell the thawing earth. He felt somewhat light-headed as he switchbacked up the first, steep segment of trail, but he had no trouble breathing. He wondered idly why he had felt no appetite the past three days and why, despite no sleep for two days and an empty stomach, he felt strong and fit, almost buoyant.

The trail evened out to run along the rising ridgeline and Baedecker paused to look out over low piñon and ponderosa pines to admire the view to the north and east. About a third of the way up he began noticing bits of cloth, tiny colored rags, tied to low bushes along the trail. He stopped and touched one of them as it fluttered in the warm breeze.

"Hello."

Baedecker spun around. The man was sitting in a low area near the cliff edge about fifteen feet from the trail. It was a natural campsite, sheltered from the north and west winds by rocks and trees but open to the view on three sides.

"Hello," said Baedecker and walked closer. "I didn't see you over here."

Baedecker had no doubt that the old man was an Indian. His skin was a burnt copper, his eyes were so dark as to appear black, the wrinkles on his brow radiated from a broad blade of a nose, and he was wearing a loose, blue-print shirt, had a red headband pulled tight, and had tied his long, graying hair into pigtails. He wore a single ring of some deep blue stone. Only his tattered, green-canvas sneakers were out of character. "I didn't mean to intrude here," said Baedecker. He looked beyond the old man to where a tan canvas tent had been erected near a lower structure built of boughs and rocks and branches. Baedecker instantly knew that the thing was a sweat lodge without knowing how he knew.

"Sit down," said the Indian. The old man himself was seated on a rock, not cross-legged but with one leg over the other in a comfortable, almost feminine pose. "I am Robert Sweet Medicine," he said. His voice was husky, amused, as if he were on the verge of chuckling at some unstated joke.

"Richard Baedecker."

The old man nodded as if this was redundant information. "Nice day to climb the mountain, Baedecker."

"Very nice day," said Baedecker. "Although I'm not sure I'm going all the way to the top."

The Indian shrugged. "I have been coming here a very long time and have never been to the top. It is not always necessary." He was using a pocketknife to whittle at a short stick. There were various twigs, roots, and stones on the ground in front of him. Baedecker noticed the bones of some small animal in the heap. Some of the stones had been painted bright colors.

Baedecker looked out at the miles of prairie to the north. From this vantage point he could see no highways and only small pockets of trees showed where ranches huddled. He had a sudden, visceral sense of the physical freedom the Plains Indians must have felt a century and a half earlier when they had roamed without restriction across that seemingly boundless land. "Are you a Sioux?" he asked, not knowing whether the question was polite but wanting to know the answer.

Robert Sweet Medicine shook his head. "Cheyenne."

"Oh, for some reason I thought the Sioux lived in this part of South Dakota."

"They do," said the old man. "They ran us out of this region long ago. They think this mountain is sacred. So do we. We just have to commute farther."

"Do you live near here?" asked Baedecker.

The Indian took his knife and cut off a small section of new cactus growing between the rocks, peeled it, and set the leaf on his tongue like a woodwind player readying his reed. "No. I travel a long way to come here. It is my job to teach things to young men who will someday teach them to other young men. But my young man is a little late."

"Oh?" Baedecker looked down at the distant parking lot. His Civic was still the only vehicle there. "When were you expecting him?"

"Five weeks ago," said Robert Sweet Medicine. "The *Tsistsistas* have no sense of time."

"The who?" said Baedecker.

"*The People,*" said the old man in his amused, husky voice.

"Oh."

"You also have traveled a long way," said the other.

Baedecker thought about that and nodded.

"My ancestors such as Mutsoyef traveled a long way," said Robert Sweet Medicine. "Then they fasted, purified themselves, and climbed the Sacred Mountain to see if a vision would present itself. Sometimes Maiyun would speak to them. More often he would not."

"What kind of visions?" asked Baedecker.

"Do you know of Mutsoyef and the cave and the Gift of the Four Arrows?"

"No."

"No matter," said Robert Sweet Medicine. "That does not concern you, Baedecker."

"You say the mountain is also sacred to the Sioux?"

The old man shrugged. "The Arapahoes received a medicine here they could burn to make sweet smoke for their rituals. The Apaches received the gift of a magic horse medicine; the Kiowas the sacred kidney of a bear. The Sioux say they received a pipe from the mountain, but I do not believe them. They made that up because they were jealous. The Sioux lie frequently."

Baedecker shifted his weight and smiled.

Robert Sweet Medicine ceased his whittling and looked at Baedecker. "The Sioux did claim to have seen a great bird on the mountain, a true Thunderbird, with wings a mile across and with a voice like the end of the world. But this is no great medicine. This is *Wihio* trickery. Any man with even a little bit of medicine can call up the Thunderbird."

"Can you?" asked Baedecker.

The old man snapped his fingers.

Two seconds later the earth shook with a roar that seemed to come from the sky and ground at the same time. Baedecker caught a glimpse of something huge and gleaming behind him, its shadow hurtling toward them and covering entire hillsides, and then he was up on one knee and watching as the B-52H finished its bank and roared off to the north at less than five hundred feet altitude, lower than the Butte, its eight jet engines leaving a black wake of smoke in the afternoon air. Baedecker sat back down, still feeling the vibrations of the aircraft's passing in the rocks under his thighs.

"Sorry, Baedecker," said the old man. His teeth were yellow and strong looking, with only one of the lower ones missing. "That was a cheap *Wihio* trick. They come by here from Ellsworth Base every day at this time. I am told they use this mountain to make sure their radar device tells them the truth as they travel."

"What's a *Wihio*?" asked Baedecker.

"It is our word for the Trickster," said the Cheyenne, cutting and chewing a new cactus leaf. "*Wihio* is Indian when he wants to be, animal when he wants to be, and always is up to no good. He can show a very cruel sense of humor. It is the same word we use for spider and for White Man."

"Oh," said Baedecker.

"Many of us also suspect that he is the Creator."

Baedecker thought about this.

"When Mutsoyef came down off this mountain," said the old man and paused a second to remove a bit of plant from his tongue. "When he came down, he brought with him the Gift of the Sacred Arrows, he taught us the Four Songs, he told us our future—even of the passing of the buffalo and the coming of the White Men to take our place—and then he gave his friends the Arrows and said, 'This is my body I'm giving you. Always remember me.' What do you think of this, Baedecker?"

"It sounds familiar," he said.

"Yes," said the old man. He had been cutting a root into small pieces, and now he frowned at it. "Sometimes I worry that my grandfather and great-grandfather borrowed a good story when they heard it. It does not matter. Here, put this in your mouth." He handed Baedecker a small piece of root with the outer layer removed.

Baedecker held it in his hand. "What is it?"

"A piece of root." The old man's voice was patient.

Baedecker put the small chunk in his mouth. There was a faint bitterness.

"Do not chew it or suck on it," said Robert Sweet Medicine and put a slightly larger piece of root in his own mouth. He worked it around until it bulged like a small wad of tobacco in his cheek. "Do not swallow it," added the old man.

Baedecker sat a minute in silence, feeling the sun on his face and hands. "What is this supposed to do?" he said eventually.

The old man shrugged. "It keeps me from getting too thirsty," he said. "My water bottle is empty and it is a long walk down to the pump by the visitors' center."

"Could I ask you something?"

The old man paused in his cutting of more root and nodded.

"I have a friend," said Baedecker, "someone I love and suspect is very wise, who believes in the richness and mystery of the universe and does not believe in the supernatural."

Robert Sweet Medicine waited. After a minute he said, "What is the question?"

Baedecker touched his forehead, feeling the sunburn there. He shrugged slightly, thinking of Scott as he did so. "I just wondered what you thought of that," he said.

The old man cut two more pieces of root and popped them in his mouth, moving them to the other cheek and speaking slowly and clearly. "I think your friend is wise."

Baedecker squinted. It might have been the result of several days without food or the time he had spent in the sun, or both, but the air between him and the elderly Cheyenne seemed to be shimmering, rippling like heat waves above a highway on a summer day. "You don't believe in the supernatural?" asked Baedecker.

Robert Sweet Medicine looked out to the east. Baedecker followed his gaze. Far out on the plains, sunlight glinted on a window or windshield. "You may know more science than I do," said the old man. "If the natural world is the universe, how much do you think we know of it, understand it? One percent?"

"No," said Baedecker. "Not that much."

"One percent of one percent?"

"Perhaps," said Baedecker although as soon as he said it he doubted it. He did not believe that the universe was infinitely complex—one ten-thousandth of an infinite set was still an infinite set—but he felt in his gut that even in the limited realm of basic physical laws, humans probably had not glimpsed a ten-thousandth part of the permutations and possibilities. "Less than that," he said.

Robert Sweet Medicine pocketed his folding knife and opened his hands, fingers spreading like petals in new sunlight. "Your friend is wise," he said. "Help me up, Baedecker."

He stood and grasped the older man by the arms, prepared to lift hard, but Robert Sweet Medicine weighed nothing at all. The old man came to his feet with no effort from either of them, and Baedecker had to thrust a leg back to keep from falling backwards. His forearms tingled where the Cheyenne's fingers gripped him. Baedecker felt that if they were not holding on to each other, they could have floated off the ground at that instant, two untethered balloons drifting over the South Dakota prairie.

The Indian squeezed Baedecker's forearms once and released him. "Have a good walk up the mountain, Baedecker," he said. "I have to go all the way down the hill to get water and to use their smelly outhouse. I hate squatting in the bushes; it is not civilized."

The old man picked up a three-gallon plastic jug and moved slowly down the hill, walking in a comical, flatfooted shuffle. He stopped once and called back, "Baedecker, if you find a deep cave up there, a very deep one, tell me about it on the way down."

Baedecker nodded and watched the old man shuffle away. It did not occur to him to say good-bye until Robert Sweet Medicine was out of sight around a curve in the trail.

It took Baedecker forty-five minutes to reach the summit. Not once did he feel winded or tired. He did not find a cave.

∾

The view from the top was the finest he had ever seen from the earth itself. The mountains of the Black Hills filled the south, an occasional snowy peak rising above forested folds. Overhead a succession of weightless cumulus marched from west to east, reminding Baedecker of the flocks of sheep he and Maggie had watched on the Uncompahgre Plateau. To the north, the plains stretched off in brown-and-green undulations until they blended with the haze of distance.

Baedecker found a natural chair made of two small boulders and a fallen log. He settled into it and closed his eyes, feeling the sunlight on his eyelids. The pleasant emptiness in his stomach spread through his body and mind. At that second he was going nowhere, planning nothing, thinking nothing, wanting nothing. The sun was quite warm, but in a minute even that warmth was a distant thing, and then even it was gone.

Baedecker slept. And as he slept he dreamed.

His father was holding him, teaching him to swim, but they were not at North Avenue Beach in the shallows of Lake Michigan; they were on top of Bear Butte and the light was very strange, soft and brown yet very rich, as clear as the summer heat lightning that had once illuminated the patrons of the Free Show in Glen Oak's little park, freezing them all in time, preserving the instant with a single, stroboscopic flash of silent light.

There was no lake to swim in atop Bear Butte, but Baedecker noticed that the air itself was as thick and buoyant as water, more so, and his father was holding him horizontal, one arm under Baedecker's chest, another under his legs, and was saying, "The trick is to relax, Richard. Don't be afraid to put your face down. Hold your breath a second. You'll float. And if you don't, I'm here to hold you up."

Baedecker obediently put his face down. But first he looked at his father, looked closely at the familiar face inches away, the mouth he would always know, the lines around the mouth, the dark eyes and dark hair he had not inherited, the half smile he had inherited. He looked at his father in his baggy swimming trunks, the dark tan line ending on the upper arms, the slight pot belly, the pale chest beginning to curve in at the center as age approached. Baedecker put his face down obediently but first, as he had done before, he lifted his face to the hollow of his father's neck, smelling the soap and tobacco smell of him, feeling the slight scratch of tomorrow's whiskers, and then, as he had not done before, *had not done*, he lifted both arms around his father's neck and hugged him, lifting his cheek to his father's cheek, hugged hard and felt the hug returned.

Then he put his face down and held his breath, bringing his arms out in front of him, straightening his legs, holding his body in a single plane, rigid but relaxed.

And he floated.

"There, it's easy, isn't it?" said his father. "Go on. I'll catch you if you get in trouble."

Baedecker floated higher, rising easily above the rock and pine summit of the butte, floating with no effort on the gentle currents, and when he looked below, his father was gone.

Baedecker let out a breath, took in a breath, struck out calmly with arms and legs, and swam upward with long, sure strokes. The currents were warmer higher up. He passed between two flat-bottomed cumuli and continued on, feeling no need to rest. He swam higher, seeing the mountain dwindle below until it was only a dark pattern glimpsed between the carpet of clouds, indistinguishable from the geometries of plains and forests and rivers and other mountains. When the currents grew noticeably stronger and colder, Baedecker paused to tread the thick, buoyant air with easy motions of arms and legs. The wonderful light allowed him to see very well. The long, graceful curve of the horizon to the south and east offered no obstacle to his sight.

Baedecker looked and saw the space shuttle sitting on its pad with gantries pulled away and the blue crest of the Atlantic beyond it. The people in the bleachers by the tall white building were all standing now, many with their arms raised above them, as brilliant flames ignited under the rocket and caused it to rise, slowly at first on its pillar of clear flame, then very quickly, arching like a great, white arrow fired from the earth's bow, turning now as it climbed, the fire from its passing dividing into long columns and billows of fragrant smoke. Baedecker watched the white ship soar on until it turned away from him, falling confidently over a far curve of sea and air, and then he turned his gaze back to find Scott in the multitude of watchers, found him easily, and saw then that Scott's arms were also raised, fists closed, mouth open in the same silent prayer the others were offering as they helped the white arrowhead of the spacecraft on its way, and Baedecker could see the tears on his son's joyous face.

He swam higher. He could feel the cold biting at him now, but he ignored it, working hard to overcome the riptides and pressures, which threatened to pull him back. And then, suddenly, there was no further need for effort and Baedecker hovered far up, seeing the planet again as the blue-and-white ball it was, curtained in black velvet, small enough and beautiful enough for him to put his arms around. Closer, tantalizingly close, was the great white-and-gray serrated curve of his other world. But even as he pivoted and prepared to stroke across the short distance remaining, he knew that this one thing was denied to him. No, not denied he realized, for once it had been allowed. Only return was denied. But then, as if in recompense, he was floating over the familiar white peaks and shadowed craters, and he could see even more clearly than before.

He could see the gold-and-silver devices his friend and he had left, dead metal, useless now, their minimum warmth and mindless activity leeched away by years of baking days and freezing nights. But he also saw the more important things they had left, his friend and he, not the tumbled flag or dust-covered machines, but their footprints, as deep and sharp-edged as the second they had lifted their boots away, and a few true artifacts catching the rising sun—a small photograph, a belt buckle set to face the crescent earth.

Then, before returning, chilled and shivering, Baedecker saw one more thing. Crossing the band between light and dark where knife-black shadows cut ragged holes in the faint earthlight, Baedecker saw the lights. Strings of lights. Circles of lights. Lights of cities and transportways and quarries and communities, some burrowing, some spreading proudly across the dark *mare* and highlands, all waiting tenaciously for the dawn.

And then Baedecker returned. He paused a few times, paddling to stay in place, but mostly he allowed the great tug of the earth to pull him in, gently, inexorably. It was only then, holding his breath for a short while at the end, floating gently above the high shoal of the butte and seeing the blue pickup stop below, watching the young woman emerge and break into a run up the tiny trail . . . it was only then that he finally accepted the pull of the earth and saw clearly that it was more than the mindless call of matter to matter. And with that realization, Baedecker felt the same energy in himself, flowing through him and from him, bringing together and binding people as well as things.

Baedecker hovered there, but even as he did so he felt the return of the warmth of the sun on his face, knew that he was sleeping, heard the familiar voice calling in the distance, and knew that in a second he would wake and rise and call back to Maggie. But for a few more seconds he was content to hover there, neither earthbound nor free, waiting, knowing there was much to be learned and happy to be waiting and willing to learn.

Then Baedecker touched the mountain, smiled, and opened his eyes.

COLOPHON

PHASES OF GRAVITY is set in Adobe Garamond. Some of the most widely used typefaces in history are those of the sixteenth-century type designer Claude Garamond. Robert Slimbach visited Plantin-Moretus museum in Antwerp, Belgium, to study the original Garamond typefaces. These served as the basis for the Adobe Garamond romans, the face used for the body of this book. Running heads and chapter openings are Formata.

Designed and set in the foothills of the Adirondacks by Syllables using Adobe software which provided electronic files used to create plates for printing.